SCARS

OF THE

RAVEN

T.C. Smith

This book contains the following content which may be distressing to some readers:

Alcohol, Animal Death, Anxiety, Blood and Gore, Bones, Death, Decapitation, Depictions of PTSD, Panic attacks, Racism/Xenophobia, Graphic Depictions of Violence, War

This book contains mentions of the following content which may be distressing to some readers:

Child Death, Harm to Children, Forced Experimentation, Genocide, Kidnapping

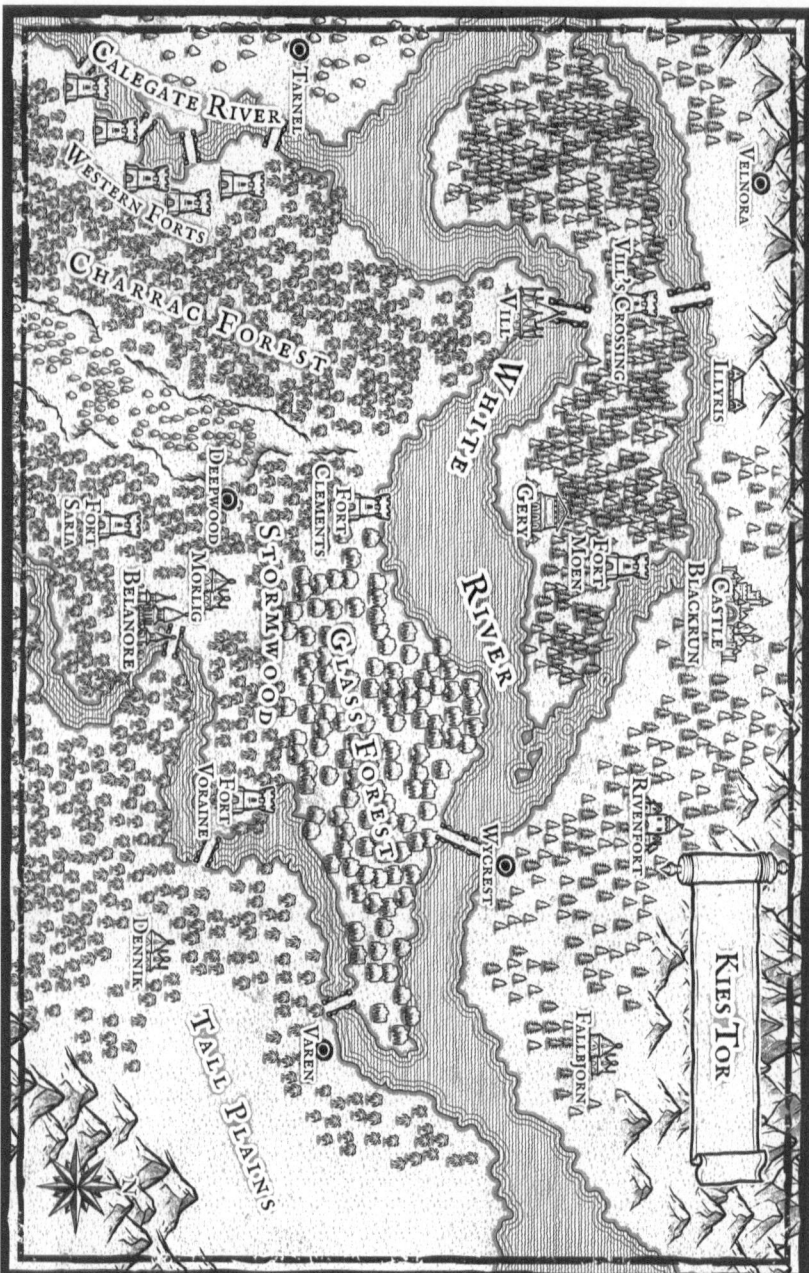

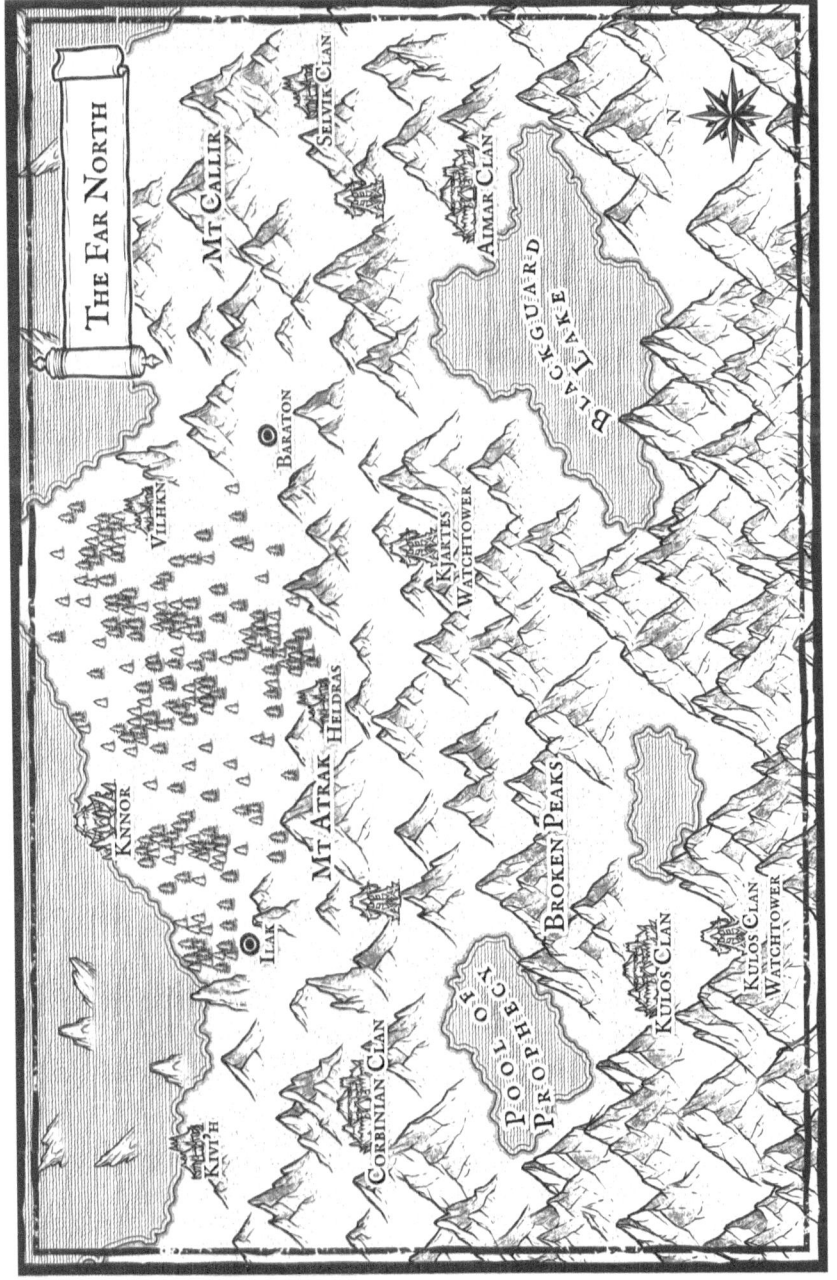

THE FAR NORTH

MT CALLIR

SELVIK CLAN

AIMAR CLAN

BLACKGUARD LAKE

N

BARATON

VILHKN

MT KNNOR

ILAK

KJARTES WATCHTOWER

MT ATRAK

HELDRAS

KIWTH

CORBINIAN CLAN

POOL OF PROPHECY

BROKEN PEAKS

KULOS CLAN

KULOS CLAN WATCHTOWER

K ies Tor was a strange place now.

He could see it at every turn, every village he passed, every fading battlefield where grass and flowers had buried the rusted steel of broken weapons and decayed remains of the dead. Where once he would have expected to pass through a ghost town, he found children instead, running after him asking if he was a giant or a knight, or otherwise chasing each other through side streets and unpaved, dusty roads. It felt good, knowing the war had been won, but this was a version of Kies Tor he had never seen before. He had never felt so lost.

The queen's letter had arrived under the guise of a simple message, encoded in the cryptic written script of Old Torrian. In it, he understood the plight. *I need you back here.*

No explanation had been provided, no context or reason for the urgent letter, but the warrant she had sent with it said enough. Something was amiss.

The world had changed in fifteen years. His travels through the south so far had made that painfully clear. He wondered, not for the first time, whether he should have returned; there was no doubt he would be even less welcome in the kingdom now as an exiled criminal. But years of skulking in the shadows at the border had taught him how to hide, and Kadis at least still welcomed him in El'Vane.

Fillius' decision to pass on the title of emperor had left the young prince in charge of everything from the northern deserts to the far western shores. Red Wolf had free reign in the Draconian lands to wander where he pleased, exploring the furthest reaches of the Empire, trying to forget everything he'd left behind.

But it didn't feel like home.

He was close now, after a month of riding. The tall, white spires of the palace towers were finally visible above the canopy of Stormwood, and he recognised a few villages he and Talin had passed when they went west all those years ago. The war hadn't touched them, thankfully. Children ran after him as he rode through, hoping for a chance to touch his horse. A pure white stallion was considered lucky by the more superstitious folk and made good fairy tales for the young ones. He slowed to let them crowd in and stroke its mane before spurring it on again. It was another five days' travel through Stormwood, and he couldn't linger.

He came across a dying fox some time later, laying beside a thick bush with a deep bite wound in its neck. He knew at a glance that a wolf had done it. His kin had clearly taken over the forests after his departure. He drew a knife and put the fox out of its misery.

Even these forests have changed.

At the northern gates of Belanore, he was finally stopped and searched by two Chained Owls who demanded he lower his hood. For a moment, he considered obeying, but then he recognised one of the guards and knew the man would remember him.

"I have papers from the queen," he said, producing the warrant. "Please. I can't be seen."

"The queen, hey?" One of the guards squinted at his warrant. He doubted the man could read any of the writing.

"The royal seal is right here." He tapped the wax in the bottom corner and watched the guards squirm. "Do we have a problem, gentlemen?"

"Not at all," the second guard stammered. "Right this way."

He was led through the wooden side gate and allowed to ride on. Behind him, the guards made their exit and locked the gate again after him.

And, just like that, he was in the city.

Red Wolf dug his heels into the stallion's sides and sent it off at an easy trot toward the glittering palace.

Three weeks ago...

***

Fifteen years ago today, Talin had said her goodbyes to Red Wolf for the final time.

She tried not to dwell on it too much as she slowly worked through the city's troubles, granting trading permits to merchants and resolving petty disputes between neighbours. Even now, five years after her victory at Castle Blackrun, her people felt the sting of war and loss. Sometimes she wondered if she could ever fully rebuild Kies Tor.

True, she had accomplished plenty since the Siege of Belanore, starting with the abolishment of the death sentence and later shutting down a series of dangerous fighting arenas in the north after the end of the war. But it felt like none of her accomplishments had anything to do with undoing the damage wrought by the Hellhounds.

Until we meet again, my queen.

At first, she had held out hope that they would see each other again. But weeks had turned into months, and then years. As the war had dragged on, she came to the realisation that Red Wolf was gone for good, that perhaps waiting for an opportunity to reunite had been a futile effort. With growing pressure from her council and the public to find a suitor, she supposed it was only a matter of time before she had to find *someone*. It was fortunate, and perhaps good timing, that King Darien had come to her rescue with an offer—his brother Aldrus' hand in marriage in exchange for an alliance with the Fae.

"You're distracted today."

Talin almost jumped when she felt a hand on her shoulder, firm but gentle. Aldrus let out a quiet chuckle and withdrew his hand again.

"This is the second time you've forgotten to call in the next person. See what I mean?"

"I'm just tired," she said. It was true; between holding court, organising a tourney, and investigating a failed assassination attempt two months ago, she was exhausted. But she knew she couldn't afford to slack off on her duties when the entire kingdom was at stake.

"You need a break," her husband said.

"I need to hold court," Talin said, waving in the next person.

"Stubborn."

"I'll be fine, really."

"You do understand that in order to hold court, *you* need to be in good health too, yes?" Aldrus said. "Deal with the man you just called in, then. I'll tell them we're finishing early."

Talin sighed. Much as she hated to admit it, she did need a break; they'd been here for two hours now, and she wanted nothing more than to sleep. The man before her now was a Drakel labourer looking for work in Kies Tor.

A straightforward matter, at least.

She took the man's details and application and passed them on to Lord Folen, her head of civil affairs since Lord Karl's arrest and imprisonment fifteen years prior. To the labourer, she explained that his work permit may take some time to go through, and to return in two weeks if he hadn't yet received any word. Guards moved to usher people from the palace grounds once he was gone.

"Your Majesty, a bird from General Ettrias," Golmin said, appearing at her side. Talin stood and took the letter from him with a nod of thanks. Her brother had been with the Fae for the last six weeks, investigating the origins of her mystery assassin. She hadn't particularly wanted him to go, but he had insisted, and Aldrus had sided with him immediately. Though she hated to admit it, his investigations made sense; Aldrus had identified the assassin as Fae in the moments before the man had fled and they had no other leads.

Not that his investigating will do much.

"Any news?" Aldrus asked.

"He's returning. Empty-handed, it would seem." Talin handed him the parchment to read for himself.

Something was wrong. Ettrias had said he would be investigating for at least two months, so returning home without any other news... It was highly unusual behaviour, to say the least. She suspected that he had indeed found something and was reluctant to write down his report.

"It was worth a try," Aldrus said as they walked. "Has Lord Highett found anything?"

Talin shook her head. "Whoever he was and whoever hired him were very good. They left nothing behind. Ettrias is—*was*—our only lead."

"I'm worried that they'll try again..." Aldrus's voice trailed off. "I know you have your reasons. But not appointing a new lord commander—"

Talin had heard enough. "Captain Golmin does not want the position. I have no-one else who can take it."

Keep telling yourself that.

She knew it was a foolish excuse; she could easily offer the position to Ashera or have someone make the recruitment rounds across Kies Tor. Fifteen years had passed since Red Wolf was exiled. Plenty of time to find a replacement.

Is that all he is? A tool to be replaced? Talin winced at the thought. He wasn't, and that was the problem. She couldn't bear to simply 'replace' him.

Gods, I need to move on.

"You've grown quiet," her husband said. "If it's because of what I said..."

"No, not at all," Talin said. They had reached the stairs leading to the upper levels.

"I've had the servants draw you a bath already," Aldrus said. "And don't worry about your paperwork. I can take care of it."

"Thank you." Talin smiled. "Though there was one matter that I'd prefer to deal with myself. Lady Blackrun wrote to us asking for assistance in an investigation into some recent disappearances across the north. I'd prefer to respond in person, given the...current tensions."

"Of course, I'll leave that to you, then. I think Arkiel will be happy you've got the evening off," Aldrus said. They parted ways there, with him continuing up the stairs to their chambers and his office to do the paperwork while Talin headed for the private bath on the second floor. The water had already been drawn up, as Aldrus had said, and she sank into it gratefully, leaving her clothes for one of her handmaids to take away. Talin unbraided her hair and sank further into the tub.

Gods, Aldrus was right—she needed a break. In the five years since the war ended, she had tried to pick up whatever was left of Kies Tor and rebuild it. Though most of the south hadn't seen battle for almost eight years now, the north was still recovering, and she could see evidence of broken towns and charred buildings all across the Highlands. She visited every year to see if she could do anything more. Lady Blackrun's hospitality was generous, as always, but they both knew there was little the Crown could give that would mend the north. Arkiel, meanwhile, was too young to even remember a time when resources were scarce and the entire kingdom struggled to get by. Talin craved that kind of innocence from when she had been a child, so blissfully ignorant of the invading Hellhounds.

That night at the Draconian border still haunted her sometimes. Even against a small team of hunters, they had been hopelessly out-numbered and outmatched. With the full moon bearing down and fuelling the Hellhounds' powers, their only option had been to run.

If it weren't for Red Wolf, I'd be dead.

The bathwater suddenly felt cold. Talin stepped out, grabbing the towel that had been left for her before changing into a light dress with semi-transparent sleeves. With the storm season almost over, temperatures were already beginning to rise; she could feel the dry heat of an early drought even through the cool marble brickwork of the palace. She had no doubt that this year's dry season would be particularly harsh across the south.

Heading downstairs again, she found Arkiel in the library as expected, writing notes while Corvan lectured him on history. The old man was a good storyteller, there was no doubt about it; he had been partially responsible for Talin's interest in books back in the day with his captivating tales and stories of old legends long forgotten. Today, he was teaching Arkiel about the Draconian alliance and how it had formed fifteen years ago. Ancient history for a child, no doubt. Talin remembered it all painfully well and the events that followed their return to Kies Tor.

"Mother did all of that?" Arkiel asked, eyes wide. "Woah."

"It was our newfound alliance with the Drakels that saved this kingdom," Corvan said. "The capital was at its breaking point when Prince—*Emperor* Kadis arrived with reinforcements." He spotted Talin watching and bowed. "Your Majesty."

"Mother!" Arkiel jumped to his feet and ran to her. "Corvan told me about how you rode west with Uncle Ettrias and Ashera to form an alliance with the Drakels. Is it all true?"

Talin cracked a faint smile. "Yes. It was a very long journey. We set out at night, under cover of darkness, because I wanted to ensure that your uncle wasn't executed in my absence. Red Wolf..." She hesitated, then corrected herself. "A good friend of mine came with us. He was one of the greatest warriors in Kies Tor. We would never have made it as far as we did without him."

"What happened to him?" Arkiel asked.

"He was...exiled. For something he did a long time ago."

"Oh." Arkiel looked disappointed. "That means he can't ever come back to Kies Tor, right? Unless you give him special permission?"

"Your father would have to give him permission," Talin said. "I can't intervene with the court's decision, according to the law. As the representative of the Crown, I have what we would call a 'conflict of interest'."

"But you can *change* the law," Arkiel said.

"Yes, but there are many laws that are there to make sure the Crown doesn't overstep its boundaries," Talin explained. "Use its power for bad things."

"I see." Arkiel's face scrunched up, as if he was trying to look like he was thinking.

"Come on now. Thank Corvan for the lesson." Talin nodded at the old healer.

"Thank you, Master Corvan," Arkiel said.

Corvan bowed again. "The pleasure was mine, Your Highness. We'll continue tomorrow." He gathered his things and put his books away before taking his leave.

"Father said you have the whole evening off," Arkiel said. "Will you read me a story?"

"Of course. Go pick a book." Talin nudged him towards the bookshelves, and he darted off to find something. She watched him disappear behind one of the shelves and settled herself on a nearby couch.

The library was oddly empty tonight. She would have expected Corvan to remain here, doing his own reading, but perhaps the old man needed his rest. Lord Cassius should be here too unless he was still trying to follow the dead ends that her would-be assassin had left him with. And the guards...

There should be two guards at the doors.

Something was wrong.

Talin got to her feet and leaned to see where Arkiel was between the shelves, but the boy had run out of sight. She wasn't armed. If it came to a fight, she would have to reveal her magic to him.

"Arkiel?" she called.

"Still looking, Mother!" he said.

Talin took a second to feel the wild magic around her, readying herself for any threats that came their way. She crept between the shelves to find Arkiel. The boy had wandered further than she had expected; she heard him flipping pages along the back shelf, trying to find a book that interested him. He looked up as she approached and put the book back where he'd found it.

"These all sound so dull and boring," he said. "Maybe you can tell me a story instead?"

"If you like." Talin forced a smile. "Come, we'll settle in the reading area."

The reading area, where she'd just come from, was the only open part of the library where her view wasn't blocked by endless shelves of books. That, and she'd be able to see the windows.

"Will you tell me more about that friend of yours? The one who was exiled?" Arkiel asked. "He seems like a nice person, if he helped you all those years ago."

"Well..." Talin's brow creased. She hadn't talked about Red Wolf in years, had done her best to forget about him and get on with her life as queen. But try as she might, she couldn't forget.

"It's alright if you don't want to tell me about him. You must have plenty of stories from the war, right?" Arkiel said.

"Of course," Talin said, breathing an inward sigh of relief. "I'll..."

Metal glinted behind Arkiel for a fraction of a second. Talin threw out an arm and shoved her son aside just in time to avoid an assassin's flashing knife. He swung again, and this time, she glimpsed his hood and mask. The same outfit as the assassin who'd attacked her before.

No, that's impossible. Why would they—

The assassin slammed the pommel of his weapon into her face, sending her staggering. Arkiel shouted for her as the man grabbed him and prepared to deal the killing blow. Talin lunged forward instinctively and grabbed the blade, gasping as it cut into her palm, twisting it away from Arkiel. It was enough to give the boy time to wriggle free.

"Get help!" Talin shouted before ducking under a wild swing. The assassin was getting desperate. She jumped back again to avoid a fast jab and finally saw an opening for her fingertips to touch his sleeve.

Lightning darted across her hand and through the assassin, lighting up the room for a split second. The man flew backwards between the shelves and landed on his back with a grunt. Talin crouched down beside him and charged another attack, in case he fought back.

"Who sent you?" she demanded. The man was silent. "I'm not in the mood for this. Give me a name."

The library doors slammed open, and she heard half a dozen guards in plate armour thunder in followed by a set of footsteps she recognised as Aldrus'. They surrounded the assassin and allowed her to pass.

"You're unhurt?" her husband asked.

Talin examined her bleeding hand. "I'll live. Arkiel?"

"Here, Mother," the boy said. "I'm alright."

Talin sighed and kissed the top of his head. "You did well to get the guards."

"We'll take this rat to the dungeons, Your Majesty," Golmin said as two of his guards dragged the assassin away. "I'll talk to Lord Cassius and find out what we can."

"Thank you," Talin said. "I want to know who hired him and why he was after Arkiel. If he won't talk, make him."

"The library should have been guarded," Aldrus added with a scowl. "You better have an explanation, Captain."

"Deepest apologies, Majesty." Golmin bowed. "Talin. I'll investigate this too, of course."

Talin dismissed him with a halfhearted wave and looked at her hand again. She was starting to notice the stinging pain now that she had calmed down from the scuffle and realised she was bleeding all over the floor. Aldrus offered her a handkerchief to help stem the bleeding for now, and she took it with a nod of thanks.

"Send Corvan to my study," she told the remaining guards. "Tell your captain to join me there as soon as possible and bring his second-in-command."

"As Your Majesty commands." The guards disappeared through the doors as well, leaving her with Aldrus and Arkiel in the library.

"Can I...can I stay in your room tonight?" the boy asked.

"Of course," Aldrus said. "If it makes you feel safer."

Talin pinched the bridge of her nose. "Assassins after me, I can understand. I can't make everyone happy. But Arkiel...Who would do something like this?"

"You did handle the assassin well enough." Aldrus shrugged. "If you would just...find a lord commander..."

"Aldrus—"

"I'm not talking about Captain Golmin. Find someone else, someone you can trust," Aldrus said. "To protect Arkiel if nothing else."

Talin sighed. He was right; she couldn't be with Arkiel all the time to keep him safe. But there were precious few people she could trust to do the job. Maybe if she insisted that Golmin take the promotion...

There is another option. One you cannot act upon.

"Come," she said. "We'll discuss this more with Corvan and the others."

"I take it you have a plan," Aldrus said.

"Yes."

"And I'm not going to like this plan."

"No," Talin confessed. "But I don't have a better one."

Don't you? Or are you just saying that because you want this one to work?

Talin hushed the voice. There was one person she trusted to protect Arkiel more than herself, more than Aldrus, and he was somewhere miles and miles away, across the border in a foreign land where he didn't belong.

Sending for him was a fool's errand.

T alin didn't often have this many people in her study, never mind this many people who looked like they didn't want to be here. Golmin leaned against the wall to her right, muttering something about how he should be investigating the situation with his royal guards, while Corvan treated her injured hand. Aldrus paced back and forth before her irritably. Even Ashera, who had earned her blue cloak some years ago now, looked like she would rather be enjoying her evening off. The only one who seemed at ease was Arkiel. He lay on the floor in the corner, acting out a pretend battle with toy soldiers.

"Golmin, please just take the promotion," Aldrus finally said and stopped pacing.

"I may be a good captain, but I'm afraid I'd disappoint as your lord commander," Golmin said. "Send for Red Wolf if you trust no one else."

A hush fell over the room as all eyes turned to him.

"Ooh, you said the name..." Ashera grinned at him. Talin winced. She *had* been thinking the exact same thing, had even wanted to bring it up as a last resort when they eventually ran out of ideas...

"I can't," she said.

"You can't, or you won't?" Aldrus muttered under his breath.

Talin shot him a tired glare.

"I think we should look to an...alternative solution," Corvan said. "Red Wolf is not exactly welcomed by the common folk in Kies Tor. Things may turn ugly even if he was to return under the Crown's protection."

"Thank you—something we can agree on," Talin said. "We know my enemies are determined, or they wouldn't have sent this new assassin. We gained no information from their first attempt. This mistake might give us something."

"How do you know the two events are connected? What if these two assassins were sent by two different parties?" Ashera asked.

"It's a possibility, but I very much doubt that a guild would accept a second contract on the same target. Not after their first man almost failed to make it out of the palace in one piece, anyway," Talin said. "We just need to find out who they are and where they came from."

"I can tell you the latter." Aldrus crossed his arms. "They come from a guild in the far south—they're contractors for the highest bidder."

"*What?*" Talin stared at him.

"The uniforms they wore, the design... I've not met these assassins in person, but I know the stories," Aldrus said.

Talin let out a long breath. "And you...didn't think to mention this a month ago?"

"I thought it was just a coincidence. Some assassin gets paid enough to kill you, of all people, of course they'll buy the best clothes they can afford," Aldrus said. "But two of these men, dressed the same? Someone in Astaria wants you dead."

"Private assassins, Your Majesty?" Golmin asked.

"The rich and mighty can afford anything these days," Aldrus said. "Especially the Fae nobility."

Talin got to her feet and brought a bottle of wine out from a cabinet in the corner. Corvan and Ashera both declined a drink.

"I'm not sober enough for this," Golmin muttered.

"But if Ettrias has found nothing from his investigation, then whoever is behind this must have enough influence among your people to keep things quiet," Talin said.

"Oh, believe me, that doesn't narrow it down." Aldrus took a sip of wine.

Talin put a hand on her chin. She suspected that Ettrias had found out exactly who was behind these assassination attempts and couldn't risk sharing it in a letter.

And Aldrus must be linked to it somehow.

She glanced at her husband. Ettrias usually wasn't so secretive in front of him; he knew that whatever information he put in his letters would quickly make its way to Aldrus. They normally got along well enough, and she was certain they would never keep secrets from each other.

But this was different.

Aldrus had insisted that she took the evening off, volunteered to do her paperwork to put her in the library with Arkiel. Was it simply coincidence that she ended up facing the assassin this evening, or had he planned everything beforehand?

"I'll talk to my brother," Aldrus said. "Maybe his network of spies can uncover something. He's involved in this now—he'd better take some responsibility."

Talin poured herself another cup. "I'll have Hesar put the Owls on high alert. If they're operating in Belanore, they won't be leaving anytime soon."

"And Arkiel?" Golmin asked. "The problem still remains. You need to appoint a new bodyguard. For him, if nothing else."

Talin stared at her drink. He was right; they hadn't fixed the problem at all. Solving this mystery wouldn't change the fact that she had put Arkiel in danger because she couldn't let go of Red Wolf and still couldn't.

"Aldrus..." She looked up. Her husband seemed to know exactly what she was thinking.

"You want to bring him back," he said.

Talin tipped back the rest of her wine. "I trust him. More than anything. He won't fail."

"That's not what I'm worried about," Aldrus said.

"Aldrus, please," Talin said. "If there was someone else who could do this, I would send for them instead. But there isn't, and I..." *I would be abusing my power if I asked you to pardon him.* She bit back the rest of the sentence.

"You feel guilty about asking me." Aldrus lifted his eyebrows. "You know you can't go through the Court; they'll never approve your request. Asking *me* to do it directly...is cheating the system."

Talin sighed. "And I normally wouldn't ask. Would never ask. But this is different."

"Think about what will happen," Aldus said. "As far as I'm aware, Red Wolf never had many supporters. If you bring him back..."

"I *know*," Talin said. "Fifteen years ago, I chose to let him go because I had to set a precedent for the Crown and court to remain impartial. If I'm ever to bring him back, it would be because I had no other choice. Aldrus, please, you know I wouldn't ask this of you if there was another way."

Aldrus rubbed his chin. "I'll...think about it."

Talin got the feeling he knew far more than he was letting on.

"Golmin, double the guard around Arkiel's chambers," she said. "Arrange for a guard to accompany him at all times, at least until I appoint a new lord commander. I won't risk something like this happening again."

"Of course, Your Majesty." Golmin dipped his head.

"I can accompany him," Ashera said. "Save the good captain some time trying to pick out of every man in the Royal Guard."

"If I have the queen's approval..." Golmin looked to Talin, who nodded. "Then it's settled. Ashera will guard Arkiel for the time being. I will investigate this incident among my men and find out who was supposed to be on duty in the library. We'll catch the culprit soon."

"I hope you're right." Talin glanced at Arkiel, still absorbed in his pretend battle, before looking at Golmin again. "You two are dismissed. Get back to the barracks, get some rest. Arkiel will be with Aldrus and I tonight."

Golmin and Ashera both stood, bowing to her and then Aldrus. The door clicked shut behind them.

"Aldrus, if you would put Arkiel to bed..." she began.

"Consider it done." Aldrus gave her a reassuring smile. "Come on, Ark, it's time for bed."

"Alright. Can I bring my toys?" Arkiel asked.

"Of course." Aldrus helped him pack up his toy soldiers and led him from the room. Talin waited until she was certain they were both out of earshot.

"Corvan, I can't be the only one who senses that something is wrong," she said. "My brother's letter, now this..."

"Ah, you'll have to forgive me. I've not had a chance to read that letter yet," Corvan said. Talin pulled the parchment from a drawer and handed it to him. She saw the old healer's brow crease as he read.

"It is unusual, yes," he confessed. "I suspect he has found something he does not wish to divulge in a letter."

"My thoughts exactly," Talin said. "Of course, he also knows Aldrus and I are the first two people who will read his letters. The only two, if I wished."

"You believe Aldrus is involved in this assassination attempt?" Corvan asked.

"Maybe. I think he knows a lot more than he is telling me," Talin said.

"I know your marriage was purely political, but you two have always gotten along..." Corvan trailed off, hesitating. "Ah, but I wouldn't want to speak out of turn. I am just an old man, after all."

"I miss Red Wolf." Admitting it felt odd. "Aldrus knows how close we were. If he's jealous... Well, I guess I'd know about it for a start." She paused and stared at Corvan. "He rarely disagrees with anything I do. Red Wolf always had something to say about how I was handling things at court. The only time he's objected...was just then. About Red Wolf."

"Correct me if I'm wrong, but hasn't he been pushing you to appoint a new lord commander?"

"Yes, but we never argued about it. He obviously doesn't want Red Wolf back here. But why?" Talin rubbed her eyes. "Things aren't adding up. If Aldrus is involved and doesn't want Red Wolf here, then I...I must forge the paperwork he needs to return."

"I know your reasons, but I would strongly advise *against* such a foolish move," Corvan said. "If Aldrus is involved and you bring Red Wolf back here illegally, he can use that against you. He's popular with the common folk and most of the southern nobility. They'll likely listen to him over you once Red Wolf is involved."

As much as she hated to admit it, the healer was right. Red Wolf would only serve to make things more complicated if she tried to bring him back illegally. Talin looked at her empty cup and refrained from pouring more wine.

"I don't think Aldrus means any ill intention toward you," Corvan said. "But if you like, I will take it upon myself to keep an eye on him."

"No, Corvan, I won't bother you with something like this," Talin said. "I'll have Lord Highett spy on him. *If* the situation calls for it. We'll see in a few weeks when my brother returns home. You should get some rest, too."

"As Your Majesty commands." Corvan backed out of the room, leaving her with her thoughts.

Talin put the wine away and took her necklace out to examine it. Red Wolf had gifted it to her on the day he left Belanore, so long ago, telling her that it held some kind of Hellhound magic he had never been able to figure out. Its jewelled wolf eyes stared back at her unblinkingly.

If this thing is magic, it's unlike any magic we've ever known.

She tucked it back under her dress and adjusted the chain to hide it better. Red Wolf's letter still sat at the bottom of one of her drawers, rarely touched. Talin wasn't sure why she'd kept it other than to re-read it every now and then.

She paused with her hand hovering near the open drawer.

Red Wolf is gone. He's moved on by now—it's time you did the same.

Talin slammed the drawer shut again and withdrew her hand. She would not entertain the thought of bringing him back to Kies Tor. He had been exiled for fifteen years, and they were fated never to meet again.

But he would know what to do.

She picked up a spare oil lamp, lit it with a spark of lightning, and tried to banish the thoughts as she made her way to bed.

IX

B elanore hadn't changed much, at least.

Red Wolf took some comfort in this as he made his way out of the inn and down Baker Lane, keeping his head down and his senses sharp. He had taken this route many times before with Talin; she enjoyed these early morning walks past the shops with their freshly baked loaves of bread. But he knew he couldn't let the scent overwhelm his nose. There were other things he needed to keep track of—such as the patrol making its way up the lane opposite him.

"Fresh loaves! Get yer fresh loaves here!" shouted a vendor. "Sweet buns, honey cakes, only two yarii each!" Another vendor chimed in with similar offers. Red Wolf heard the patrol drawing closer and turned towards the nearest baker, pretending to fumble in his pockets for the coin. He paid the woman for a honey cake and continued on his way. The patrol officers didn't spare him a second glance.

Talin's papers had seemed suspicious, at best, and he had considered ignoring the summons altogether at first. But she had sent the encoded message for a reason, and if the situation was dire enough that she would send for him in the first place, he had to return. At the time, he had told himself it was his duty. After all, he'd made a promise to return if she ever needed him.

Now I'm just making excuses.

He had to admit it, he supposed. The real reason he had ignored his own suspicions and endured a month's travel back to Belanore was because he wanted to see her again. But now that he had returned, he wasn't sure she even wanted to see him. The papers must have been forged; she'd never send for him, not like this.

Red Wolf pondered all the possibilities. He had no intention of going to the palace yet, not until he was certain he could enter safely. The Owls at the gate may not have thought too much about the warrant, but the royal guards were trained to spot fake documents, and if Talin or someone else had forged his papers, he would be arrested on the spot. He needed information.

The local gossip had it that a second intruder had been apprehended at the palace, after an assassin was sent to kill the queen last month. Red Wolf doubted that she would send for him over such a trivial matter. She was more than capable of dealing with assassins now, after a long journey to the Drakels and back, after winning a war. If only she'd included more in her message...

Red Wolf turned off Baker Lane and headed towards the market square. He wondered if a part of him was simply trying to convince him that Talin didn't want to see him, so he was coming up with these excuses subconsciously.

If the papers are real, the court must think the situation is dire enough. If Talin forged them, she must be desperate. If someone else did, Talin is in danger.

He pinched the bridge of his nose. All those scenarios led him to returning to the palace, but how? The safe choice was to sneak back in through one of the secret passages, assuming they hadn't been sealed off permanently and that they weren't guarded. With the city being evacuated through them during the Siege of Belanore, he doubted they were much of a secret anymore, but sealing them would rob the palace of an emergency escape. He had no doubt he could handle a few guards, but inside the palace, it would be much more difficult to sneak into Talin's office. Assuming Aldrus had his own place to work.

Things have changed so much since I was gone.

Would she even remember him? He hoped so, but he wasn't so sure. He couldn't blame her for moving on. She had a kingdom to keep afloat, and in the end, he was nobody special.

Red Wolf cursed and turned back the way he came, heading for the palace. The least he could do was scout the area, see if the guards' positions had changed, find some entry points.

He could smell a gang of thugs laying in ambush at the next alley he passed, no doubt waiting to mug an unsuspecting citizen or worse. He paused there and considered springing the trap, then walked on. He didn't owe the city anything, and he was perfectly content to let these boys do whatever they wished. He had lost faith in Belanore long before his exile.

This is Talin's city. She would have done something.

Red Wolf stopped again and turned back just as another young man turned down the alley, clutching a map in one hand. He wore a crisp tunic and his hair had been slicked back. Lost on his way to the palace, no doubt.

"Oh, for the love of the gods," he hissed through his teeth and followed the man.

It didn't take him long to catch up; the young man kept glancing down at his map as he walked and barely paid any attention to his surroundings. Red Wolf managed to cut in front of him just before he could stumble into the ambush zone.

"I wouldn't go that way if I were you," the ex-bodyguard said.

"Wha…" The man blinked at him for a moment, then moved to step around. "I need to get to the palace. Excuse me, please."

"Just wait," Red Wolf began, but the man had already ducked past, made it two steps into the ambush zone, and froze with a knife at his throat. Two thugs had stepped out to bar his path, both with knives in their hands, while two more slipped behind Red Wolf to cut off his escape. That was fine by him. Preventing the unfortunate victim before him from getting his throat slit, on the other hand…

The thugs in front of him were clearly trained. He could tell from their posture and feet that they had some combat experience, perhaps as ex-militia fighting alongside the royal army during the war. The two behind were less confident.

Might as well take a page from Talin's book and try negotiation.

"Whatever you want from us, I'm sure my—the queen could provide you with *legally*," he said. "She's a generous woman. I hear there's a veterans' compensation for ex-militia and soldiers if you went to the palace to apply."

"It's not *enough*," one of the thugs hissed. "It runs out. And we have no way of earning more coin."

"Don't even like the queen." A thug behind him spat on the ground. "She's too soft. At least the king has been pushing for *useful* laws instead of getting rid of the death penalty."

Red Wolf felt a surge of anger and tried his best to push it down. He couldn't let his emotions get the best of him here, not if he wanted to prevent bloodshed.

"I don't have anything of value," he said instead. "I'm not sure the man you have at knife point has any coin, either, if he's on his way to the palace."

The young man gave a small nod at that. "I really don't have anything, please..."

"Don't believe you. You're dressed too fine," said the thug behind him. He was a burly-looking man, with a scar on his cheek and a faded red tunic.

"I wanted to dress well for the queen," the young man squeaked. "This is my best shirt."

"Hand over the coin, or we'll take it off your corpses!" the thug snapped.

"I have no coin beyond a few coppers," Red Wolf said. "You can come search my pockets if you like." He took a cautious step forward, bringing himself within arms' reach of the young man.

One of the thugs behind him stepped forward to pat him down. Red Wolf leaned in slightly to talk to the young man.

"Whatever happens, don't pull away from my hand," he said softly.

He grabbed the man's wrist and held on tight as he drove a back elbow into the red-shirted thug.

The man went down instantly, clutching a broken nose, while the two ex-militia moved in. The taller one drove his knife towards the young man's throat. There was a flash of gold as the blade skittered harmlessly off Red Wolf's shield. He gave the young man a shove, send-ing him stumbling out of the fray, and took the second thug's knife to the chest with a grunt. A hard body kick sent him to the ground soundlessly.

"I don't want to fight," Red Wolf said. "Let us go, and nobody else gets hurt."

The remaining two thugs both rushed him at the same time. He kicked the knife out of the tall one's hand and threw him, then stepped around the other and followed through with a punch to the face. He crumpled in an instant. Red Wolf moved just in time to stop his head from hitting the cobblestones.

Gods, I'm sorry. You'll have an awful headache when you wake.

The tall thug climbed to his feet and rushed forwards again. Red Wolf took the knife to the gut and wrapped his arms around the man's neck, bringing him to the ground as they struggled. He went limp a few seconds later.

"Come on," the ex-bodyguard said, dragging the young man to his feet and smoothing down his shirt. "The palace is this way. You should still have time."

"You're...you're a Weaver. You used magic," the man said. "And then you...healed. Like those *things*. Like the Hellhounds." He backed away. "Get away from me, freak!"

"I'm not..." He knew then that he would receive no gratitude. "*Tch*. Maybe I should've left you alone with those thugs instead."

Leaving the man behind, he continued up the main road to the palace, dodging guards whenever they passed. His height attracted enough attention as it was, but with his hood turned up and his head down, he could pass for an ordinary citizen going about his day. The guards didn't have the time or reason to stop and search every single tall person in the city.

The palace exterior looked largely the same as it had fifteen years ago. Guards still stood at their usual posts, and a quick scan over the outer walls showed the blind spots where they had always been. The number of guards, however, appeared to be double the usual number, no doubt as a response to the intruder who had been apprehended. Scaling the walls would be difficult but not impossible.

Red Wolf did a lap around the entire palace to map out the area before deciding to check the secret tunnels. He doubted they would yield any more promising results than the main gates and ramparts, but there was no harm in taking a look.

The tunnel behind Thieves Lane was closest to the inn and likely the most accessible, but to his dismay, Talin had sealed it at some point after the siege. He could move the debris himself, he supposed, but there was no telling whether he'd be able to do it without collapsing the entire tunnel on top of him. The tunnel near the city square was in a similar state, blocked off just past the fork that separated the exit to the palace cellar and the exit to Stormwood. He remembered that they had collapsed the roof on purpose after Hellhounds found their way inside. He doubted Talin was planning on opening it again; such a huge amount of rubble would be almost impossible to clear without bringing more of the ceiling on top of the workers. He knew of other passages leading to the palace, ones that Talin hopefully didn't and therefore couldn't order sealed.

Knowing Talin, she would have studied the original palace blueprints and sealed most, if not all, of the secret tunnels. He didn't have time to run around the entire city on the off chance one of them was still open.

But he did know she wouldn't seal the final exit to Stormwood. Doing so would rob them of an escape in case of a siege. He would have to leave through the northern gate again to find it, and for that, he needed his papers. Red Wolf turned and headed back to the inn.

The innkeep was serving up lunch when he returned, and he briefly considered paying for a meal but decided against it. Finding the tunnel would likely take him all afternoon, and he needed to return before dark in case he came up with nothing. He jogged up the stairs without a word and fumbled for his key.

Wait. Red Wolf sniffed. *Someone's been here.*

He caught a fresh scent that wasn't his own leading directly to his room. Perhaps the housekeeper had come through to clean the place? But he didn't smell soap.

This is bad.

He slammed open the door to his room. The scent was strongest near his pack, and from the way his belongings had been overturned and strewn all over the floor, someone had been looking for something specific. But his sword still rested in the corner, his coin pouch left untouched. A chill went through Red Wolf as he opened the side compartment of his pack and saw nothing inside.

The papers from Talin were gone.

T hree weeks came and went uneventfully, though the attempt on Arkiel's life had Talin more on edge than usual; she often caught herself double-checking dark corners and open windows for any lurking intruders. Ashera accompanied him as agreed, and the extra guards Golmin had put around the palace meant there was no shortage of security, but still, she couldn't help but feel like something could go wrong.

Arkiel, for his part, seemed to be faring better. Despite being shaken up after the incident, he was soon back to his usual self, chatting to the guards on duty and reading his books. He still avoided the library, which was understandable, so Talin had one of the spare rooms cleared out and turned into a classroom for his lessons. He didn't seem to mind.

"I'm glad young Master Arkiel is still in high spirits despite the situation," Corvan remarked after one of their daily lessons. "I'm not sure you would have fared as well at his age. I don't mean any offence, of course."

"No, you're probably right." Talin allowed herself a brief smile. "Ettrias and I grew up oblivious to the war, Arkiel will grow up seeing the aftermath. I just hope...I'm doing things right. For him."

"You're doing a fine job, Your Majesty," Corvan said, stealing a glance at the boy, fiddling with the hem of his tunic. "You should be proud of yourself."

"I...appreciate it. Thank you."

"I take it you've not found anything linked to your assassin yet?"

"No, not yet," Talin said. "We'll know more when Ettrias returns." She doubted that whatever Ettrias had found would be of much use, considering the Fae's mysterious nature and Darien's reluctance to involve himself in what appears to be an internal affair. Still, it was their only lead. She hoped it would be enough.

"Are you holding court today, Mother?" Arkiel asked, looking up.

"I am." Talin was surprised by his sudden interest.

"Can I come?"

"Of course." She figured that he only wanted to come because he felt safer with her, but that was fine. Aldrus could keep an eye on him while she sorted out whatever grievances the common folk had. Ashera still followed him everywhere, too, acting as a temporary lord commander of sorts; she was no more than a shadow in the background, barely noticeable. Keeping him entertained couldn't possibly be that difficult.

She began to regret that decision half an hour in.

Half a dozen people had come and gone, and Arkiel already looked bored out of his mind. Aldrus hovered nearby, trying his best to distract the boy, but he kept fidgeting in his seat and tugging at her sleeve. She managed to send off a miner with compensation for his stolen tools after he claimed the City Watch wouldn't help him.

"Arkiel, I thought you said you wanted to be here," she said quietly when he tugged on her arm again, looking for something to do.

"Well, yes, but...all these people's problems are so boring," he said. "Don't people come to court if they have interesting problems? Like if someone's an outsider and their neighbours are rude to them just because of that, you do something about it."

"Sometimes, yes, but it's these little problems that sometimes mean the most," Talin said. "A farmer losing some cattle may not sound so important to you because you don't need to worry about cattle in the palace, but to them, it is the only way they can feed their family."

"So...if we give the farmers money to buy more cattle, they won't starve," Arkiel said. "That's a nice thing to do."

"Yes. A kingdom is nothing without its people. If you let your citizens starve while you sit on mountains of gold, then you have nothing to rule," Talin said. "You are responsible for the lives of your citizens. All of them. And one day, you will sit on this throne, and it will be your duty to listen and act."

"When I'm king, I'm going to make sure nobody starves ever," Arkiel declared.

Talin smiled. "I'm sure you could."

The session continued, and this time, the boy seemed a little more attentive to what was going on. Talin allowed another dozen or so people to come through and tried to do what she could. There was no way for her to address some of the problems her people had; in the aftermath of the war, there was too much destruction and too little time. But it was her duty to rebuild this kingdom, she knew that much, just as it had been her duty to defeat the Hellhounds. That responsibility had been passed on to her from her father.

Red Wolf had told her that she would be a good ruler just before her coronation all those years ago. She remembered that conversation with him clear as day, because her heart had been racing the entire morning and he had managed to calm her, if only a little. He'd said that she didn't seek the power that came with ruling. He was right, in a way. She cared not for the crown, nor the idea of being queen.

Now, fifteen years later, she fully understood. Knew that ruling the kingdom was more than a crown, more than a title and some lands. Being queen was a duty to all her people. Being queen demanded she serve her people and make sacrifices where necessary.

That had been her first lesson when she sent Red Wolf away.

"Your Majesty..." Ashera leaned over and dropped her voice. Talin saw Golmin disappear through a door at the edge of her vision. "Ettrias has returned. Captain Golmin has let him into the meeting hall. He says it's urgent and asks that you come alone."

"Close the gates," Talin said. The guards moved to usher everyone out.

"Can I come with you?" Arkiel asked when she stood.

"Not this time, I'm afraid," Talin said. "Your uncle has returned, and there are matters I must discuss with him in private. Besides, you have swordplay now with Quartermaster Brakis."

"I don't *like* swordplay," Arkiel said. "History with Master Corvan is much more interesting."

Talin smiled. *Gods, I used to be the same.* "You need to learn how to use a sword to defend yourself if the occasion ever arises."

"Like if another assassin comes?" Arkiel asked, and Talin's gaze shot towards the guards at the throne room doors to make sure they were still there.

"Yes." She nodded. "Or you might have to travel around the kingdom when you become king, and there might be bandits lurking on the road, and you mustn't rely on guards to defend you all the time."

"And if there's a war, I'll have to lead an army into battle, right?" Arkiel said.

"Let's hope you never have to."

"But that would be so epic and exciting! Like you. You fought against the Hellhounds and *won*."

Talin didn't respond. Arkiel had never seen the broken defence lines in the north nor the Western Forts before they regained control. She wasn't sure she would describe any of it as exciting.

Let the boy dream. He's still so young. So innocent.

"Go on, now, you'll be late," she said, and Arkiel rushed off with renewed excitement, forcing Ashera to keep up.

"I'll be in my study," Aldrus said. Talin gave a brief nod, and they parted ways at the corridor.

She hoped Ettrias had some news for her, good or bad. That he would return so soon was odd, to say the least, especially since he had been the one who insisted on riding south to investigate things.

Ettrias was waiting in the meeting hall for her as expected, having changed out of his travelling clothes into court attire. One of the servants had served him some chilled liquor, which he was nursing at the long table. It was odd, seeing the table without its maps and documents, but Talin was glad to see him again.

"I trust your journey wasn't too unpleasant," she said.

"Well, not many people are dumb enough to attack half a dozen royal guards and the Royal Army *General*," Ettrias said, getting to his feet. Talin allowed herself to be wrapped in a hug. "Good to see you again."

"Likewise." She glanced at the guards standing by the main doors. "Leave us, please."

The guards looked at each other, then bowed and backed out of the room.

"You got my letter?" Ettrias asked.

"Yes. It was...cryptic, to say the least," Talin said.

"I couldn't say too much. I didn't know if Aldrus would read it too," Ettrias said.

I was right, Talin thought. "I'd suspected he might be involved. Did Golmin catch you up on what happened while you were away?"

"He thought it best if you briefed me," Ettrias said.

Talin explained what had transpired three weeks ago, from Aldrus conveniently placing her in the library with Arkiel to the attempt on her son's life. Ettrias' face paled as she went on. She wasn't sure she had ever managed to render him this speechless before.

"Arkiel... Gods, this is worse than I thought," he stammered. "Is he alright?"

"He was unhurt, yes," Talin said. "The assassin is in the dungeons now, but Golmin has failed to make him talk so far."

"Your assassin will tell you what I already know if he does crack," Ettrias explained. "Talin...Darien's reluctance to help isn't because he believes this to be an internal affair. He's the one who sent the assassins."

Talin stared at him. She wasn't sure she had heard right. "What."

"You heard me."

"But…" Talin rubbed her eyes with one hand. "No, that can't be right. Why would he want to kill me and Arkiel? And why now?"

"I don't know, but I wager it's because he wants Kies Tor for himself," Ettrias said. "He's realised that the Fae hold no power on the Torrian throne with you in charge. Aldrus' influence only stretches so far. As for the second assassin…I'm guessing he must have decided that taking you out wasn't enough. Aldrus would only become king regent until Arkiel came of age."

"Then Aldrus *is* involved?" Talin heard herself ask.

"I don't know. We have to assume so," Ettrias said. "I would have found out more, but I had to return early. My main concern in Astaria was that Darien would start targeting *me* in case I had any thoughts on taking the crown after you."

Talin hissed through her teeth. "That must be why Aldrus protested so strongly against Red Wolf's return. They know they'll never succeed with him in the palace."

"Red Wolf…" Ettrias' eyes widened. "No. I heard something about Darien wanting Red Wolf in Belanore."

"What? That doesn't make any sense."

"*Talin.* They want to bring him back under *your name*. Aldrus objected because he knows he can use the others as witnesses."

"Oh, gods." Talin felt her blood turn to ice. *Have I made a terrible mistake?*

"Talin?"

"I think I already sprung the trap. We need to—"

The doors to the meeting hall slammed open, revealing Aldrus, flanked by half a dozen guards armed with crossbows. Talin stole a glance at her brother and readied herself for a fight.

"I was tipped off this morning by a member of the City Watch who told me a certain fugitive was seen in Belanore," her husband said. "I didn't believe him at first, but he handed over the documents as proof. Talin, General Ettrias, you're both under arrest for conspiracy to aid a known criminal and enemy of the state."

"I don't seem to recall aiding any criminals recently; you'll have to specify," Ettrias said.

"Really? Because these—" Aldrus held up a warrant bearing Talin's signature and seal— "are the documents I spoke of."

"I never..." Talin began. "I never signed a warrant like that. Aldrus—"

Aldrus ignored her and read from the parchment. "'The individual named in this warrant shall be given passage into and out of any gated city in Kies Tor without question, may refuse searches by any City Watch member or patrolman, et cetera, et cetera... By decree of the State, with full approval from the High Court of Kies Tor, signed Talin Zylvaris II.' Would you look at that? It even has the court stamp. Oh, and there's his name."

"Aldrus..." Talin said, but he held up a finger, silencing her.

"This privileged individual is none other than the disgraced Lord Commander Red Wolf. Your ex-bodyguard."

Things are unravelling so much faster than I imagined.

Aldrus had ordered them to be taken up to one of the palace towers, which were only accessible from the top floor, but the distance did nothing to help Talin come up with a plan of any sort. With Golmin elsewhere in the palace and Ashera no doubt with Arkiel in the courtyard, there was no way to contact either of them for help. Corvan spent most of his time tinkering and experimenting in his own tower, while Lord Cassius was probably in the city at this hour, receiving new intelligence from his spy network.

They were alone here. Just her, Ettrias, and half a dozen royal guards wielding crossbows. She knew they had some of the best aim in the kingdom, surpassed only by the Royal Army archers. Red Wolf and Golmin had proven that countless times.

"Do all of you truly believe Aldrus over me?" Talin asked the guards. "He accuses me of conspiring with an enemy of the state, yet I would never do such a thing."

"I'm sorry, Your Majesty," one guard said. He seemed to be the youngest of the group, with pointed ears and tanned skin that marked him as a southerner. "King Aldrus has the documents bearing your signature and seal. He has an arrest warrant from the *High Court*. We're only doing what we've been instructed. Whether you and General Ettrias are innocent is up to the court to judge, not us."

"Who did you receive your orders from? Captain Golmin?" Ettrias asked.

"No, sir, from the king directly," the guard said. He looked apologetic. "We were off-duty. King Aldrus came to the barracks and asked that we accompany him somewhere, and he explained the situation on the way. We're not really supposed to talk to you, either, so I'd...appreciate it if you didn't ask any more questions."

Talin exchanged a knowing look with her brother. Aldrus must have known that passing his instructions down through the chain of command would alert Golmin to the fact that something was wrong, which would give him time to warn Ettrias. Bypassing the captain was the only way he could do this, which meant that Golmin didn't know these guards were here.

"The afternoon guard shift is about to swap over," Ettrias said in a low voice, leaning in to avoid being overheard. "Rufus will notice the missing guards at roll-call."

We need to stall for time, he meant.

"You're aware that standard protocol would have you receive the instructions from your captain or lieutenant, yes?" Talin asked. "It doesn't strike you as odd that Aldrus would bypass the chain of command?"

"Well…" the guard began.

"We're not supposed to talk to the prisoners," an older guard said.

"Just think about it, please," Talin said. "I don't care if you don't believe me, but *surely* you must all notice that something seems odd about the situation."

The young guard frowned. "I…well, King Aldrus…didn't actually show us the arrest warrant he'd obtained…right, Corporal?"

The guards slowed to a halt as they looked between themselves for confirmation.

"We have orders," the sergeant at the front finally said. "It doesn't matter who they're from. Defying an order from the king is one thing. Ignoring a *High Court warrant* is another."

"Aldrus cannot have acquired an arrest warrant so quickly," Talin said. "He was with me *holding court* for most of the morning."

"He could have obtained it before today," the sergeant said. "I'm sorry, Your Majesty, but it doesn't prove anyth—"

"Hold it, Sergeant."

Talin looked past the guards to see Golmin striding towards them. He didn't look happy.

"The six of you should be in the barracks, reporting for afternoon shift," the captain said.

"We were given orders from King Aldrus, sir," the sergeant said. "He has an arrest warrant for the queen and the general for conspiracy to aid an enemy of the state."

Golmin's gaze flickered towards Ettrias, who gave a barely perceptible nod.

"I'll take it from here, Sergeant," the captain said. "Get back to the barracks and receive your orders for the afternoon rotation."

The sergeant hesitated. Talin noticed a glint in his eye and recognised it as defiance.

He's working with Aldrus.

The sergeant raised his crossbow as if to shoot. Ettrias rammed his shoulder into the man and sent him staggering just in time, sending the bolt flying past Golmin's shoulder to embed itself in the ceiling. Talin spun, drawing on the wild magic around her, and managed to touch the nearest guard's gauntlet.

Lightning lashed out across the hallway, jumping between the guards' metal armour, dropping them all in an instant. Golmin dived out of range just in time.

"Are they alright?" he asked.

Talin winced. "They'll be unconscious for a while, but they'll be fine. Thanks for the rescue."

"You couldn't have done this *before* Rufus almost got shot?" Ettrias grumbled.

"I *was* hoping to talk to them." Talin crouched beside the young guard and double-checked to make sure he was still breathing, letting out a sigh of relief when it became apparent that he was alright. "Attacking half a dozen royal guards does no favours for our innocence."

"We need to get out of here," Golmin said. "I don't know what in the seven hells is going on, but all this is starting to feel uncomfortably similar to what happened fifteen years ago."

He was right, of course. Fifteen years ago, the late Master of Coin, Felix Wormwood, had conspired to take the crown for himself, and Talin had almost been executed without trial as a result. Now, with the death penalty abolished, she was certain they weren't in such serious mortal danger, but if Aldrus was allowed to take over, he would no doubt undo all the work she had done over the past fifteen years.

"We need to fetch Arkiel," Talin said. "He should still be in the courtyard with Ashera and Brakis. I can't risk leaving him here, not when Aldrus might be involved in the assassination attempts."

"I'll find him. If any of the other guards have orders to arrest you, you won't make it far," Golmin said. "We'll meet in the Stormwood tunnel."

Talin gave a nod. She knew the guard captain was right. "Quickly, then."

She made her way to the rear courtyard with Ettrias while Golmin detoured towards the central courtyard instead, keeping out of sight of any guard patrols in case they were also working with Aldrus. Her brother was uncharacteristically silent as they climbed down the ladder into the tunnel.

"You're quieter than usual," she said, taking a torch from a nearby bracket and lighting it with a spark of her magic.

"Something's been bothering me about those documents," Ettrias said as they walked. "Talin, I need you to—"

They were interrupted by a sound from the tunnel hatch. Talin turned and saw Golmin descending the ladder, followed soon by Arkiel and Ashera. The three of them quickly joined her at the bottom, and Golmin took the torch from her to lead the way.

"Mother!" Arkiel exclaimed. "What's going on? Where are we going?"

Talin let out a long breath and crouched down in front of him. "It's not safe for us here. We'll need to leave Belanore—it's the only way I can protect you from more assassins. I promise I'll explain everything, but for now, I need you to be brave and stay close. Understand?"

Arkiel sniffed and nodded. Talin stood and kissed the top of his head before taking his hand, and the five of them continued on through the tunnel. She explained the situation to Golmin and Ashera as they walked.

"If Aldrus really is involved, he must have forged those papers to make it look like you brought Red Wolf back to Kies Tor illegally," the young woman said. "It would make sense. The Fae specialised in illusory magic before Braenern began his purge of magic. It's not a stretch to say some of those skills translate to forging official documents in this day and age."

Talin didn't respond. She had her suspicions about where those papers came from, but without any way to confirm them, she kept quiet for now.

What she did know, however, was that it didn't make sense for Aldrus to have made a move so recently—as far as she was aware, Red Wolf was all the way in the Draconian capital of El'Vane, five weeks' travel from Belanore. Only three weeks had passed since the second assassination attempt and the meeting in her office. Nowhere near enough time to make it look like she brought him back to Kies Tor.

"Does Father really want to hurt us?" Arkiel whispered.

"It's...possible," Talin said carefully. "What we do know for sure is that your Uncle Darien sent the assassins and that your father knew at least some part of his plan but chose not to say anything."

"But...why?" Arkiel asked.

"I don't know," Talin said. "But I won't let *anybody* hurt you. I promise."

"Talin, before we continue, I want the truth." Ettrias stopped and turned to face her. "I told you earlier that something was bothering me about those documents that Aldrus showed us. They were written perfectly in your hand. Did you write to Red Wolf?"

"...what? No! We both know I wouldn't do that," Talin said.

"Not without good reason," Ettrias said. "The truth, Talin."

"I didn't write to Red Wolf," Talin said.

Ettrias' eyes darted across her face as if searching for answers, but he eventually gave a nod and faced the front again. "Alright. I believe you."

"Do you think Red Wolf might be in Belanore?" Ashera suddenly asked, breaking the tension. Talin opened her mouth to say something but had no response ready.

"How could he be in Belanore?" Ettrias asked.

"Aldrus knows those papers alone won't be enough to incriminate you," Ashera said. "Even if they were forged perfectly, the court won't rule out a possibility that someone else could have written them, not when it comes to trial. He needs more evidence."

It took a few moments for that to sink in. Talin felt a surge of...*something*...that wasn't quite hope.

"They would have to have been forged well over a month ago, and neither Aldrus nor Darien know anything of Red Wolf's whereabouts," Golmin said.

"Yes, precisely," Talin jumped in. "There's...surely no way either of them could have planned for the timing to occur perfectly." She looked to Ettrias to further back up the argument.

"That, and...uh...he's probably smart enough to recognise them as fakes and wouldn't come even if he did receive them," her brother said. "Exactly...what I was thinking. There's no way."

"If you say so." Ashera shrugged and kept walking.

"We can't go back to find him either way." Talin winced. "And I don't know whether I'd prefer if he was in the city or not."

"If he's in the city, he'll follow, trust me," Golmin said. "We'll find out in a few days."

They emerged in Stormwood a few minutes later, under an unmanned watchtower along the outer wall. Golmin snuffed out the torch and buried it in a shallow hole. Talin took the lead from there, following the narrow path she'd carved through the undergrowth. They arrived at the refurbished hunting cabin not long after, and she dug the key out of a hollow tree trunk nearby.

"Does Aldrus know of this key?" Ettrias asked.

"No." Talin let them inside. "I made plans for the kind of situation we find ourselves in. We were betrayed on our return to Belanore fifteen years ago. Wormwood turned half of my council against me, and you had nothing when you escaped. I wasn't going to let it happen again." She opened a hidden hatch in the floor and led them into a basement of sorts. Inside, there was a small stash of weapons and armour nailed down inside wooden crates. Her own weapons lay in the armoury above them with the rest of the hunting equipment, hidden in plain sight.

"Take what you need, but travel light," she said as Golmin grabbed a nearby pry-bar and set to opening the crates. Ettrias began unbuttoning his tunic while Ashera stripped her mail and plate.

"Do I have to change into armour?" Arkiel asked.

"There's nothing here that will fit you," Talin said. "Come, I'll find you some hunting clothes in the cabin." She grabbed a set of leather travelling armour and led her son back upstairs into the cabin's sleeping quarters. There, she rummaged through the wardrobe, trying to find a set of clothes that would fit him. She eventually settled on a slightly oversized tunic, a pair of simple trousers, and a long travelling cloak. A knife to the fabric cut it down to size easily. Arkiel struggled into his new clothes while she changed into her armour, ditching her dress on the floor.

"Where will we go?" Arkiel asked.

"East, for now," Talin said. "Your father will assume regency of the kingdom after our escape. He'll be sending people to hunt us down and capture us. He will be expecting us to ride west for the Draconian border to seek help from Emperor Kadis."

"Why does he want to arrest us? We haven't done anything wrong, have we?" Arkiel said.

"No. We haven't." Talin paused there, struggling to find the right words. "Sometimes, people get desperate for power. It makes them feel like they're better than everyone else, and it changes them. They start to believe they deserve to have more. They get greedy and do terrible things to get what they want."

"Oh. I see." Arkiel looked sad. "And this happened to Father? Is there a way we can make him good again?"

"I'm not sure," Talin confessed. "It will be difficult. I don't know if appealing to his good side will do much."

"Well...I think I want to try and talk to him," Arkiel said. "If we ever get the chance. I don't want to fight."

Talin cracked a faint smile. "Me neither."

"You're both ready?" Ettrias called. He poked his head through the doorway a moment later.

"Ready as I'll ever be," Talin said. Her brother handed over her bow and quiver, as well as an arming sword and dagger. She buckled everything to her belt and slung the bow across her back.

Ettrias passed Arkiel another dagger. "Here, you'll want a weapon too."

"Why?"

"To defend yourself. Just in case."

Arkiel frowned but took the weapon anyway, wrapping the belt around his waist. "What if I don't want to use it?"

"We will do everything we can to protect you, Arkiel, but it might not be enough," Ettrias said. "You are the future King of Kies Tor. We can't risk it. Besides, your mother would kill me if I let anything happen to you." He grinned. Talin smacked him on the arm lightly on their way out of the cabin.

"I had a look at the maps," Ashera said. "We're not far from Athron. It's a decently sized village a few hours' ride from here. I'm sure they'll have horses we can buy."

"Ettrias and I will be recognised there," Talin said. "You'll have to enter with Golmin to buy the horses. You took the gold out of the stash?"

"Aye, we did," Golmin said. "As much food as we can carry, too. Just in case."

"Good."

"We'll also need supplies to make camp," Ashera said. "We'll buy those while we're in town, with your permission."

"Of course." Talin gave a nod. "Whatever you think we need. I trust you both. We need to put some distance between ourselves and Belanore. The sooner you get the horses, the sooner we can set off. Meet us on the south road when you're done."

"Aye," Golmin said. Ashera tossed him the coin pouch and the two of them disappeared into the bushes, heading for town. Talin turned up the hood of her cloak.

"You have a plan yet?" Ettrias asked.

"No," Talin confessed. "But I will."

They made camp that night in a small clearing, far from the nearest settlement. Talin had hoped to keep to the roads at first, but after Golmin and Ashera returned from Athron having sighted search parties on horseback, the five of them had quickly detoured into the forest again. They'd managed to acquire four horses, however, as well as two tents and bedrolls for everyone. Supper was dried meat and spiced nuts from the supplies they'd brought. Lighting a fire would only serve to make things worse with the dry season now upon them, so Talin had brought two oil lamps with them from the hunting cabin and used those as their main source of light. She put Arkiel to bed shortly after supper and ducked back out of the tent to rejoin the others.

"Not much of a campfire, I'm afraid," Ettrias said when she took a seat on the ground beside him. He lowered the hood of the lamp to avoid waking Arkiel.

"We're more than warm enough without one," Talin said. "I can take the first watch, if no one else is willing."

"Aye, I'll take the final shift," Golmin said.

"Hey, I wanted final shift." Ashera pouted.

Golmin shrugged. "I was first. You can have the final shift tomorrow."

"Fine," Ashera said. "I'll take third shift, then."

"I guess that leaves the second shift for me," Ettrias said. "Now, about Red Wolf."

"If he was in the city as Ashera predicted, then he'll have heard the news by now and set off after us," Golmin explained. "Given how long it would take to travel to Belanore on foot, I'd assume he has a horse. I'm willing to give him the benefit of the doubt and keep an eye out for him for a few days, but truth be told, I'm not hopeful. The full moon is tonight. Even if he set out immediately after us, it'll take him time to pick up a trail. He'll lose at least half a day's worth of travel time, and that's *if* Aldrus doesn't find him first."

Talin wasn't sure if she was looking forward to the wait or dreading it. "We can't afford to slow for him either way. Every opportunity we give him to catch up is also an opportunity we give to Aldrus and his search parties. If Red Wolf is in Kies Tor, he will have to find us on his own. I know he can do it."

"And what will we do in the meantime?" Ettrias asked.

"Keep riding east until we hit the Tall Plains, then turn north for the Highlands. I need allies, and I know House Blackrun has never been on the best terms with Aldrus. It was a pain to deal with back then, but now, we can use it to our advantage."

"We'll need more than the Highlands if you ever plan to retake Belanore," Ashera said. "Just putting it out there."

"If Lady Blackrun is willing to support us, she has the power to rally the northern banners. The Highlander nobility have sworn their allegiance to her as Ambassador for the North," Talin explained. "We'll deprive Aldrus of most of the royal army's cavalry."

"But if Aldrus has Darien's support from the south…" Ettrias began.

"He won't risk it. If Darien marches into Kies Tor with an invading army, the Drakels will rally to us. No other army has ever withstood the full force of the Draconian Legion."

"I'll give it to you. You thought of everything."

"A lot can still happen," Talin said. "The situation could change in an instant."

"A conversation for another time." Golmin yawned. "I think I'll turn in. Need to be up early for my shift. Goodnight."

"Likewise," Talin said, and the captain disappeared into the first tent.

Ashera stood next. "It is getting late. Wake me when it's time for my shift." She ducked into the other tent, leaving Talin alone with her brother.

"Not tired?" she asked.

"Something's on your mind," Ettrias said.

"Nothing important."

"Ah, so it is about Red Wolf."

Talin sighed. "It's been fifteen years. I don't know if he still cares enough to follow me, even if he was in Belanore."

"If he was in Belanore, then he obviously cared enough to return when he believed you needed him," Ettrias said.

"That's not what I meant," Talin said.

"Ah." Ettrias huffed a half-laugh. "You really think he would've returned because he felt it was his *duty*?"

"I...don't know," Talin confessed. "I gave up thinking we'd see each other again. Maybe he did too and moved on."

"Talin, he would've returned for you," Ettrias said. "He's the only one stubborn enough to make the five-week trip all the way back to Belanore just to see you."

Maybe.

She wasn't sure she was ready to see him again.

H e'd...panicked at first. It wasn't something he liked to admit.

Because with his papers gone, it could only mean that he'd been right about them being forged by a third party, and he had sprung the trap by answering the summons. Now, he was too late to stop it.

But Red Wolf knew Talin better than her adversaries, or so he hoped, and he knew that she would have a plan to escape the city if things went south. He needed to get into the palace *now* and warn her—assuming it wasn't too late for that, too.

Collecting himself again, he packed his things and headed downstairs for his horse. A minute later, he was riding towards the palace at a gallop, hood turned up to hide his face. He considered his options again, tried to figure out the most likely scenario, and came up blank. Red Wolf cursed himself for returning. This was a foe he knew nothing about.

The line outside the palace gates was gone when he arrived. Dismounting, he approached one of the guards, doing his best to hunch and look smaller.

"Good morning to you, sir," he said. "I was under the impression that the gates would be open today for court."

The guard looked bored. "They were. You're late. The general returned from his trip, so Queen Talin has ordered the gates closed earlier than usual. Come line up before they open next time."

"I see. Sorry to trouble you." Red Wolf turned away from the guard. He knew Ettrias had gone south to investigate the assassination attempt on Talin three months ago, and if his return had prompted Talin to close the gates, it must mean that he'd found something. That meant the Fae were involved somehow. He wasn't sure he liked it. Still, Ettrias being with the queen made him feel a little better. The twins had grown close again after their reunion fifteen years ago, and he knew they would look after each other if anything happened.

In the meantime, he needed another way in. Scaling the walls in broad daylight would get him spotted for sure, and Talin's enemies would probably accelerate their plans in response. He needed some other way in...

Red Wolf mounted his horse and made to leave.

"Wait," the guard said.

He recognises me.

Red Wolf turned his horse back around slowly. "Have I done something wrong, sir?"

"You seem familiar. Did you serve in the palace once?" the guard asked.

"No, sir, I'm a nobody. You must be confusing me with someone else," Red Wolf said. "Sorry to trouble you." He wheeled his horse around and left the guard behind before he could raise any more suspicion.

Gods, if only I knew what was happening in the palace...

Passing through the city square, he saw that the Chained Owls had been put on alert. Guards stood at almost every street entrance, every junction, every alleyway where fugitives might think to hide. Hesar was briefing his men in the middle of the square. Red Wolf dismounted slowly and led his horse away. The Commander of the City Watch was a decent man, but he was also the type to follow whatever orders were given to him by whoever held authority at the moment, and if that meant arresting an old acquaintance, he would do it without question. Red Wolf needed to find someone loyal to the queen. Heading for the northern gate on foot, he blended in perfectly with the afternoon crowd, dodging guards when he needed to.

Someone I trust had better be there.

He was in luck. Lord Cassius Highett was in an alley nearby, dressed in plain clothes, talking to what looked like a group of young boys. He sent them all off with a coin in hand and looked around cautiously to see if anyone was watching the exchange. Red Wolf approached, keeping his head down, trying not to draw the attention of the City Watch guards stationed right at the gate.

"Lord Cassius, a moment of your time," he said in a low voice.

"Who's asking..." Cassius stared at him for a moment, and then his eyes went wide. He gasped.

"Keep it down." Red Wolf pulled him further away from the guards. "What's the situation in the palace?"

"Truth be told, I'm not entirely sure either," Cassius confessed. "All I know is that Aldrus got his hands on some papers addressed to you from the queen. Warrants for you to return. He claims she forged the

High Court stamp. They went to arrest her and General Ettrias, but the two of them escaped."

"They'll be well away from here by now," Red Wolf said. "Talin never forged those papers—someone else did. The Fae are involved in this somehow. What of Corvan? Rufus?"

"From what I've heard, Captain Golmin aided Ettrias and the queen in attacking the guards," Cassius said. "The three of them should be together. Corvan isn't involved as far as I know."

"Corvan didn't ride west with us fifteen years ago. Neither did you. Aldrus probably thinks you two will swear your loyalties to him." Red Wolf's brow furrowed. "Talin could use that."

"I take it you have a plan?"

"Of sorts."

"And how much of this plan are you planning on sharing with me?" Cassius asked.

"Not much." Red Wolf shrugged. "I trust you will do what you can to slow the search from Belanore."

"I'll certainly try. Corvan might have a few ideas, crafty as he is," Cassius said.

"Good. I cannot stay here. If they arrest me, then nothing that Talin says will convince the court of her innocence," Red Wolf said. "Take a page from Corvan and ally yourselves with Aldrus for now. You'll know to rally to us when the time comes."

"Very well." Lord Cassius beckoned for the two guards at the gate. Red Wolf slipped away. "You two, why aren't there more guards at the gate? Are you aware that the city is under lockdown? Nobody is to leave without permission until the lockdown is lifted. How are you supposed to enforce that with only two guards? You..."

Red Wolf watched the guards become more and more flustered and smiled. Cassius always did have a knack for fast-talking his way through situations. Turning the mechanism just far enough for his horse to get through, he slipped out and headed into Stormwood before the guards could turn back around. There was an old hunting cabin in the forest just north of Belanore; he remembered Corvan picking it out as a safe place to hole up after they escaped from prison fifteen years ago. If he knew Talin at all, she would have refurbished it and hidden some supplies in there for situations exactly like this.

He wandered through the forest for fifteen minutes before finally catching a scent. It was faint, barely still perceptible, but following it brought him to the cabin. The door was locked. Red Wolf dug through the nearby tree trunks and found the key.

They've been here for sure.

The scent was stronger here, and focusing on it told him that five people had passed through. Checking the cabin's sleeping quarters first, he found an ice-blue dress abandoned on the bed next to a fine-looking tunic and pair of trousers. Two pairs of shoes were strewn on the floor. Red Wolf picked up the tunic and guessed it to fit an average eight-year-old.

Talin's son. What's his name again? Arkiel?

Red Wolf brought the tunic close to his face and drew in a deep breath, committing the scent to memory. If the boy was travelling with her, finding him would be the same as finding Talin. He put the tunic back down and sniffed the dress as well.

Talin.

Red Wolf closed his eyes and committed her scent to memory, too. If she had been separated from Arkiel somehow, he would be able to find them both.

Ettrias also escaped. Where are his clothes?

He went back out into the main room. Talin's scent led back to an empty corner and downward into the floorboards. He felt the floor in that corner and lifted open a hidden hatch.

There it is.

He descended the stairs into the basement and picked up one of the swords in the open crates to examine it. Elven Steel, excellent quality, but nothing particularly exquisite. The empty space in the crates told him that some of the equipment had been removed. Nearby, he could see three sets of clothes piled together, along with two blue cloaks. Golmin and...Ashera?

Red Wolf wondered how the girl was doing. When he left Belanore, she had been just a squire, barely more than a child. Judging from the cloak he saw now, her dreams of joining the Royal Guard must have come true. He missed her and wished he'd been there to see her grow.

There was no way he could keep track of five different scents at the same time, so he gathered up their clothes and any belongings they'd left behind and burned them in front of the cabin. Aldrus' men were likely to come through later with hunting dogs to track their scent, and he wasn't about to let them have that advantage. He scattered the ashes when he was done and locked the cabin again, putting the key back where he'd found it. If they were lucky, Aldrus would arrive here, assume that Talin hadn't come through after all, and move on without checking the area. Red Wolf doubted the Fae would overlook it so easily, but with so little evidence that they had been here at all, perhaps he would look to alternative ways of tracking them down. Either way, he had no intention of staying here to find out. Mounting his horse again, he took off after the trail that Talin had left behind.

He came across a small village not long after, finding that Talin had stopped by the road just outside for some time. They'd clearly purchased horses here, or at least Golmin and Ashera had, judging by the hoof-prints he could see in the dirt. For a moment, Red Wolf debated on going into town to confirm that the villagers there had seen Golmin and Ashera here, but then he decided against it. Aldrus might stop by here as well, and he didn't want to leave his own breadcrumb trail for someone to follow.

Full moon's tonight. Need to move faster.

Red Wolf cursed. His damned shapeshifting had never been anything but trouble. He could only hope to gain as much distance as possible before dusk, for he would lose half a day's worth of travel just to find his own belongings the next morning.

Talin's scent continued into the forest to the east, as he'd expected. Kadis was of no help in this matter, and Aldrus would expect her to ride west. Red Wolf guessed that she would reach the Tall Plains and then turn north for the Highlands.

I'm coming, Talin. Just wait.

Red Wolf turned his horse around and continued deeper into the forest.

Waking up after the full moon had passed always felt like waking from some kind of fever dream.

Slowly, gingerly, he pushed himself to his feet, clutching his head as the world spun. His limbs felt like soft pudding. Red Wolf glanced up at the sunrise before taking in his surroundings.

He was utterly lost, as he usually was whenever the wolf was allowed to roam wild in the southern tropics. This deep into the forest, the trees stood untouched by all civilisation, stretching far towards the sky above him. Everything looked the same.

You couldn't have taken me somewhere more recognisable?

It took him a few minutes of scanning the ground before he finally uncovered a set of shallow paw prints that could only have belonged to the wolf. Tracing his steps backwards, he managed to make it an hour before the tracks gave way to thick undergrowth. Here, decomposing plant matter covered the soft soil beneath, making it near-impossible to leave behind tracks, forcing him to his hands and knees once again as he searched for signs of the wolf having passed through.

"Gods have mercy," he muttered to himself. Every minute he wasted trying to find where he'd tethered his horse and left his clothes was a minute that Talin would be using to put distance between herself and Belanore. Every minute he lagged behind was a minute that Aldrus and his search parties could use to find him first.

A broken twig here, some disturbed undergrowth there. He inched forwards slowly as he continued tracing the wolf's path through the forest.

A flash of memory cut through his mind as he passed a particularly imposing tree, and he knew then that he was on the right track. The wolf had dashed through this area last night on a hunt.

I must be close, surely.

Red Wolf spotted his horse another hour later, still tethered to the tree where he'd left his pack and clothes. He quickly dressed and ate some dried meat while he undid the ropes.

"I hope you didn't run into any trouble," he said to the horse. "Apologies for taking so long."

His horse huffed through its nostrils and pawed the ground with one hoof. Red Wolf swung himself into the saddle effortlessly.

"Let's go, then."

Talin's trail had quickly veered off the road and into the forest yesterday, forcing him to rely on his nose and tracking skills to stay on her tail. He'd managed to follow it for a few hours before he had to stop and ditch his horse and clothes to shift. Her scent would be long gone by now, blown off course by the wind, and from the difficulty he'd had in tracking his own movements last night, he knew that their tracks would be near-impossible to spot. Red Wolf continued in the same direction as he'd been travelling yesterday and hoped to the gods that he would find some kind of clue.

There, in the ground.

Red Wolf dismounted and crouched before a pile of dung. Prodding it with a stick, he ascertained that it belonged to a horse and continued moving on foot, leading his own steed through the thick vegetation.

"Talin!" he called.

No such luck. His only response was a flock of birds startling out of a nearby tree and taking off.

He took a swig from his flask. With temperatures already climbing, he knew he would need to make a detour soon, find some source of water in the forest. Much as he wanted to catch up with Talin as soon as possible, he would hardly be of any help to anyone if he collapsed from thirst.

It was late afternoon by the time he came across a small clearing, almost completely hidden by the thick bush and trees around it. A glance at the disturbed vegetation nearby told him that someone had been through here, cutting a gap through the ferns to get to the clearing. Here, Talin and Arkiel's scents still lingered faintly, confirming his suspicions. They had made camp here last night and moved on at first light.

There wasn't much he could do about the broken ferns, but he did cover the entire clearing back up with dirt and leaves, hiding any remaining trace of Talin's camp. That done, he mounted his horse again, spurring it on towards the eastern edge of Stormwood.

What if she's moved on? What if she doesn't want you running after her?

Red Wolf forced the thought from his mind. What Talin thought about their relationship now shouldn't matter. He had to help her stop Aldrus and clear her name. Afterwards, if she felt so inclined, they could discuss where their relationship stood.

And if she truly has moved on from you?

He supposed he could live with that. As long as she was happy.

It was nightfall by the time he reached a small creek in the forest, quickly confirming that Talin's group had passed through from a stray footprint they must have missed while covering their tracks. He swept it away with mud and set up a small camp for himself nearby, refilling his water canteens. He didn't bother with any source of light; his enhanced eyesight in the dark let him see perfectly fine, and he didn't want to leave any more of a breadcrumb trail than he had to.

"I wish I could get word to her," he said as his horse settled down nearby. "Or any of them. Feels like a lifetime ago when I was sparring with Rufus or Ashera in the yard, or trailing after my queen on her way to a council meeting."

I miss them, he didn't say.

Red Wolf finished his supper in silence before consulting his map. There was a village at the edge of the forest, right before the Tall Plains, and if his hunch was right, Talin would make a stop there, then turn north for the White River. He'd find more clues there either way.

There's no way they'll go through the Tall Plains in the dry season.

It made the most sense; only a fool would risk the Tall Plains in this kind of heat. He could start moving northeast tomorrow and bypass the village completely or stay on their tail in hopes of catching up with them. The former might get him ahead of Talin, but he would have to rely on luck—there was no telling the exact route they would take and which villages they might stop at. But staying on their tail wasn't likely to get him any closer to them, with the amount of time he'd already lost. Red Wolf tucked his map away with a sigh.

Something to worry about tomorrow.

He lay down on his bedroll and tried to sleep.

The immediate aftermath of the queen's escape had been...pandemonium, to say the least.

Lord Cassius had wasted no time in contacting his spy network and ensuring the eastern roads were monitored. If his suspicions were right, the queen and her companions would ride until they hit the Tall Plains and then turn north for the Highlands.

For now, all he could do was delay the king's search parties.

He knew the queen had prepared for situations such as this; she would be foolish not to after the events of Wormwood's attempted coup fifteen years ago. They had come to the agreement that he and Master Corvan would keep an eye on the situation in Belanore whenever she was absent from the city. She would send word once she could establish communications with the capital again and include instructions on how to contact her if possible.

But neither of them had accounted for Red Wolf's reappearance. Being approached by the former lord commander the day the queen fled had been a shock, to be sure. But if what the man had told him was true, then someone else had forged his return papers, deceiving him into riding back into Kies Tor.

Who could have forged such official documents so perfectly?

Cassius pondered this as he made his way to the council meeting. The Fae were experts in illusory magic before King Braenern outlawed all magic and the rest of the world followed suit. It wasn't unreasonable that the king or one of his contacts had the skill or necessary equipment to falsify the papers.

The rest of the Royal Council had already gathered by the time he reached the small hall; only the king was still absent. Cassius took his usual seat beside Lord Folen Wyndove, the appointed head of civil affairs after Lord Karl's arrest fifteen years ago. The late Lord Wormwood had also been quickly replaced after things settled down; sitting in the Coin-Master's spot now was Lord Tybalt Mornus from the northern nobility.

"Any idea why we've been summoned?" Cassius asked the table at large.

"Not a clue," Lord Wyndove said.

"I hear the king wants to send search parties to the east and the north," Lord Mornus said.

"What reason would the queen have to flee east?" Lord Wyndove asked. "Her alliance is with the Drakels. If you ask me, we're wasting resources and time."

"Lady Blackrun is a good friend of the queen, despite her strained relations with the Crown. I have many reasons to suspect she will seek out allies in the north."

Every head in the room turned as King Aldrus strode in, silk cape fluttering behind him. A gold circlet adorned his head, glinting in the morning light. He took his seat at the head of the meeting table.

"Apologies, Your Majesty, I did not mean to undermine your judgement," Lord Wyndove said. "I was only—"

"It matters not." The king waved him off. "The queen knows I am aware of her friendship with Emperor Kadis and she expected me to send my search parties west. Yet, after almost two weeks, there has been no word of her passing through any settlements west of Belanore. At this stage, if she is not found soon, I must turn to the High Court."

"Am I to understand, Your Majesty, that you intend to seek approval from the court for regency of the kingdom?" Corvan asked.

"Yes," the king said. "I am...hesitant...to officially accuse Queen Talin of misconduct and forgery, but given the circumstances, I feel I have no choice. An innocent person would not have fled." He let out a deep breath and flattened his palms on the table. "My lords, I ask you to put aside any personal feelings you may have about this situation. I know that most of you, if not all, believe the queen to be innocent. But until she returns to Belanore to face the allegations against her, Kies Tor needs a ruler."

Cassius didn't like where this was going. "Your Majesty, I would caution against such a decision without concrete proof of the queen's wrongdoing," he said. "Queen Talin has been popular among the common folk since she led the city against the Hellhounds in the Siege of Belanore fifteen years ago. Having the High Court's support does not guarantee you will have the *people's* support."

"I agree," Corvan said. "Despite what progress Her Majesty has been able to make, Kies Tor remains wary of outsiders at best. You'll not sway the crowd without sufficient evidence."

"Of course, you're both right, sirs." The king offered them an easy smile. "But I see no choice. The Crown's administrative matters have come to a standstill in the queen's absence, and Torrian law forbids me from taking over unless I can assume regency of the kingdom."

"It's...true that we require someone able to make administrative decisions in Belanore," Corvan admitted. "I recently received another message from Lady Blackrun; she is once again requesting aid in investigating a series of disappearances in the north—disappearances that she believes to be kidnappings. But the queen left explicit instructions for all of us that she would handle the matter personally, so...legally, we can do nothing without a regent."

"Then we understand the necessity of what I wish to do," Aldrus said, flattening his palms on the table. "I also have reason to believe that the fugitive Red Wolf is in Kies Tor at this very moment. His arrest should prove sufficient evidence for both the High Court and the public."

Cassius felt his blood run cold.

How does Aldrus know about Red Wolf being in Kies Tor? How could he possibly know?

"All the same, Your Majesty," he began, "I would advise caution. Red Wolf is...a highly skilled fighter, even without his Hellhound abilities."

"I'm aware," the king said. "But even he cannot resist the Draconian torslek." He stood and unrolled a map of the kingdom. "My search parties are currently split. Half are en route back from the villages to the west of Stormwood. The rest have been dispatched from Fort Voraine and are currently searching the eastern villages. But it is as Lord Cassius and Master Corvan have said: I require more evidence. That is where all of you come in."

Of course, Cassius thought. Though his and Corvan's allegiances lay with Queen Talin, their *duties* dictated that they serve the Crown and its people. And with the current allegations against the queen, it fell upon her council to investigate. He would have to work against her, like it or not.

The king was quick to delegate the investigation work; as expected, much of it was assigned to Cassius as the head of intelligence. His spy network would uncover more than the rest of the council combined. He left the meeting in a considerably worse mood than when he entered.

Was there a possibility that the queen truly *had* forged those papers for Red Wolf's return? He knew they had been close, but as far as he was concerned, their relationship was no different from the generations of rulers and royal bodyguards who had come before them. What reason could she possibly have to bring him back?

Whatever the case, it was clear to him that now more than ever, he needed to recruit Hesar into his spy network. The City Watch Commander had always rejected his recruitment attempts before, citing a need for the Chained Owls to remain neutral in whatever political struggles occurred in Belanore, but given how they had turned on the queen and her companions fifteen years prior...

He knew he couldn't take that risk again.

Much of the chatter on the street was still about the queen and her brother's arrest and subsequent escape, as expected. Cassius kept an ear open for unusual gossip as he made his way to the Chained Owls' headquarters.

The guard on duty outside the headquarters gave him a nod as he approached and stood aside to let him through. He jogged up the steps to the front doors, making a beeline for Hesar's office as soon as he was inside.

"Lord Cassius? What a pleasant surprise. You should have sent word ahead; my men could have given you a proper welcome."

Cassius turned as Hesar appeared at the top of a staircase leading to the upper levels, black cloak trailing behind him. He quickly made his way down and gestured for the spymaster to enter his office first.

"There have been...new developments," Cassius said, stepping into the room. "Apologies for the unannounced visit, but I think you know why I'm here."

"Ah. Of course." Hesar closed the door behind him and went to the cabinet by the window, pouring out two cups of spiced wine. Cassius took one with a nod of thanks. "I've told you countless times, my lord, I care not for your politics. The role of the Chained Owls is to protect Belanore and uphold our laws in this fine city. I cannot agree to spy for you."

"King Aldrus has requested the Royal Council's aid in uncovering evidence of the queen's misconduct," Cassius said. "As Commander of the City Watch, you are in charge of filtering through the countless reports and complaints filed by the common folk. I only require your assistance to investigate."

"And here I thought you were loyal to Queen Talin." Hesar raised his eyebrows.

Cassius winced. "I am. But my duty is to the Crown. To its people."

"Yet your spy network operates entirely independently from the Crown," Hesar said. "Tell me, does *Her Majesty* even know who all of your contacts are?"

"Of course not," Cassius said. "But their identities are no secret to her or the king if they wished to know. What I ask of you now falls under the Crown's jurisdiction. I must get to the bottom of these accusations." He felt a little bad, using the investigation as a means to recruit the City Watch Commander, but it couldn't be helped. He needed Hesar's eyes and ears in Belanore.

Hesar pinched the bridge of his nose. "Fine, I'll help—under one condition. I will only report to you on matters relating to your investigation and only until this whole business is over and done with."

Cassius could work with that. "Thank you. First things first, I must know if your men have spotted any...particularly tall, suspicious persons in the city before the queen's arrest."

"You're asking after the former lord commander?" Hesar blinked. "No, I don't believe there have been any reports of the sort. If there were confirmed sightings of a fugitive in the city, I would have heard about it immediately."

That's good. Then the king has no solid proof that Red Wolf was in Belanore.

"Very well," Cassius said. "That's all for now. I'll let you know if my spies turn up anything else requiring investigation. Thank you for the drink."

"Wait," Hesar said as the spymaster stood to leave. "There's something else you should know. Whether it helps your investigation is up to you."

Something told Cassius that he wasn't going to like this.

"My men have been hearing rumours," Hesar continued. "They started circulating this morning. Nothing you'd hear in public—I don't believe any would dare speak of them so openly."

"And...what do these rumours say?"

"There have been whispers about the queen's relationship with her former lord commander. People say the reason she never appointed a new royal bodyguard...was because she was romantically involved with Red Wolf. They were lovers."

The next two weeks of travel were surprisingly quiet. Talin had expected Aldrus' search parties to find them somehow, or perhaps raiders and outlaws would try to rob them for whatever valuables they carried. But no danger came save for the scorching heat of the dry season and dangerously low supplies of water.

She knew they couldn't stay off the road for much longer; the Tall Plains were not to be underestimated, especially in the dry season. With long grass that could grow taller than a person and an assortment of snakes, it had taken many a foolish traveller. Talin had briefly considered covering their trail by going through the Plains and turning north at the border, but she knew it was suicide in this heat.

"Bloody awful start to the dry season, pardon the language," Golmin muttered. He stripped off his cloak and used it to wipe his brow. "We don't have enough water to last another day."

"I know." Talin had her nose buried in the map as they led the horses through uneven terrain. Trees surrounded them, some as old as the giants, stretching into the sky. "There's a small town at the edge of the forest. We should reach it before nightfall, provided nothing slows us down."

"I know this heat makes it dangerous, but perhaps we still ought to consider going through the Tall Plains," Golmin said. "It's the best way to cover our tracks and lose any unwanted tails we might have."

"Don't know about you, Rufus, but I'd rather not die of dehydration halfway through," Ettrias said. "There won't be another village until we reach the other side and no source of water unless it rains."

Talin checked the map and found that her brother was right. There were no villages marked in the Tall Plains, and the only source of water anywhere nearby was the creek they had passed earlier this morning.

"We'll ask the locals," she said. "They know more about the land and its surrounds. Perhaps they will know whether it's safer to head north and ride along White River."

"Aye, I agree," Golmin said.

"Why are the Plains so dangerous?" Arkiel asked.

"The heat." Ettrias jerked his head upward to indicate the sun. "Hot day like this, we need more water than usual. The Tall Plains has no steady source of water. No rivers, no creeks, nothing. If you run out of water in the middle of the Plains, you won't last very long."

"Don't forget the venomous snakes," Ashera added. "They'll wait in the long grass until some animal comes near, and then...BANG!" She stretched an arm out and grabbed Arkiel. "And if you step on one by accident..."

"Oh." The boy's eyes went wide. "I don't want to get bitten by a snake!"

Ashera laughed. "Don't worry. We won't let anything like that happen."

"I wouldn't worry about the snakes. We're more likely to run out of water before anyone gets bitten," Talin said.

"Aldrus couldn't have waited for a better time to drive us out of Belanore?" Ettrias muttered. Ashera snickered.

"I'll give anything to avoid going through the flooded plains to the west," she said.

"Oh, wouldn't we all..."

"Stop." Talin grabbed her bow and nocked an arrow in half a heartbeat. She could swear she had just seen something elf-shaped moving out of the corner of her eye. And just when she'd thought they were safe...

She caught the movement again, for certain this time, and loosed a warning shot. It struck the trunk of a tree barely an inch from the stranger's face, forcing him to a stop. He wore a simple hood and cloak over his leather armour, and beneath the hood, she caught a glimpse of a youthful face.

He's barely more than a child.

"We don't want any trouble," Talin called, readying another arrow. "But if you mean us any harm, you should know I'm a good shot."

"Behind us, two more," Golmin said in a low voice. Talin saw out of the corner of her eye that he had also drawn his bow.

"Another two on our left," Ettrias said. "Probably more in the bushes. Outlaws, is my guess."

"Oh, good, then it's even," Ashera said.

Ettrias paused. "There are four of us."

"Let's count, shall we? Two of us are royal guard officers, one of us has a reputation for being one of the best swordsmen in the kingdom, and one of us is possibly the kingdom's greatest archer," Ashera said. "Seems like even odds to me."

"The aim is not for this to escalate into a fight," Talin hissed through her teeth. "If it does, we protect Arkiel."

"This part of the forest is our territory," said the outlaw in front of Talin. "You want to pass? You pay the fee."

"How much is this...fee?" Talin asked.

"Whatever coin you have, you'll pay it," the outlaw said.

"And if we don't have any coin?"

"Then, uh..." The outlaw seemed puzzled at this. Clearly, he wasn't expecting such a response. "You'll pay with your life!"

"Alright." Talin nodded and made a show of contemplating her options. "Or, seeing as I have an arrow aimed at your face, I could kill you, the leader of this bunch I'd assume, and we all go on our merry way without paying."

"Well..." The outlaw was totally stumped now. "You're surrounded. If you shoot me, my men will kill all of you before you have time to loose a second arrow."

"I'll risk it." Talin jerked the bowstring a fraction, not enough to pull back and loose her arrow but enough for it to twitch. The outlaw visibly flinched. A second passed before he realised that she still held her arrow at the ready.

"Tell your men to stand down," she said with a smile. "We'll be on our way."

The outlaw's shoulders sagged as he waved for his men to stand down.

"But boss—" one of the others began.

"This isn't worth dying for," the outlaw said. "I value my life and all of yours more than some stupid gold." He didn't look at Talin.

"You should think about visiting Belanore once things have settled down," she told him. "I'm sure the Crown would be more than willing to help if you're in need of money."

. "I..." The outlaw still didn't meet her gaze. "Just go."

"Mother, that was *amazing*," Arkiel said once they were clear of the outlaws. "You didn't even have to shoot them! You just...convinced him to let us go!"

Talin couldn't help but smile. "It doesn't always have to come to a fight, you know. If you're good at persuading people to see things your way, you can avoid a great deal of conflict."

"Like...when I'm king? And someone wants to start a war with us? But I can talk them out of it," Arkiel said.

"Yes, exactly," Talin said. "But if it doesn't work, you must still be ready to fight."

They reached the edge of the forest just before sunset, with the relentless dry season heat still bearing down on them and precious little water left. Talin gave Arkiel what was left in her second flask as they made for the village at the start of the Tall Plains. It was a fairly small place, Talin saw as they drew closer, a few farms and houses spread along either side of a narrow, dirt path branching off the main road. The village centre wasn't much more to look at, either; she spied a well for fresh water and a little town hall for gatherings. She doubted any of them would recognise her as the queen, but the five of them entered with their hoods turned up just in case.

"Do you have food and water here?" Golmin asked a passer-by.

"Aye, but the market's closed already," the villager said. "Opens tomorrow morning. You can get your water from the well."

"Thank you," Golmin said.

"Is there an inn where we might be able to stay for the night?" Talin asked. "If the market's closed..."

"Down there, last building on the right," the villager said.

"Much appreciated," Talin said.

"I'll go pay for our rooms. The rest of you can perhaps find out if it's safe to cross the Tall Plains," Ettrias said.

"Aye, sounds good," Golmin said. "We'll get water from the well while we're at it."

They parted ways there, and the captain crossed the narrow dirt path to pull up the bucket. Talin filled their canteens and took a long drink of water.

"Ah, adventurers heading east, I presume?" an old man asked as he approached the well with a bucket of his own. He looked so frail and thin Talin thought he might break his legs just by shuffling up the path, and his white hair had almost completely fallen out.

"Well, actually—" Arkiel began.

"We are," Ashera cut him off neatly while Talin motioned for him to stay quiet. "We were hoping to make our way through the Tall Plains, but my friend here says it's not safe in this heat." She indicated Talin.

"Hmm." The old man went to pull up the bucket, and Golmin quickly moved to assist. "Oh, thank you, son." They filled the old man's own bucket together. "It might be too dangerous as it is, yes. This drought isn't likely to go away for a while. You'll run out of water long before you can make it across the Plains."

"Isn't there any way through? A...lesser known path, perhaps?" Golmin asked.

"Not as far as I know," the old man said. "Better to take the safe route, eh! All you young folks these days crave too much adventure to think about the consequences." He shuffled off again with his water.

"There we have it, then," Talin said. "We'll have to turn north."

"Well, I'd rather be caught and thrown into the dungeons than die of thirst and left to dry out in the Plains," Ashera said with a shrug. "But I wouldn't worry. Red Wolf is probably still on our tail, cleaning up our mess."

"And if he's not?"

"Oh, stop worrying. He'll turn up. Now, I'm craving a decent supper, so how about we meet up with your brother at the inn?"

Talin grudgingly obliged, though she couldn't shake her worries. She reminded herself that she didn't need him; she had gone fifteen years without his guidance, without him by her side. Ashera was simply trying to get her hopes up, nothing more. They all knew the chances of Red Wolf actually being in Kies Tor were astronomically slim. And though she was cut off from any allies she might have in the capital, it wasn't as if she was alone; Golmin and Ashera were both with her, along with Ettrias. She had no doubt that Aldrus would order her Royal Council to investigate the allegations against her, but Corvan and Lord Cassius were loyal to her, and she knew they would do everything they could to clear her name. All she needed to do was avoid getting caught, find allies in the Highlands, and prove her innocence by uncovering the mastermind behind this mess.

With or without Red Wolf, she had to push on.

A glint of blue caught Red Wolf's eye.

Under normal circumstances, he would have ignored it and opted to continue following the scent that had led him on a winding trail through the forest, but he distinctly remembered that there were no blue flowers in this part of Stormwood. The fletching on Talin's arrows, though, were a bright blue and white.

Red Wolf pushed aside some of the shrubbery to examine the glint. Sure enough, he found an arrow buried deep in the trunk of a massive tree that was easily broader than he was. Red Wolf grabbed the shaft and yanked it free. Talin had loosed a shot at someone here but missed.

She doesn't easily miss.

A warning shot, then. He turned the arrow over in his hands and sniffed it. Good quality Highlander pinewood, the fletching done by experienced hands in a distinctive southern style. The lack of blood

in his immediate surrounds indicated that the encounter had ended
without a fight. Red Wolf was impressed. Looking around, he saw that
parts of the foliage had been disturbed. People had lain in ambush
here, probably hoping to surprise passers-by and demand payment. He
slipped the arrow into his own quiver and pressed on, determined to
cover the trail that Talin had left.

Judging from how faint her scent was, he guessed that he still had to
be a few hours behind, but he had been able to regain the time he'd lost
on the night of the full moon. Now, two weeks later, he was close to
the edge of Stormwood. If he could reach Dennik by tonight, his search
might finally be over.

She sent me away. She doesn't want me back.

Red Wolf pushed the thought from his mind. It had been his idea to
appeal to the court for his own exile, not hers; Talin had been prepared
to lie to the whole kingdom to ensure his freedom.

Yet a part of him wondered how things had changed. Was it her duty
that drove her to marry Aldrus, or was it love?

It doesn't matter.

By her summons or not, his return had caused a ripple effect with
Talin at the heart of it all. It was his duty now to fix things.

The sun had gone down by the time he reached the village at the
edge of the Tall Plains. Here, the scent he was following was much
stronger, lingering by the well before veering towards the inn. Red Wolf
dismounted and led his horse on through the main street. Talin had
passed through here barely an hour ago, judging from how easily he was
able to follow the trail. But he also knew that Aldrus was no fool. There
were bound to be Royal Army search parties nearby, if not already in
the village itself, and the tiniest slip-up could be disastrous for him and
Talin both.

Danger!

It wasn't often that he felt the wolf's instincts overtake his own, but as he pushed open the door to the inn, he felt a sense of *wrongness* only the wolf could place. He rested a hand on the dagger at his belt and scanned the empty downstairs tavern. No doubt all the patrons had retired to their rooms already. He tugged his hood further over his head and approached the reception.

"Looking for a room, good sir?" the innkeeper asked.

"I'm searching for someone, actually," Red Wolf said. "A young woman. Southerner, blue eyes. She would have been travelling with a boy and three others. I know they're here."

Danger!

"I can't give out my guests' information, sir," the innkeeper said. "But if you'd like a room for tonight, I can let them know you're here when they sign out tomorrow morning."

Danger! Danger!

Hoof-beats pounded along the dusty road outside. Red Wolf drew his dagger and sword. The innkeeper gasped.

"Did you sell them out?" the ex-bodyguard growled.

"I...I'm sorry. The soldiers, they promised so much gold..." The innkeeper held up his hands in surrender. "Please..."

"*Orrlát,*" Red Wolf hissed through his teeth. "Their room numbers. Now!"

"I can't. The soldiers, they'll—" The innkeeper was cut off when the door opened again and two southerners in mail and plate strode in. Their tabards were dyed crimson, with a white raven emblazoned on the front. Royal Army soldiers. They saw Red Wolf and drew their weapons.

Red Wolf contemplated his options. He could make a break for the upstairs rooms and kick down doors until he found Talin or one of the others, but the soldiers would pursue them out of the village and catch up eventually. Their escape was far more important than his longing to see her.

"You're too late," Red Wolf said. "I tipped them off. They're long gone." He twirled the sword in his hand. "And I'm going to make sure none of you make it out of this village to pursue."

He swung his blade in a wide arc, forcing the nearest soldier to jump back and parry. The weapons collided with a sharp ring of steel that seemed to echo through the entire building.

That should alert them.

Red Wolf swung again without missing a beat, forcing the two soldiers on the defensive, driving them towards the door as the innkeeper cowered behind the counter. One of them quickly broke off to run outside, presumably to warn the rest of the search party. Red Wolf knocked aside the other soldier's weapon and kicked him through the door after his companion.

"Is this the best the Royal Army can offer?" He spat on the ground near the soldier's head. "Get up and die with some dignity."

The soldier scrambled to his feet as another half-dozen swordsmen surrounded them, all with blades drawn. Red Wolf glanced towards the inn's upstairs windows and saw a curtain move ever so slightly.

They need more time.

He sidestepped a thrust and drove his dagger into the nearest soldier's armpit, between the steel plates of his armour. The blade stopped against chainmail, but the soldier staggered with a grunt regardless, giving Red Wolf an opening to slip out from the ring of soldiers. They turned to face him in unison, putting their backs to the inn. He bared his teeth at them and lunged at the nearest man. The soldier met his strike with a deft parry and countered with a slash to his arm. He took the hit without bothering to defend and slammed the pommel of his sword into his opponent's head. He crumpled almost immediately.

I'm sorry about the headache.

He immediately regretted the decision. True, Talin wouldn't have wanted him to resort to lethal force, but leaving the soldiers alive would only mean more witnesses who could testify against them if it ever came to a trial. But for now, Talin and her companions needed an escape route, and it fell upon him to provide the diversion. Keeping the soldiers alive might work out in the end. Time would tell.

Hoof-beats on the road. More soldiers.

Red Wolf backed away from the inn, drawing the search party and reinforcements towards him. One of the new arrivals aimed a crossbow at his face. His magic sprang up into a shield around himself, and the bolt splintered against it. The crossbowman struggled to reload. He closed the distance between them in a few strides, sliced through the bowstring with his dagger, and nailed a punch at the man's nose that sent him staggering.

Two more swordsmen came at him from either side. He parried the first strike with his dagger and ducked under the second. Out of the corner of his eye, he saw five cloaked figures on horseback slip past and make for the northern edge of town. The boy glanced back as they rode off, and for a moment, made eye contact with him.

Electric-blue eyes. Talin's son—there's no doubt about it.

A part of him longed to charge past these soldiers and follow them—it would be *easy* given his healing powers—but he knew he couldn't risk their capture just so he could see her again. Besides, with so many soldiers, there was no way he could stop them all without resorting to lethal force.

"We have orders to take you alive," the squad sergeant said. "Put your weapons down and come with us."

They need more time, Red Wolf thought. If he allowed these soldiers to continue their search, they would follow Talin north along the road and quickly catch up. He needed another plan—and fast.

"The white raven is the emblem of House Zylvaris," he said, nodding at the man's tabard. "Yet you follow the orders of an outsider like King Aldrus?"

"We serve the Crown," the sergeant said. "Queen Talin led us to victory in the war, it's true. But if she's suspected of conspiring with an outlaw like you, then it's our job to bring her in to face the allegations. Come with us. If the queen is innocent, you can explain that to the court."

"And if I told you that she's been framed? That Aldrus' so-called 'evidence' is fake?" Red Wolf asked.

"That's not for any of us to judge," the sergeant said. "As it stands, you've attacked a whole squad of my men. The court could easily add assault to your growing list of charges, Red Wolf."

Red Wolf contemplated escape again. He had the element of surprise here and his Hellhound abilities on top of it all; it wouldn't be a stretch to think that he could get away without casualties if he moved fast enough. But there were too many soldiers here, and deep down, he knew he would have to kill some of them to have any real shot of getting away.

But if I let them arrest me...

It was a risky plan, though he didn't see any other option. At the very least, the soldiers would drag him back to Belanore instead of continuing to pursue Talin north. All he needed to do was find some way to escape before they put him on trial.

"Take me back to Belanore, then," Red Wolf said. "But I want you to answer me this. Has the king dispatched more search parties east?"

"He has," the sergeant said. "They're stationed at every major town along the White River, and more search parties are being dispatched into the Highlands. Your queen won't get far. Neither will you if you try to run."

Red Wolf dropped his weapons. Two soldiers came forward to tie his hands with rope. "If Aldrus thinks he can stop her like that, he doesn't know her at all."

The last thing he felt was a heavy blow against his head before everything turned black.

They must have travelled for hours, first along the main road, then veering northwest back into Stormwood before Talin finally dared to call a halt. Her heart still hammered wildly in her chest as Golmin and Ashera set up their tents, illuminated only by the dim light of their oil lanterns and a tiny sliver of the waxing moon.

How could the soldiers have found us so quickly? Did the innkeeper tip them off?

Either way, she supposed they had to thank whoever alerted them in Dennik; she had been struggling out of her travelling armour when she heard the ring of steel from downstairs and knew immediately that something was wrong.

"I know what we're all thinking," Ettrias said as he unbuckled the saddlebags and grabbed their personal packs to take stock of their inventory. "Especially you, Talin."

"I didn't say anything," Talin protested, though she knew exactly what he was talking about and did her best to push the thought from her mind.

Red Wolf is the only one who has any motive to be on our tail and cause a diversion for us.

"If it *is* him, he'll be fine," Ettrias continued. "He took two arrows and a knife to the chest and survived, and that was after he was poisoned with torslek."

Talin glared at him. "I don't want to talk about it."

"Suit yourself," Ettrias said.

"Mother, who was that man at the village?" Arkiel asked.

"I'm not sure," Talin said. "None of us got a good look at him. But whoever they are, we can only assume they're an ally, at least for now."

"I got a good look at him!" Arkiel said. "He was really tall. But he had his hood up, so I didn't really see his face."

It can't be him. There are other elves who are close to his height...

"We'll talk more of it in the morning," Talin said. "For now, you should get some sleep."

Arkiel yawned as she steered him towards the tent. "Alright..."

"It does sound like Red Wolf, you have to admit," Ettrias said when she returned.

"I said I don't want to talk about it."

"Alright, alright." Ettrias raised his hands in defeat and went back to their inventory. He frowned at the bags, then opened them one by one to look inside. His frown deepened as he counted and recounted something under his breath.

"Something wrong?" Golmin asked, joining him.

"Yes." Ettrias looked up. "We don't have the pack with our spare rations."

Talin cursed. "It must still be at Dennik—we were in too much of a hurry to get out of there. I should have double-checked that we had all our supplies. What about our personal rations?"

"Maybe two full meals if we pool our rations together," Ettrias said. "But there are plenty of villages between Dennik and the White River. We shouldn't have any trouble finding one before dusk tomorrow."

"Going into town will be risky," Talin said. "We know now that there are search parties looking for us in the east. I've no doubt we'll run into more soldiers, especially with Fort Voraine so close."

"I could sneak in and buy some supplies," Ashera said. "I'm the least likely to be recognised out of all of us, and the Royal Army will be looking for a group of five travellers, not a single person."

"If you're caught—"

"Oh, come on, what's the worst that could happen?"

"I promised Red Wolf I'd look after you."

"Pfft. I'm not a child anymore."

"Sending Ashera might well be our best bet," Golmin said. "I'm likely to be recognised as Captain of the Royal Guard, and I'd bet all my yarii that half the Royal Army would recognise you and Ettrias on sight."

"Besides, we need those supplies," Ettrias added. "Two meals' worth of rations isn't even going to get us to the White River, let alone all the way into the Highlands."

Talin gave a sigh of defeat. "I guess I'm outvoted, then. Though I have to admit that I don't know about continuing north anymore." She dug out the map and held it near one of the lamps to examine it. "We know Aldrus' search parties have made their way east. It stands to reason that they've been dispatched into the HIghlands, too—and they've probably been ordered to set up a checkpoint at the bridge near

Varen, where we would have to cross in order to make it to the Wycrest bridge."

"What's the new plan, then?" Ashera asked.

"I'm...not entirely certain yet," Talin admitted. "But I'll figure something out. I usually do."

True to Ettrias' prediction, they came across a tiny village just off the main road at dusk, and Ashera made her way in while the rest of them hid behind a thick cluster of trees to wait. The young woman was quick to return with two large, wrapped parcels.

"I pretty much cleared out the grocer's stock," she said, "but there wasn't much left. This late in the afternoon, the shops were about to close."

"It'll do." Talin sighed. "I hate this hiding and skulking around. It reminds me too much of what happened fifteen years ago. Wormwood taking over, us wanted in every town and village..."

"You're more prepared this time," Ettrias said. "And Aldrus doesn't have the same influence that Wormwood did. They'll never believe his word over yours once you come forward with witnesses and allies who can vouch for you."

"It's not that simple."

Ettrias' eyes narrowed, but thankfully, he kept his mouth shut.

"In any case, we need to decide what we're going to do now," Golmin said. "I'm assuming there weren't any Royal Army soldiers at the village?"

"If there were, I didn't see any," Ashera said. "And those red uniforms are hard to miss."

"Then there's a chance they haven't been dispatched this far north yet," Golmin said. "I wager we could risk crossing into the Highlands, but I leave the decisions to you, Your Majesty."

"I wish we had some news from home," Ettrias said. "Or even local gossip to tell us something about the Royal Army's movements." He looked at Ashera. "I don't suppose you picked up anything on your way through the village."

"I...did hear a few things," Ashera said. Her gaze flickered momentarily to Talin and Arkiel. "Nothing that will help us."

How much worse could the situation get? Talin thought.

"Gossip? Rumours?" Golmin asked.

"You could say that." Ashera looked at Arkiel again. "But we should get out of here first. I'll tell you all about it after we set up camp for the night."

"Something tells me I'm not going to like this," Talin muttered under her breath.

They quickly left the village behind and continued on, winding through the forest off the road to avoid leaving any sort of trail. It was dusk by the time Golmin halted them again, in another clearing near-identical to the last. Talin put Arkiel to bed after a quick supper of dried meat and biscuits.

"We'd be completely lost in these woods without your help, Rufus," Ettrias was saying when she rejoined the group.

"You give me too much credit," Golmin said. "I'm used to navigating in the Highlands, not here, where the canopy is so thick you can barely make out the stars."

"All the same, we rely on you."

Golmin coughed and looked away.

"Aww, are you embarrassed? Take the praise—you deserve it."

Talin took a seat around the makeshift campfire to watch their interaction. She didn't have the heart to interrupt.

"What was that story you told me about the Battle of Rivenfort?" Ettrias asked. "You tracked the ambushing vanguard for a *week* through the snow and alerted Lord Whitehall's bannermen before they could walk into a trap."

"It was three days, not a week." Golmin smiled. "But it *is* one of my career highlights in the army, I'll give you that." He let out a long breath. "But now's not the time for sharing stories. Ashera, I assume whatever you overheard this morning isn't something to be shared with Prince Arkiel?"

"I heard rumours, yes, if you can call them that," Ashera said. She looked at Talin. "I assume they started in Belanore and got out of hand. But whoever leaked them...knows about your relationship with Red Wolf, Your Majesty."

Talin felt as if all the air had been knocked out of her. Her fingertips suddenly felt cold. "What kinds of rumours?"

"People say you'd been in love with each other for years before the Wormwood incident. They back it up by saying that rumours had gone around the royal palace for all those years, that *King Arnas* knew about it and did nothing."

That's impossible.

"Nobody outside the palace should know anything about those rumours," Ettrias said. "After Father's death, Rufus and Red Wolf went around dispelling them. How could *anybody* have gotten hold of that kind of information?"

"It's not impossible that one of the palace servants let slip," Golmin said. "This is Belanore we're talking about—rumours spread like wildfires."

"Oh, it gets worse," Ashera continued. "There are, apparently, eyewitness accounts from those who fought in the Siege of Belanore.

Civilians and soldiers who swear they saw the two of you kiss. There's also some talk of you...how shall I put it? Sharing the lord commander's bed. Suffice it to say, people are now questioning whether Arkiel is a legitimate heir to the throne, even though we all know he's not nearly old enough to be Red Wolf's son."

So, it's come to this. Talin said nothing.

"We have to ride north for Blackrun's help," Ettrias said. "Aldrus must have leaked all this to ruin your reputation and garner more support for himself. I mean, these rumours are ridiculous! Red Wolf has been exiled for fifteen years, and Arkiel is only *eight*. Not to mention that there was *no* opportunity for you to have slept with your lord commander before—"

"Aldrus couldn't have leaked anything, I never told him the details of the siege. In any case, I can't contest any of the rumours...because they're true."

She was pretty sure she could see the gears turning in her companions' heads as they processed what they'd just heard.

"Alright, we need to talk about this—"

"What do you *mean* they're true—"

"You slept with him and never told me?" Ettrias exclaimed.

"I... What? No!" Talin pinched the bridge of her nose. "It's not like that. You'll remember that during the siege, we lost access to the upper levels of the palace because we needed to shelter the evacuating civilians somewhere while we got them through the tunnels."

Her brother crossed his arms. "And?"

"Red Wolf offered me his chambers. I asked him to stay so he wouldn't have to sleep on the floor. We didn't... We weren't intimate. We just...slept in the same bed."

"Of course. And whoever leaked the rumours either doesn't know the full context or doesn't care. What about the rest?"

"I kissed him in the front courtyard after the Drakels arrived. There were probably a few dozen witnesses," Talin admitted. "As for being in love for years... That's certainly true for Red Wolf. But Arkiel is Aldrus' son and the rightful heir to the Torrian throne."

"In hindsight, I can see why you were so determined to keep things under wraps." Ettrias rubbed his eyes with one hand. "What now? There's no reining in these rumours, *especially* if they hold some ring of truth. We need to gather our allies and return home as soon as we can."

"Like I said, it's not that simple," Talin said. She hesitated. "If Aldrus can convince the court that I forged those papers, and I'm willing to bet they'll listen to him over me, there's nothing I can do to convince them of my innocence. As it stands, going directly north is too risky—if we're caught, it's all over. But I do have a new plan."

"Let's hear it, then."

"The White River disappears underground further upstream, past the border," Talin explained. "We'll ride east, as far into the mountains as we can, then turn north. We'll cross the river above land and then loop back into the Highlands."

"That's a long detour," Ettrias said.

"I know. But it's our safest bet," Talin said. "I know the eastern range is impassable, but I've heard stories of Weavers fleeing into the mountains to the east during Braenern's purge of magic. There has to be some truth to it."

"Well, if you're sure, we're all with you," Ettrias said. Golmin and Ashera both nodded.

"Good." Talin stood. "Get some rest, then, all of you. We'll move on at first light."

XIII

The first thing Red Wolf felt upon waking was a wave of dizzying nausea as he tried to reorient himself to his new surroundings.

The second thing he felt was a growing sense of dread—not because he had been captured, but because, judging by the moon and stars above them, they were heading north, not west.

They're not taking me back to Belanore. Why?

The answer came to him almost immediately. It made more sense for the soldiers to drag him along while they continued to search for Talin; taking him all the way back to Belanore and then heading out again would waste far too much time and resources.

This was a mistake.

Saving Talin had been at the forefront of his mind back in Dennik, but now, as he wriggled the ropes that bound his hands, he realised that his stunt had bought her little time, if any. He had instead delivered himself, a crucial piece of evidence, right into Aldrus' hands.

"Oh, he's awake," a soldier said, looking up from his spot at a nearby campfire. "Don't know what you're all so afraid of. He's harmless when he's tied up, isn't he?"

"Why don't you come a bit closer, and I'll show you how harmless I am?" Red Wolf growled. "Traitors. All of you."

"We serve the Crown." Another soldier crouched before him and held out a piece of bread in front of his face. "Open up."

Red Wolf's gaze flickered to the man's weapons belt. He *was* crouched awfully close...

The ex-bodyguard opened his mouth and allowed the soldier to feed him. They all burst into laughter as he chewed and swallowed.

"Look at him. He really is just like a dog—" the first soldier began.

He was stopped short when Red Wolf headbutted the man in front of him and ripped his dagger free from its sheath. His hands were free a moment later, and any cuts he'd accidentally inflicted on himself were already closing.

"I'm guessing a dog can't do that trick." He deflected a sword strike from the nearest soldier as they advanced on him. A slash to the leg dropped him instantly. The rest were smart enough to circle him and cut off any chance he might have of simply making a run for the trees. One of the soldiers fumbled for his horn and blew it.

Fools.

It was a tactic that might have worked on anyone else, not someone trained by Hellhounds and taught, through countless brutal drills, how to fight against a circling pack. Besides, all he needed to do was protect his head and maybe his neck, assuming any of these soldiers were even capable of decapitating him with a single hit.

Red Wolf sidestepped one of the soldiers and took him out with a kick to the knee. There was a sharp *crack* as the joint dislocated. Two more came at him from either side while a third tried to grab him from behind. He slipped out between them, ignoring their blades as they dug into flesh, and slashed at the nearest soldier's wrist. He dropped his weapon with a gasp.

More are coming.

He paid no heed to the gathering footsteps; there were only a handful of soldiers here, and he would be well away before the rest of the camp showed up to intercept him. He danced around his remaining opponents and took out two more with precise slashes to the legs.

Danger—

He barely registered the final soldier's mace swinging at him before it clocked him in the side of the head, sending him sprawling. His vision went dark for a moment.

"Get the shackles on him!" someone shouted. Red Wolf tried to push himself to his feet but only succeeded in receiving a boot to the face. Half a dozen soldiers piled onto him, restraining him as he struggled. He managed to throw one off, but the man was quickly replaced by one of his comrades. One of the soldiers wrestled a set of manacles around his wrists, but they couldn't hold him still enough to snap the iron bands shut.

"By the gods, how strong is he—" another soldier said. Red Wolf elbowed him in the nose and heard a satisfying *crack* as bone broke. The man stumbled away with a howl of pain and allowed him an extra half-inch of wiggle room before two more replaced him. He growled at the newcomers.

"Hit him in the head again," someone else suggested. Red Wolf felt his head being shoved down against the ground.

Oh, gods—

A stab of irrational panic shot through him. He suddenly found himself back in the alchemists' labs, struggling as they pinned him down. They were so much stronger than he had been back then; two Hellhound alchemists were enough to completely immobilise him without any need for restraints.

"Got it!"

He was released a moment later. By the time he regained his bearings again, they had dragged him to the nearest tree and locked his excess chains around the trunk, preventing him from going anywhere. He didn't struggle. Blood pounded in his ears, drowning out almost every other noise. The panic from earlier lingered in his chest and throat. He could barely think.

Stupid. Should've held it together. Maybe I'd have overpowered them.

But he supposed it was too late for regrets. For now, he was back where he started, bound even more securely than before with his hands stuck behind his back. He knew an escape opportunity would come eventually, but until then, all he would be able to do was bide his time and wait.

Odd that none of the soldiers' weapons are coated in torslek.

He watched as a healer attended to the soldiers he'd injured during the scuffle. Aldrus surely knew of his powers and how dangerous he could be, even on a night such as this, with the moon barely more than a sliver in the sky. He was equally sure that every garrison, outpost, and major fortification in Kies Tor had some supply of the Draconian venom; Kadis would have supplied them with more than enough in their war against the Hellhounds.

Then again, maybe it was for the best that they hadn't coated their weapons, given how easily he was able to steal a dagger and cripple so many soldiers. He figured this was the exact reason that they'd elected to leave their weapons clean—a torslek-coated blade would have been inconvenient for him but fatal for anyone else in the search party unfortunate enough to be on the receiving end.

Wherever Talin is now, I hope she can stay hidden.

The soldiers set out again at dawn, this time ensuring that half a dozen guards accompanied him at all times during the day and chaining him to a tree with two sentries to watch him at night. He was hand-fed whatever leftovers they had from dinner, and he entertained himself by trying to scare whichever poor private was assigned the job in the evenings.

But a week passed on the road, and the search parties returned each day empty-handed.

He supposed that was a good thing. The longer they spent failing to find Talin, the more time she had to make her way to Blackrun and seek refuge in the Highlands.

One evening, after most of the soldiers had gone to sleep and night sentries had been placed around the perimeter, one of the two guards watching him approached to hand him a fresh bread roll and feed him some dried meat—a luxury for him, considering the stale bread leftovers he'd been eating.

"You realise I can't eat the bread if you put it in my hand," he said.

"Regards from Lord Cassius," the soldier whispered into his ear. He rejoined his companion before Red Wolf could ask any questions.

"What was that about?" his companion asked. "Don't tell me you've gone all soft on the prisoner. He wounded, what, at least half a dozen of our men?"

"I just want to stay on his good side in case he escapes again."

"Huh. You know what, you might actually have a point there..."

Red Wolf fumbled with the bread roll for a few moments before he was able to rip it open, feeling something cold and hard within. It was small, oddly shaped, small enough to fit into his palm with a narrow shaft and teeth at one end.

The key for his manacles.

He contemplated the best way to escape. It wasn't enough for him to make a break for it; he needed his sword if he truly wanted to deprive Aldrus of any evidence of his return. The dark patterned Draconian steel of the lord commander's sword was far too recognisable.

"What are you going to do with my weapons?" he asked the guards.

"Not for us to decide," the first guard said. "Aldrus will probably want it for himself. It *is* a nice sword."

"Don't worry, we're keeping it safe," Cassius' spy said. "It's with the quartermaster at the edge of camp." He jerked his head towards one of the tents in the distance. "Although I suppose it's not *with* the quartermaster right now, I mean, most of the camp is asleep."

His companion elbowed him in the ribs. "Watch your mouth around him."

"What? It's not like he's going to break out of the chains right this instant," the spy said. "I've fought Hellhounds before. They're not *that* strong."

Red Wolf only shrugged. The two guards lost interest in him after a few seconds and turned back around. He fumbled with the key in his hands and managed to slot it into the keyhole with some difficulty. From there, it was a simple matter to turn it and unlock the shackles. The guards didn't seem to react as he slipped away behind them, though he did notice the spy's gaze flicker towards him ever so briefly. The man quickly struck up a conversation with his companion about their company not being supplied new gear like they'd been promised.

He heard a shout as he reached the quartermaster's tent; the guards must have seen that he was missing by now and raised the alarm. Red Wolf ducked inside and quickly grabbed his belongings.

Time to leave.

There was a soldier waiting for him as he stepped out of the tent. He ducked under the man's sword swing, bashed him in the face with the hilt of his sword, and took off running without missing a beat.

A crossbow bolt struck the tree next to him as he tore through the thicket, forcing him to flinch away. He ducked around another tree trunk and tried to place as many obstacles between himself and the crossbowmen as possible.

Lose them in the thick undergrowth. It's the only way.

He vaulted over a large, fallen log, stealing a glance back as soon as he landed. Two more crossbow bolts came flying at him. Red Wolf felt his magic spring into existence around him and deflect them both.

"You can't run forever!" one of the soldiers called back.

I can try, he thought. Another bolt brushed past his arm close enough that he felt the gust of air that followed. The next one punched clean into his side and sent him to one knee with a grunt.

"Stay down!"

Red Wolf staggered to his feet and scrambled onto the nearest tree branch. A bolt embedded itself in the wood next to his head. He didn't pause to check on his pursuers and kept climbing, trusting the foliage to camouflage his movements. His torso burned where the bolt had dug into flesh. He ripped it free without thinking.

Wait—

He realised his mistake too late as blood immediately seeped across his tunic. He looked at the crossbow bolt in his hand and cursed.

The search parties knew that coating their melee weapons could prove disastrous if Red Wolf were to get his hands on a sword or dagger, and so they had left them clean to protect themselves. But crossbows were slow to load and the quarrels they shot were unlikely to be his first choice of weapon in the melee—it had been a smart move to dip those in torslek instead.

Can't do anything about the bleeding now. Have to get away first.

He hauled himself onto the next branch with some difficulty. Below him, he could hear the soldiers spreading out, likely positioning themselves around the nearby trees in case he tried to get back down. A small group had hoisted themselves onto the lowest branch beneath him and were trying to make their way up higher. He knew they had no chance wearing their heavy plate and chainmail, especially without the enhanced strength he possessed, but they would make their way up to him eventually if he did nothing. Red Wolf spied a branch leading to a neighbouring tree and leapt across to it.

Slowly, agonisingly so, he climbed his way across the treetops and away from his pursuers. His torso burned with each movement he made, but he dared not stop. A single mistake could land him back in their hands.

He climbed for what felt like hours, moving through the thick canopy of Stormwood, trusting the darkness to conceal him. His wound was what eventually forced him to stop on a thick branch, leaning against the tree trunk, clutching his side.

Everything hurt. His muscles ached from the climb.

He supposed, if there was an upside, the lack of noise from the forest floor meant that he'd shaken his pursuers for now. His priority now should be to find a healer willing to treat his injuries *without* turning him in to Aldrus' men. For now, he ripped up some cloth from the bottom of his cloak and packed the injury with it. With most of his supplies still at the soldiers' camp and only his weapons belt to help him, this would have to do.

Red Wolf reminded himself that it was too late for regrets. He needed to continue moving, or he would bleed out in the middle of Storm-wood—not the most dignified way to die if he was honest with himself. He climbed his way down the tree to continue his journey on foot. At the very least, walking would be easier on his injury than swinging through the trees.

Need rest.

Gods, he was exhausted. Given the strength of the moon's pull on him, it must be well past midnight, and he knew he needed sleep. There was no use forcing himself onwards if it would only result in him collapsing in the middle of the forest. But if he closed his eyes and slept now, what were the chances that he would wake up? What if he succumbed to his injuries in his sleep?

Have to keep going. Try to find a road, head east, split the search parties so they don't go north to find Talin.

It took him several more hours of stumbling through the under-growth before he finally came across the familiar packed dirt that marked a road through Stormwood. There, he sank to his knees, look-ing up at the steadily brightening sky and praying to whatever gods were watching to deliver him to the nearest town.

Red Wolf felt his consciousness slipping and didn't try to fight it.

T alin was beginning to regret stopping here.

      She had tried to skirt around most of the villages on their route after their close call in Dennik, but their journey always led them, inevitably, back to a village well or some other source of water. With the unrelenting heat of the dry season, keeping their water canteens filled was near-impossible; they often found themselves running empty by nightfall despite filling up the day before. Ashera had eventually volunteered to stop by the market at the next village and purchase some extra canteens while the rest of them waited on the outskirts. Running into another search party had been bad luck.

      The soldiers deployed here had left them well alone at first, but after they did their usual interrogating and prepared to head out again, one of the cavalrymen had given them a second glance and clearly must have decided that they fit the description of the runaway group from

Belanore. Talin saw her brother reach for a sword as they approached and silently motioned for him to stop.

"Travellers, I presume?" the sergeant asked.

"Aye," Golmin said. "Is something the matter?"

"We've been ordered to search all travellers passing through these parts," the sergeant explained. "Remove your hoods, please."

Talin stole a sideways glance at Ettrias, then lowered her hood. Her companions did likewise, including Arkiel, who was mostly hidden behind her. The sergeant noticed the boy and leaned over to talk to him.

"What's your name, boy?" he asked.

Talin reached back and put a hand on his leg, hoping he would understand the gesture. "This is my nephew, William. You'll have to forgive him, sir; he's quite shy."

"That so," the sergeant said. "It's alright, William, no need to be shy. We're just here on official duty. The king is looking for some fugitives."

"We're not fugitives," Arkiel said quietly.

"Of course not." The sergeant smiled. "But you'll be good and let the soldiers know if you see something amiss, won't you?"

"Y-yes, sir," Arkiel said.

"That's good." The sergeant straightened. "Well, I'm sorry to trouble you lot. Take care now." He wheeled his horse around and signalled for his men to move out. Talin let out a breath she didn't realise she'd been holding.

"What was that about?" Ashera asked, appearing beside her with four extra canteens and staring after the fading outlines of the search party.

"We should leave," Talin said.

"No complaints here."

Talin led the way onwards, turning off the road to avoid running into any more search parties, keeping a brisk pace as the horses tried to navigate the difficult terrain. She was eventually forced to slow when it became apparent that their mounts were growing tired.

"Good thing that search party didn't recognise us," Ettrias said as they dismounted and continued on foot, detouring towards the White River.

"I wouldn't make any bets," Golmin muttered. "You saw their colours—they're soldiers from the Fort Voraine garrison. I'd be willing to bet they *fought with the queen* during the war."

Talin had been thinking the same thing. "There's a good chance the sergeant already suspected who I was before he approached. Why else would he double back?"

"Then why would they let us go...?" Ettrias frowned.

"Oh, come on, we'd easily outmatch them," Ashera said. "You're one of the best swordsmen in the kingdom. Golmin and I are royal guards. The queen is a crack shot with a bow *and* shoots lightning out of her hands. That search party wasn't even a full squad—I saw four soldiers, including the sergeant."

"If my hunch is correct, they're riding ahead to regroup and cut us off at the border," Talin said. "We can't double back with search parties on our tail. We've already passed Varen and the final bridge into the north. They want to capture us before we make it into the mountains."

They stopped at the edge of the White River to let their mounts drink. At this time of year, the river had lost much of its height, sitting several inches below the bank. The horses were forced to lean down in order to reach the water.

"We'll be at the border tonight if we keep up our current pace," Golmin said, examining their map. "If your theory is correct, there will be *dozens* of soldiers waiting to stop us."

"But if we turn back now, we'll run into the search parties pushing east from behind," Ashera said. "We're outnumbered either way."

"If we turn back, there's a chance we run into Red Wolf," Talin said softly. "If he's in Kies Tor and following us."

Golmin and Ettrias exchanged looks. Talin knew what they were thinking even before her brother opened his mouth.

"It's been weeks. If he was on our tail, he would have caught up by now," Ettrias said. "Either that or something happened to him. At this point, I wouldn't...get my hopes up."

Talin winced. She knew he was right; all logic dictated that Red Wolf *couldn't* still be on their trail. Yet there was a stubborn streak at the back of her mind that refused to give up on him despite the odds.

It's not worth risking everyone's lives.

"You're right," she said, though she wasn't sure if she was telling Ettrias or herself. "Damn it. We have to push for the border. We're so close..."

Golmin tucked his map away. "Let's get moving, then. With any luck, we can cut through Stormwood and outpace the soldiers to the border."

The five of them mounted their horses again and continued on, led by Golmin this time. Talin found herself pondering all the possible scenarios as they rode. How many troops had Aldrus mustered to stop them? What would happen to Arkiel if they were caught?

She pushed the thoughts from her mind. There was no way for her to know the answers to her questions; anything was possible when they reached the border.

It was nearly midnight by the time they reached the foothills of the mountain range that marked the eastern border. They had agreed unanimously to keep riding through the night in case they were being tailed by any search parties waiting for them to settle down before springing an ambush. Arkiel had fallen asleep in the saddle, and so Talin had wrapped an arm around his midsection to keep him from sliding off the horse. Trees gave way to low shrubland as they rode on before most of the vegetation disappeared altogether, leaving nothing but short grass and precious few flowers. Under the dim light of the moon, Talin could just make out the outlines of a large camp situated off the road. No fires were lit. Perhaps the soldiers had gone to bed.

"There's a camp just off the road, up there." She pointed. "It's huge, but I don't see any others. We could sneak past."

"I see it," Golmin said. "Don't let the lack of light fool you. They probably have guard dogs and sentries posted around the perimeter. We could go off the path to avoid them..."

"They might have anticipated that and put sentries out along the flanks," Ettrias said. "We need to plan this out carefully."

Ashera put a hand on her chin. "I'm thinking I can run ahead to scout the camp on foot. I'll report back with their numbers and sentry locations, and we can work out the best way to approach."

Talin gave a nod. "Agreed. If you do spot any sentries, don't engage them. Come straight back to us."

"You got it." Ashera dismounted and handed the reins to Golmin and continued forwards on foot, faintly silhouetted in the dim moonlight. Talin watched the young woman until her outline grew too small for any of them to see.

Gods, I'm exhausted.

A month on the road, avoiding search parties at every opportunity, constantly looking over her shoulder...she hated it. She hated the situation she'd been put into, unable to prove her innocence. Aldrus had played his hand perfectly. How did she never catch on?

There was a shout up ahead. Talin reached for her bow reflexively and shook Arkiel awake gently, motioning for the boy to hold on to the saddle. She nocked an arrow but didn't draw the bow, watching to see what was happening ahead. Ettrias drew his sword. On her right, Golmin also readied an arrow.

"There," her brother hissed, pointing with his weapon. Talin saw Ashera running back towards them, pursued by half a dozen swordsmen. She cursed and loosed a warning shot that missed the closest soldier by half an inch.

"I don't think they care much for warning shots, Talin!" her brother snapped, charging forward to lend Ashera a hand.

"Don't kill them!" Talin called after him.

"What's..." Arkiel yawned. "Are there soldiers trying to stop us?"

"Yes. Hold onto the saddle tight." Talin spurred her horse forwards and loosed another warning shot. The soldier she'd aimed at flinched away reflexively. None of them slowed.

"They're not going to stop..." Golmin hissed.

Damn it.

Talin changed targets and sent her next arrow through the nearest soldier's leg. He dropped instantly with an audible scream as Ettrias reached Ashera and forced the others to scatter to avoid being trampled. It gave the young woman enough time to duck past and reach her horse.

"They saw me approaching, I'm sorry," she said. "One of them ran off to get reinforcements. I didn't have time to shoot him down before the rest attacked."

"Never mind that. We just need to make it past the border," Talin said. "Ettrias, take the front; stop anyone who gets close. Golmin, Ashera, deal with whoever slips past. I'll cover you all with my bow."

More soldiers were forming into position up ahead, armed with pikes to stop their charge. Ettrias veered off the road instead to dodge around them. Talin aimed for non-lethal targets, crippling soldiers before they could any of them could get a swing at one of their horses.

"Up ahead, archers!" Golmin yelled. Talin barely heard him over the thundering hoofbeats. "Keep your heads down!"

An arrow sailed past them, brushing Talin's hair with a light breeze, and she found herself missing Red Wolf's protection magic. On her left, Ashera parried a strike from a charging cavalryman and sliced through the straps of his saddle, sending him tumbling.

We just need to make it past the border. We can lose them in the mountains...

An arrow found its mark in Ettrias' shoulder and sent him tumbling off his horse. Talin shot down the archer responsible and turned back around; in the few seconds that it all happened, she'd overtaken her brother.

"Go, just...go!" Ettrias tried to stand but quickly dropped to one knee again. Golmin spun his horse around as well and reached down, hoisting him back up. Ashera cut down a swordsman who'd gotten close while Talin was distracted.

"Can you still ride?" Golmin asked.

"I'll be fine." Ettrias pulled the arrow free, and Talin saw with relief that his leather travelling armour had stopped the tip from penetrating skin. She shot another two archers to give her brother an opportunity to mount his horse again. Ashera had crossed the border. Golmin hung back near Ettrias to help fend off the approaching swordsmen.

"Crossbows!" the captain shouted.

"Keep going—we can get out of their range!" Talin loosed one more arrow before wheeling around to follow Ashera. She heard a cry of pain from Arkiel as something jostled them both in the saddle but didn't slow. Ettrias and Golmin soon caught up, and they made for the top of the first hill, putting distance between themselves and the crossbowmen. Talin didn't dare stop until she was certain they were out of sight, hidden by the rocky terrain and darkness. Hoof-beats faded into the distance as the Royal Army soldiers left the area—no doubt returning to camp to regroup and search for them in the morning. They had plenty of time to disappear.

"We're safe," Ashera said. "For now, anyway. Ettrias, how's the leg?"

"I think I broke something." Ettrias winced. "Nothing too serious, though...we'll find somewhere safe to spend the night first."

"Mother?" Arkiel whispered, turning in the saddle. Talin looked down at him. In the moonlight, it was difficult to make out his face, but his features were twisted in a grimace. Her gaze travelled down to his leg, eyes registering what she was seeing before her brain could fully process the dark liquid on his fingers.

"*Kust*," Ettrias muttered under his breath. Talin felt a cold chill run down her spine as she realised what had happened.

Arkiel's fingers were covered in blood.

C assius felt as if he was living in some sort of nightmare, one in which all of his worst fears had come true.

He wasn't entirely sure what to feel—other than anger—as he made his way out of the small hall. Aldrus had called another meeting, asking for updates on the investigation, and had announced to them that the High Court had officially ruled to name him King Regent of Kies Tor. All of the queen's power would be stripped while she was under investigation, and she would only be reinstated if there was a lack of evidence to prove her guilt.

That Aldrus had gone against the council's advice was no surprise. Talin herself had done it on many occasions, mostly when she had her mind already set on something and that infuriating stubborn streak of hers refused to listen to any reason from her advisors. But King Aldrus himself had agreed that such a move may not be well-received by the general public, and especially not by Lady Blackrun.

Then again, it's not like we have a choice. Everything has come to a standstill. Someone needs to take charge.

"You seem troubled, Lord Cassius," Corvan said, falling into step beside him.

Cassius sighed. There was no use in denying it. "I hate this," he said. "King Aldrus now has absolute power over the kingdom—only the High Court will hold him accountable. It's a shoddy move, especially with tensions running so high. Didn't you receive another letter from Lady Blackrun just *yesterday* asking for help? How likely do you think King Aldrus is to comply? He's devoted to completing this investigation as quickly as possible. The longer we delay sending someone north, the more likely it is for Lady Blackrun to do something drastic." He pinched the bridge of his nose. "I always did object to the queen simply...handing over...so much power to the court. This is exactly what I was worried about."

"One could argue it's a good thing," Corvan said. "Accountability is good. If the queen truly *is* guilty of misconduct, we have a way to uncover it. Not that I believe she is, of course. I only speak hypothetically."

"I know." Cassius sighed. "There must be more that we can do. My spies have been trying to rein in all those rumours, but..."

Corvan put a hand on his chin. "Well, this may be a long shot, but..."

"Yes?"

"I have heard from both Lord Wyndove and Lord Mornus that they have their...shall we say disagreements about Aldrus' administration. They share our sentiment—that he will only serve to provoke Lady Blackrun into turning on the Crown and, by extension, the entire north."

"You truly believe that Blackrun can turn all the Highlander nobles against us?" Cassius asked.

"It's not unfeasible," Corvan said. "They're loyal to her and trust her to represent them in the political sphere. If she believes that following the Crown is no longer the best course of action for the north, who are they to argue?"

Cassius hissed through his teeth. Things were clearly much worse than he'd anticipated. "We must do something about the situation, then. If we can somehow get word to Blackrun, or...settle the situation here..." A thought occurred to him. "I may have a plan. Corvan, how do you feel about using your tower to host a...secret meeting?"

"I...would not be opposed to it," Corvan said. "But why there?"

"It's out of the way. Nobody is likely to spy on us or overhear anything by accident. The alternative is meeting in the cellar, which was Wormwood's idea, and my brother's, and their plot was uncovered by a patrolling guard captain—entirely by accident, I might add."

"You do have a point," Corvan admitted. "Pick a time and date—I'll make sure my tower is ready for you."

"Appreciate it, Corvan."

They parted ways at the next fork, with Cassius making his way down the hall to his office. There, he quickly scribbled out two identical notes—one each for Lord Wyndove and Lord Mornus requesting them to meet in Corvan's tower tomorrow. That done, he headed out again, deliberately taking a longer route to the kitchens, passing a patrolling guard on the way. He discreetly handed the first note to the man with a whisper to deliver it to Lord Mornus. The second note, he left on one of the pantry shelves, knowing that one of the serving ladies would come by in a few minutes to take stock of their inventory for lunch and would see the slip of parchment immediately.

All that's left to do now is wait.

He returned to his study with a wrapped parcel of baked goods to snack on, giving himself an excuse to visit the kitchens in the first place, and began sifting through the latest intelligence reports from his network.

The rumours seem to be dying down. That's probably a good thing.

Part of him did wonder, blasphemous as it might be, whether they held any ring of truth, for most of the rumours in Belanore always did. Could the queen and her bodyguard truly have been lovers? It would certainly explain the way they interacted with each other, especially following their return from the Draconian lands. But if the rumours *were* true, why did she let the court sentence Red Wolf to a lifetime of exile? He tried to make sense of it all but only found himself with more questions than answers.

Cassius decided to drop the matter. Investigating this was not his job, and he wasn't sure he even wanted to know the answers to some of his questions. Besides, the queen's personal life was none of his business.

There was a tiny corner of his mind that wondered, just a little, how much he could get away with by simply asking her or Red Wolf about the truth.

Another report detailed that the queen had been spotted in the eastern villages, moving along the White River to the border. Cassius read over it twice more to make sure he hadn't misunderstood.

What in the seven hells is she doing? Aldrus has search parties all over the east by now. She should have turned north.

But perhaps she had been cut off at Varen. The Royal Army had moved in from just about every direction—forcing her down the only route where she wouldn't run straight into their waiting arms.

The report continued on to explain that some of the townsfolk believed that the queen was actually dead, given the length of the searches,
and that Prince Arkiel had been stolen away by General Ettrias and his
co-conspirators in an attempt to undermine Aldrus' rule of Kies Tor.
Cassius decided not to stem this latest round of local gossip. At the
very least, they would serve to complicate the narrative and make things
more difficult for the search parties.

The next morning, after breakfast had been served and he was sure
that Corvan had retired to his tower once more to work, he made his
way up the winding staircase and into the old man's study. Wyndove
and Mornus joined him not long after—with an unexpected visitor.
Cassius' brow creased when he saw the tall, dark-skinned elf trailing
behind Wyndove. Lord Elyr Varkis.

Cassius had never met him in person before, but he knew the man's
reputation; House Varkis had always been a staunch supporter of the
royal family ever since the ancient civil war that saw House Zylvaris
seated on the throne of Kies Tor. These days, Lord Varkis owned a
massive stretch of land that encompassed the top half of the Western
Forts.

"I wasn't aware that we were bringing friends," Cassius said drily.

"I trust Lord Elyr with my life," Wyndove said. "My lord was visiting Belanore on business, and I'm sure you're aware of the close ties
between House Varkis and the royal family. I believe it was fated that he
should be here."

"I only wish to help, my lord," Varkis said. "Lord Folen has briefed
me on everything. I know the situation is tense."

Cassius let out a long sigh. "Very well. I suppose it can't be helped
now, anyway." He inclined his head and indicated the couch. The three
men sat while he pulled up Corvan's wooden chair. "Master Corvan

tells me that we all share similar sentiments regarding the High Court's latest ruling. Treasonous sentiments, perhaps, if one were to say them in the open."

"You speak of King Aldrus and his administration?" Lord Mornus asked.

"I do." Cassius produced a bottle of wine and poured three glasses. "I'm of the opinion that we cannot allow the current situation to continue. Things will only escalate from here, and our relations with the north will continue to disintegrate until tensions reach a boiling point."

"And what exactly do you propose, my lord?" Wyndove asked. "What you speak of is high treason."

"Yet I hear no objection from you," Cassius said.

Wyndove shrugged. "We serve the Crown. One could argue this is in the Crown's best interests."

The corner of Cassius' mouth quirked. "Of course. I am, at the end of the day, only a humble Head of Intelligence. I can only do what I do best—spy."

"You suggest we spy on the king regent himself?" Mornus exclaimed. "This is madness."

"Perhaps," Cassius admitted. "But as it stands, King Aldrus holds absolute power over the kingdom. We can do nothing overtly, not without him finding out about it."

Varkis put a hand on his chin. "I'm afraid I won't be of much help, then—I'm staying in the inner district, not in the palace itself. But I could find more supporters for you among the nobility who reside there."

"It would be helpful, I agree," Cassius said. "Thank you."

"Before I agree to this mad plan, I'd like to know one thing," Mornus said. "Why must we spy on Aldrus? Why not continue the investigation as planned, or work to prove Queen Talin's innocence so the court will reinstate her?"

"This *will* prove her innocence if my hunch is right," Cassius said. "I have reason to believe that someone else forged the papers for the former lord commander's return and that King Aldrus might be involved." He didn't mention that his source had been Red Wolf himself; complicating the narrative right now was the last thing he wanted.

"Gods, I can't believe I'm agreeing to this." Wyndove pinched the bridge of his nose and downed a large gulp of wine. "Fine. If your suspicions hold any kind of truth, Aldrus cannot be allowed to remain in power. I'll help."

"Lord Tybalt?" Cassius looked to Mornus.

"Spymaster, you truly are mad." The silver-haired man let out a long breath. "If my companions here believe in you, then I suppose I must have some faith as well. I will help you."

This is it, then, Cassius thought. There was no backing out now.

"Thank you for the support, gentlemen," he said. "Let's get started."

How long has it been?

He forced his eyes open slowly, fighting the urge to slip back into a peaceful slumber, and found himself staring up at a simple, wooden ceiling. He was in a bed. The mattress wasn't particularly comfortable.

Where am I?

He hadn't been brought back to Belanore; that much was evident. The room was completely unfamiliar to him, and when he stumbled out of bed to try the door, he discovered that it was unlocked. His weapons had been left propped up against the wall beside his bed, his coins left untouched in their pouch. Red Wolf examined the bandages wrapped around his midsection before struggling into the spare tunic left for him. That done, he snatched up his weapons and headed out to gather his bearings.

A countryside inn, then.

Red Wolf made his way down the stairs at a slow limp, the positioning of his wound making it difficult to place weight on his left side.

Full moon is rising. I haven't healed yet. Should be safe for now, but I need to get out of here soon.

The ground floor of the inn opened up into an attached tavern with the reception desk at the front. A young woman was busy wiping down tables while an older gentleman counted coins behind the desk. Evidently, the tavern had just closed.

"You're awake!" the woman exclaimed, straightening when she saw him. "I found you collapsed on the road while I was on my way back from delivering ingredients. My father here decided it best if we lent you one of our rooms while the village healer dealt with your wound. We...weren't sure you'd make it."

"Thank you. Both of you." Red Wolf made it to the nearest chair and sat, clutching his torso. "Where are we? How long have I been here? Who are you people?"

"You're in a tiny little village near Varen—it's off the main road and doesn't even show up on the maps. You've been passed out for a week," the woman said.

"A *week*?" Red Wolf blinked.

I knew that. The full moon is rising.

He shook his head. The wolf's instincts thrashed against the back of his mind, desperate to take over. There was no telling what might happen if he transformed here. He needed to leave.

"Anyway," the woman continued, "I'm Laura. That's my father, Ralph. We run the inn together." She indicated the man at the reception.

Ralph grunted but didn't stop counting coins.

"I'm..." Red Wolf hesitated. "William. William Higgins."

"Well, William," Laura said, "supper is already finished, but I can ask the chef to cook you something extra if you'd like. You must be hungry."

"I...need to leave. You're not safe with me here." Red Wolf stepped towards the door.

"Are...are you sure?" Laura asked, cutting in front of him awkwardly. "It's just, well, you should keep up your strength."

Maybe it's for the best. The wolf is less likely to go after anyone if he's already full.

Red Wolf offered her a stiff smile. "Alright. I suppose you're right."

"Do you want anything in particular? We have some leftover soup, but I know that's not the most filling meal. There's also some kind of meat dish."

"If it's not too much trouble...the meat would be good."

Laura set down her cleaning rag. "I'll let the chef know." She disappeared through a set of double doors at the back of the tavern.

"I'm sorry for the trouble," Red Wolf said to Ralph. "I'll be out of here as soon as I can. I, uh...don't suppose you know anyone nearby who's selling a horse."

"If you're offering to buy, I can sell you my old horse." Ralph looked up. "Used to pull the wagon, but he's getting old, so I've bought a new one. He's yours for six hundred yarii."

"For an old pack horse? Don't be ridiculous." Red Wolf checked the coin pouch attached to his belt and found only three gold coins inside, other than a few silvers' worth of spare change. "You can't do...three hundred?"

"Six hundred. Take it or leave it." Ralph went back to counting his coins.

"I only have three hundred. My belongings were taken," Red Wolf said.

"Then you'd best find someone else to buy a horse from," Ralph said.

Laura soon returned with a bowl of beef drenched in a spiced sauce, explaining that these were all the leftovers from supper service that the chef would have to throw out otherwise to stop it from getting anyone sick. Red Wolf accepted the food gratefully.

"I...well, I saw the healer treating your injuries," Laura said, blushing a deep shade of scarlet. "Are you a soldier?"

Red Wolf looked up from his food briefly. "No."

"But you must have fought hundreds of battles to get those scars, surely," Laura said.

"I don't want to talk about it."

"I'm sorry."

"Don't be." Red Wolf swallowed another bite of beef. "I don't suppose I could trouble you for some ale? I can pay."

Laura quickly went behind the bar and filled a flagon. "Don't worry about payment. It's on the house."

Red Wolf's brow creased. "I don't deserve this kindness."

"Well, I can't be a judge of that," Laura said, "but my mama said to always treat everyone with the kindness you would want shown to you. Especially if they're in need."

"Wise words to live by."

A shout from outside made him swivel, ears straining to pick up more sound. Hoofbeats echoed on a dirt road. Lighter footsteps sounded on wooden floorboards as Laura crossed to the nearest window and peeked through it.

"It's the soldiers!" she said.

"The Royal Army?" Red Wolf asked.

"Yes." Ralph looked dejected. They arrived here a few days ago, searching for the queen and her associates. Instead of actually going out to find them, these soldiers have set up a temporary base here and seem to relish tormenting us for extra 'taxes' and threatening to punish anyone who disobeys them. They take what they want and do what they want."

"We can't make them leave," Laura whispered. "They sometimes make all the village girls line up on the road and pick one out to take back to their camp. I don't know what the soldiers do with them."

"Nothing good." Red Wolf joined her at the window, watching the soldiers go around to each house to threaten the inhabitants. He ought to find a villager selling a horse and leave; he had no business getting involved here. Talin was hardly likely to wait for him to deal with whatever troubles these villagers had, and the wolf was certainly not going to wait until he finished his business here before transforming. Besides, these soldiers lazing around instead of actually searching for the queen should be a good thing...

She would help them. She would never leave them to this fate.

"I'll have a word with them when they come knocking," Red Wolf said.

"You? But..." Laura quietened with a little surprised squeak when the soldiers started banging on their door.

"C'mon, innkeep! We know you're in there!" a soldier yelled. "Time to pay up!"

Red Wolf tapped the sword at his belt and opened the door.

"Weren't you dispatched here to search for the queen and her associates?" he asked. "Doesn't seem like you're doing any of that."

"*Tch*. What's it to you?" The sergeant at the front scoffed.

"Nothing. Maybe I'm just a follower of the chivalrous knightly oath." Red Wolf shrugged. "You have no right to charge these people a fee of any kind, legally or otherwise."

"And who in the seven hells do you think you are?" the sergeant drawled. "We'll charge a fee because we can. Think of it as a...soldiers' tax." The men behind him snickered. "And since you thought it such a good idea to talk back, we'll have to make an example out of you."

Red Wolf twisted aside when the sergeant reached for the front of his tunic and nailed a punch at the man's face, sending him staggering backwards and into two of his men. He followed through with a second hit that broke his opponent's nose.

"You're dead, *abiyo!*" the sergeant screamed. He came forwards again, flanked by his men this time, and Red Wolf drew his sword without skipping a beat. The sergeant's hand barely made it to his own weapon before Red Wolf rested the edge of the blade against his throat.

"Walk away. Don't come back. Nobody has to get hurt."

The sergeant's nostrils flared, but he didn't move.

"Last. Warning." Red Wolf's sword inched forward and drew blood.

The sergeant let go of his weapon with a scowl and backed up slowly, hands above his head. Red Wolf kept his sword trained on the man, watching the rest of the soldiers out of the corner of his eye in case they decided to attack. They never dared to get close.

"You're Red Wolf, aren't you?" the sergeant asked. "The exiled lord commander. The queen's greatest failure."

Red Wolf scoffed. "You're all a bloody disgrace to the Royal Army. Do not speak to me of failure when you would rather prey on the innocent than do the jobs you were assigned."

"All we'll receive is praise when we hand you over to King Aldrus."

"Good luck with that."

Two of the soldiers lunged at him. He dodged the first swing and met the second with a deft parry. His riposte tore clean into the man's leg and dropped him instantly. The sergeant drew his own weapon, and Red Wolf spun, unsheathing his dagger at the same time. He brought the smaller blade up in time to block a downward strike.

"You should have stayed out of this," he told the sergeant.

The sergeant came forwards again. Red Wolf parried his low swing and stepped in, tripping him easily, and turned again as the first soldier rushed him. He sidestepped and sliced through the tendons in his opponent's arm in a single movement.

How do you do it? Ashera had asked him once. *How do you end a sword fight without killing the other person?*

Perhaps it was his Hellhound instincts, or perhaps it was Kehlvor's training. Either way, he had always known how best to target his opponents' weaknesses. To incapacitate or kill.

The next soldier who came at him received a blade to the hamstring when Red Wolf stepped around him. Another swung at him while his back was turned, but he heard the movement and ducked. The blade brushed over his head harmlessly. He retaliated by thrusting his dagger into the man's shoulder, between the armour plates. The soldier dropped with a scream.

The final two approached more cautiously, circling him, perhaps trying to flank him or surprise him from behind. He paid no attention to the one before him and listened for the movements of the other.

Pathetic. They think they can best a wolf.

Red Wolf shut the voice from his mind. He refused to think like the Hellhounds, refused to be the ruthless killer they'd trained him to become.

Stop denying your true nature, the wolf seemed to say. *This fight is beneath you. It's trivial.*

The remaining two soldiers rushed him at the same time. He dodged the first one, crippled him with a slash to the legs, and parried the second strike with his dagger. His riposte sliced through his opponent's wrist and forced him to drop his weapon with a gasp of pain.

"You're a...monster," the sergeant hissed, scrambling to his feet with his sword and backing away. Red Wolf kept distance with him easily. "You're one of *them*."

The ex-bodyguard scowled. "Say it. Go on."

The sergeant fell silent.

"Smart choice. Now drop your sword and run along."

The sergeant did as he was bid and scarpered. Red Wolf glanced down at the bleeding soldiers around him.

"It's nothing personal," he told them. "But I can't let any of you find the queen." He wiped his sword down and was about to sheath it when he saw Ralph climb to his feet and step around the reception counter with a crossbow pointed at his chest.

"I should have known," the innkeeper said. "You're a fugitive. An outlaw."

"Don't do this," Red Wolf said.

"Father—" Laura began.

"You stay out of this, Laura!" Ralph snapped. "Foolish child. I always said you were too damn soft. Now you've brought a *criminal* to our home! How am I to explain this to the Royal Army? We housed a fugitive who wounded half a dozen Royal Army soldiers!"

Laura closed her mouth again and looked down at her feet. Red Wolf's gaze flickered towards the open door. Maybe he could make it out of here before Ralph hit him with a potentially fatal shot.

This is bad. I'm running out of time.

"Ralph, I don't want any trouble," he said. "You don't understand the situation. Put the crossbow down. I need to leave—right now. For the safety of everyone in the village."

"Laura, go find the rest of the soldiers! Tell them I have one of the fugitives they're looking for held up at the inn," Ralph said. Laura hesitated, briefly meeting Red Wolf's gaze, but then she ducked past them both and disappeared outside.

"You don't need to send her," Red Wolf said. "The sergeant will return with enough soldiers to move their wounded out of here. There's no telling how well she'll be received at the camp."

"Not another word from you. Sit down, *abiyo*." Ralph nodded at the nearest chair. Red Wolf didn't budge.

"You won't kill me," the ex-bodyguard said. "If you know who I am, you should know what I am."

"Not. Another. Word."

Red Wolf brought a hand to his side and realised that his wound had healed.

That's not good.

"Ralph. Please. You need to let me leav—ARGH!"

Pain exploded across his vision—a familiar, soul-rending pain, not the pain of being shot. A bowstring *twanged* somewhere. He fought against it, trying desperately to wrestle back control, but it was no use; he saw only red haze as the wolf took over...and then he saw nothing at all.

Blood and screams. So much blood. He was wading in it.

He awoke to a dizzying headache and the scent of iron, the overwhelming taste of blood in his mouth. The first thing he saw when he looked down at himself was that he was covered in blood. So much so that his hands were soaked in it.

Oh, gods. No.

The taste of iron lingered on his tongue. He turned and threw up into a bush.

Where—

What happened—

Why is there a—

He almost jumped at the sight of a chewed-up arm, almost mauled beyond recognition. There was no sign of its owner or where they might be. He was in the middle of nowhere, deep in the middle of Stormwood once again, with no notion of how he arrived or what happened the previous night. The wolf had, however, left a trail of blood as he'd dragged the limb to its current location. Red Wolf followed it back through the forest with a knot in the pit of his stomach.

The trail led him, as he'd expected, all the way back to the outskirts of a tiny village, to a large military camp that looked more like the aftermath of a battlefield. Here, he found the owner of the severed arm—it was the sergeant he'd talked to and defeated the previous night. He lay motionless on his back with his throat slashed open and the stub of his left arm hanging uselessly out to the side. Judging from the bloodied drag marks on the ground, the wolf had hauled his corpse all the way from within the village itself, almost as if parading him through the camp.

Red Wolf felt sick as he rummaged through the camp for some clothes he could wear.

How did I...

He continued into the village dressed in an outfit slightly too small for his bulk. More corpses littered his path, mostly Royal Army soldiers. He saw a handful of civilian bodies holding makeshift weapons too—pitchforks, sickles, a blacksmithing hammer. He sank to his knees in the middle of the village square, surrounded by bodies butchered almost too far beyond recognition.

What did I do?

XVII

T alin didn't sleep that night.

They had found a cave a little further up the mountain that would serve as a temporary shelter while Golmin rode on to find help and Ashera scavenged for their food, and with Ettrias and Arkiel both settled, they had agreed to split up in the morning. Talin had instead spent the night comforting her son and doing what she could to make him more comfortable. They had managed to stop the bleeding in his leg after half an hour of terrifying suspense, but without any medical supplies or a map of any settlements past the border, his chances of survival were slim. The bolt had clipped his leg instead of going directly in, dealing far more damage. Talin had been worried that it had severed an artery, but Golmin had assured her that it was impossible with the position of the wound.

"Mother? Are you still there?" Arkiel said weakly. Talin jolted awake; it seemed that she'd drifted off again.

"I'm here," she said. "Golmin has gone to find help. You'll be alright, I promise."

"We don't even know if...there's any civilisation in these mountains." Nearby, Ettrias sat up with a grimace, injured leg stretched out in front of him. "He might not find anything."

"Ettrias." Talin shot him a glare.

"Oh! Uh, what I mean is, uh...I'm sure Rufus will find help, whatever the odds," her brother said, hastily covering up.

"But what if...what if he takes too long?" Arkiel said quietly. "Will I die?"

"No, no, of course not." Talin pulled him into a hug gently. "I will not let that happen to you. Ever."

Arkiel seemed to relax a little at those words. "Can I have some water? I'm thirsty."

"Here." Talin passed him a canteen.

"We're running low." Ettrias gave his own canteen a little shake. Nothing swished inside. "Ashera won't be back until dark."

Talin sighed. "Look after Arkiel. I'll fetch some more." She grabbed the canteens and ducked out of the cave. There was a freshwater spring a short hike from their shelter that provided an unlimited source of water, and thanks to the altitude, the weather was more bearable compared to the tropics. She refilled everyone's canteens and returned to the cave.

"...and then, just when we thought it was too late, Red Wolf comes charging in out of nowhere and distracts everyone for long enough for your mother to escape," Ettrias was saying. "But then there were all these guards, and it was almost sunset, so all they had to do was keep Red Wolf in the city square for a few more minutes until he shifted. And it worked. Everyone saw him turn into a big wolf and kill Wormwood."

"I see you've been coaxed into telling a story," Talin said, setting his canteen down beside him.

"I asked Uncle Ettrias about Red Wolf," Arkiel said. "His stories are very good. It makes my leg hurt a bit less."

"Red Wolf." Talin sat down beside him. "What do you want to know?"

"Well..." Arkiel frowned. "He must have known that if he came to help you that night, he'd probably shift in front of everyone, and they'd all think he was a Hellhound. But he did it anyway. He must have really liked you, right?"

You have no idea, Arkiel.

"He was bound by his sense of duty," Talin said. "No matter what. He felt like he had to help."

"I think he liked you," Arkiel said with a teasing smile.

Talin laughed. "There's no fooling you, is there?"

"Did you like him too?" Arkiel asked.

Talin's smile faltered a little. "I...did. Very much."

"*Anyway,*" Ettrias said. "Seeing as there's not much to do around here, why don't we play a game?"

"What game?" Arkiel asked, immediately perking up. Talin glanced at her brother and met his gaze in a silent 'thank you'.

"Well, it's a game your mother and I used to play as children. We'll go around in turns and think of something from a certain category," Ettrias explained. "For example, the category might be 'animals', and I would have to say an animal on my turn. You're not allowed to repeat the same thing, so if I say 'tiger' on my turn, nobody else is allowed to say 'tiger' anymore. If you do, then you're out."

"That sounds fun," Arkiel said. "What happens if you can't think of anything?"

"Then you're also out," Ettrias said. "Last person standing wins. Or...sitting, I guess."

"Will you play, Mother? Please?" Arkiel looked at Talin.

"I suppose I could." She smiled.

Ettrias picked out the first category, which was 'towns and cities in Kies Tor'. Talin felt that Arkiel had a disadvantage in that field, given that she and Ettrias had spent countless hours staring at maps and memorising town names during the war, but as it turned out, the boy did surprisingly well. She suspected that Corvan had been giving him extra geography tutoring. The next category was magical creatures, which Arkiel easily won, having spent so much time in the library reading books about forest fairies and ancient dragons and the giant clans of the Far North. He eventually grew bored of playing and resorted to begging for more stories again. Ettrias obliged him with some of his stories of the war.

"When I grow up, I'm going to be the strongest warrior in the world," Arkiel declared. "That way, nobody would think of starting wars with us." He shifted in his spot and winced. "My leg hurts again..."

Talin rummaged through her pack and found the last of the powdered glass leaf they'd bought in Kies Tor. She mixed it with some water and gave it to him.

"This will last until tomorrow morning," she said. "After that, there's...not much that will numb the pain. I'm sorry, Ark."

Arkiel downed the concoction in one gulp and made a face. "Ew."

"There's no telling when Rufus will be back," Ettrias said.

"I know." Talin ran a hand down her face and leaned back against the cave wall. "We just have to hold out."

If Arkiel's wound festers—

She pushed the thought from her mind. Arkiel and Ettrias would receive the help they needed. She refused to let anything happen to them on this mountain.

Ashera returned to their shelter at dusk, as Ettrias had predicted, bringing three rabbits expertly caught in her traps. She roasted them over the fire while Talin divvied up some of their dried nuts to accompany the meal.

"No sign of Rufus?" Ashera asked.

"No," Ettrias said. "Doubt he'll be back for a while. We're on our own for now."

"How are you and Arkiel?"

"We'll be fine. Thanks for the rabbits."

Talin was silent as she chewed on her food. If Golmin failed to find any nearby settlements past the border, they needed another plan; she was responsible for the group's safety and survival. Turning back down the mountain would only send them straight into the Royal Army soldiers, no doubt still camped in the foothills, or straight into the search parties scouring the mountainside by now.

She knew their hiding spot wouldn't remain hidden forever. Though it was far enough up the mountain that navigating to this location would be difficult for the search parties, they would risk the rocky terrain sooner or later. The four of them were dependent entirely on Golmin finding some kind of help before the soldiers reached them.

"If Golmin doesn't find help up here, we have to head northwest, back into Kies Tor," Talin said. "Our only hope is that the Highlander nobility will grant us passage and safe refuge in the north."

"And if they arrest you on sight?" Ettrias asked.

"Better than any of us dying up here."

"You make it sound so grim." Ettrias snorted. "But you make a good point."

"Get some rest tonight," Talin said. "You and Arkiel both. Ashera and I will watch the camp."

"You're sure?" Ettrias asked. "Night shift with two people isn't going to be easy."

"We're in no hurry to travel anywhere," Talin said. "I don't think we lose anything by sleeping in."

"Alright. Look after yourselves, then."

Talin put Arkiel to bed, then lay down on her bedroll and tried to snatch a few precious hours of sleep before she had to take over Ashera's shift for the night. It was almost impossible. Between worrying about Arkiel and turning over their options in her head, she couldn't hope to settle down enough to fall asleep. She eventually dozed off thinking about Red Wolf and the Hellhounds and the war.

Blood and steel. The sounds of screams filling the air. Civilian bodies trapped in the crumbling ruins of Vill's Crossing. She could have saved them if she hadn't been so naive or foolish to trust Wormwood.

"Talin." Someone was shaking her awake. "Wake up."

Talin's hand flew to her sword before she registered that it was Ashera. She let out a long breath and released her grip on the weapon.

"Bad dream?" the young woman asked.

"Something like that." Talin climbed to her feet and rubbed her eyes. "Thanks for the wake. Get some sleep."

"Want to talk about it?" Ashera said.

"I'll be fine. But thank you."

She took her spot at the cave entrance while Ashera settled down by the fire, stringing her recurve bow in case she needed it.

We're alone on this mountain. There are no threats here.

Yet she couldn't shake the feeling of unease that had settled over her when she woke, sending her on high alert. It wasn't an unfamiliar feeling—she often felt the irrational need to watch for danger when she woke from a nightmare. Beyond waiting for the feeling to pass, there wasn't much she could do.

What if something happened to Red Wolf? What if he was in Kies Tor and Aldrus' men captured him?

Ettrias' words rang in the back of her mind, reminding her of the possibility that her former lord commander may be in trouble. All while she was helpless here, hiding from Royal Army soldiers herself.

He'll be fine. He can look after himself.

The thought didn't do much to shake her worry and guilt.

Ettrias joined her at the cave entrance at sunrise, using the wall to hobble over and seat himself on a rock next to her. She noticed that he'd put his weapons belt on.

"You should sleep," he said. "I can watch the camp for a few hours."

"I'm not tired," Talin said.

"Talin."

"Ettrias."

Her brother sighed. "Another bad dream?"

"Yes." She didn't see any point in denying it.

"I thought they were getting better," Ettrias said.

"They were. Maybe it's just this whole situation," Talin said. "I feel so...helpless. It's just like what happened with Wormwood. I should have seen it coming."

"You couldn't have predicted this, nor could you have predicted Wormwood's plan," Ettrias said. "By the gods, Wormwood even deceived *me*. Aldrus used your trust against you. And if he's not the one behind everything, then the real mastermind is someone we didn't even know was a threat. They outplayed us."

"I just..."

"It's not your fault."

Talin let out a long breath. "You're right. Thank you."

"Go sleep." Ettrias nudged her. "I'll call for help if there's trouble."

"You sure?"

"Come on, I only hurt my leg. I can still look for danger."

Knowing that it was pointless to continue arguing, Talin unstrung her bow and moved back into the shelter of the cave, to the dying embers of their campfire. She quickly fell into a dreamless slumber.

She was woken some hours later by the faint sounds of conversation nearby. Rubbing her eyes with one hand, she forced herself into a sitting position, fighting the lingering fatigue on her body as she scanned her surroundings. Ashera was chatting away to a stranger with dark hair and rounded ears. Golmin, meanwhile, had returned to their camp and was busy now fussing over Ettrias' leg. Arkiel slept on by the remains of the fire, no doubt still drowsy from the powdered glass leaf concoction.

"What's..." Talin yawned and climbed to her feet, strapping on her weapons belt. "Golmin?"

"Your Majesty." Golmin dipped his head. "There's a village half a day's ride from here. I talked to the elder in charge, and she's agreed to shelter us for the time being. I've brought back their healer, Undel, to look at Arkiel and Ettrias' injuries. Ashera was just explaining what happened while we waited for you or Arkiel to wake."

Talin felt a weight lift from her shoulders. "I'm glad." She glanced past the captain and saw that Ettrias' leg had already been splinted. "I'll wake Arkiel. We should get his injury treated as soon as possible."

She stepped over the smouldering fire pit and crouched in front of her son, shaking him awake gently. He groaned and turned over without opening his eyes.

"Five more minutes..."

"Arkiel. Come on," Talin said. "There's a healer here to look at your leg."

Arkiel yawned and sat up grudgingly. "Did Captain Golmin find help?"

"Yes," Talin said. "Here." She helped him prop himself up with his back against the cave wall. The healer finished talking to Ashera and approached.

"Master Undel." He stretched out a hand. "You must be Raia."

Talin quickly understood the situation and shook his hand. "Yes. Thank you for coming. I owe you my thanks."

"Just trying to help." Undel smiled. He turned to Arkiel. "I'm going to take a look at your leg and fix it up as much as I can. Is that alright? You can say no."

"It's alright," Arkiel said in a small voice.

Undel crouched beside the boy and undid the bandages around his leg, revealing the extent of the injury. He hummed and reached into his medicine bag for supplies. Talin squeezed her son's shoulder gently while the healer worked, taking advantage of the powdered glass leaf still in Arkiel's system to clean the wound with alcohol and suture it closed.

"There, that should do it," Undel said, getting to his feet again. "But you'll need somewhere clean and comfortable to rest. I believe your companion has already talked with the village elder, so I am ready to depart whenever you are."

"I see no reason to delay," Talin said. "Golmin, if you'll be so kind as to help my brother onto his horse. Ashera, we'll pack the camp. How far is the village?"

"We'll be there by nightfall if we keep a good pace," Undel said.

"That's good to hear. Let's get moving."

XXIII

The villagers didn't go near him as he tried to piece together what had happened last night. Red Wolf couldn't blame them.

What he did know was that the wolf had cleaved a path of bloody murder through the village, defending himself, presumably, from the Royal Army reinforcements that showed up after he transformed. He just didn't understand what initiated the rampage.

The trail of bodies led him back to the inn where he'd been staying, where he saw Ralph's lifeless body sprawled face-down on the wooden floorboards, throat slashed open so deep that he was almost decapitated. His right hand had also been mutilated beyond recognition. A broken crossbow lay on the floor beside him.

I remember...

Rage.

No, there has to be more.

He saw, through the red haze of fury, a crossbow bolt being shot at him. It sailed high as he dropped to all fours and clipped the top of his head instead, only it was no longer him by that point.

The wolf had taken offence to that attack.

Then the soldiers...

Laura must have run into the sergeant with his reinforcements outside the inn, and they had returned to a grisly mess and the wolf standing over his kill. A dozen Royal Army soldiers were sprawled across the floor close to the door. He recognised some of them as the men he'd dispatched while defending the innkeeper and his daughter—going for non-lethal strikes. But with the wolf's rampage, they had tried to fight or stop him and had paid the price for it. Those who didn't fight had posed no threat to the wolf, and they had no doubt crawled to safety.

Where's the girl?

Red Wolf bent down gingerly and picked up his weapons belt. The buckle had broken when his transformation shredded his clothes, so he pocketed his coin pouch and stripped the dagger and sword off the belt to hold onto instead. Another blood trail started nearby and went behind the reception area. When he went around the counter, he saw Laura huddled there, white as a sheet and shaking, clutching a bleeding leg. Four deep claw marks ran across it, shredding the limb into a mangled mess. Drying blood pooled underneath.

"I'm...I'm sorry. I'm sorry. I'm so sorry." His voice cracked as he crouched before her and looked her over for any other injuries. "You need to...get this fixed. Can I carry you to the healer?"

"I don't want your help," Laura said. He flinched at the coldness of her voice.

"You've lost a lot of blood. You'll die," he said.

Laura didn't respond. Red Wolf grabbed his broken belt and tied it around her upper thigh as tight as he could. That done, he scooped her up and carried her out of the inn, wandering down the main street until he found the sign that indicated the healer's house. The door opened as he was making his way up the steps.

"First room on your left," came a woman's voice. "Put her in one of the beds and get out."

Red Wolf did as he was bid. The healer didn't show herself. Returning to the inn, he found the pack horse that Ralph had been talking about and left his three gold coins on the counter inside before saddling it up. He needed to get away from this place, this bloodbath, away from all of his guilt. There was nothing he could do here that would help.

He stopped by the edge of the White River eventually, at a section of the riverbank where the ground sloped downward gently and allowed him to wade into the water without being swept away by the rapids. Here, he splashed water onto his face and tried his best to scrub the blood from his skin.

By the gods, he should have just left the village immediately instead of accepting Laura's offer of food and then trying to play the hero. What he ended up doing was far worse than anything the soldiers were ever capable of.

There was still blood on his hands. He scrubbed until his skin was raw and as clean as it would ever be, but still, he felt the blood on his hands, sticking between his fingers and in the crevices of his palms. No amount of scrubbing would remove it.

He splashed more water onto his face. That didn't help either.

Red Wolf heard a guttural yell rip from his throat as he sank to his knees in the shallows.

I could have prevented all of those deaths.

He let his hands drop to his sides, and for the first time in his memory, he wept for the dead.

He wasn't sure how long he spent there, but he eventually forced himself to step out of the shallows and keep moving. Remorse and guilt would not help Talin. His best bet without any sort of trail to follow had to be to continue east in the hopes of splitting the Royal Army, assuming that Talin was in the Highlands by now. And if, for whatever incomprehensible reason, she had elected to travel in the same direction as him, he should be able to pick up a trail once more if he was patient.

Tracking Talin directly was impossible by now, but he was eventually able to deduce a few things upon arriving at Varen the next day and purchasing supplies and a map. For one, Talin could not have gone north, given that the local gossip was all about 'another search party' moving *east* instead of crossing the bridge to the Glass Forest. For another, there was speculation that the search parties were, in fact, reinforcements called to a large camp at the eastern border, in the foothills of the impassable mountain range that cut them off from any civilisation that might exist beyond.

Talin didn't go directly north because of the Royal Army soldiers being deployed into the Highlands, likely to the bridge at Wycrest to cut her off. She knew as well as anyone that there was no hope of crossing the eastern mountain range. There was also talk about rising tensions between the north and south—Lady Blackrun, apparently, didn't particularly like the idea of Aldrus being in charge. All gossip that Talin would have picked up on, no doubt.

She knew for sure that she would be safe in the north if she could just slip past the search parties. She intended to circle back into the Highlands from the east.

It was the only thing that made sense; turning back would only send her into the search parties' clutches, which meant that she had only one option. And with no more major settlements on the map between Varen and the border, he supposed that they would have opted to continue along the White River. The only thing he could not determine was how long ago they had passed through.

Could she be in the mountains by now? Or is she still travelling along the river?

He hated not knowing where she was. Whether she was safe.

"Come on," he told himself, dismounting his horse again to purchase some proper clothes at the tailor. "No use worrying."

His route along the White River yielded no new clues, nor did he pick up any trail. He supposed it was a good thing; it meant that Talin's group had well outpaced any search parties trying to follow them.

Yet perhaps more strange was the fact that he hadn't encountered a single Royal Army soldier since setting out from Varen. Had the search been called off? Had Talin been captured at the border somehow?

Whatever the case, I'll know more once I reach the border.

It was almost dark by the time Red Wolf reached the edge of the treeline east of Stormwood, discovering that a huge campsite had been set up in the foothills just ahead. Royal Army banners billowed in the evening wind, bright red in the fading sunlight. Red Wolf quickly dismounted and slunk back into the cover of the trees to observe.

This must be the camp that the townspeople were talking about.

But their presence here still yielded no answers. Had Talin managed to cross the border? Or were these soldiers here to cut off her escape, and he had overtaken her without realising?

Upon closer inspection, however, he realised that there were no sentries posted along the western perimeter of the camp. That was even more unusual. Surely the soldiers would be on the lookout for...

They're not looking for fugitives on this side of the border.

Red Wolf's head spun. That was the most likely explanation, yes, but it only complicated things further. Talin had made it across the border, though whether her companions had been captured was another thing entirely. He had no chance of picking up any kind of trail on the rocky terrain, even if he could get past the soldiers here. He could go around the camp and try to pick up a scent once he'd passed the border, but there was no guarantee that he would find Talin at all. Most of the eastern range was unmapped territory; he would have to rely on his instincts to guide him.

"*Orrlát.* Couldn't make things easy for me, could you?" Red Wolf hissed through his teeth. He had to turn back; there was nothing more he could do here. There had to be another way for him to catch up to her—or intercept her on her way through the Highlands.

Red Wolf steered his horse back through Stormwood, looking for a clearing where he could set up camp for the night, a plan beginning to form in his head. Talin must be in the Highlands by now, and if she wasn't, she would cross back into Kies Tor soon enough. At the risk of exposing his whereabouts to Aldrus, if he could make himself known at enough inns and taverns across the north, then word would spread about his travels, and Talin would get wind of his whereabouts.

Far from a perfect plan.

But it was all he had. Even if his whereabouts were exposed, if he could find her, it would all be worth the risk.

Red Wolf settled down in the dim moonlight and began marking a travel route on his map.

The village they were taken to was a tiny cluster of houses
built precariously along the mountainside, staggering upwards
steeply with crude paths carved through the stone to allow for travel.
Undel led the way forwards, explaining that there were many isolated
communities like this just past the border, created when Weavers fled
persecution in Kies Tor during King Braenern's reign of terror. But
the king's Inquisitors had reached them anyway, and over the years, the
Weavers in these settlements had died out too.

"Why not return to Kies Tor?" Ettrias asked. "Why remain up here
in the mountains?"

"Those who live on the fringes of society often find themselves there
because society does not welcome them," Undel said. "So it is for us too.
We are outsiders now, after a thousand years away from our ancestors'

homeland. We belong here, where the people's prejudice will not reach us
."

Perhaps it's for the best that Golmin didn't give our true identities,
Talin thought. She doubted she would be welcome here otherwise.

"Here. This is where you can stay," Undel said, gesturing to a small
hut as they approached the middle of the village. "Elder Parya had this
empty hut cleaned for you. Get settled inside, and I can take a closer
look at your companions' injuries."

"Thank you," Talin said. "I won't forget this kindness."

"My people understand how unforgiving these mountains are,"
Undel said. "It is our duty to help those who are lost."

"All the same, thank you." Talin carried Arkiel into the hut and
settled him in an available bed while Golmin supported Ettrias. Undel
went to treat their injuries properly, and the rest of them were left to
their own devices.

"I don't know about the two of you, but I could do with some sleep."
Golmin yawned.

"The past few weeks have been exhausting, I agree," Talin said. "Still,
our troubles aren't over. Rest up tonight. We'll need to discuss our next
plan of action tomorrow."

Undel was quick to finish his work, promising to return in a few days
to check on them. Talin thanked him again for his help before he left.

"We're one bed short," Ashera said, ducking briefly into the two
bedchambers. "Someone's going to have to sleep on the floor."

"I will." Talin opened her pack and bedroll and began setting up.
"You two can claim the beds."

"Wh— Your Majesty, with all due respect, you're still our queen,"
Golmin said. "We cannot allow you to sleep on the floor when there
are beds available."

"I should not be entitled to anything just because of my status," Talin said. "You and Ashera have both done far more for me than I could ever thank you for. Please, take the beds. I insist."

Golmin and Ashera exchanged a glance but didn't budge. Talin finished setting up her sleeping area and unclasped her cloak, and the latter finally gave a sigh of defeat.

"You know, I think you're too selfless for your own good sometimes." The young woman huffed a half-laugh. "Come on, Rufus. Might as well take the queen up on her offer."

She disappeared down the narrow hallway with Golmin. Talin bundled her cloak neatly and set it down as a pillow before ducking into Arkiel's room to tuck him in. Ashera was already busy setting up her own bed and didn't pay them much mind.

"Comfortable?" Talin asked. Arkiel nodded. "How's your leg?"

"It's alright. A little better," the boy said. "The healer gave me a potion to drink. It tasted awful, but it made my leg not hurt."

"That's good." Talin kissed his forehead. "Make sure you get some rest tonight, alright? Your leg won't heal if you don't rest properly."

"Yes, Mother," Arkiel said.

"I'll be in the front room. Just let Ashera know if you need anything." Talin straightened and made a move to leave.

"Wait, Mother..." Arkiel called. "Can you...tell me a story? About Red Wolf? He sounds *amazing* from what Uncle Ettrias told me."

Ashera momentarily stilled on the other side of the room. Talin herself was taken aback by the question; she hadn't expected him to show such an interest in the former lord commander after a single story from Ettrias.

"I...of course," she said. "What do you want to know?"

"You said he was exiled for something. *Way* back, when we were still in the palace," Arkiel said. "That's a pretty serious thing, isn't it? People only get exiled if they do something really bad. What did he do?"

Talin paused. How could she possibly explain the events that had led to his trial and exile? And how was she supposed to justify to an eight-year-old child that what she did had been necessary when she had difficulty justifying it to herself?

"He...did some terrible things in your grandfather's name," she said eventually. "It started with me and your Uncle Ettrias, actually..."

She recounted everything that had transpired fifteen years ago, from Ettrias' return to Wormwood's treachery and eventual downfall. She left out the more graphic parts of the story, of course, but she did explain how she'd gotten the bite scars on her left shoulder. Arkiel listened to every word of it, eyes wide. It felt oddly relieving to get everything off her chest, even if she skipped over some details and tried to play down the magnitude of the feat she'd accomplished. Everyone else she trusted was there when it all happened, and she'd only really shared the details of their journey with Corvan after Red Wolf's exile.

"So...you had to exile Red Wolf because he really did kill those two people, and it's not fair if he gets to go unpunished if others commit the same crime and do get punished," Arkiel said. "But you didn't want to. It's like...when I get into trouble for doing something I'm not supposed to, and you have to make me sit in my room as a punishment, but you don't really *like* doing it."

"I..." Talin had never considered it like that. "I suppose so."

It was more complicated than that, because sending Red Wolf away would have meant that they might never see each other again, with the war still raging in Kies Tor. But Arkiel did have a point.

"Well...I think he's forgiven you by now, Mother, if he was even angry about it in the first place," Arkiel said.

Talin couldn't help but smile. "Thank you. Get some sleep now, Arkiel. It's late."

"Aww, but I'm not..." Arkiel yawned. "...that tired, Mother. Can't you tell me one more story?"

"Goodnight, Ark." Talin kissed his forehead again and moved towards the door.

"Goodnight, Mother..." Arkiel mumbled, sounding like he was already drifting off. Talin made her way back to her bedroll and lay down on it, staring up at the ceiling.

"How do you plead?"

"Guilty."

Talin shut the memory out. She refused to entertain thoughts of that day in any capacity, refused to remember their final goodbye. And yet...

Try as she might, she couldn't forget him. The memories of their journey west had been etched forever into her mind, reminding her over and over again of what she'd lost. She'd seen a side of him in those few months that he had never shown anybody, and she had come close enough to stare into the wolf's eyes and recognise him in them.

Poetic, in a way, that the first time I saw his wolf form, he would save my life.

She remembered that night at the border painfully clearly. Staring down the jaws of death, thinking it was the end, utterly helpless—only for the wolf to save her.

Talin jolted awake with a start, heart pounding, ringing steel echoing faintly in her ears. For once, she couldn't recall the dream, but the feeling of tension and danger it left behind suggested that it hadn't been anything good. Struggling to her feet, she made for the window and pulled back the curtains to discover that it was still dark outside. The others must still be asleep.

After some contemplation, she threw on a coat and headed out for a walk. She was unlikely to get any more sleep at this rate, and sitting in the dark in the hut would do nothing for her racing mind.

When will these nightmares end?

Part of her had grown used to them by now. The journey west, the ensuing siege at Belanore, eight *years* on the front lines of war...she supposed she would be lying if she pretended that none of it affected her. She sat herself down on a cliff at the edge of the village to watch the first traces of light creep past the mountain peaks.

Maybe I'm just not strong enough.

A raven flew past overhead, riding the upcurrents, wings cutting through the air like razor blades. Talin's gaze followed it as it tucked its wings and dropped, only to open them again halfway down and ride the current back up. It repeated the movement several times before flying down and disappearing behind another cliff. Talin almost wished she could turn into a bird and escape all her problems.

But running away from her problems had never solved anything. She would have to face Aldrus and the High Court eventually, regardless of whether she wanted to or not. She could only hope that fifteen years under her administration had rendered the court fully impartial.

Talin stood again and turned back for the village. The sun was almost up by now, and knowing her companions, they would be awake soon. She preferred *not* letting them know about her excursion outside or her nightmares. Ettrias would only worry. Stopping just outside the hut, she listened for any indication that they were already awake. The hut was silent. She pushed open the door carefully and stepped in.

"Aww, and you didn't think to invite me on your little walk?"

"Wh— *orrlát*, Ettrias, what in the seven hells?" Talin jumped. Her brother was already seated at the wooden table in the corner of the hut, injured leg stretched out in front of him.

"Care to at least enlighten me on what you were doing?" Ettrias asked.

"I..." Talin hissed through her teeth. "How long have you been sitting in the dark? Aren't you supposed to be resting your leg?"

"Avoiding the question, I see," Ettrias said.

"I was just going for a morning walk. Like I do most days in the palace."

"Talin."

Talin let out a sigh of defeat. "I couldn't sleep."

"Do you want to talk about it, at least?" Ettrias asked.

"There's nothing to discuss." Talin stripped off her cloak and sat down on her bedroll. "I don't even remember what the dream was about."

"It bothers you, clearly," Ettrias said.

"I... Yes. Of course it bothers me." Talin huffed a humourless laugh. "I thought the end of the war was the end of my troubles. But I can't...forget...any of it. And I should be able to. Everyone else has moved on. It's not...fair."

"You spent most of the war visiting the front lines and helping where you could," Ettrias said. He stood and hobbled over to join her. "That's more than any of the Royal Army. By the gods, you were on the front longer than your own *general*, and I spent a good portion of my time actively fighting. I think you're too hard on yourself."

Talin let out a long breath. "You actively fought in the war. I was just...there...for most of it."

"Oh, come on, you fought plenty. We secured the Western Forts thanks to your help. The bridge at Wycrest was only rebuilt because *you* were willing to make over a dozen round trips for emergency rations when the roads flooded."

"But that wasn't..."

"Talin, you have done far more for the war effort than you know," Ettrias said. "It's not your fault that you're still haunted by all the things you saw."

"I...don't know. Maybe you have a point." Talin offered him a stiff smile. "How's your leg?"

"I'll be fine. Have you come up with a plan yet?"

"Of sorts. Granted, it's not much of a plan, but it's a start."

They were soon joined by Golmin and Ashera, both yawning and clearly still half-asleep, and they divvied up their remaining rations for a quick breakfast. Talin explained the beginnings of her plan as they ate.

"I know that things have been...tense, for lack of a better word, with Lady Blackrun for the past few years," Talin said. "For all the rebuilding we've done since the end of the war, much of the Highlands still remains uninhabitable. Ghost towns are still speckled across the countryside. Blackrun believes the Crown should be doing more."

"Aren't you friends with Blackrun?" Ettrias asked.

"Yes. Which is the only reason I suspect she made an effort to maintain cordial relationships with the Crown," Talin said. "The High Court, hopefully, has learned a thing or two from my administration and maintains a degree of impartiality despite the accusations against me. I hate to rely on guesswork, but it's all we can do at the moment."

Ettrias' brow furrowed; clearly, he was already catching on. "If the Head of State is under investigation, they cannot remain in power. You passed that law fifteen years ago."

"Yes. Arkiel is presently with us, and even if he was still in Belanore, he has not yet come of ruling age," Talin continued. "The court would rule that he was too young to take the throne. Given that Aldrus is not the Head of State but is still king, it would only be natural that he becomes regent."

"Blackrun will be pissed, if you'll pardon the language," Golmin said.

"I'm counting on it."

Ashera and Golmin exchanged confused looks.

"I'm not sure I follow," the latter said.

"I know Blackrun, and I suspect she would never follow Aldrus based on a ruling by the High Court," Talin said.

"You intend to rally the northern banners." Ashera's eyes widened. "We're not just seeking refuge; you're looking to clear your name."

"Witnesses, yes," Talin said. "If I can prove my innocence to the High Court, they will have no choice but to reinstate my authority as Head of State."

"And if...tensions reach a breaking point?" Ettrias asked.

Talin understood what he was asking. While she wasn't keen on taking back Kies Tor by force, it was unlikely that Blackrun would share her sentiment. There was always the chance that the north would decide to split from Kies Tor entirely, returning things to what they had been before the unification of the kingdom.

"I'm hoping my presence in the Highlands will dissuade Blackrun from such a ridiculous move," she said.

"I guess we'll see," Ettrias said.

There was a light rap on the door. Talin crossed the room to open it, revealing an elderly woman with silvery hair tied back in a high bun. She carried a wooden cane in one hand.

"Good morning," she said. "We didn't have a chance to talk yesterday. I am Elder Parya—I run this little village."

"Madam. It's an honour." Talin inclined her head and stepped aside to let the woman in. "Allow me to extend my gratitude for giving us shelter here. It means more than you know. I'm Raia. This is my brother, Taj, and—"

Elder Parya only smiled and seated herself in the armchair. "I know who you are, White Raven."

What?

"I'm...not sure I follow," Talin said.

"You are Queen Talin, ruler of Kies Tor," Elder Parya said. "Your brother is Prince Ettrias, General of the Royal Army. You are both of House Zylvaris—the house of the white raven."

"Are the search parties here?" Talin asked.

"They were. I sent them on their way with some nonsense about you meeting your unfortunate demise to some hungry bears," Elder Parya said. "Allow me to preface what I'm about to say by assuring you that your presence here is not an intrusion. Quite the contrary, in fact."

Talin sat on the sofa opposite her.

"Why did you call me the White Raven?" she asked.

"Because I believe that is what you are," the elder said. "Are you aware of the superstition surrounding white ravens?"

"No. I didn't think they were real birds." Talin frowned.

"Very rarely, a raven in the mountains is born with snowy white feathers instead of jet black like the rest of its kin," Elder Parya explained. "Because these birds are the colour of snow in a land where snow is the most ruthless killer of nature, the superstitious folk believe that seeing such a bird means death will soon follow."

Talin felt like she'd been hit by a charging bull. She was suddenly reminded of General Virion and his decision to betray Kies Tor to side with the Hellhounds. In the years that followed the Siege of Belanore, she had tried to understand what they could have told him to change his mind, questioning him many times, but her interrogations had yielded no results. Virion only glared at her, and on the few occasions he did talk, he only spoke in riddles about the Torrian Crown, only ever referring to it as the 'White Raven', and Braenern's purge of magic—an event that he had begun to refer to as the Inquisition.

"Years ago," she began, "during our war, the Hellhounds told my previous general about some sort of 'truth' that swayed him to their side. I tried questioning him, but he wouldn't tell me much. Is this it?"

Elder Parya put a hand on her chin. "I'm not sure how the Hellhounds came across this information, but he is right not to tell you. The exact details of the prophecy are a closely guarded secret, known only to a select few records-keepers in the Far North. If you wish to know the truth, you must seek out the clans there."

"The...Far North?" Talin's head spun. "That's past the Torrian border..."

"Yes," Elder Parya said. "Outside the influence of the Torrian Crown. Outside the influence of the White Raven."

"Why tell me all of this?" Talin asked as the woman stood to leave. "What is this prophecy you speak of? Why is it relevant to me?"

"Because, like most, I believe in fate," Elder Parya said. "I believe that your presence here is no coincidence. I only wish to warn you."

The door clicked shut behind her.

"What in the seven hells was that about?" Ettrias asked.

Talin stared after the elderly woman. "I have no idea."

Much as she wanted answers about why the Hellhounds attacked, about the Inquisition, about this supposed 'prophecy', she knew she couldn't afford to follow those breadcrumb trails now. Her goals should remain the same: make her way to Castle Blackrun and seek help in clearing her name. Once things had settled, perhaps then she could turn her attention to the Far North.

"What's the plan?" Ashera asked. "This whole 'prophecy' thing sounds important. Do you want to go into the Far North?"

"No," Talin said and was surprised by how confident she sounded. "Our priority remains the same. We make for Castle Blackrun as soon as Ettrias and Arkiel are well enough to travel. I have to talk to Katherine."

R ed Wolf hadn't been in the Highlands in a long time.

North of the White River, the weather was considerably cooler despite it being the middle of summer, making for a welcome reprieve from the scorching heat of the dry season. When he looked back at the edge of Wycrest, he saw fields of greenery and the Glass Forest in the distance, transparent leaves glittering in the afternoon sun. He'd hoped to take Talin there at some point after the Siege of Belanore. But reflecting on it now, he realised it was never much of an option. His fate was sealed the night he killed the Harrison siblings.

Was she still in hiding past the border? Had she gone to seek out Blackrun's help? Red Wolf wondered. He hated not having a trail to follow, forced to travel blind in circles until he turned up some information about her whereabouts. The Highlands made up almost half of Kies Tor, and most of it was mountains and foothills. Plenty of places for a group of people to disappear. He looked at his map and resolved to stick to his plan.

His travels through the north took him through several ghost towns where he'd initially hoped to find work for a few yarii and someplace to sleep, but he had instead been forced to camp beneath the stars and go through his quickly dwindling rations.

Red Wolf remembered some of these towns; the Hellhounds had torn through most of the smaller settlements in the Highlands and the western villages and burned it all to the ground, and he'd rode north with Arnas on several occasions to try and save what they could. For the most part, though, people had been forced to flee to safety or be eaten.

If only we'd known about the Hellhounds' weaknesses sooner.

Despite Talin's efforts to rebuild, it was evident that the Hellhounds' rampage through the north had left some of the settlements completely devastated. No doubt the survivors had decided to seek refuge elsewhere—if there were any survivors at all.

He remembered Talin's hand on his shoulder as she told him the fate that had befallen Velnora. The only link he had to his past and the Hellhounds had destroyed it all, just as they had destroyed these towns. He felt a flash of anger that was quickly drowned by dull grief. Red Wolf pushed the thoughts from his mind and rode on towards Fallbjorn.

A lone travelling merchant passed him along the road, heading south west for Wycrest, no doubt. Red Wolf stopped when he saw the man was selling dried meat and bought a small packet of it.

"How far to Fallbjorn?" he asked.

"A few more hours," the merchant responded in a heavy northern accent. "You'll get there before dark."

"Thank you." Red Wolf left the merchant behind and continued onward.

Talin must have been busy these last few years.

He supposed he had to give her some credit; thanks to her efforts, much of the south looked like the war had never touched it at all. But he knew that one person alone could not hope to rebuild an entire kingdom, no matter how much power they held. The war had taken too much of a toll on Kies Tor already.

He made it to the settlements at Fallbjorn at dusk and quickly gained directions to the market and the nearest inn. The last time he had been here, the entire town had been razed by Hellhounds, but he could see that it had been rebuilt in the years since the war's end. In the back of his mind, he remembered that dying woman, whose name he would never know but to whom he had made a promise anyway.

Protect my daughter, sir. Please.

He wondered how Ashera was doing nowadays.

Pushing the thoughts aside, he pulled out his map and set about asking where the nearest unmarked villages were. One of the locals, an ore trader, was kind enough to point out the ones he knew of, and Red Wolf thanked the man before heading for the inn. A stableboy took his horse to be watered and fed.

"What'll it be?" the innkeep asked when he entered.

"Just a room for the night," Red Wolf said, digging out his coins. "And supper, please." He glanced around to make sure there were eavesdroppers who'd catch wind of the conversation before leaning in. "I'm looking for a group of travellers. Two southerners, two northerners, and a boy. The southerners both have light hair, brother and sister. One of the northerners should be quite tall, black hair and a beard. The other is a young woman with green eyes. The boy has...blue eyes, same as the southerners. Seen anyone fitting that description?"

"Can't say I have..." The innkeep counted out Red Wolf's coins for the night and opened his ledger. "Name?"

"William Higgins," the ex-bodyguard said. He tossed in an extra silver. "If you see these travellers, would you mind telling them I'm looking for them?"

The innkeep swiped his silver and smiled. "Of course."

Red Wolf dipped his head and went to find a seat at the corner table. He caught two other patrons who'd been listening in, who quickly went back to their meals when they saw him glance over.

Good. Once I've been to enough inns and taverns, word will spread.

The innkeep soon brought his supper, stew with an assortment of meat and vegetables in it and some bread to go with. Red Wolf sipped it slowly, keeping his hood up and his head down. He could feel one of the patrons staring at him as he ate and elected to ignore the man. Finishing his meal, he stood and left the inn quickly, heading to the tavern to catch the local gossip.

I'm drawing too much attention to myself.

Despite his attempts to keep a low profile as he moved through the streets, he could feel the stares he got from passers-by; Fallbjorn was still bustling at this hour on account of its famous night market. He could only hope the attention would benefit his goal in the long run instead of just making it easier for Aldrus to track him down.

He seated himself in the corner and ordered a flagon of ale from a passing barmaid, straining his ears and doing his utmost to filter out individual conversations through all the chatter. There was some talk about serial disappearances continuing to happen, and Blackrun bannermen being deployed to investigate. He also heard something about Lady Blackrun herself seeking help from Aldrus but receiving no reply. He was trying to catch more of the conversation when the doors flung wide open, and a messenger strode in.

"News from Belanore," the man said.

The tavern fell silent. Red Wolf felt the mood shift from lively to sombre before the messenger even opened his mouth.

"The queen is dead. Reports from the search parties say that she was killed in the mountains past the border and that General Ettrias and his co-conspirators have whisked away the Crown Prince to hide him from authorities. Aldrus has officially been named King Regent until Prince Arkiel is found and becomes old enough to rule."

Red Wolf felt like all the wind was suddenly knocked from his body. Shock quickly turned to panic and despair. *That couldn't be true, Aldrus wouldn't kill them, he needs Talin to confess to bringing me back...*

No. Aldrus knew that remaining as king regent for so long would lose him some of the support from the southern nobles and make him an enemy of the Highlands entirely. He would never risk such a thing when he could bring back Talin alive and delegitimise her rule. Something must have happened up in those mountains to the east.

Then she really is dead?

He refused to believe it. Talin was smart; she would have known to keep out of trouble, she couldn't have...

Red Wolf downed the rest of his ale. It didn't do much for his racing heart.

If Talin was gone, then the others might still return to Kies Tor. There was no reason for him not to continue his search; if he found Ettrias or Arkiel, there was a chance he could still turn things around and reinstate the rightful heir of Kies Tor. Either way, they would need support from the north. His objective should still remain the same. Find the others and go to Castle Blackrun.

What's the point in doing this without Talin?

He cursed himself for even thinking it. Talin would want him to carry on, to do the right thing. Find her son and see him seated on the throne, and carry on protecting the Crown.

Part of his subconscious registered that the tavern chatter had returned; most of the patrons were gathered around the messenger now, peppering the man with questions or talking about his announcement. The shock of the news settled over him like a thick fog, choking his lungs.

She can't be dead. There must be some mistake.

Red Wolf finished his drink and left the tavern, mind still reeling. Whether or not the news was true, Aldrus now had total control of the south, and it would be impossible for him or the others to return there without being arrested immediately. The only way home now was to reclaim the throne, and he doubted that Aldrus was going to give it up without a fight. For now, he could only act on the assumption that Talin *was* still alive and continue with his plan.

Assuming that Aldrus didn't find him first.

K ing Aldrus was entertaining an Astarian diplomatic party today. Among the Fae nobles was none other than King Darien himself, ruler of Astaria and the far south. Accompanying him was most of his Royal Council and no shortage of guards, and after some talks behind closed doors, the council members were dismissed, and Aldrus and Darien had continued their conversation in private.

Cassius was immediately suspicious. And given that Lord Mornus was currently unoccupied with his duties, the two of them had quickly decided to eavesdrop.

"I don't know how you can suffer the indignity," Mornus grumbled, leaning against the wall while Cassius turned the handle ever so slightly and inched the door open just far enough for sound to carry through the crack. He put a finger to his lips in a silent gesture to tell his fellow lord to shut up.

"...expected more progress from you," Darien was saying. "It's been eight years, almost nine. You said you'd be able to do this your way, and you have nothing to show for it."

"I'm not playing your ridiculous game anymore," Aldrus hissed. "I know you sent those assassins. Killing her isn't going to make the people rally to me; it'll make her a martyr. For the love of the gods, you even tried to kill my son! He's only *eight*. He is of no threat to your plans. Why target him?"

"Let's not forget why you agreed to this in the first place," Darien said. "This benefits you as much as it does me. Think about it. You hold absolute power over Kies Tor. Yours is the *highest* authority in these lands. Tell me, brother, doesn't it feel good?"

Aldrus growled. "I had all of that the moment I married into the royal family here."

"And with Talin as queen, you'll forever be in her shadow," Darien said. Footsteps rang through the room as he paced. "How much power did you truly hold under her administration?"

There was a beat of silence.

"That's what I thought," Darien said. "Besides, you're in too deep now. Things have already been set in motion. All you need to do is continue playing your part."

"*Tch*. I suppose you expect me to just...forget about the attempt on my son's life, then?"

"All I did was kick things off. Gave all of the pieces a little nudge, as it were. Your 'family' was never in any true danger."

"You mean by manipulating Talin into sending those papers? How presumptuous of you to think that I needed any help with that," Aldrus said icily.

"*Eight years*, little brother. That's how long you've had to 'do things your way', as you so elegantly put it," Darien sneered. "If it were up to me, Kies Tor would have joined Astaria long ago."

"You really expect to emerge victorious by simply marching into Kies Tor with an army?" Aldrus scoffed. "The elves have the Drakels on their side. The legions will rally the moment you set foot across the border. I offered you an alternative eight years ago by playing politics. And now, thanks to your convenient meddling, I have the perfect opening to finish what we started."

"I'm no fool to think that I can defeat the Draconian legions," Darien said. "But it doesn't mean I like your method any better. It's slow, and quite frankly, I don't see why you feel the need to play by the books."

"The people rally to Queen Talin," Aldrus said. "They still believe in her. And with Arkiel still missing, you can imagine that they're eager to see him found and seated on the throne once he comes of ruling age. If I do things 'by the books', they'll have no reason to doubt me."

"Then get it sorted," Darien snapped. "I'll visit again soon. You better have an update for me then."

Cassius heard footsteps rapidly approaching the door and pulled Mornus away, half-leading, half-dragging his fellow lord down the hallway. They miraculously got a good enough distance away that Darien didn't pay them much attention as he passed them.

That was too close.

"What in the seven hells..." Mornus stared after the Fae king as he disappeared around a corner. "This is..."

"Not here. We'll meet in Corvan's tower. I believe Lord Varkis has an update for us," Cassius said.

"An update? I wasn't aware that Lord Varkis had visited the palace recently," Mornus said.

Cassius only smiled. His network of spies could pass word through the kingdom faster than some of the official correspondence between the palace and county lords; getting an update about what Lord Varkis had been up to was hardly a difficult feat. Really, Mornus should know better than to ask about how he gets information, for his network was more of an open secret than anything else.

"What happens if the identity of one of your spies gets discovered, then?" Mornus asked. "If this network is supposedly so secretive, what happens when a secret gets out?"

Cassius huffed a laugh. "If I told you *that*, it would no longer be a secret, would it?"

"Is that what you tell the king regent?" Mornus asked.

"The king regent, yes—at the moment. The queen...well, she's privy to whatever she wants to know. My network serves the Crown, at the end of the day, and she is still its representative in my eyes."

"You think she's still alive?"

"Naturally."

"A lot of loyalty and faith to be coming from one man."

Cassius laughed again. "I take it you've never met the former lord commander."

"Never had the pleasure. Or misfortune. Haven't made up my mind about him yet."

The two of them climbed the steps to Corvan's tower in silence. In the study, Corvan was busy preparing a pot of his herbal tea while Varkis and Wyndove both sipped cups of wine from a bottle taken from the cellars.

"To be clear, I don't like meeting in the same location more than once," Cassius said, crossing the room immediately to pour himself some of the wine. "But I suppose it can't be helped. Any progress on stemming those rumours?"

"They're dying down, slowly but steadily," Lord Varkis said. "But...I'm afraid they weren't started by one particular individual. This was secret, behind-closed-doors gossip that has been circulating since the Siege of Belanore."

"What? That doesn't make any sense—" Cassius began. *My spies would have picked up on these rumours if they were so old.*

"I dug into the source," Varkis continued. "Did some of my own questioning. Apparently, there are eyewitnesses from the Siege of Belanore who swear on their lives that they saw the queen and her bodyguard kiss. I can only assume, with so many to corroborate the claim, that it's true."

"It would seem so." Cassius let out a long breath. He hadn't wanted to believe it at first, for he had been certain his spies would have been able to confirm the veracity of any rumours that circulated the city. But it seemed like the queen and the former lord commander were able to hide their relationship even from him. He had to give them credit for outplaying him.

"There's no point disputing that rumour, then." He sipped his wine and began to pace. "But we need to do *something* to explain it."

"Not to worry, I'll deal with it. King Aldrus already asked me to come up with something," Wyndove said. "It's odd. I would have thought that these rumours would be beneficial to him—as far as we're aware, he *is* trying to destroy her reputation and public image. But he was clear to me that the rumours had to stop."

"Maybe he feels it's no longer necessary," Corvan said. "We all heard the bells. Aldrus declared a day of mourning, and the reports from the east all say the same thing. The queen is dead—you should accept it, Lord Highett."

"*Tch.* I have my own reasons to doubt her death," Cassius said. "For one, they never found a body up there. Maybe Aldrus truly believes that she's dead, but I don't buy it." He didn't mention the report he'd received detailing local gossip surrounding the queen's death *before* any of the search parties' reports made it back to Belanore. If he had to guess, the rumours were nonsense, and someone aiding the queen had taken advantage of them to convince the search parties to abandon their search.

The others exchanged looks.

Cassius sighed. "Look, I didn't come here to debate the king's claims. Any other news for me?"

"I had the fortune of talking to King Darien's Royal Council," Wyndove said. "Lord Bayesh, in particular, shared some fascinating insight into Astaria's reigning monarch."

Cassius knew that Lord Bayesh was Darien's head of civil affairs—Lord Wyndove's equivalent in Astaria. He'd never formally met the man, but from Talin's descriptions of him, he imagined that Bayesh was a decent enough fellow.

"And what does Lord Bayesh say?" Mornus asked.

"He tells me that much of the Royal Council share a...somewhat negative perception of King Darien," Wyndove said. "Lord Bayesh was of the opinion that Aldrus would have made a far better ruler than his tyrant brother, going so far as to say that he wished the previous king had decided to pass the crown to the younger sibling instead. He wanted to warn me, actually, though I suspect his words border on treason. According to him, Darien is incompetent and has set his eyes on conquest, wishing to build an empire to rival that of the Drakels, neglecting to take care of his own people in his pursuit of power. My guess is that Darien has set his eyes on Kies Tor."

This is concerning news, Cassius thought, remembering the conversation he and Lord Mornus had overheard.

"Surely he knows that Kies Tor is allied with the Drakels," Lord Varkis said. "Kadis' legions could wipe out entire kingdoms—Darien stands no chance against him."

"Oh, he's well aware," Wyndove said. "Lord Bayesh tells me that Darien is known for meddling in other nations' politics when open war is too risky. It's what he did to the far south—it eventually crumbled, and he swept in to 'save the day', as it were, by offering them protection and security under Astarian rule."

Then Aldrus must be the seed he's planted in our administration to undermine everything we've worked towards for the last fifteen years. Cassius didn't need to voice it aloud. He knew they were all thinking the same.

"Lord Tybalt and I can confirm," he said. "We overheard Darien and Aldrus talking about a takeover of Kies Tor."

Lord Varkis swore. "Of course, and the High Court has just granted Aldrus full power over the kingdom! Gods, we were fools."

Cassius poured another cup of wine. He put his free hand on his chin.

We need a way to stop Darien from extending his influence, or at least keeping it to a minimum, he thought. But as far as he was aware, with the supposed death of Queen Talin and rumours of General Ettrias hiding Prince Arkiel away, most of the southern nobles just wanted to see the Crown Prince found. Aldrus was their only hope of seeing the future King of Kies Tor returned safely to Belanore.

Katherine Blackrun, on the other hand, didn't *quite* share their sentiment.

"I may have an idea," he announced. "Or, at the very least, a way to stall things out until Arkiel is found and we can expose the truth."

The other lords looked to him expectantly.

"It's a simple matter," Cassius explained. "We'll not receive much support from the southern lords, if any. But Katherine Blackrun hates Aldrus' current administration and believes the north is not receiving the attention it needs. If tensions continue as they are, they will reach a tipping point soon—civil war." He exhaled. "I wish to give her a little p ush."

"You're mad," Mornus said. "We've barely recovered from our last war. You wish for the north to turn its blades against us?"

"Not exactly." Cassius winced. "I know that civil war is the last thing we all want right now. But consider: if Blackrun finds Prince Arkiel first and marches south with an army, Aldrus is sure to call upon Darien's forces for backup. The Drakels will rally against them once Blackrun explains who she is fighting for."

"It's...risky, I'll grant you that." Corvan frowned. "Then again, we don't have many options. This could certainly buy us the time we need. But how can we provoke Blackrun? She is a good friend of the late queen—I doubt she would declare civil war so readily. She is well aware of Queen Talin's disdain for violence."

"The north has been dealing with a series of disappearances," Cassius said. "If we can discourage Aldrus from sending aid—"

"Begging your pardon, my lord, but I may be able to...expedite your plans," Lord Varkis said. "House Varkis contributes a significant number of reserve bannermen to the Royal Army, and we hold half of the Western Forts. If I was to rally my banners and march north to pledge my allegiance to the Highlands against Aldrus...it would strengthen Blackrun's resolve that she doesn't need the south's administration."

The room fell silent. Cassius himself was stunned; such a bold move was open treason and could lose House Varkis *everything* if things went wrong. That the man had even suggested such a thing was sheer madness.

And yet...he couldn't deny that the offer was tempting.

"You...you cannot be serious," Lord Mornus spluttered. "You speak of...of...turning on the Crown *itself*. Starting a war. It's..."

"Please trust me," Varkis said. "I know what's at stake. But I don't believe either side will march to war so readily."

Mornus' lips pursed, but he said nothing.

"Are you sure?" Cassius asked. "If this doesn't go according to plan, the court has the power to strip your titles, your lands, your entire house's status as one of the nobility. You'd lose *everything*. Is your long-standing friendship with House Zylvaris worth that much?"

"It is to me."

Cassius let out a long breath. "Far be it for me to stop you, then."

"I'd best leave as soon as possible. Can you get word to the Western Forts through your spy network?"

"It shouldn't be difficult."

Lord Varkis stood. "I'll have the note for you by this evening." He was out of the door a moment later, leaving Cassius to stare after him.

This is pure madness. Provoking civil war, risking everything, all to stop Darien from extending his influence on Kies Tor...

Whatever the case, none of them could back out now. It was clear to him that things had been set in motion long before any of them were aware of the full picture, and with so many things moving in the political sphere, all he could do was stay informed of the situation.

Cassius hoped that he was doing the right thing.

XXII

F ollowing Elder Parya's directions, they made good time down the
mountainside, keeping to the path that Golmin had planned out.
The five of them made camp under a familiar Torrian sky on the second
night and continued west to the nearest road in the morning. Arkiel's
leg had completely healed by now, and Ettrias had also recovered to the
point that he could limp around if he wasn't on horseback, so Talin had
made the decision to ride out for Castle Blackrun as quickly as possible.
The others had been quick to agree.

"We're not far from Fallbjorn," her brother said, poring over their
map as Golmin led the way forwards.

"It'll be another two days' travel at least," the captain said. "There are
unmarked border villages much closer to our position. We're better off
spending the night in one of those."

"I haven't returned to Fallbjorn since Red Wolf rescued me from the Hellhounds," Ashera said quietly.

"We could skirt around." Golmin gestured for the map, and Ettrias passed it up silently. "It'll be an extra day's travel."

"No, I think...it'll be good to see the town again," Ashera said. "I heard even the night market is back in business. Mother used to take me all the time. I liked it there. I remember there was a baker who always brought his unsold goods from the daytime, and he'd always give me a honey cake if I asked." She frowned. "I hope he made it out before they burned everything down."

"The last time I was at Fallbjorn, it was still under Hellhound occupation," Talin said. "Feels like a lifetime ago. I'd also like to see how it's doing now."

"We'll pass through Fallbjorn, then." Golmin put away his map. "Though, if my hunch is correct, we'll happen across a village before nightfall. A room at the inn beats sleeping on the road, in my opinion."

"No complaints from me," Talin said.

As Golmin had predicted, the five of them did arrive at a village at dusk, though the crumbling buildings around them indicated that nobody had returned after the Hellhounds tore through the place. They picked through the rubble for anything that might identify where they were and came up with nothing.

"I thought the Highlands had recovered from the war by now." Ashera frowned. "Guess not."

Talin winced. "It's been a long road. The Hellhounds had occupied parts of the north since before Ettrias and I were even *born*. There's just...no saving some of these places, despite mine and Lady Blackrun's efforts."

They camped for the night on the village outskirts, eating a simple supper of dried meat and fruit from their rations, and set off again at dawn for Fallbjorn. Arkiel nagged Ettrias for more stories. Talin tried to keep her mind off the rebuilding efforts in the north and unsuccessfully tried to convince herself that she had done all she could.

It was dusk by the time they reached Fallbjorn, finding it still bustling with people despite the hour. Golmin slowed his horse to a steady walk as the sun dipped close to the western horizon. "Well, here we are, then. It *is* quite lively."

"It looks...different," Ashera said.

"Good different or bad different?" Golmin asked.

"Neither. Just...different." Ashera's gaze swept across the town and quickly landed on the night market. "I think there's an inn not far from the market. Mother and I used to walk past it all the time when she took me to buy food."

"I'll ask for directions to the next inhabited settlement," Ettrias said. "Order me some supper."

They parted ways at the inn, Talin leading the way inside while her brother turned away for the night market. She paid for their rooms and requested an extra bowl of soup for Ettrias.

"Five of you, then?" the innkeeper asked, counting out their coins.

"Yes, my brother is just asking about the nearby settlements..." Talin's voice trailed off. "Why do you ask?"

"A strange gentleman came through here some time ago," the innkeeper said. He flicked through his guest logbook. "A...William Higgins. Said to tell you he was looking for you. Quite a generous fellow, he was. I might not have remembered him if he hadn't tipped me an extra silver."

"William Higgins?" Talin racked her memory for where she'd last heard that name.

Red Wolf's first squire. He died beside King Arnas in the Glass Forest.

"This gentleman... He was quite tall?" she asked.

"Aye. If I didn't know better, I'd say he was a giant," the innkeeper replied.

"Golden eyes?"

"Aye."

Oh, gods.

"Thank you," Talin said. She tipped him an extra three coppers and went upstairs to drop off her belongings. Her hands shook as she fumbled for the key to her room.

"He was *here*," Ashera hissed once they were out of earshot of any nosy patrons. "You know what this means. He's still looking for us. For you."

"But how can he *be* here?" Talin's head spun. "If he was in Belanore, then surely he would have caught up to us before we reached the border. But how else would he know to search for us in the Highlands?"

"Well, if he's been in Kies Tor this whole time, he must have heard the news about Aldrus being granted regency of the kingdom," Ashera said. "He's smart enough to figure that Blackrun might shelter you in the north, or at least she'd hate Aldrus enough not to turn you in immediately. I bet he has a plan to find you, and we've already walked into it."

Talin ran a hand over her mouth and nose. *It's not possible. How is he here? Why? Did Aldrus lure him here?*

"Have faith, Your Majesty," Golmin said. "If I know Red Wolf at all, he'll find us."

They took their supper downstairs at a corner table, keeping an open ear for local gossip. Ettrias joined them not long after, and Golmin caught him up on the news of Red Wolf. He seemed to agree with the others—that the former lord commander would find them eventually.

"I discovered something else, too," he continued as the server brought them their round of ale. Arkiel was given cider instead. "There have been thugs targeting travellers closer to Rivenfort and Castle Blackrun. They're...stealing people away for something. Most of the missing travellers have been adults, but recently there have been reports that children are going missing too. Blackrun has sent out soldiers to investigate, but they've not made much progress so far."

Talin put a hand on her chin. "I recall receiving similar reports of some serial disappearances back in Belanore. I'd planned on organising some people to investigate before this whole mess happened."

Arkiel's eyes widened. "Are the thugs...going to take me away?"

"We would never let that happen," Golmin said. "Ashera and I have sworn an oath to protect you with our lives, and I am sure your mother would do anything to keep you safe."

"I won't let them take you." Talin squeezed his shoulder. "I promise."

"Either way, we must exercise caution," Golmin said. "I'll take the same precautions I did when we were in the south and cover our tracks, but we should avoid splitting up, just in case."

Supper arrived not long after, and the five of them ate in silence, staying alert for any important gossip. Talin caught a few snatches of conversation about Aldrus and some sort of memorial service being planned in Belanore but didn't get the context.

"Do you think Red Wolf will find us?" Arkiel asked that night, bundled up in his blankets.

"I'm...hopeful that he will," Talin said. The idea that they might see each other again after all this time sent a spike of hopeful anticipation and nervousness through her.

Maybe I'm not ready. But I want to see him again all the same.

"I hope so, too," Arkiel said. "He seems like a good person. I'd like to meet him."

Talin tried and failed to hold back a smile. "He is."

Morning brought with it a light shower of rain and bad news—Ettrias, in examining a more detailed map of the Highlands purchased from the market, had discovered that they would not come across another inhabited town until they reached Rivenfort. And given the reports of thugs along all the major trade routes, their path to Castle Blackrun would no doubt take a dangerous turn.

"We'll have to be careful," Golmin said. "There are four of us who can fight, but these thugs could easily outnumber us or outmanoeuvre us somehow. I wish we could take a safer road, but this is, unfortunately, the most direct route to Castle Blackrun."

"We can get through this so long as we stay alert," Talin said.

They spent their next few days looking over their shoulders and jumping at any suspicious movement that caught their attention. It was exhausting; by the fourth morning, Talin had just about had enough, travelling on three hours of sleep and unable to shake the feeling that they were being followed. Golmin examined their maps while she tried not to fall asleep in the saddle.

"We can turn south at the next fork and take a detour down a less-travelled road," the guard captain finally said. "That'll bring us to a few smaller settlements before we hit Rivenfort. I cannot handle another night of sleeplessness."

"Me neither." Talin yawned. "Please tell me we'll be at a village by tonight if we take the fork."

"Looks like it."

"Good."

True to Golmin's word, they made it to a small village not far from the crossroads before dusk. There, they heard a similar story to the innkeeper's account at Fallbjorn—that a giant with golden eyes had passed through and asked after their whereabouts. Talin slept much better that night, knowing they didn't have to worry about thugs in the inn. They set off at dawn with plans to camp off the road that night and reach the next village on the third day.

"I don't suppose Red Wolf's 'plan' is to simply enter as many towns and villages as possible in hopes of finding you," Ashera muttered as she helped pitch the tents. "We'll be chasing him for weeks if that's the case."

"I'm worried about that too," Talin confessed. "If we knew where he was likely to go next, it wouldn't be a problem, but we don't. And he has no lead on us, from what I've been able to tell. To make matters worse, half the town gossip is about Lady Blackrun's decision to split from Kies Tor and whatever else." She shook her head. "If he would just go straight to Castle Blackrun, we could meet him there, but..."

"He doesn't even know if you're still alive," Golmin said. "That innkeeper said he'd headed northeast, back the way we came. Aldrus must have announced by now that you've fled past the eastern border. He's...panicking, for lack of a better word."

I wish there was a way to tell him where we are. Talin didn't voice it out loud.

"Cold night tonight," she said instead, changing the topic. "I suppose we should light a fire."

"I'll gather some firewood, then." Ashera stood.

"Can I come?" Arkiel asked.

"No," Talin said before any of the others could open their mouths. "It's too dangerous. Those thugs we've heard about could be lurking around."

"Oh, come on. We haven't heard a peep from these thugs since we turned south," Ettrias said. "Let the boy explore a little."

"I'll go too," Golmin said. "They're hardly likely to touch him with two guards at his side."

"Mother, please? We won't go too far, right, Ashera?" Arkiel said.

"We'll stay nearby," Ashera said.

Talin glanced at her son, then at the two royal guards on either side of him. "Very well. But be back before dark."

Arkiel skipped off excitedly with his two bodyguards in tow.

"Well, they're off. What are we to do in the meantime?" Talin asked.

Her brother shrugged. "Sparring always seems like a good idea. It's been a while."

"You sure? Your leg isn't fully healed yet," Talin said.

"I'll be fine. Barely even hurts anymore," Ettrias said.

Talin drew her sword after a few moments of hesitation. Ettrias did likewise.

"I'll let you have the first strike because I'm—" he began. Talin swung at him before he had the chance to finish. He jumped back with a start and parried.

"That's not fair!" he exclaimed.

"All's fair in war."

"Red Wolf's rubbed off on you."

Ettrias came back around with an attack of his own. Talin side-stepped him and feinted to the right. He saw her blow at the last second and knocked it aside. She changed angles, trying to catch him off-guard, but he followed her movements with ease and parried her sequence of strikes without much effort. He was on the offensive a moment later. Talin ducked under a swing and parried a second strike before feinting again. He saw the movement and dodged.

"You'll have to do better than that, dear sister," he said with a grin.

"Show-off."

The two of them went back and forth in the clearing for a few minutes longer before Ettrias ended the fight with his blade at Talin's neck, looking smug as ever. She knocked his weapon away and sheathed hers.

"Not bad," he said. "Your parries could do with some work, but other than that, I see you've kept up with your training. Don't be so obvious with those feints. As Red Wolf would say, I could see what you're trying to do from a mile away."

"I'm surprised I lasted that long with your reputation," Talin said.

Ettrias shrugged and took a swig from his canteen. "I was going easy on you."

Talin snorted and smacked him on the arm lightly.

"When we get to Castle Blackrun and meet up with Red Wolf, I'll enjoy watching him give you a few new bruises with a training blade," she told him.

Ettrias laughed. "Oh, please, I'd beat him. You forget that I duelled him after my trial and landed what would normally be a killing blow."

Talin was about to open her mouth to retaliate when a twig cracked somewhere nearby. She straightened immediately, hand flying to her sword again, and Ettrias began scanning their surrounds.

"That wasn't any of the others, was it?" she asked.

"Can't be. It's too soon." Ettrias drew his sword. "I'll take a look nearby. Could just be an animal." He stepped around a thicket of bushes and quickly disappeared from sight.

"Don't take too long—" Talin began.

Someone clamped a rag tight over her nose and mouth. A sickly-sweet scent flooded her nostrils immediately, followed by a wave of nausea. She reached for her sword, but a strong hand pinned her arms to stop her from moving.

"Best you don't resist, darling. It'll make our jobs a whole lot easier," a voice said from behind her. Talin struggled against whoever had grabbed her to no avail. Her eyelids felt unnaturally heavy. She wanted nothing more than to slip into a blissful slumber. She struggled to stay awake, willing her eyes to remain open, but with the sickly-sweet scent of the rag still flooding her nostrils, staying awake was useless.

Talin felt a pair of cold hands hoist her up over someone's shoulder, and then she felt nothing at all.

XXIII

"Mister Higgins? Is that you, sir?"

It took a moment for Red Wolf to register that he was the one being referred to, and that the man who'd just called him had rushed out of the inn where he'd stayed several weeks ago. He hadn't planned on returning here so soon, but his route through the towns east of Castle Blackrun had led him back through this village on his way to a settlement he'd not yet visited. Part of him had been ready to give up; over a month had passed since he set out and he had shifted again just last week. He despaired more with each day that passed.

Perhaps, in the end, it was fate that dictated he should return.

"I didn't think you'd be back," the innkeeper said.

"What is it?" Red Wolf asked.

"You're still looking for those friends of yours, aren't you?" the innkeeper asked.

"I am. You have news?" Red Wolf didn't dare hope.

"They came through last night. Stayed right at my inn," the innkeeper said. "You just missed them."

"Last night?" Red Wolf asked. He felt a flicker of...*something* in his chest that wasn't quite hope. "You're sure it was them?"

"Absolutely certain," the innkeeper said. "Two southerners, looked like siblings, light brown hair. Exactly as you described. Tall, bearded Highlander travelling with them and a northerner woman as well. There was a southerner kid with them."

By the gods, it really is them. Talin's alive.

"Which way did they go? West towards Castle Blackrun?"

"Aye, I think I overheard 'em talking about going that way."

"Thank you." Red Wolf mounted his horse and spurred it on through the village. Some distance from the outskirts, he finally picked up a trail, and closer examination confirmed that it belonged to Talin and her companions. He followed it along the road as the sun dipped below the horizon.

I'm so close. I can feel it.

The sun had set completely by the time he picked up a scent. It was faint, barely recognisable through the tangle of other people and horses who had passed through recently, but his nose picked it out without any difficulty. Red Wolf followed it along the road for another hour before it veered off into the forest to his left. He dismounted and led his horse into the dense thicket of trees. This close to her, he could pick out the scent more accurately and shut out everything else to focus on it, moving deeper into the forest.

There was a campfire ahead. Red Wolf slowed, approaching deliberately, making enough noise that his movements would be noticed. He could make out a lone guard standing by the edge of a clearing; past him were three sleeping figures.

"Hold it there," the guard said softly without turning. Red Wolf recognised the voice as Golmin's. "Not a step closer, or things will get ugly for you."

He stopped. "Rufus, it's me."

Golmin slowly swivelled to face him, arrow nocked in his bow. Red Wolf held up his hands and stepped into the dim glow of the campfire.

"Red Wolf?"

"Evening."

The bow clattered from Golmin's hands as he came forwards and pulled the former bodyguard into an embrace.

"I missed you," the guard captain said.

"I'm sorry it's taken me this long."

Golmin pulled away and thumped him on the shoulder. "Gods, I am glad to see you." He broke into a grin. "You haven't changed a bit."

"Neither have you." Red Wolf smiled. "There are only four of you?" He leaned past the captain to take note of the sleeping figures by the campfire. Ettrias and a young woman who could only be Ashera, and a boy he'd never seen before—probably Arkiel. "Where's Talin?"

The grin disappeared from Golmin's face in an instant, and Red Wolf felt his blood turn to ice. "Best if you take a seat. Try not to wake the others, we've all had a long evening."

Red Wolf took a seat by the fire. Golmin sat opposite him and fell silent for a moment, as if contemplating how best to explain the situation.

"You might have heard about thugs along this part of the road," the captain said. "Kidnappers, outlaws, call them what you will. They're taking people away somewhere."

Red Wolf said nothing.

"They took her, Red Wolf. We were fools. We took the main road towards Castle Blackrun but grew paranoid and detoured south. Stayed at an inn last night, let our guards down, and...well, we only have ourselves to blame for splitting up." Golmin sighed. "We should have known they'd strike again. We spent most of the evening trying to find a trail, but they were good. *Experienced*. This was all they left behind—probably dropped in a hurry." He held out a handkerchief.

Red Wolf fought the surge of panic in his chest. He'd been so close, *so close*, but she had slipped from his grasp again. If he'd gotten here faster, maybe he would've been able to stop this. Maybe he could've saved her. *Done something*, at the very least. His jaw tightened as he took the handkerchief from Golmin and sniffed, and was immediately hit by a wave of nausea as the sickly-sweet scent overpowered his nose.

"Someone dipped this into a sedative," he said, handing it back. "Very distinct scent." He sniffed the air. "There's a trace of it still around here, but I can only track where the handkerchief has been, not where she's going. I followed her scent here. If I leave now, I might be able to continue following it a little further, but it's a few hours old already. Won't be long before it fades."

Golmin put a hand on his shoulder. "We'll find her."

"I know." Red Wolf hissed through his teeth. "I should have gotten here faster."

"Don't blame yourself. We'll set out tomorrow at dawn," Golmin said. "See if we can't pick up some tracks when there's light." He tucked the handkerchief away. "We heard you were looking for us at both inns we stayed at. How in the seven hells did you end up here and how long have you been trying to find us?"

Red Wolf sighed and explained everything from the beginning, with the fake papers that had brought him into Belanore and how they had been stolen the day that Talin went on the run. He told Golmin about how he'd lost their trail and about the incident at the village near Varen, and then his subsequent plan to scour the Highlands until he caught some news of Talin and her group.

"You've been busy," the captain said once he was done. "We suspected it was you at Dennik but couldn't confirm. I suppose we all owe you for stalling back there."

"I'm not sure if it was worth the risk," Red Wolf said. "If the soldiers had successfully delivered me to Aldrus, then nothing would have convinced the High Court of Talin's innocence."

"And that village..." Golmin trailed off. "Gods, you must feel awful. There was nothing you could have done. It wasn't your fault."

Red Wolf winced. "But it *was* my fault in a way, wasn't it? I decided to stay when I knew I was about to shift. That girl and her father offered me their hospitality and I—" He broke off there and drew in a shaky breath.

"We can debate matters of responsibility and blame some other time," Golmin said, laying a hand on his shoulder. "Get some sleep before dawn. You look like you've been dragged through the seven hells."

Red Wolf let out a short exhale. "I feel like I have. Need someone to pick up the dawn shift?"

"I'll be fine. You need rest."

"Hellhounds don't need as much sleep as you lot. But I take your point."

Dawn came eventually, and Red Wolf woke early to join Golmin by the fire. They discussed their options and decided that he would try to find any tracks the thugs had left behind and follow those if possible. Golmin and the others would follow just behind, staying out of sight to avoid detection. Red Wolf was unlikely to look like a threat if he wandered into the thugs' camp or headquarters alone, and they would be able to set up an ambush. Ashera and Ettrias woke not long after.

"Alright, let's go find my sister," the prince said. "Did you have any earth-shattering revelations last night, Rufus? Any new clues? When I find those kidnappers, I'm going to..." His voice trailed off when he looked towards the campfire and saw Red Wolf.

"Morning, Ettrias."

"Wh..." Ettrias blinked and rubbed his eyes. "Am I dreaming right now?"

"No, unfortunately." Red Wolf sipped the soup that Golmin had made. "I'm here. And real. Soup?" He held out a second bowl.

Ettrias sat up fully and absentmindedly accepted it.

"Red Wolf?" Ashera leaned past him to look.

"Ashera." Red Wolf dipped his head. "You've...grown. I seem to remember you being a lot shorter when I left."

"You..." Ashera stared at him for a few moments, but then she jumped to her feet and barrelled into him with a hug. "I missed you. It's been so long."

Red Wolf froze for a moment, stunned at the sudden show of affection, but then he laughed and broke into a smile. "Well, you haven't changed much. I missed you too."

"How did you find us?" Ashera asked, separating herself.

Red Wolf shrugged. "It's a long story."

"I'm sure." Ashera sat by the fire and accepted her meal.

"We have a plan," Golmin said, once they'd both settled down. "Now that Red Wolf is here, we may have an easier time finding a track or some kind of trail. He will follow it while we tag along at the back, staying out of sight. If we run into the kidnappers, we will set up an ambush."

"Sounds good," Ettrias said. "What if we hit a dead end?"

"The handkerchief they dropped still reeks of whatever sleeping potion they used on Talin," Red Wolf explained. "It has a distinct scent. I believe if we were to find the nearest healer or alchemist, they would be able to tell us what it is and where it came from."

"And...if that fails?" Ashera asked.

"Then, as much as I hate to admit, we must rely on Lady Blackrun to get to the bottom of this situation and find the kidnappers herself." Red Wolf tried not to let his worry show. His job as lord commander had always been to protect the royal family from his spot at their side, not tracking down breadcrumb trails in hopes of finding Talin at the end of it.

"We'll set off as soon as we're packed up, then," Ettrias said. "Before you run off ahead..." He indicated Arkiel, still asleep behind him. "Consider introducing yourself?"

"I..." Red Wolf wasn't sure he deserved to introduce himself, but looking at the boy's small figure, he was reminded of a distant memory. One that he couldn't grasp but that always ended with screams and blood.

"We've been taking turns telling him stories about you." Ashera grinned. "He could never get enough."

"I don't deserve that much," Red Wolf said softly.

Ettrias sipped his soup. "If you're still looking for redemption, I think you redeemed yourself when you confessed your sins in front of the High Court fifteen years ago. Come on. He looks up to you."

The boy yawned almost as soon as he finished speaking and sat up, rubbing his eyes. He looked around wildly.

"Mother? Did you guys find Mother?" he asked.

"Not yet. I'm sorry, Ark." Ettrias put a hand on his shoulder.

"Oh." Arkiel sniffed. "I see. I miss Mother."

Ashera nudged Red Wolf in the ribs, and he reluctantly turned to face the boy. "Your Highness. We've...not met. But I...believe you've heard of me—"

"You're Red Wolf!" Arkiel exclaimed, jumping to his feet. "Mother's told me all sorts of stories about you! We'll be fine now, won't we? You'll find her."

Red Wolf wasn't sure how to respond. "She...told you stories about me?"

"Yes!" Arkiel looked about as excited as a young child might when meeting some famed hero or another for the first time. "Well, at first, she didn't really want to, because I think she was still sad about having to send you away. But when she did start telling me stories, she must have remembered how much she enjoyed spending time with you and going on that big adventure together."

"Uh..." Red Wolf cleared his throat. He wasn't sure why this news didn't make him happier; he'd spent all this time convincing himself that she had moved on. "Well, I'm...honoured that you think of me this way, Your Highness."

"Everyone calls me that. It gets awfully dull after some time," Arkiel said. "It's so *formal*. There's nothing wrong with using my name if you want to."

Red Wolf couldn't help but laugh. "I remember your mother was never one for palace protocol, either." He stretched out a hand, and the boy shook it eagerly. "It's an honour to meet you, Arkiel. I must ride out now, to find any trail that might have been left by the kidnappers. We'll find her, I promise."

There was still the faintest trace of a scent when he set out. Red Wolf knew it wouldn't be enough for him to follow, especially given how much the wind must have blown it off-course by now, but it gave him an idea of which direction they had taken her. He doubled back towards the road and discovered that the scent had, indeed, continued west.

Golmin was right, he thought. *They're very experienced.*

They must have followed her and the others since they turned off the road to be able to double back like this. Not only that, he could smell the scent branching off in multiple directions, almost certainly spread on purpose to throw off any sniffer dogs sent after them. In the light, he could now also see fresh tracks in the road, two deep grooves running parallel to each other. Between the grooves were two sets of hoof-prints. A horse-drawn wagon, then, bearing a heavy load. One of the beasts had taken a dump just before they set off, and it had been hurriedly shovelled up and tossed into a nearby bush. Red Wolf sniffed it out and picked up a fallen stick to get a sample. As unpleasant as the smell was, he committed it to memory and tossed the stick aside.

"Found anything?" Golmin asked, riding up and dismounting.

"Good news." Red Wolf pointed at the tracks in the road. "One of the horses decided to relieve itself right before they set off. They had to shovel it aside quick and hide the evidence." He pointed at the bushes. "A sniffer dog and tracking party probably wouldn't spare it much thought. I've found a trail."

"This wagon..." Golmin crouched to examine the tracks. "It must have been loaded with goods, to make an impression like that."

"Goods...or people." Red Wolf sniffed the air. "I'm picking up a mess of scents here. They continued west for some distance without stopping. I think you'll be safe to ride alongside me for now without giving yourselves away."

"Aye, I'll keep an extra eye out for tracks," Golmin said. "Lead the way."

They continued along the road for another two hours, Red Wolf following the horse's trail while Golmin kept his eyes to the ground, making sure the tracks didn't veer off-course and scanning for any additional clues the thugs had left behind. Their trail led them all the way to Rivenfort, to a stable on the outskirts of the town, where Red Wolf found the horses that had been pulling the wagon.

"They changed horses." He growled and turned away from the stables. "In the middle of the night, too...I doubt anyone here would have seen them. And with so much traffic going through this place, their tracks have long been trampled."

"We might be able to find out who owns these stables and who they're rented to. It might not be much, but it's something," Ashera said.

Golmin nodded. "I'll ask around. In the meantime, I believe I saw a healer's hut on our way here. Perhaps it would be worthwhile to ask after that sleeping potion."

"I'm on it." Ashera grabbed the handkerchief and dashed off.

"Look, up ahead. Soldiers." Arkiel pointed. "Should we leave?"

"Wait." Red Wolf gestured for the boy to stay put. These were not Royal Army soldiers; rather, they bore the grey and gold colours of House Blackrun. The soldiers before them were Lady Blackrun's reserve bannermen.

"What are reserve bannermen doing out here?" Ettrias' eyes narrowed. "Blackrun's reserve banners are all deployed to the Royal Army garrisons. They should have no reason to be here, unless..."

He didn't need to finish the sentence. Red Wolf understood perfectly what the prince was referring to—the deployment of reserve bannermen, under their own colours, meant that Blackrun had no intention of continuing to cooperate with Aldrus.

"I'll talk to them. Wait here." The ex-bodyguard dismounted and handed the reins to Ettrias before approaching cautiously. One of the soldiers—a captain, judging from his uniform—turned to face him, having just finished talking to an old man.

"Good morning, sirs," the former bodyguard said conversationally. "Am I right in assuming this is one of the search parties investigating the recent kidnappings on the road to Castle Blackrun?"

"Aye, that's us," the captain said. He was a stocky man with a deep voice and chin stubble. "Captain Hurst. Leader of the first reserve cavalry division in Lady Blackrun's army."

"I take it you're investigating a wagon that passed through here last night with a suspiciously heavy load," Red Wolf said. "The horses who drew the wagon are in the stables over there—" he pointed— "and you've not had any luck in discovering which two horses they were exchanged for."

Hurst's eyebrows shot up. "That's right. You know something?"

"Correct me if I'm wrong, sir, but I take it the deployment of reserve bannermen in these investigations means that Lady Blackrun will no longer cooperate with King Aldrus or recognise his rule of Kies Tor," Red Wolf continued.

"Correct. Make your point." Hurst crossed his arms.

"I would also assume, then, that Lady Blackrun has no intention of cooperating with King Aldrus' search for Queen Talin?"

"Word is that the queen's dead, but yes."

"Excellent. I'm Red Wolf."

Captain Hurst looked like a deer freezing up at the sight of a hungry predator.

"I believe we can help each other out here, sir," Red Wolf said.

To his credit, the good captain recovered quickly. "Aye, I believe we can. Come with me." He turned and beckoned. "I think it best if we talked somewhere more private."

XXIV

T alin woke in the back of a moving wagon with no notion of the time, nor where she was or where she was going. A dozen or so other people were huddled in the wagon with her, all of them chained together. She looked down and saw that similar shackles adorned her own wrists, attaching her to the rest of the prisoners here. There was a door at the back that was no doubt locked, and even if she could get free, she would have to bring every one of these people with her. Realistically, it was never going to happen.

From the light streaming through the single, barred window, however, she could tell it was daytime. A few of the prisoners' faces were illuminated, though one stood out from the others. This prisoner had scaly, reptile-like skin and a distinct lizard face.

A Drakel? How did she end up here? Talin squinted, and upon closer inspection, realised that she knew this woman.

"Aelia?" she said softly. "Aelia Cato?"

The Drakel looked up and saw her, and her eyes widened. To her credit, though, she kept her mouth shut. "Well, it's good to see a familiar face, at least."

Aelia was one of Blackrun's advisors back when Talin had made her usual trips to the Highlands. She had worked for Kadis, for a time, before the Draconian Emperor offered to let her serve the Highlands after the war. She had accepted immediately. As far as Talin was concerned, Aelia was unstoppable with a sword in hand. They'd often sparred together when she visited.

"How did you end up here?" she asked.

"I could ask you the same question," Aelia said with a laugh. "It's a long story, really, and not one I'd like to share at present. I suspect your story is similarly long."

"Do you know where they plan to take us?" Talin asked.

Aelia shrugged, but there was a glint in her eye that indicated she knew exactly what she was talking about. "I've heard rumours. There's an...extremist group who believe the fighting arenas in the Highlands should never have closed. Folk say they're running these illegal arenas in secret locations far away from any of the major towns or cities to avoid drawing suspicion."

"Fighting arenas?" Talin had a bad feeling about this.

"The ones y—Queen Talin—closed down way back, yes," Aelia said. "I always said you couldn't please everyone, but these people have taken it to the extremes. They believe these blood sports should be glorified, and worse, that they can and should be fought to the death."

Talin could hardly believe what she was hearing. "How long have they been running these illegal arenas?"

"Almost a year now," Aelia said. "We think they started before the disappearances began, and that they used to recruit in secret. Tried to find people who were willing to fight and who weren't likely to expose the arena's secrets. But they've been lacking good fighters recently, and I suspect that's why they've turned to abducting people." She sighed. "I was going to bring it up the next time the queen visited. It's been a while. I know...she's trying, but she's...let things slide here."

Talin saw that now. She'd been too preoccupied with trying to make things as they were before the war that she had stopped paying attention to new problems that arose in the kingdom, and these people, including her, were now paying the price.

"I'll find a way out of this," she said.

"I know." Aelia gave her a faint smile, indicating that she understood. "But enough about this whole situation. You might have heard rumours that the queen is *dead*?"

"No..." Talin's brow creased. "Surely not. Why would Aldrus..."

"Blackrun didn't believe them either," Aelia said. "It's why she's no longer recognising the king's authority. She wants to split from the south entirely."

Gods, things are so much worse than I thought.

"You'll have to catch me up on what's been happening in the political sphere of Kies Tor," Talin said. "I haven't had contact with reliable sources of information for weeks."

The wagon jolted to a halt. There was a shout from outside, and then the door was opened, revealing a man with a cloth covering his mouth and nose. He gestured for the prisoners to move out. Talin found herself walking beside Aelia as they were marched through an open field towards a crudely built fighting arena. Half a dozen other thugs flanked them, preventing their escape.

"Looks like most of it is underground, that's how they were able to hide these places from the authorities," Aelia said.

"Quiet," hissed one of the men.

Inside, they were marched down a narrow corridor barely wide enough for them to walk side by side before being taken to a small auditorium. Their chains were finally unlocked there, and the thugs took up guard positions around the room.

Find a seat," one of the men said. "Don't try to run."

One of the prisoners had the bright idea to do the exact opposite and fled back towards the auditorium entrance. The nearest thug drew a sword and cut him down in a swift, decisive strike.

"*Tch.*" The first thug scoffed. "They always do that."

Talin took a seat beside Aelia. A well-dressed man with dark hair and a long tailcoat made his way to the front.

"Now, then," he said, voice echoing through the room. "You may be wondering why you're here. Don't fret, I am about to answer all your questions." He flashed them an easy smile. "My name is Royce Hargrave. I'm the one running this arena. Now, a few ground rules before we get started. I know many of you perhaps do not wish to be here. I understand, it's normal to be nervous for those of you unfamiliar with these fighting arenas. But I don't want to see any attempted escapes or anything of the sort. Nobody, and I mean *nobody*, has escaped from this arena before. If you try, you will die."

"Nobody leaves the arena?" Talin whispered to Aelia.

"No. Even when these places were run legally, nobody was ever allowed to leave," the Drakel said. "To sign up as a fighter was to devote the rest of your life to the arena. You fight for the crowd's entertainment until you die."

"I knew I was right in shutting these down," Talin muttered.

"Those of you who fight well will be rewarded," Royce Hargrave continued. "Some of our esteemed viewers like to sponsor particularly outstanding fighters. Get on their good side, and you may find yourself receiving better equipment and even accommodations. Of course, as an arena master, I am not allowed to sponsor fighters, so don't go around trying to suck up to me." He paused to let that sink in before continuing. "You will be shown to the fighters' quarters after this...briefing. Rest up. Tomorrow, you will be split into groups and your prowess in battle will be tested against some of our better fighters. This will be just a taste of what your new lives will be like. We will see each other again sometime...if you survive."

The thugs hustled them out of the auditorium and back down the narrow corridor. Talin, Aelia, and another woman were separated from the main group and taken to the women's quarters on the other side of the arena. The Drakel immediately went to one of the beds against the wall, where there was a little more privacy. Talin joined her and settled on the corner bed next to hers.

"You seem to know a lot about these arenas," she said.

Aelia nodded. "Well, now that we have some degree of privacy, I suppose I should tell you everything."

"I'm listening," Talin said, though they both fell silent when they were approached by a dark-skinned Highlander woman with long braids in her hair.

"New fighters?" she asked.

"Yes," Aelia said, and stretched out a hand. "Aelia Cato. And you are...?"

"Icari Carricus Valaia." The two of them shook. "Who's your friend?"

"Ah..." Aelia spared a sideways glance at Talin.

"I'm..." She knew she couldn't give her real name. "Raia."

Icari shook her hand too. "Well, pleased to meet you. Make your-selves at home here, we don't get a lot of women fighters. I have a fight now, but we'll talk more after." She smiled. "If I live."

Aelia waited until she was out of earshot before continuing where they'd left off. "Blackrun knows I'm good with a blade. She was running out of options, too; every time we got close to tracking the thugs to one of these arenas, they'd give us the slip, and Aldrus wasn't sending us any help. So...when all else failed...I volunteered to be 'abducted' and taken to one of the arenas myself. A search party was supposed to follow and shut down the operation, but I think the thugs have managed to trick them somehow. Now I'm stuck here for the foreseeable future."

"That's a risky plan," Talin said. "If you're killed in the arena—"

"I know. It's a risk I was willing to take then, and still am." Aelia shrugged. "Kadis always said he'd never let me lead his legions on ac-count of me being too reckless. I can't say I disagree."

"Do they always fight to the death in the arena?" Talin asked.

"No, not against sponsored fighters. New fighters like us? They couldn't care less." Aelia scoffed. "I know you don't like killing. But out there, you may not have a choice."

Talin had hoped that Aelia wouldn't say it, though she knew the Drakel was right. Here, in these illegal arenas, anything went. She might have to wade through an ocean of blood if she wanted to stay alive.

How am I supposed to kill so ruthlessly, without mercy, for entertain-ment?

She knew it was necessary. Red Wolf would tell her the same.

But as she sat on her bed and watched the other fighters mill about, she wondered what else she would have to sacrifice in the arena. She had fought a war against the Hellhounds and won, and she'd seen far worse things on the battlefield than fighters duelling to the death for sport. Many of the other 'fighters' who'd been abducted barely looked like they knew how to hold a blade, let alone hold their own in the arena. She had training on her side and years of experience in battle.

It had to be enough.

"So, you're telling me that your 'plan' was to send one of Blackrun's advisors to get *herself* abducted by the thugs?" Red Wolf looked at the captain incredulously. "And now, let me guess, you've lost the trail you were following and have no backup plan."

They had sat down at the edge of the village so Hurst could explain everything he knew and the two of them could exchange information, but as Red Wolf was quickly finding out, the search party had little intelligence that could be of use. Golmin and Ashera joined them not long after with news about both the horses that were swapped out and the sleeping potion used on the handkerchief.

"These thugs are professionals," Hurst admitted. "They knew exactly how to cover their tracks, to shake us off. We...underestimated them. You've done more work in one morning than all of us put together, much as I hate to admit."

"The horses they swapped belonged to the men who rented the stables, so no leads there," Golmin said. "I got a name...sort of. Tomas. The thugs clearly thought to use a cover name for everything."

Of course, count on the thugs to use one of the most common names in the Highlands. Red Wolf let out a long breath and crossed his arms.

"And the potion?" he asked.

"The healer recognised it as Black Byer extract," Ashera said. "It's a powerful sedative often used for performing surgery. Whoever is buying the potion must be rich."

"That makes sense, if we're dealing with arena masters," Hurst said. "It doesn't narrow things down by much."

"Then we've hit a dead end." Red Wolf scowled. "There has to be something else. The thugs clearly passed through here last night. If I could just find a trail somehow..."

"Perhaps it would help if you came with us back to camp," Hurst said. "We set up a temporary base of operations a few hours' ride from this village, and all the information we have so far on the thugs are there. A man of your...reputation...surely has ways of making use of anything we can't."

Red Wolf sighed. He knew when to admit defeat. They had all underestimated the kidnappers, it seemed, and the thugs had slipped away from right underneath them.

"Very well, lead the way," he said. "I'd be interested in looking over what you have."

They arrived at the camp in the early afternoon, after the sun had passed overhead and was beginning to dip towards the horizon. Hurst led them past rows of tents and other search parties who had clearly just returned and showed them into the command tent in the middle of camp.

"Well, here's all the information we've gathered these past few days," he said, gesturing to the map table and noticeboard. "A former patron of the arenas let slip their existence—it's how we were even able to begin our search."

"You didn't get anything else from him? A location, information on the thugs, who their boss is?" Red Wolf asked.

"Not much. A group of thugs attacked us before we could question him any further and killed the poor man," Hurst said. "I've no doubt he was their true target. Whoever these people are, they're...prepared to do anything to keep the arenas running."

Red Wolf hummed. "And your own searches have turned up nothing?"

"It does feel that way." Hurst sighed. "Our intel seems to indicate that the kidnappings originated further away from Castle Blackrun than where we just were." He pointed at a section of road close to one of the villages Red Wolf remembered staying at. "Recently, they've started targeting people closer to the castle, no doubt getting bolder, expanding their territory."

"No. All we found at the village indicates the thugs were moving *towards* Castle Blackrun. If they were expanding their territory, then their route would not make sense—they should be moving *away* from the castle, towards their arenas," Red Wolf said. "They must be operating somewhere between where we were camped last night and Castle Blackrun. That narrows the search down, but we still have half a region to check, and it could take months to comb through the entire place bit by bit."

"Well, we could start by checking the villages..." Hurst said.

"If these arenas are as brutal as you describe, we don't have that kind of time. There are dozens of villages dotted along these roads, and even if you could send your men out to each one, there are too many places left unaccounted for. My bet is that the arena isn't even at a village but built somewhere more remote, where it would be easier to hide from your search parties."

"Very well," Hurst said. "What do you suggest?"

"Much as I hate to say it, we must wait," Red Wolf said. "Do nothing."

"Nothing? Are you out of your mind?" Hurst exclaimed.

"Quite the opposite. We'll set up some more bait for these kidnappers," Red Wolf said. "And then we wait. Give them a few more days to haul in more victims. Take note of where the kidnappings take place and which direction they're headed. That will further narrow our search. We also know they cannot be operating too close to Castle Blackrun, or Lady Blackrun would have discovered them by now."

"What kind of bait did you have in mind?" Hurst asked. "I'd advise against using another *person* as bait, given what's happened already."

"No, I was thinking we spread some more rumours around..." Red Wolf put a hand on his chin. "The thugs are careful not to leave behind any trails that might be followed because they know the search parties are hunting them. I suspect it's also the reason they've not dared to get much closer to Castle Blackrun."

"We spread stories around that the investigations have stopped!" Arkiel exclaimed. "That way, the bad men will think they're safer and start moving closer to Castle Blackrun, and they might be willing to take less precautions because we're not looking for them."

Red Wolf smiled. "As the boy has stated, this is exactly what I plan to do."

Gods, he takes after Talin. Ever the strategist, preferring stories and books over swordplay and fighting.

"You think they'll fall for it?" Hurst asked.

"When enough people begin to spout the same news, even the most implausible lies may take some ring of truth," Red Wolf told him. "We *are* halting our searches, after all, and resorting to a different approach, but the kidnappers do not need to know this."

"I will instruct my men to begin spreading the word, then," Hurst said.

"We shall do the same. It may take a while, but I have faith." Red Wolf turned away from the map table. "I know your men have to travel together in units, which slows their movements somewhat. My companions and I can travel much faster in that regard and reach the furthest villages in our search area. We'll reconvene here in a week."

"You're setting out now?" Hurst asked. "It will be dark soon. The Highlands sees sunset much quicker than the south."

"Aye, it'd be best if we rested tonight and set off at dawn," Golmin said.

"We don't have time," Red Wolf said.

"I know you wish to find her. We all do. But she would never want any of us overextending ourselves for her sake," Golmin said. "Captain, I don't suppose we could trouble you for somewhere to sleep."

"Of course, I'll have someone find you all a spare tent," Hurst said. "Ashera, I'm sure you're aware military protocol dictates that you sleep elsewhere. I will have one of my officers take you to the women's section."

Red Wolf glanced at Ashera, and she gave him a reassuring smile.

"I'll be fine," she said teasingly. "Our side of camp is better than yours anyway."

Red Wolf snorted. "If you say so."

They were escorted out by two officers and split up at the next row of tents, with the female officer taking Ashera to their own section of the camp. The officer that remained showed them into an empty tent near the command centre and left them to unpack.

"You've put a lot of thought into this plan, I'll grant you that," Golmin said as he threw his pack onto the nearest bed. "I suspect, therefore, that you already have an idea of where to start."

"The main trade route between Castle Blackrun and the outer villages. We can move closer to the castle than Hurst and his men because we can travel faster," Red Wolf said. "I say we ride as close to Castle Blackrun as we can, spread the word that the soldiers have halted their searches, then turn back here."

Golmin gave a nod. "Wherever you lead us, I will follow."

"So will I," Ettrias said.

"You'll take me too, won't you? I don't want to be stuck here at camp waiting for you all to return," Arkiel said.

"Here is where you're safest, Your Highness," Red Wolf said. "These soldiers will protect you."

"But I want to come!" Arkiel protested. "*You* can protect me, like you used to protect Mother!"

"That was a long time ago, Arkiel." Red Wolf turned away and went to the bed at the back. "I don't... I'm not that kind of person anymore."

"If you really believe that, then you wouldn't be helping us..." Arkiel's voice faltered. "Right?"

The boy has a point. Why are you doing this, if not to protect her?

"I...don't know." He frowned. "But I promise we'll find her. Whatever it takes."

M orning came, and with it came the lists for today's fights.
There was only one copy of the lists, located in the communal
recreation rooms between the men's and women's quarters, and Talin
had made the mistake of being two minutes late. Fighters had crowded
around the lists by the time she made her way there after a simple breakfast in the mess hall—from her spot near the doors, she was completely
cut off and unable to even see the parchment. Some of the fighters had
already begun shoving each other aside to see the lists first. She decided
to hang near the back with Aelia and Icari.

"You two have been split up," the dark-skinned woman said. "They
organised all the new arrivals from yesterday into two groups of twelve.
I heard the information from my sponsor, who heard it from his
friends, the arena masters. The first group, *your* group…" She pointed at
Aelia. You'll be up against a group who survived yesterday's initiation

fight." She paused and glanced at Talin. "The rest of you will be up against half a dozen cavalry, led by one of the other sponsored fighters. The masters weren't keen to discuss who. Probably wants to keep it a surprise."

"Are we...getting horses ourselves?" Talin asked.

"No."

"What?! That's a death sentence!" Aelia exclaimed, and was quickly shushed by Icari when several fighters looked their way.

"They clearly split you up into the 'capable' fighters and the... How shall I put it? 'Less capable' fighters," Icari said. "A fool could tell. The masters aren't expecting the second group to walk out alive. It's more of an...entertainment fight, to make the sponsored fighter look good."

Aelia began to pace. "If we swap groups...I could take your place...but you'll have to face twice as many enemies..."

"Why in the seven hells would you want to swap?" Icari looked at the Drakel incredulously.

"I'll find a way," Talin said. "I fought Hellhounds during the Siege of Belanore, at the White River, Illyris..." Icari was staring at the two of them. "I know what I'm doing."

"You fought in the war?" the fighter asked.

"In the...cavalry division," Talin tried to cover up. "As a...mounted archer, not as an officer, or anything, or..." *The leader of the Royal Army.* She decided she'd overshared quite enough. Any more information, and she might as well announce to Icari that she was the queen.

"Well, you seem to know what you're talking about, in any case," Icari said. "Drakel, your fight is up first. You'll want to go now. Down the main hallway; the masters will direct you."

"Are there viewing stands for the fighters?" Talin asked, as Aelia peered at the list to make sure Icari's information was correct.

"There are, but you'll want to go with your friend," Icari said. "The waiting room and armoury are connected, and you'll want to see what weapons are available."

"It can't hurt, I suppose." Talin followed Aelia out of the recreation room and down the narrow corridor, where two of the arena masters in their long tailcoats ushered the Drakel into the waiting room and halted Talin.

"You're not in this fight," one of them said.

"I'm in the next one," Talin explained. "Thought I'd take a look at what's in the armoury."

The masters talked amongst themselves for a moment before they ushered her inside as well.

"Any, uh...suggestions?" Aelia asked when she joined the Drakel in the armoury.

"You're up against infantry. Pick the best armour you can find," Talin said. "That chainmail, put that on." Aelia quickly grabbed a chainmail shirt and struggled into it before anyone else could claim the armour. Talin looked around and saw a steel helmet that would probably never fit on Aelia's lizard-like head. *A shame, really,* she thought, as another fighter saw it and snatched it up.

"Try to protect your head," she continued. "None of the helmets here will fit you, so you're at a disadvantage there." She grabbed a steel breastplate and handed it to Aelia. "This will be handy."

"And weapons?" the Drakel asked.

Talin looked around again. "You know how to use a spear?"

"Of course. But I don't exactly train with them on a regular basis," Aelia admitted.

"Never mind, then. Longsword or arming sword and shield. Dagger if you lose your sword." She spied a bow and quiver of arrows in the corner, unclaimed by any of the other fighters. It was no surprise, given how Highlanders were known for their cavalry units rather than archers. Even Aelia, who had served under Kadis before coming to Kies Tor, would likely have little use for the weapon. Talin took it instead and tested the weight of the draw on a training mannequin in the waiting room. Too slow for close combat. She might get two or three horses before the rest of them trampled her; having the bow would immediately make her the most obvious threat to take out. Talin took the arrows out of the mannequin and put it back.

"Really? You don't want that?" Aelia asked when she returned.

"Too risky," Talin said.

"Fighters! Five minutes left! Pick your weapons and leave!" one of the masters called. Talin put a hand on Aelia's shoulder.

"Be careful," she said.

"I'll see you after."

Talin browsed through the weapons in the armoury while Aelia and the other fighters were ushered through a metal portcullis into another waiting area. Through it, she could just barely see the arena grounds and the white sands that covered it.

White sand to make the blood stand out.

Talin had been to an arena fight before as a child, back when Arnas still ruled, and the fights were still legal. They had gone to Eshor Taesi, the largest fighting arena in the Highlands, situated in the heart of Gery and just three days' ride from the nearby Fort Moen. She had seen the brutality of combat in the arena and questioned the necessity of it. Why should two fighters be pitted against each other in mortal combat if there was such a high chance that one or both of them could die? Why spill so much blood in the arena, all for the entertainment of the masses?

The portcullis on the other side of Aelia's group was raised, and they entered the arena for their fight. Talin watched from the armoury.

The arena truly is a lawless place.

She could already see blood in the sand. Aelia cut down one of the fighters as she watched. Another came to stab her in the back, but one of the fighters on her side used that opportunity to kill the man while he was distracted.

Talin wasn't sure what she would do if Aelia died here. She was confident in the Drakel's abilities, true, but the only time she'd ever seen those skills put to practice was on the training grounds at Castle Blackrun—not in a brutal battle to the death in the arena.

Slowly, the fighters fell, until only a handful of them remained standing. Talin recognised Aelia among them and the two other fighters in her group. They cut down the last few enemies while she looked on.

They won. She's alive.

She would have liked to greet Aelia when they all returned to the waiting room, but as it turned out, the fighters left through a different gate instead, probably to avoid cluttering up the armoury too much. Talin resolved to find the Drakel after her own fight if she survived.

The rest of her group had filed into the armoury while she'd been distracted by the fight. She quickly grabbed the sword and dagger she'd spied earlier and picked up a spear before all the good equipment could be claimed.

"Fighters!" the arena master cleared his throat. "You'll be up against six cavalrymen today. One of these men will be a sponsored fighter with better equipment than what we have here at the armoury. Good luck, die well."

Chattering began amongst the group. Talin saw several fighters begin to fight over who should get the best armour while two others went for the pikes propped against the wall.

"You two." Talin approached the pikemen. Both looked fairly young. "You know what you're doing."

"My brother fought in the war," one of the men said. "He told me a story once about how they stopped a huge Hellhound charge just with a solid pike formation."

Talin nodded. "When we get out there, tell the others to form a circle. It won't stop them, but it should make them think twice about a charge."

The two men nodded and went to stand at the portcullis. Talin looked around for anything else she might need and snatched up a round, wooden shield, fitting it to her left arm. There may not be much sense in wearing armour against a cavalry charge that could trample a man in just a few seconds, but a shield and some chainmail should provide her with some degree of protection.

"Fighters, five minutes left! Grab your gear and move out!" the master said, and the portcullis was raised. Talin wedged herself between one of the pikemen and a thin man who looked like he was about to piss himself. The portcullis shut behind them.

"We'll form a circle near the middle of the arena," Talin whispered to the thin man. "It will stop them from charging straight away. Pass it on."

The skinny lad stared at her for a moment, then leaned over to whisper to the next person. She heard the two pikemen doing the same.

"...and on the left side of the ring, we have a dozen brand new recruits, here for their initiation fight!" boomed the voice of Royce Hargrave from the arena. The gate in front of them was raised, and they stepped onto the blood-splattered sands to the roar of the cheering crowd. Talin remembered this fear. The rush of blood-frenzy before the battle. She saw the crowd, but their cheers and movements seemed slowed, as if she was moving through a dream.

They took their positions on the battlefield, forming a circle as she'd instructed. The gate directly opposite her opened and half a dozen cavalrymen spilled out, each wielding a lance with a sword at their belts. The man at the head of the formation bore a shield instead and a flail. She saw the spiked head swinging lazily on its chain as he paced the horse back and forth.

This is it.

She remembered the day they had taken back Belanore, how Kadis and his cavalry had torn through the Hellhound ranks like a rushing river sweeping away everything in its path. It had taken a minute, perhaps less, for the tables to turn at the edge of Stormwood. Talin remembered staring into the eyes of death, only to be saved a moment later.

The riders split, with three circling towards their left while the other two, led by the man with the flail, circled towards the right. She braced for a charge, but none came. The riders continued circling them, watching. Waiting. Testing their resolve.

They're trying to panic us. Catch us off-guard.

It was working. Though Talin had seen the tactic before used by groups of Hellhounds, her allies here had not. She saw one of the fighters trembling out of the corner of her eye.

"Hold!" she yelled. Her voice carried across the arena.

Two of the riders had enough waiting and charged.

They aimed for gaps in their defense, as she'd predicted, avoiding her spear and the two pikemen and barrelling into their circles on opposite sides. The crowd burst into cheers and shouts as blood splashed onto the sand. The two riders dodged out of the way before any of them could get a swing at the horses. Talin tightened her grip on her spear and watched the flail rider. She heard another charge behind her but didn't dare to look. There was a yell, followed by the screams of a dying horse, and the crowd cheered again. Talin risked a glance back and saw that one of the pikemen had impaled the charging horse through the neck while one of the other fighters finished off its rider. The flail rider continued to circle them, letting the spiked ball swing on its chain, almost hypnotising.

Beside her, another rider charged. The other pikeman angled his weapon slightly and thrust forward. The rider saw him move too late and tried to turn. There was a sickening crunch as the pike drove deep into the horse's shoulder, sending the rider flying. He landed in front of Talin, and she speared him through the chest before she could give herself time to take pity on him and show mercy. The flail rider looked at her, and the two of them locked eyes for a moment. She saw a pair of grey eyes behind his helmet, filled with bloodlust. Not a sight she was unfamiliar with on the battlefield.

Steel rang together behind her, but she didn't dare look back now. She had underestimated that kind of bloodlust before. A fighter fell to her right, blood spraying from his chest, but he had taken down a rider with him—Talin saw the dead cavalryman lying in a heap as his horse fled to the edge of the arena. Around them, the crowd cheered on. The flail rider circled them once more before making up his mind. Talin saw his focus shift to her as he lined up a charge.

She remembered charging Hellhounds at Belanore and Vill's Crossing, driven by a kind of hate that she had never seen before. They were nearly unstoppable that way, fuelled by their rage and the power of the moon. The only way to survive such a charge was to dodge out of the way and hope for the best.

Talin glanced at the spear in her hand, then at the flail rider. He carried a shield on his left arm and seemed to be sizing her up, trying to gauge how much of a threat she posed. She had no doubt she could hit his horse with a well-aimed spear throw, but even unseated, the flail rider could pose a threat. The only way to stop him was to aim for his chest and hope she didn't miss.

The flail rider charged, and Talin knew she was out of time. She switched her grip on the spear and flung it as hard as she could. The flail rider brought his shield up to block and the tip of the weapon buried itself in the wood with a solid thunk. The crowd roared its approval. Talin cursed and drew her sword as the flail rider dropped his shield and continued his charge without slowing. She saw the spiked ball swing towards her and jumped out of the way just in time. He changed direction abruptly to avoid her sword, quickly circling back for a second hit. Talin backed up towards the middle of the circle. The flail rider apparently had other ideas, however, and turned his attention on the pikeman next to her at the last second. Talin shouted a warning too late. The spiked flail slammed into the fighter's head, and there was a crunch as bone shattered and blood sprayed everywhere. The crowd roared its approval once more. The flail rider readied himself for a third charge, and Talin realised the arena had grown oddly silent. It quickly dawned on her that they were now the only two combatants still alive.

I have to unseat him somehow. She looked at the fallen pike by her feet. Too heavy for her to wield effectively, even if she had formal training in how to use one. All she had here was a sword and her wits. Talin spied a chestnut stallion at the edge of the arena—the same horse she'd seen fleeing the combat earlier. A little further from her was a spear dropped by another combatant.

Oh, I must be mad.

Talin sprinted for the spear as the flail rider charged towards her, reaching it just in time. She flipped it and dragged the end across the sand in a wide arc, sending sand into the air and into the rider's face. He steered his horse away with a curse, disappearing into the dust cloud that followed, and Talin sprinted for the riderless horse. She grabbed the saddle and swung herself onto its back before the dust could clear and waited for the flail rider to re-emerge.

The arena was silent. Talin tried to get a glimpse of the flail rider through the dust.

Horse hooves pounded to her right. She turned just in time to see the rider galloping towards her and knew that there was no time for her to meet his charge. He swung the flail. She brought her shield up just in time to block the attack. There was a sharp *crack* as the weapon skittered against it, splitting a crack through the wood and sending blinding pain lancing through her arm. Talin shook the shield off with a wince and prepared to meet his second charge. Hooves drummed together on the arena sand as they drew closer. She aimed her spear forward, eyes fixed on the gap between his pauldron and breastplate. Time slowed, and she saw his spinning flail in the split second before they met.

This is going to hurt.

The two of them collided together in a sharp screech of metal and screaming horses. Talin found herself flying forwards, weaponless and dazed, her left arm burning when she landed on her shoulder. She rolled onto her stomach quickly and pulled herself up, drawing her sword as she searched for her opponent.

She was quick to spot him, sprawled on his back on the ground a few feet away, the broken tip of her spear lodged deep in his shoulder. His helmet had been knocked off somehow in the fall, and his weapon lay useless beside him, splattered with the blood from her horse. It was already dead; his blow had turned its skull into a disfigured pulp. His own horse had stopped in the middle of the arena, looking uncertain of what to do next. Talin approached and kicked the flail out of his reach.

"Well, go on, then. Kill me," the rider spat. "Or wait for the crowd to decide. Not that I care."

Talin waited, watching the crowd. A minute passed that felt like an eternity. She heard whispers in the stands that quickly escalated into a chant.

"Kill. Kill. Kill. Kill."

The rider looked up at her and closed his eyes. "Make it quick."

Talin stepped closer. The crowd fell silent.

"No."

She let the sword slip from her fingers. It clattered to the ground with a soft thud, muffled by the bloodstained sands of the arena, and the warrior at her feet opened his eyes again.

"Thank you," he said hoarsely. Talin didn't respond. Instead, she turned soundlessly and walked away, the deafening silence of the arena ringing behind her.

XVII

Talin took her supper that evening with Icari and Aelia. They sat at the furthest table in the mess hall, as far from the crowd of fighters as possible, but she could still see some of them shoot her a glance every now and then when they thought she wasn't paying attention. Her decision to spare the sponsored fighter—Marcus, his name was—had come with some controversy; that she waited for the crowd to decide but went against their wishes was not unheard of, but it was generally considered bad form. And sparing the fighter despite the crowd's decision, on her first day, no less...well, it had been seen as a statement that she refused to kill or play by the arena's rules. Some of the fighters had begun to question the amount of choice they had in the arena. If she could spare her opponent after the masses had yearned for an execution, perhaps there was a choice in whether they had to kill for the crowd's entertainment, too.

The arena masters didn't like that line of reasoning, of course.

Talin had kept out of their way for the rest of the day. Even in the fights directly after hers, the fighters had been more reluctant to fight, to spill blood. Some still went for a fatal blow at the crowd's behest. Others chose to walk away. She knew the arena masters blamed her for showing mercy against the odds; Royce Hargrave himself had cornered her earlier and told her, rather unpleasantly, that she would kill for the crowd without question.

She decided that she didn't like him very much.

"I've fought in the arena for almost a year now," Icari said, watching the fighters flock around the hall. "The energy in here has never changed much. Today, it feels different. I'm not sure why, but it is as if you've...made us realise something."

"What's that?" Talin asked. She hadn't thought much of her actions at the time; the only reason she'd spared Marcus was because she refused to fall that far.

"We have a choice. More than what the masters have given us. *Much* more. If you did not have to kill to satisfy the crowd, is there not a possibility that we do not have to fight at all?" Icari lifted her brow. "The masters have always told us that we fight to the death. If you are defeated, you die with dignity. If you are lucky, the crowd will spare you. But you walked out there today and defied the odds to survive, and then you defied the crowd. Whether you meant it or not, it was a statement."

"I didn't think..." Talin began.

"It doesn't matter. What you did today was a good thing." Icari looked deep in thought. "This place has turned into a lawless wasteland. Once upon a time, being an arena fighter *meant* something in the north. Now we fight to survive, and only the strongest do. Change is on the horizon, Raia. I sense a revolution brewing in the depths."

"I only spared a man's life," Talin said.

"Perhaps, in your eyes. But the masters see it as dissent," Icari said.

"Doesn't sound fair," Aelia muttered.

"It isn't. But whatever the masters say goes. They only care to please the crowd, that they may reap the rewards."

Talin looked at one of the thugs guarding the mess hall. *The masters must be rich indeed if they can hire mercenaries for this kind of thing.*

"You say there's a revolution brewing." She turned back to her supper when the thug glanced her way.

"Yes," Icari said. "What of it?"

"Say the fighters really did revolt. Could we bring this place down?" Talin asked.

Icari barked a laugh. "It's hard to say."

"There are plenty of fighters here. Surely we could overpower the guards and the masters," Talin said.

"Perhaps we could overpower them here. But the masters have a whole army of mercenaries at the ready, waiting outside the arena. From what I hear, they're a new faction that appeared after the war, made up of Royal Army veterans and ex-militia," Icari explained. "They're highly trained, and they will come at the first sign of trouble. You would need to offer them a much higher sum than what the masters are already paying for them to get them to switch sides. And none of us have that sort of coin, obviously."

Talin thought about it. If she could count on Ettrias and the others to be looking for her, then they must have gone to Blackrun for help. And if they could track the thugs here, perhaps it would be possible to pay the mercenaries off and convince them not to come to the masters' aid while the fighters took over from the inside.

"I know some people who might be able to help," Talin said. "People on the outside. But I have no way of contacting them from in here."

"Well, then, therein lies your problem." Icari shrugged. "We have no contact with the outside world from in here. Those of us who are sponsored with families to write to, we can send the occasional message. But those are heavily monitored and checked before they are sent out."

"I'll find a way," Talin said. "Nothing is foolproof. There must be a way to get a letter past the masters."

Icari tapped her chin. "My sponsor is a decent man. He's grown to dislike the arena just as much as me. The only reason he's still sponsoring me is because he's trying to get inside intelligence on how the place operates and where exactly we're situated."

"Keep your friends close and your enemies closer. I like it." Talin had to admit she was impressed. "You think he could smuggle out a letter for...Lady Blackrun, perhaps?"

Icari nearly choked on her drink. "These people you know work with *Lady Blackrun*?"

"Sort of." Aelia stole a quick glance at Talin. "I know them too. There may be a way to get their attention directly."

"I have a meeting with my sponsor tomorrow morning," Icari said. "Whatever you plan to do, you must write the letter tonight."

"Do they supply ink and parchment?" Talin asked.

"No, but you can win some." Icari gestured towards the recreation room. "I hear Marcus has parchment and ink that you can use. If you can beat him at Tavern Cards."

"I've never played—" Talin began, before Aelia cut in.

"I'll play him," she said, flashing Talin a knowing look.

"Hey, Marcus!" Icari called. The fighter that Talin had spared looked up from a nearby table. She saw bandages under his tunic, just barely visible, and his arm was in a sling.

"What'd you want?" he yelled back in a thick northern accent.

"Got a fighter here who thinks she can beat you at Tavern Cards!" Icari said with a grin. "What do you say? Bet some of your ink and parchment?"

Marcus excused himself from his group and approached. "I'm never one to turn down a game. What do you have to bet?"

"Uh..." Aelia scratched her head.

"I'll give you my archery gloves if she loses," Icari said. "It's sponsored gear. Pretty valuable."

"Oh? Never thought I'd see a sponsored fighter become a sponsor herself." Marcus raised his eyebrows. "Alright, if you're that confident."

He stalked off towards the recreation room, Aelia in tow. Talin and Icari followed just behind.

"Why do you want ink and parchment anyway?" he asked as they walked. "You realise the masters only allow sponsored fighters to write home."

"It's...for my art," Aelia said.

"You draw?" Marcus asked. "I hope you'll show me when you're done. And you." He looked at Talin. "I suppose I owe you for sparing m e."

"You don't owe me anything," Talin said.

"Perhaps not in your eyes."

They reached the cards table, and Icari quickly set about shuffling the deck while Marcus and Aelia took their seats. Talin watched the fighter deal their hands and the two began to play. She understood very little of the rules and what they were doing; having grown up in the palace, she was only ever taught how to play Rack-and-Ruin, as Tavern Cards was considered a commoners' game and not fit for nobility. She supposed that was why Aelia had cut her off before she could say she'd never played. It would have given away her status as one of the Torrian nobility, and Icari might catch on to who she was.

"Ah, looks like I win," Aelia said, laying her cards on the table for all to see. Marcus put his cards down with a sigh.

"I know when I'm beaten," he said. "Very well, I'll fetch my ink and parchment. Wait here."

He stood and disappeared down the hall towards the men's quarters while Icari packed the cards and shuffled them again.

"I'm impressed," she said. "Marcus is pretty good at this game. I've only been able to beat him a handful of times."

"What can I say, I just got lucky," Aelia said. Marcus returned momentarily with some parchment and an inkwell, and a simple quill to go with it, and disappeared back into the men's quarters.

Icari looked around and saw that more fighters had flocked into the room, having finished their supper. "Come, we'd best not linger here."

They returned to Talin's bed in the women's quarters, where she propped the parchment against the wall and scribbled a coded note in Old Torrian.

> *Mercenaries guarding the gate. Planning takeover from inside but need to persuade them with money. Neutralise them and wait for our move.*

She folded the parchment and passed it to Icari.

"That's funny," the fighter said, as she tucked it under her tunic. "I know only two groups of people who know how to read and write Old

Torrian. The first is the northernmost villages in the Highlands, where I'm from. The second is the palace nobility in Belanore."

Talin and Aelia glanced at each other.

"I'm..." the queen began.

"Not from one of the villages, trust me, I know," Icari said. "That, and you say you fought in the war as a mounted archer. Your Majesty."

"You could at least keep your voice down..." Talin looked around to make sure there were no eavesdroppers in the vicinity. "Fine. I was on the run before I ended up here. I was on my way to seek help from Blackrun before the thugs captured me. Now, are you planning on keeping a secret or do I have to resort to some other means of remaining unnoticed?"

Icari smiled. "See, someone like you wouldn't resort to such methods, Your Majesty. You spared Marcus in the arena because you have no wish to kill for the crowd's entertainment. I wish to see this arena shut down, and so we have a common purpose. Escape. I will deliver the letter to my sponsor. Where will he take it?"

"There's a camp, a few hours' ride south of Rivenfort," Aelia said. "It's where Blackrun's men have gathered. Make *sure* it reaches Captain Todd Hurst directly."

"Hurst won't be able to read the message," Talin added. "But my brother can. If Ettrias is not already with them, he won't be far from Castle Blackrun—he might even be at the castle already. Have Hurst find him and pass on the message to him."

"I'll let my sponsor know," Icari said. "In the meantime, we should..."

The three of them fell silent as one of the arena masters swept through the women's quarters, long coat trailing behind her. She caught sight of them huddled together at Talin's bed and narrowed her eyes. Talin felt her gaze on them as she did her rounds and promptly left.

"...be careful about who we trust," Icari finished. "The only way we could initiate a takeover from the inside is if we get the cooperation of the fighters. And some of them are not keen on leaving this place."

"You've been here longest. Any ideas on who to talk to?" Talin asked.

"Ask the fighters whether they came here by choice or whether they were abducted," Icari said. "Usually it's the latter who are more willing to see this place torn down."

"Then Aelia and I will start talking to the fighters," Talin said. "You deliver the letter. Give them time to deal with the mercenaries. How long should we expect to wait?"

Icari shrugged. "I have no idea. I'm meeting with my sponsor tomorrow, but it could take him anywhere between a day to several *months* to get this to your people."

"Let me think, then..." Talin tapped her chin. "I was taken somewhere between Rivenfort and Fallbjorn. It took us less than a day to reach the arena from there..."

"That checks out," Aelia said. "The spot we'd set up for me to be taken was also close to Rivenfort."

"It shouldn't take more than a week for your sponsor to deliver the message, then," Talin said to Icari. "That's not a lot of time to incite a rebellion." Her brow furrowed. "Wait. Give me back the parchment, I'll add something." Icari did as she asked, and she scribbled out an extra line about a simple hand signal used by the Royal Army to indicate friendly forces. They'd used it in the war to differentiate between Torrians and Hellhounds from a distance, and she figured it would help Blackrun's men tell the difference between their rebellious fighters and the arena masters and guards. She also added the information about their proximity to Rivenfort, reasoning that if anyone could deduce their location, it would be Golmin. That done, she explained everything to the other two, and quickly taught them the signal.

"We'll give them two weeks to act on the information, then," Icari said, taking the message again. "I imagine if Blackrun's men can't persuade the mercenaries with money, they'll have other ways to eliminate the outside threat."

"I expect so," Aelia said. "Let's reconvene in a week to check on each other's progress."

Talin gave a nod. "Icari, if your sponsor can't get the message out, let us know as soon as possible. The plan hinges on alerting Blackrun's men."

Icari let out a long breath. "Alright. I hope you both know what you're doing."

XXVIII

Lord Cassius had only vague memories of the last memorial service he'd attended. It had been a sweltering dry season day, not unlike today's weather, and the front row seats of the funeral house had been reserved for King Arnas' Royal Council. Talin, who was still a princess then, had given quite the moving eulogy, praising his bravery and sacrifice.

How ironic, then, that the seats were packed full today and not then.

Lord Wyndove was currently giving some speech about the queen's involvement in the war—it was well-known, after all, that she had remained on the front lines far longer than Arnas had before her. Cassius paid little attention to it; much as he liked the man giving the speech, they all knew it was out of necessity that such eulogies were given at all. Certainly, in Talin's case, the praises were well-deserved. But for Arnas, knowing the things he'd done...

"You don't seem keen on being here, my lord," Corvan said in a low voice, leaning in to avoid being overheard.

Cassius tilted his head to acknowledge the healer. "They're always the same. Empty praises from people with no understanding of the magnitude of the feats the deceased has accomplished. Or undeserved praise for some gods-forsaken *abijo* who never did a single act of good in their entire life."

"I understand what you mean." Corvan turned his attention back to Lord Wyndove and his speech. They spent the rest of the service in silence.

It was another hour before the last of the proceedings finished, and the funeral house began to empty as townsfolk went back to their daily lives. Cassius accompanied Corvan back to the palace and parted ways with him at the stables—at least for the moment. He headed upstairs to go through some of his paperwork before making his way into the city again.

By now, Lord Varkis should have pulled his reserve banners from the Royal Army and begun the march north. He needed to talk to his remaining loyalists to discuss their next move.

He had been the one to pick out their meeting spot this time, a secluded little inn located in the poorer half of Belanore, and he had instructed his fellow lords to dress down and disguise themselves as one of the common folk. The innkeeper didn't spare him a second glance as he made his way upstairs into one of the rooms.

"You couldn't have picked a better inn for this meeting?" Lord Wyndove asked as soon as he stepped foot inside and closed the door.

"The point of these meetings is to remain discreet," Cassius said. "Nobody would suspect a group of nobles to gather in a seedy inn such as this one. It's the perfect disguise. What's the latest news?"

"I received a bird from Lady Blackrun this morning, shortly before the memorial service," Corvan said. "It does not bode well." He produced the letter.

To King Aldrus of House Dalkarth, Regent of Kies Tor

I have requested your aid in resolving the case of the serial disappearances across the Highlands and have received no reply. It is my understanding that prior to the unjust accusations against Queen Talin and her supposed death in the eastern range, she had planned to send Royal Army reinforcements to help my men investigate. However, given the situation, it has become apparent that we cannot maintain a cordial working relationship.

I have pulled back my reserve banners and reallocated them to the investigation in the Highlands. Through them, I have uncovered rumours of illegal fighting arenas being re-opened and operating in secret, which I believe is the reason for the disappearances. My reserve banners cannot hope to finish their investigation alone. I write to you once again to request assistance—but know that the Highlands will no longer recognise your rule should my letter go unanswered once more.

Signed,
Lady Katherine Blackrun

Cassius hissed through his teeth. The situation had escalated so much faster than he had anticipated; his intention had been to stall Darien's influence on the south, not actually start a civil war in Kies Tor. But with Lord Varkis and some two thousand men marching north right now like a lit fuse, they had no way of stopping the inevitable explosion.

"This is exactly what I was worried about," Lord Mornus snapped. "I knew we shouldn't have stirred the pot. Things were better when we didn't meddle in these politics."

"Peace, Lord Tybalt," Lord Wyndove said. "This may not be entirely a bad thing. At this stage, civil war may be the only way to resolve the tensions between the north and south—and the fastest way to put Prince Arkiel on the throne."

"We don't even know if he's been found," Mornus said. "And even if it works out, a civil war could cost the lives of millions of innocents. It's too great a risk. There has to be a way to de-escalate the situation."

"It's out of our hands now," Wyndove said. "Besides, Aldrus has been acting on edge ever since King Darien and his council returned to Astaria. He's hiding something else, I can sense it. Letting him and Blackrun have at each other's throats might force the truth out about everything."

"I...I'm sorry. I didn't sign up for this." Mornus swallowed.

"As I've told you countless times, my lord, it's too late to back out now," Cassius said. "We all knew the risks, coming into this. You must accept th—"

The door slammed open with a sharp *crack*, revealing a royal guard holding a small battering ram in both hands. Half a dozen of his comrades streamed in past him with spears held at the ready.

And behind them all, striding into the room purposefully, was King Aldrus himself.

How did he find out about all of this? Cassius thought. He had left no trace of his activities behind, had made *sure* he was not seen with any of the other lords in this room before he left the palace...

"Well, then," Aldrus said. "This is an interesting turnout." His gaze landed on Lord Mornus, who quickly looked away. "Excellent work, my lord."

Cassius glared. "You damn snake."

"I'm sorry," Mornus said. "But like I said, I didn't sign up to start a war. I couldn't be a part of it any longer—not after Lord Varkis decided to do what he's doing now."

Cassius glanced around the room. It was cramped in here with half a dozen royal guards crammed inside, forming a semicircle in front of the door to prevent their escape. There wouldn't be much room to fight or dodge around them. He knew that the space beneath the window held a small flower bed, dense enough to break his fall if he were to leap out, but he doubted the guards would give him the opportunity. What he needed was a diversion.

One of Corvan's potions would be useful right now, he thought, gaze flickering toward the old healer. Surely the man had *something* hidden in his robes as a backup plan...

"You can't do this," Wyndove said as two of the guards seized him and dragged him towards the door. "We've been doing exactly as you instructed—investigating the queen's case. You're not above the law, Aldrus!"

The remaining guards moved to grab Corvan and Cassius, and he saw the healer bat one of the guards' hands away—a potion slipping free from his sleeve as he did so. Cassius watched in fascination as it tumbled, almost in slow motion, and shattered against the floorboards. Thick white smoke immediately filled the room as the liquid held within reacted with the air. It smelled putrid and burned his lungs.

I knew I could count on you.

Cassius covered his mouth and nose with his sleeve, took a running leap, and crashed through the window with his shoulder.

He landed in the garden bed as predicted with a grunt, the air going out of his lungs. Footsteps thundered in the room above as the guards fled from the room to avoid the smoke. Cassius picked himself up and sprinted for his horse. He knew well enough that Corvan had no hope of outrunning the guards, nor landing safely in the garden bed, and with Wyndove already in custody, he was on his own. No doubt the Royal Guard and the City Watch would both be placed on high alert within the hour. He needed to get out of Belanore *now.*

And go where? a voice in his head asked.

Cassius didn't care. For now, his priority was escape, for he was the only one who knew the truth of the situation. Red Wolf was looking for Talin in the Highlands. One of his spies had seen the queen with her own eyes barely a few days ago. She was, without a shadow of a doubt, *alive.*

He needed to link up with Lord Varkis near the Western Forts and ride for Castle Blackrun as soon as possible. Their only chance of preventing a full-scale civil war now rested solely on Kies Tor's rightful queen.

XXIX

"**H**ave you seen the lists?"

"This has to be a joke, right?"

"He's just a *child*...there's no way they'd pair him with *her*..."

The crowd parted slowly, like a wave. Talin shouldered her way through to see the listings for the day's fights. She could feel the stares as she moved and tried to ignore it.

There it was—her name printed at the very top of the list in neat handwriting. Next to it read, 'Edward of Rivenfort'. Her heart sank.

Edd had been one of the abducted fighters who'd survived the ring alongside Aelia, and had quickly risen in popularity over the past week thanks in part to his young age and unmatched skill with an axe—a combination loved by the crowd. Talin herself had some popularity owing to her sparing Marcus and a second fight last week against a group of infantry, where she'd shown off her marksmanship. But her reputation was nothing compared to Edd's. Truthfully, it wasn't a stretch to say that he was already one of the crowd favourites.

Outside the fighting pit, Edd was popular with the other fighters, too; he was adept at telling stories and cracking jokes. He'd once graced the communal lounge with a rendition of *Blackbird's Melody*—only he'd swapped the lyrics out for something more...obscene. It had been an amusing evening, to say the least.

But despite whatever skills the boy might possess on or off the battlefield, he was still just that—a boy.

And Talin was now expected to duel him in a fight to the death.

She left for the armoury feeling numb. Edd was a good fighter, certainly, but he'd only ever been pitted against untrained opponents who relied on power instead of technique. She had seen him fight and was certain she could defeat him without any difficulty. Surely the arena masters also knew that it wasn't a fair match...

But perhaps that was precisely why they paired him with her. They wanted to force her to kill an untrained boy as a twisted form of punishment for sparing Marcus.

I will not stoop that low.

She pulled on a chainmail shirt and whatever plate armour was available to her, as well as a steel helm to protect her head, and grabbed a sword and shield on her way out to the waiting area. There had to be a way out of this without spilling blood. She was going to find it.

Somewhere in the back of her mind, she registered Royce Hargrave announcing their upcoming fight. She barely paid any attention.

There *was* a chance, she supposed, that the crowd would decide to spare Edd. He was one of the favourites, after all, and they'd likely want to see more of him in the arena. But she also knew that Hargrave could order a fighter to go for a kill if he so desired. The crowd's pleas might not be enough to save Edd then.

The portcullis gate opened before her, and she knew she was out of time. Talin tightened her grip on her sword and strode out to the approving roars of the crowd. Opposite her, another gate opened, revealing Edd, outfitted in plate and mail and wielding an axe in each hand.

Gods, he's too young.

"We don't have to kill each other!" she called. "The crowd only came for a fight. Let's give them one."

"I don't know, I think we do," Edd said. "That's what this arena was built for."

"It doesn't have to be like that." Talin kept her shield raised as they neared each other, ready to block whatever attack he threw.

"Stop talking and *fight.*" Edd lunged at her with a swing. Talin stepped back and blocked. The boy's axe skittered off her shield harmlessly. As expected, he didn't follow up with another strike as a trained fighter might do, opting instead to dance back again and continue circling her.

"Please don't make me do this," she said.

"If you won't fight me, I'll just have to kill you." Edd twirled his axes and swung at her again. She blocked both strikes and saw an opening for an easy kill—and shoved him back with her shield before he could expose himself a second time.

Killing him would be so easy. Frighteningly so.

She parried another strike and countered with a slash to his left arm, forcing him to drop an axe with a hiss of pain. Blood splashed onto the arena sands.

"I don't want to kill you, Edd," Talin said.

"It's either you or me, Raia," Edd called back. "Kill or be killed. If you're so adamant about not killing me, you're free to surrender. But that wouldn't be any fun."

Talin sidestepped a wild swing. A cut to the leg sent the boy staggering. He came at her again, but she was faster, knocking aside his weapon and shoving him back with her shield for the second time. Her blade was at his throat a moment later. He froze there, and she caught a glimpse of genuine terror in his eyes, as if he had only just now realised that his life was in true danger.

Reason and battle experience told her to finish him there and then and be done with this fight. Every inch of her conscience screamed at her to spare him.

She hesitated—perhaps foolishly so.

"What's the matter? Can't bear to take a fellow fighter's life?" Hargrave asked. Talin saw him move up to the announcer's stand out of the corner of her eye, looking as smug as ever. "Let me make this an easy choice for you. Young Edward! Kill your opponent, and I shall see to it that you're well-rewarded."

Edd, thankfully, was smart enough not to move.

"There is no glory to be found in this arena," Talin said. "Only death. The arena masters will demand everything from you, and when you've given all you have, they'll demand more still. We don't have to fight."

"They won't let us both walk out of here alive," Edd said.

"I'll figure something out," Talin said. She lowered her sword. "This is what I do. I think of solutions."

"You can't defeat the masters."

"We can make a stand *here*."

"I'm sorry."

"Don't—"

Edd raised his weapon to strike. Talin moved reflexively and parried. Countered with a riposte.

He dropped his axe and crumpled with a half-gasp, gurgling on his own blood, clutching his slit throat as if that might stop the bleeding. Talin looked away when she saw the fear and sheer panic in his eyes. Blood splashed onto the arena sands, pooling around them both.

"I'm sorry it had to come to this," she said softly. Above them, in the announcer's stand, she saw Hargrave smile, and wondered what kind of twisted person he had to be to *revel* in others' misery. She made a move for the portcullis gate with a knot in her stomach.

"Not so fast!" Hargrave called. "Seeing as that was such a short fight, I'm sure the crowd wants to see more! What do you all say?"

The crowd cheered, and Talin felt a sense of dread settle in her bones. Of course there would be more. Hargrave evidently intended to make an example of her.

Whatever the case, I have to survive this first.

The portcullis gate opened, and two mercenaries strode out to face her. One wielded a sword and dagger while the other, the taller of the two, held a two-handed Highlander broadsword. Both were heavily armoured. There would be no chance for her to go for any crippling strikes here—only kills.

Another deliberate move on Hargrave's part, no doubt.

Talin parried a swing from the dual-wielder and slipped around the taller fighter, aiming directly for the armour gap around his neck. She beat his parry but missed her mark; the tip of her blade hit his gorget and glanced off harmlessly. He stepped back and swung his sword at her neck. She raised her shield just in time to block, sidestepping the dual-wielder's blow at the same time. Her second riposte found its mark under the taller fighter's arm and dropped him instantly. The crowd gave a roar of approval.

The remaining mercenary backed up a few steps, evidently more cautious now, but it made no difference to Talin. She bided her time instead, watching his movements, committing his attacks to memory as she defended each strike.

Feint. Parry and counter.

Her opponent feinted to the right exactly as she'd expected. She parried his attack from the left without skipping a beat and slit his throat before he could make another move. Blood splattered onto the armour she was wearing and sprayed across the arena sands. He fell with a choked gurgle.

There was a moment of tense silence before the crowd erupted.

Talin had never seen them in such an excited state; even the victory celebrations at Belanore seemed to pale in comparison to the cacophony unfolding around her now. She thought she heard her name being chanted amidst the yells of approval and cheering.

"I'm done here!" she yelled up at Hargrave. The crowd seemed to quieten. "I've fought an extra fight I wasn't informed of. Surely the arena's ringmaster understands that it would not be fair to pit a fatigued fighter against a third wave of opponents."

Hargrave pursed his lips, but they both knew she had won the crowd over—a third consecutive wave would only work against her, and with little promise of new entertainment.

"Naturally," the arena master finally said, putting on a forced smile that looked far too strained to be natural. "Give it up for our new up-and-coming champion of the arena, Raia of Belanore!"

The gate finally opened for her. She spared no time getting herself out of the arena.

Back in the armoury, she stripped her armour and made a beeline for the women's quarters, trying to calm her breathing. There was blood on her hands and face. She was acutely aware that some of it had also stained her clothes.

So much bloodshed, and for what?

She hated this feeling of clarity after a battle, once the blood-lust had worn off and realisation hit.

I killed Edd. I killed those two mercenaries. The sight of the boy's fearful gaze as he crumpled was burned into her memory. Talin squeezed her eyes shut, trying to purge the image from her mind, but it was all she could see.

She found a rag and set about aggressively scrubbing the blood off her skin.

Aelia found her eventually, slumped against the wall in the washroom an hour later, with the bloodied rag clutched in her hands. She barely had any recollection of what she was doing with it, but the Drakel woman took it from her and set it aside before taking a seat next to her.

"The arenas should never have shut," Aelia said. "Keeping them open, under heavy regulation...that might have discouraged these illegal fights."

"It's my fault, then." Talin huffed a humourless laugh. "What a cruel twist of fate that I should suffer the consequences in such a way."

"It's *not* your fault. I...I'm sorry, I didn't mean it like that. People were clamouring for the arenas to be shut down. Blackrun had been begging you to do something about it," Aelia said. "I think if you'd been given...enough time...you would have figured out a better solution."

"It wasn't time I needed," Talin said. "I needed..." Her voice broke there, and she had to fight to hold back a sob. "I *need* someone who truly sees me as an equal, who could look me in the eye and tell me honestly that I'm doing something *right*."

Someone like Red Wolf, was the unspoken sentence.

"I know." Aelia fell silent.

"Is it wrong to want validation?" Talin asked after a pause.

"No," Aelia said. "I think we all need it from time to time. Especially someone in your position. People are so quick to criticise authority over the smallest of mistakes that they lose sight of the good things. You've done good work. Don't forget that."

"Thank you," Talin said softly.

The two of them sat in silence for a few moments longer before the Drakel climbed to her feet and stretched a hand down. Talin allowed herself to be helped to her feet.

"We should meet up with Icari," Aelia said. "It's about time we discussed the next step of our plan. Should help keep your mind off things, at least."

They found the sponsored fighter losing to Marcus at Tavern Cards, and she quickly excused herself to join them. Marcus looked smug as he collected his winnings from her—a shiny dagger and a pair of archery gloves probably given out by her sponsor.

"Not keen on another round?" he called after them. "Who knows, you might win your stuff back!"

Icari ignored him as they made their way back to the women's quarters.

"How have things been going with recruitment?" she asked.

"You were right," Talin said. "Almost all of the abducted fighters have agreed to join us. I think we should shift our attention to recruiting some of the sponsored fighters, too. They tend to be more skilled in combat than the abducted fighters and should hopefully give us an edge."

"I'd be careful if you plan on that," Icari said. "There's been a rumour going around that one of the arena masters has been sponsoring fighters personally."

"I thought the masters weren't supposed to sponsor fighters," Talin said.

"They're not. But they know we can't do anything about it," Icari said. "Even if us fighters found out, it's not like we can get solid proof. The ones they're sponsoring certainly aren't going to fess up and lose all their privileges."

"Surely the information would lead to further dissent if it was to spread..." Aelia frowned.

"Yes. Which is why they're trying to keep it under wraps."

Talin began to pace. "Icari, you know some of the sponsored fighters, yes?"

"Of course."

"Can I count on you to try and recruit them?"

Icari lifted her eyebrows. "What are you planning?"

"I'm going to find out which arena master is sponsoring fighters," Talin said, "and I'm going to expose them. In front of the crowd."

XXX

The camp was still awake when they returned in the late hours of the evening, well past sundown and close to the soldiers' usual bedtime. Judging from the individual campfires still dotted around the site, though, Red Wolf figured that they were still enjoying their downtime.

He was glad to be returning, in a way; after a week's travel, it felt good to settle into a military setting, where he felt most comfortable, and recuperate. The four of them dismounted and led their horses through the camp on foot.

"Your plan's already working," Golmin remarked as they walked, passing soldiers still chatting by the warm glow of their campfires. "Folks in Rivenfort were talking about an increased number of kidnappings when we passed through. I only hope the people being taken can survive the arena long enough to be rescued."

They stopped in front of the command tent to find the lamps still lit within. No doubt Hurst was still going over the information they'd gathered.

"I'll let the good captain know we've returned," Red Wolf said. "The rest of you should get some sleep. Say hello to Arkiel for me, if he's still awake."

"I'll come with you," Golmin said. "It'll be good to go over what we know so far."

The two of them handed their horses' reins to Ashera and Ettrias and ducked inside.

"...after that, I'm afraid I'm a little fuzzy on the details," a man was saying. He was a well-dressed, portly fellow, with greying hair and the most well-groomed moustache that Red Wolf had ever seen, shooting outward in both directions before curling up in a neat circle at the ends. Standing opposite him was Captain Hurst. Both men were hunched over the map table.

"Captain. M'lord." Red Wolf dipped his head.

"Oh, no, I'm no lord," the portly man chuckled. He had a high-pitched laugh that sounded a little like a teakettle. "I wish I was. Alexander Teller. You two must be Red Wolf and Captain Golmin."

Red Wolf shook his hand. "An honour to meet you. What brings you here?"

"This letter." Hurst tapped an unfolded piece of parchment on the table. Red Wolf recognised Talin's handwriting immediately.

"What's this?" he asked quietly.

"I'm not sure. I can't read it." Hurst shrugged. "Mister Teller here claims it came from the arenas, where he's been sponsoring a fighter but grew dissatisfied with how they operate. He's working with the fighter now to bring it all down."

"This is Talin's hand." Red Wolf picked up the message and pulled Hurst's inkwell towards him. Her code was written in the same cipher as the letter attached to his return papers, and he'd been able to decode that with his knowledge of Old Torrian. Unscrambling this note was child's play in comparison. He turned the parchment once he was done so that it faced the captain again.

"Mercenaries? Guarding the gate..." Hurst's brow creased. "Are the arenas guarded by mercenaries?"

"I wouldn't know, but if this message says so, then it must be true," Teller said. "I received it from my fighter who told me she was working with two others—a southerner and a Drakel."

"Talin and Aelia," Golmin said.

Red Wolf began to pace. "They say it took them less than a day to get to the arena from wherever they were captured. That makes sense based on what we know about the sedative used. They couldn't have been unconscious for more than a few hours. If they moved through Rivenfort on their way to the arena..."

"Do we have anything more on the thugs' movements?" Golmin asked.

"Here." Hurst beckoned for them both to come to the other side of the table. They crowded around him, and the cavalry captain pointed at several red circles drawn on the map. One of the circles had a line mapped out from it, stopping abruptly in a forested area east of Castle Blackrun.

"The thugs struck again in these areas," Hurst said. "Much closer to Castle Blackrun. You were right. They moved west instead of east after abducting one group, and we lost them in the forest when we tried to track them."

"That's awfully close to Castle Blackrun," Red Wolf said.

"Aye, Blackrun's land ends here, right next to the path."

"Mister Teller, do you know anything of the arena's whereabouts?" Red Wolf asked.

Teller shook his head. "Not much, I'm afraid. We're always taken to the arena via privately organised transports and are never allowed to look at our surroundings until we arrive. All I know is that the majority of the arena is underground, and that they take captured fighters into it by wagon."

Golmin's brow furrowed. "May I?" He gestured towards the inkwell and map. Hurst gave a nod, and he began scribbling on the map, marking out seemingly random lines between the camp, Rivenfort, and the locations of the most recent reported kidnappings.

"They're here." He drew a circle around a small, open field, at the northern edge of the forest.

Hurst let out a long breath. "You're sure?"

"Almost certain," Golmin said.

"I can vouch for him," Red Wolf said.

"Very well." Hurst straightened. "We will move out in the morning and overpower the mercenaries. My troops should be familiar with the signal, but just in case there are some who are confused: are either of you able to teach it to the men?"

"Ettrias can," Golmin said.

"Good. We'll put him in charge of my rookies tomorrow. For now, get some rest," Hurst said. "And you, Mister Teller. Your aid will not be forgotten. Come to Castle Blackrun when all this is over, and you shall be rewarded."

"Thank you, captain," Teller said. "Though I didn't do it for the reward. Seeing the arena brought down was my only goal."

"We will reconvene in the morning, then," Red Wolf said. "Good-night, captain."

"Likewise, sir."

Red Wolf ducked out of the tent and returned to his bed, Golmin trailing behind. Inside, Ettrias had evidently fallen asleep already, though he could hear from Arkiel's breathing that the boy was still awake. Golmin dropped his pack by his own bed and collapsed into it without another word.

"Can't sleep?" Red Wolf asked softly.

Arkiel rolled over slowly to look at him. "How'd you know?"

"A wolf senses many things." Red Wolf dropped his pack on his bed. "Do you want to talk?"

"I just miss Mother," Arkiel mumbled. "I missed you guys, too. The soldiers were nice, but it would have been nicer to travel with you all."

"We must leave again in the morning," Red Wolf said. "A man came to the camp earlier today with a message from your mother. We know where she is, and we will go tomorrow to free her. You must stay here."

"I don't want to stay," Arkiel protested. "I want to be there when you find Mother."

"I know. You'll be able to see her when we return to camp," Red Wolf said. "Where we are going tomorrow is highly dangerous. If something were to happen to you there, your mother would never forgive me."

Arkiel sighed. "Very well. But you have to bring her right back. Promise?"

"I promise." Red Wolf smiled. "Now, get some rest. You don't want to be tired tomorrow when you see her, do you?"

"I guess not." Arkiel yawned. "Will you...sit here for a little while? Just until I fall asleep?"

Red Wolf hesitated. He was a monster, a failed experiment—he had no business comforting a child who never knew war or suffering.

And yet...

He needs someone right now. Give him what you never received, a voice in his head told him.

"Alright," he said, taking a seat on the bed. "Is there anything else you need?"

"If it's not too much trouble...a story would be nice," Arkiel said.

"A story." Red Wolf frowned. "What kind of story?"

"I don't know. Something happy."

Red Wolf regaled the boy with a few tales of his time as lord commander, well before the trial and his exile. Most were about the antics his guards got up to, though he also threw in a story about Ettrias and Talin when they were children. Arkiel had drifted off by the time he finished his fourth story, so he carefully moved the boy into a more comfortable position and covered him with the blanket.

He's like you, when you were a boy. Before...

"Goodnight, Arkiel," he said softly and banished the thoughts from his mind.

XXXI

T alin supposed she shouldn't have been surprised that they would put her in another fight the following day.

This morning, for once, she had arrived at the lists early enough to get a good look before all the fighters started crowding in, and her heart had immediately sunk at seeing her name in neat, cursive writing near the top. Icari was her teammate for this fight, which was a relief, but they had been pitted against half a dozen new initiates—no doubt more innocents abducted and forced to fight in the arena.

"Oh, ouch, that's not a fun one." Icari appeared beside her. "That gods-forsaken *abiyo*. He knows you and I would wipe the arena floor with those initiates. I suspect it's another case of the abducted fighters being used as cannon fodder to make us look good."

Talin was suspicious. Icari was a sponsored fighter, true, but she was not, and should be as disposable as the rest of them. Yesterday's fight against Edd had been calculated—the boy would never have beaten her, but he was talented enough that he wasn't being offered up as a sacrifice for entertainment's sake. Hargrave had wanted her to fight for her life. These abducted fighters were an easy win for her and Icari with minimal struggle, especially if she was able to get her hands on a bow in the armoury before the fight.

Hargrave didn't want to teach her another lesson here. He was up to something else.

"Whatever the case, we still have to fight," she told Icari. "See if you can't claim a light bow for me. I might have a plan."

"I'll do my best," the fighter said.

The two of them were called into the armoury an hour later to prepare for their fight, and Icari immediately went for the recurve bow laying in the corner with its quiver of arrows. Talin picked up a chain-mail shirt and arming sword for a backup melee weapon. She picked out a pair of shortswords for Icari, too, knowing that the Highlander woman favoured dual-wielding. They struggled into their armour and buckled their weapons in the waiting area.

"What's the plan, then?" Icari asked as Hargrave announced their fight.

"You be a menace up close," Talin said. "I go for non-lethal crippling shots. We might get lucky again, and Hargrave will let me spare at least one fighter. Besides, I'm told I've been getting quite popular with the crowd. Maybe they enjoy my...less violent approach."

Icari snorted. "Good luck out there."

"You too."

The portcullis creaked open before them, and they strode out to the sight of half a dozen terrified civilians wielding a mismatched assortment of weapons. One man had the good sense to put on some chainmail; Talin doubted the rest even knew how to get the armour on properly. Another man near the back of the group held a bow in his hands.

Talin sent her first arrow into his shoulder without hesitation.

The man dropped with a scream and nobody else moved to pick up his weapon, letting her know immediately that she'd taken out their only source of ranged attack. Her fingers itched to draw a handful of arrows and loose them all in quick succession, but she held her ground instead and let Icari approach. The dark-skinned fighter approached her first challenger and danced around the man's spear easily, keeping the group's attention fixed on her. Talin sent her second arrow into the spear wielder's thigh.

Just get rid of them all, part of her subconscious thought. Reason dictated that she should finish this battle as quickly as possible, to drop the remaining fighters with well-placed arrows to the joints or limbs. It would be so *easy*.

But perhaps part of her was hesitant to even maim. And perhaps she was foolish to drag this out.

The fighter with the chainmail came forwards, flanked by the rest of the group, trying to surround Icari. She parried their strikes and stayed on her feet, moving away, refusing to let them box her in.

Talin should have known it wouldn't last forever.

The chainmail fighter landed a solid strike against Icari's arm with his sword—making her drop one of her blades. And Talin realised that she couldn't afford to hesitate any longer.

Her next arrow found its mark in the chainmail fighter's knee. Her fourth shot was in the air by the time he hit the ground. Icari had barely reacted to him falling when the woman beside him also dropped. Her final two shots found their marks so quickly that the two remaining fighters seemed to drop at the same time.

The crowd erupted for her once again.

Talin hardly paid any attention to the ensuing chaos; her attention was fixed on the fighters she'd spared, writing on the ground in pain. Was it truly an act of mercy to cripple them like this? She looked at Icari, who examined her bleeding arm momentarily before picking her fallen sword back up. The fighter seemed to be looking at the gate opposite them.

"We're done here!" Talin yelled up at Hargrave. "We're sparing these fighters. Let us go."

"Oh, but I wager our dear spectators haven't had enough yet!" the arena master said. The crowd roared in agreement. "What do you say, Raia and Icari? Shall we pit you against another wave to show off those *spectacular* archery skills?"

"My fellow fighter is injured," Talin simply said, quietening the arena in an instant. "She'd be a liability in any upcoming fights—not to mention we haven't been informed of what kinds of enemies we'd be facing. There's no telling whether our current weapons and equipment will be sufficient."

Hargrave offered her one of his strained smiles. "Naturally. Give it up for our fighters of the day, Raia and Icari!"

Talin strode out of the arena without a second glance.

In the equipment drop-off area, she tossed her bow and sword and stripped off her armour as fast as she could, throwing the bow in particular with a little more force than necessary. Icari put a hand on her shoulder.

"You spared them. We did good today."

"I probably crippled them for life. I'm not sure that's much of an alternative," she said bitterly.

"Better than dying."

"I guess time will tell."

She had her supper with Icari and Aelia as usual that evening, seated in a corner table to avoid some of the fighters' glances and as close to the wall as possible to discourage anyone from approaching. She saw the six wounded fighters from today hobbling in together as the evening dragged on. They looked around the mess hall, saw her, and sat as far away as they could. None of them acknowledged her.

"Wow, cold," Aelia said, following her gaze and noticing the fighters. "At least Marcus was grateful."

"Marcus knew the risks of the arena." Talin turned her attention back to her food. "He knew what he was getting into. These fighters didn't. Why should they be grateful to an opponent who maimed them?"

The three of them continued eating in silence. One of the arena masters swept through the mess hall a few minutes later, long coattails flapping behind him, eyes darting around the room before landing on Talin. He changed direction and strode towards their table purposefully.

This cannot be good news, she thought.

"You," he said, pointing at her. "Royce Hargrave wants to talk."

"I'm eating supper," Talin said coolly.

"Don't make me say it twice," the arena master said.

Seeing no point in resisting, Talin swallowed one more bite of stew and pushed herself to her feet. She followed the master from the mess hall and down the maze of corridors.

"Why does Royce Hargrave of all people want to talk to me, then?" she asked.

"Quiet," the master snapped.

"Friendly," Talin muttered but didn't press the matter further. There was nothing to be gained from prodding the man for answers, other than to antagonise him further.

The two of them made their way past the armoury and down a flight of stairs, moving deeper and deeper into a section of the arena she had never seen before. She concentrated on memorising the route. The master led her past a closed trapdoor and up to a door at the far end of the hallway and gestured for her to enter. She stepped inside hesitantly.

The room she found herself in was something like an office, with a simple, wooden desk in the centre stacked with papers. Shelves lined the walls on either side of her, filled with scrolls and books. Hargrave himself sat behind the desk with a glass of wine in hand.

"Evening, Raia," he said, motioning for her to sit. "Drink?"

"As long as it's not poisoned." Talin slid into the chair opposite him.

"Not at all. In fact, I have a proposal for you." Hargrave poured a second glass for her.

"A proposal for me?" Talin asked.

"Yes. You've become quite popular with the crowd, as you saw the other day," Hargrave said. "Much as I...dislike what you did in your first fight of the arena, I am willing to forgive and forget."

But there's a catch. She didn't need him to say it.

"And in return?" she asked.

"You take on a sponsorship."

"A sponsorship? With whom?"

Hargrave laced his fingers together. "With me."

Of course it's him.

It made sense all of a sudden, why he'd given her such an easy fight, why he hadn't objected when she told him that she would be sparing her opponents. It had been a gesture of his goodwill and a taste of what he could offer her. And, gods, she should have seen it coming; Hargrave was exactly the kind of person who would flaunt his own arena's rules simply because he was in charge. That he wanted to offer her a sponsorship was no surprise—it would let him keep a better eye on her, and she would be obliged to stay in his good graces to receive easier fights and better equipment. She wondered how many other fighters he was sponsoring.

"I was under the impression that arena masters weren't supposed to sponsor fighters," she said.

"Ostensibly, yes," Hargrave said, flashing her an easy smile. "We don't want our clients to feel as if their favourite fighters are already taken, after all. But behind the scenes..."

"If I say no?" Talin asked.

Hargrave huffed a half-laugh. "I thought you might be stubborn. Think about it, Raia. Agree to this, and I can make it so that you never have a difficult fight in your life. You will have all the equipment you could ever need to achieve glory in the arena. I could make it so that you don't have to *kill*."

It was, much as she hated to admit, a tempting offer.

"There's a catch, isn't there?" she asked. "I know someone like you would never offer me such an easy way out."

"Well, all you need to do is answer to me," Hargrave said. "I may have...additional tasks for you to complete, but it would not be without reward."

Answer to Hargrave. Of course. Talin had no doubt that he would force her to do some questionable things to keep her sponsorship, with severe consequences if she refused. It wasn't a risk she could take.

"I'm sorry," she said. "But I must decline."

Hargrave pursed his lips. "Very well, Mister Yonik outside will show you back to the fighters' quarters. Though I think you're making a big mistake."

"I know exactly what I'm doing," Talin said. She finished her wine and stood. "Thank you. For the drink."

She could almost feel Hargrave's glare burning into the back of her neck as she left the office.

Back in the women's quarters, she relayed the details of her conversation with Hargrave to Aelia and Icari, adding that she doubted her refusal would come without some kind of retaliation. The Highlander woman scoffed at the news.

"I should have known. That damn *snake*." She scowled. "Any idea who he's sponsoring?"

"He didn't drop any hints," Talin said. "But I think we ought to be careful. Forget recruiting the sponsored fighters—it's too risky. If one of them informs *Hargrave* of what we're planning, this whole operation falls apart. Best if we keep a low profile until we're ready to strike."

"I had a meeting with my sponsor just after you were escorted out," Icari said. "He says he was able to deliver your letter successfully. Didn't see your brother, but there *was* someone there who could decipher your message. A certain...ex-bodyguard of yours, I believe."

Talin felt as if all the air had been knocked from her lungs. She sat down on the edge of her bed heavily.

He found the others? Or perhaps they found him? The news sounded almost unreal.

"Blackrun's men will be here by midday tomorrow," Icari continued. "But you refused Hargrave…"

"I know." Talin forced herself to focus on the situation at hand. "We have to go ahead with the plan as soon as possible. If we can time a riot or takeover with the arrival of Blackrun's men, it would be the perfect diversion."

"There's word that you're being pitted against another sponsored fighter tomorrow, Raia," Icari said. "That might be your chance to reveal to the crowd that Hargrave has been sponsoring fighters—and kick off the whole rebellion."

Talin nodded. "Tomorrow, then. We'll finalise the plan at breakfast."

XXXII

Talin woke early that morning for no particular reason. In the dim torchlight of the women's quarters, she could see that most of the other fighters were still asleep. Some had risen already and made their way to the mess hall to eat, likely so they could be the first ones to the lists when they came out. Talin decided to do the same. She slipped on her boots and slipped into the mess hall quietly to eat.

"Don't usually see you up at this hour."

Talin looked up to see Marcus slide into the seat opposite hers with a tray of food.

"I woke early," she said.

"How's the arm?" Marcus asked.

"It was only bruised, so I'll be fine. So long as nobody hits it with a flail again," Talin said.

Marcus snorted. "I'll try to refrain."

"How's the shoulder?"

"Better. So long as nobody drives another spear into it."

The two of them fell silent while they ate.

"Word's been going around," Marcus said after a little while. "You should be careful here. The masters could be listening to everything."

"I don't know what you mean," Talin said.

"I know you plan to rebel against the masters." Marcus took a bite of his bread. "And I would advise against it. The mercenaries outside will kill us all if they have to."

"I know some people on the outside who might be able to stop them," Talin explained. "If all goes well, we won't need to worry about the mercenaries at all."

Hopefully, anyway. She decided not to mention that they were risking everything on a gamble that Captain Hurst and his soldiers would arrive in the midst of their rebellion and deal with the mercenaries before they could come to quell her insurrection.

"That so?" Marcus' eyebrows shot up. "Well, either way, I have news."

"Concerning me? I'm flattered," Talin said.

"I'm sure you've heard by now that you'll be up against a sponsored fighter today," Marcus said. "That fighter is me."

"How do you know?" Talin asked.

Marcus hesitated there as if contemplating how much he should reveal, but then he heaved a sigh and lowered his spoon. "*Hargrave* is my sponsor."

It all made sense all of a sudden, why Marcus was given such an easy fight on her first day and not given any subsequent fights during his recovery, why he always possessed equipment and personal effects that none of the other fighters could seem to get their hands on. Talin cursed herself for not connecting the dots immediately.

"I'm guessing this is to be a fight to the death," she said.

"Look, I still owe you for sparing me. I'll refuse to fight," Marcus said. "Hargrave won't be happy, but I think I can cause enough of a scene for the rest of your lackeys to do what they need to do. The only catch is that we must act today, or one of us isn't leaving the arena, and as much as I respect what you did for me, I'd like to remain alive."

"I already know Hargrave's been sponsoring a fighter," Talin said. "And if you really feel like you owe me, why not help me and the fighters rebel?"

"What's your plan, then?"

"I want to expose Hargrave in front of the entire crowd."

"Heh." Marcus looked impressed. "I'll admit, the thought has crossed my mind. We can both refuse to fight—it should be enough of a disruption to the usual proceedings that you can say your piece before Hargrave cooks up something to stop us."

"Fine. How will we get the arena gates open so we can escape without killing each other?" she asked.

"Your lackeys could deal with that, I'm sure," Marcus said.

The two of them had finalised their plan by the time Aelia and Icari showed themselves into the mess hall. They joined her and Marcus at the table, and she quickly explained what they intended to do.

"I can probably get to one of the gate mechanisms once the fighting starts," Icari said. "I know the place well, but the two of you will have to be fast. I can't guarantee that I can keep the gate open. Position yourselves close to the usual exit."

"We will," Talin promised. "Aelia, can you start the riot?"

"Count on it," the Drakel said.

"And you two? How are you planning on drawing the masters' attention?" Icari asked.

"Leave that to us, Valaia." Marcus stood. "Now, we need to go make a show of acting all surprised when the lists come out. If I know Hargrave, he's not going to make it easy for either of us to refuse to fight."

The lists went up in the recreation room a few minutes later, and Talin saw Marcus and most of the other fighters leave to check. She made a show of continuing to chat with Icari and Aelia, asking them about their hometowns and how they ended up in the arena.

"You!" Marcus strode back into the mess hall. "Raia, was it? Have you seen the lists?"

"No..." Talin lifted a brow and pretended to act surprised in front of the thugs guarding the mess hall. "What's the matter?"

"We've been pitted against each other again," Marcus said. "Fight to the death."

Talin glanced around to see if they'd caught anyone's attention and found all the thugs staring at them. *Good. That should give Aelia and Icari enough opportunity to slip out unnoticed.* "You're not counting on me sparing you this time, are you?"

Marcus scoffed. "I'm not losing to you again. Now hurry up. We're the first fight." He strode off again without another word. Talin looked at the thugs who'd been staring at them, and they quickly averted their eyes. No alarm had been raised. Aelia and Icari were nowhere to be seen

So far, so good. Talin stood and followed Marcus from the mess hall, where they split up to their respective gates on opposite sides of the arena. In the armoury, she ignored the chainmail and steel plate, figuring that she could make more of a statement by refusing to even wear armour, and settled for a one-handed Highlander arming sword instead. She strode into the waiting area without hesitation.

On the other side of the portcullis, she heard Hargrave begin his usual spiel, thanking the crowd for gathering and promising excitement and bloodshed today before announcing their fight. Talin tightened her grip around her sword and strode out to meet Marcus.

He had dressed similarly to her for the fight, wearing the same tunic and trousers he'd worn in the mess hall, wielding nothing but his spiked flail and a small shield. She allowed herself a brief smile at the idea of sitting in the crowd and seeing two fighters entering the ring bristling with sharp and pointy weapons, completely unarmoured.

"Everything's in position?" Marcus asked as they circled each other, just out of reach of their respective weapons.

"Aelia has the fighters ready to move at a moment's notice," Talin said. "Icari should be in position soon."

"Good." Marcus threw down his flail and stepped away. Whispers started in the crowd almost immediately. Talin fought to keep her weapon directed at him now that he was unarmed.

"This fighter spared my life in our last duel," Marcus said. "The crowd decided my fate, yet she chose not to kill me." He looked directly at Talin, warning her to keep up the act for now. "So, you may ask, why are we here today? The masters of this arena have decided that to repay this kindness shown to me, I must kill her in order to walk out of here alive. I cannot do this. My fellow fighter, you may do as you wish. But I refuse to fight."

The whispers in the crowd rose to a shout. Some booed and demanded to see a fight, while others directed their outrage at the arena masters and at Hargrave. Talin dropped her own weapon and stepped away as well.

"I have no intention of killing for your entertainment," she said. "And I will not try to kill an unarmed man." She turned her attention to the crowd. "I must thank you all, too, for gathering today. I believe it's time for some confessions."

"Those of you who have watched the fights for some time will know that I'm a sponsored fighter," Marcus said. "But my sponsor is not in the crowd today. In fact, my sponsor has broken one of the few *rules* in this lawless arena—by sponsoring me as an arena master."

Talin looked up at the announcer's stand just in time to see Hargrave's face twist into an expression of rage.

"My sponsor...is none other than Royce Hargrave," Marcus finished.

The crowd erupted again. Most had now taken their side, cursing Hargrave, demanding an explanation from him. Talin watched as the man stepped forward to address the accusations.

"Peace, everyone!" he yelled. "Please. Let us maintain some level of civility in the audience. Fighter Marcus, you make a serious accusation against me, one upon which you have no basis. I'm afraid I must silence these accusations by swearing, upon my life, that I have *never* sponsored a fighter nor ever offered any sponsorship to a fighter."

Oh, this is perfect. Talin might have laughed if the situation was any less dire; he had opened himself up completely to her retaliation.

"That's not true!" she said. "Royce Hargrave offered to sponsor *me* just yesterday. We had quite the productive chat in his office. I turned him down."

The crowd was in uproar now, with most patrons on their feet, cursing Hargrave for his hypocrisy. Nobody paid any attention to her and Marcus, still in the arena. Mercenaries streamed onto the stands to try and pacify them.

"I think that did the trick," Marcus said. "Let's go."

The two of them turned to leave...only to find that the gate was still closed.

"*Touvir*, where's Icari?" Marcus hissed. "She better not have betrayed you..."

"No, she must have run into some trouble..." Talin turned her attention to the opposite side of the arena as another gate opened, and a dozen mercenaries spilled out to meet them.

Hargrave's orders, no doubt. It was clear enough that the arena master had no intention of letting them leave alive.

"Marcus..." she called. Her fellow fighter turned and followed her gaze as the mercenaries advanced.

"Well, that's a problem."

"Really, I hadn't noticed."

"Got a plan?" Marcus asked.

Talin looked around frantically. There were no other weapons in the arena save for the ones they had brought, and the mercenaries all wore chainmail and steel plate. Marcus may be able to deal with a few if he clocked them in the head hard enough, but this was a near-unwinnable fight.

No, wait.

One of the mercenaries at the back carried a bow and quiver of arrows and wore only chainmail and a light helm. If she could get hold of his weapon...

"Marcus, the archer at the back," she hissed. "I need that bow."

"Keep the others off me." Marcus snatched up his equipment and kicked up a cloud of dust to blind the mercenaries before sprinting for the archer. Talin grabbed her sword and managed to straighten just in time to parry an incoming strike. She sidestepped another swing, trying to keep her distance with the mercenaries while bringing herself closer to Marcus and the archer. She saw him block two arrows with his shield as he drew closer. The archer dropped his bow and drew a sword.

That's my chance.

Talin dropped into a roll as one of the other mercenaries swung at her, bringing herself next to the archer and abandoned bow. She drove her sword into the man's neck before he could turn and grabbed his weapon and a handful of arrows. She loosed all six shots within a few seconds and dropped six mercenaries. Marcus barrelled into the nearest and clocked him in the side of the head with his flail, giving her time to grab more ammunition. She freed another four shots. The remaining mercenaries fell.

"Good shooting," Marcus said.

But they didn't have much time to celebrate. More mercenaries were pouring out of the gate, this time clad in full plate and wielding heavy kite shields. Talin knew from experience that they would be practically arrow-proof.

"Hargrave, you gods-forsaken *abiyo*..." Marcus growled. "There's no way you'll take these mercenaries with your bow, Raia."

But Talin was barely paying attention. She could hear shouting from beyond the gate. Behind the new group of mercenaries, as the portcullis slammed back down, she saw fighters storm the armoury and snatch up weapons, making short work of the guards there.

"I think it's time to go," she said. Marcus quickly understood.

"The gate's still not open yet."

"Then we need to buy some more time."

The two of them backed towards the exit gate slowly as the mercenaries advanced. Talin grabbed the quiver from the fallen archer and quickly tied it to her belt.

"Let's...talk about this?" she tried.

"Really? You want to *talk* to them?" Marcus hissed. The mercenaries inched forward slowly, no doubt cautious of what they were capable of after seeing how quickly they dispatched the first group.

"It was worth a shot."

"We're going to die," Marcus muttered under his breath.

The gate behind them creaked open. They darted through immediately, and Icari quickly dropped it shut again, sealing the mercenaries in the arena. She lifted the inner portcullis and let them into the equipment drop-off area before moving away from the winch to greet them.

"Good timing," Marcus said. He looked down at one of the dead mercenaries by the gate mechanism and prodded him with a foot. "You were busy."

"It was a close fight," Icari said.

"Go find the other fighters. Help if you can," Talin said. "I'll track down Hargrave and prevent him from escaping."

"We'll meet outside, then?" Marcus asked.

"Outside." Talin gave a brief nod and moved off in the opposite direction.

The stands were already half-empty by the time she reached them, with most of the spectators having no doubt been ushered out by mercenaries or fled. Hargrave was nowhere to be found, which wasn't much of a surprise, if she was honest with herself. Talin shot two guards who came to stop her and pushed past a small group of fighters on her way back down the stairs. If her suspicions were correct, Hargrave had fled the moment the fighting started and gone to hide in the lower levels. She continued down the maze of corridors.

"Talin!" Aelia's voice. She turned to see the Drakel jogging to catch up.

"I'm going to find Hargrave," she said. "Icari and Marcus should be headed outside. Go help if you can. We need to make sure the fighters don't turn on each other and that Blackrun's men don't mistake them for mercenaries."

"Talin, Lady Blackrun's people are right outside," Aelia said. "Forget Hargrave, they'll be able to find him, let's just..."

"I think he's gone into the lower levels," Talin said, remembering the trapdoor she saw yesterday. "He might have some kind of escape tunnel there. I can't let him get away."

Aelia sighed. "I understand. I'll let Lady Blackrun's men know where you've gone."

Talin continued on deeper into the lower levels. The fighters had swept through here, too; she saw bodies sprawled across the corridor and tried not to step on them. At the far end, she spied a familiar figure running towards an open hatch and loosed a warning shot that landed at his feet. Hargrave skidded to a halt.

"Going somewhere?" Talin asked, readying another arrow.

"You missed," Hargrave said.

If I'd missed, that arrow would have gone through your foot," Talin said. "I can't let you leave."

Hargrave raised his hands in surrender. "Well, I suppose I don't get a say in the matter."

"Here's what's going to happen. Blackrun's men will be here any minute to arrest you, and you'll go with them, no fuss. Until then, we're going to sit right here, you and I, and if you try to escape, I'll make sure you never walk again."

"Very well," Hargrave said. "Let's not get hasty there. I'll close this hatch if you drop the bow."

Talin didn't move.

"I'm not likely to try anything, am I? Look at me, I'm unarmed," Hargrave said.

"Go on, then." Talin nodded towards the hatch, and the arena master kicked it shut. She dropped the bow and put the arrow back in its quiver.

"That's better," Hargrave said and stepped a little closer. "Perhaps we could...make a deal? Say, something that benefits us both?"

"What do you have that could possibly interest me?" Talin asked.

"Well...I may know of...other arenas, like this one," Hargrave said. "And you could get all the credit for finding out where they are if you just let me go." He took another step closer.

"Other arenas?" Talin asked. She knew she couldn't let the man walk free after all he'd done, but the fact that he had this information might be of use to Blackrun's people, and she knew she might save the man from some torture if she could get him to reveal everything here. She approached cautiously.

"Yes, there are other arenas in the Highlands, just as well hidden as this one," Hargrave explained. "I could tell you exactly where they are and how to find them. If you let me go now, I'll...get access to the arenas and...act as an inside man."

"I'm thinking if I let you go, you'll just disappear, change your name, and vanish without a trace. Good try, but no." Talin scoffed. "I'm sure Blackrun will be interested in these 'other arenas', though. You can either tell me now, or I can let her people throw you into an interrogation room until you confess everything."

"Raia..." Marcus' voice. "Get away from him!"

Talin only caught a glimpse of steel before Hargrave stuck the knife into her gut.

There was a shout. Hargrave drove the knife into her again. She barely felt the second blow and the blow after that. Hargrave's form wavered in front of her, and then he gave a soft, muffled grunt and fell. Talin barely caught a glimpse of the blue-and-white arrow fletching before she too felt herself falling. Warmth seeped across the front of her tunic, and it hit her only then that she'd been stabbed.

"Get a healer!" a familiar voice shouted as her vision darkened. "Oh, gods. Talin, stay with me. Stay with me!"

She struggled to stay conscious. It was impossible.

Wait...I know that voice.

The last thing she saw before her vision faded completely was the sheer panic and shock behind a pair of golden eyes.

XXXIII

The group huddled outside in the middle of camp was silent.

Red Wolf sat with his back against a heavy crate, knees drawn up to his chest, staring at the drying blood still on his hands. Ettrias had attempted to strike up a conversation with Arkiel to no avail, and the two of them stood beside each other in awkward silence. Clouds had gathered overhead to block the sun. Ashera busied herself with oiling her sword and dagger. Aelia had stood with them for a time but was soon called away for debriefing, and the other two fighters, who had introduced themselves as Icari and Marcus, waited with them for the new
s.

"Now that I know who spared me, I'm less surprised," Marcus finally said, breaking the silence. "I should have…"

"No use thinking about what we should have done. Could have done." Red Wolf didn't look up.

"You sound like you're telling that to yourself more than me," Marcus said.

"Maybe."

Footsteps drew to a halt before him. A damp cloth was thrust into his hands.

"Clean yourself up," Golmin said. "You'll feel better, at the very least."

Red Wolf gingerly wiped his hands on the cloth. It quickly stained crimson. He didn't bother scrubbing off the more stubborn dried blood.

"It's not your fault," Golmin said after a beat.

"I bloody well know that," Red Wolf snapped. He gave a defeated slump of his shoulders. "I'm sorry. That was uncalled for."

"It's alright. I didn't take it personally." Golmin took the cloth from him again. "I'll rinse this and bring it back." He left without another word. Red Wolf went back to staring at his hands.

The healer ducked out of the tent a few minutes later, looking grim. Everyone turned in unison. Red Wolf jumped to his feet.

"She lives, for now," the healer said. "I fear her wounds are quite severe. I've done what I can for her, but she may not survive."

Red Wolf's jaw clenched.

"She was wearing this." The healer dropped a wolf necklace into his hand. He recognised it immediately. "It was...glowing...earlier, but stopped when I took it off. I thought you might want to have it." The man excused himself and left, leaving Red Wolf standing stock-still with the necklace in his hand.

She still wore it after all this time. Why was it glowing?

He looked at the necklace. The wolf's jewelled eyes stared back, and he saw that it had been smudged with blood. He must have touched it without realising back in the arena.

"Can I...go in?" Arkiel asked quietly. He sniffed and tried to put on a brave face.

"Go ahead, Ark," Ettrias said. "Do you want me to come?"

"Yes, please," the boy whispered. Ashera stood aside to let them through.

We were so close. But I failed her after all.

"Why would this glow?" Red Wolf muttered to himself. *And why now?* He closed a fist around the necklace and ducked into the tent.

Inside, aside from a small lamp, the tent was sparsely decorated. Talin lay on the single bed at the back, motionless, covered by a blanket from the shoulders down. Arkiel sat by the bed, crying quietly while Ettrias remained standing beside him, a hand on his shoulder.

"I...hope I'm not intruding..." he began.

"No, I think..." Ettrias glanced at him, then at Talin. "I think she would want you here. By her side."

Red Wolf drew in a shaky breath and exhaled. He came forwards and fastened the wolf necklace back around her neck.

"Mother never took that off, you know..." Arkiel sniffed and looked up. "Was it from you?"

"It was." Red Wolf positioned the necklace so that it rested directly in the middle of her chest. The jewelled eyes began to give off a faint, barely perceptible ruby glow. Talin stirred a little but didn't wake.

There's the glowing that healer was talking about. But why would it do that now...?

"You know, this...wasn't exactly the reunion I'd hoped for," he said softly, running a thumb across the dull metal. "I spent all these weeks thinking about how you might feel about seeing me again, wondering if you even *wanted* to see me..." His voice broke there, and he let the rest of his sentence trail off. If he said anything else now, he was likely going to fall apart.

"Red Wolf, the necklace," Ettrias said. Red Wolf looked at it again and saw that the glow had brightened a little. It flickered before dimming again. He looked at his hands and remembered that he still had some dried blood on them.

The Hellhounds told me there was magic in this necklace, but I was never able to figure it out.

Red Wolf ran a hand over his chin and touched the necklace again, and again it flickered before dimming. He put his free hand under Talin's nose and realised her breathing was now a little deeper.

The Hellhounds liked to experiment with blood as a magical component—it was artificial Hellhound blood, after all, that gave him his powers and curse. Perhaps this necklace was just another trinket left over from one of their failed experiments, only good for show. Red Wolf straightened and headed back outside. He needed to think.

Golmin found him a few minutes later, sitting by a creek not far from camp, picking up smooth, flat stones and skipping them across the water. The guard captain picked up a similar-looking stone and tossed it, and it made a little splash as it sank.

"Never could figure out how you do it," he said.

Red Wolf picked out another stone for him. "Throw it flat. Let it spin."

Golmin tried again, and this time the stone barely skimmed off the surface of the water before dropping at the next bounce.

"Something's on your mind," he said.

"I..." Red Wolf sighed. "I have a theory. It will sound absurd. But hear me out first."

"I'm listening," Golmin said.

"The necklace I gave to Talin has some sort of Hellhound magic imbued into it." Red Wolf skipped another stone. "I never figured out how to use it...until now. It first activated when I touched it without realising, back in the arena. I had her blood on my hands."

"You think it needs...more blood?" Golmin asked.

"No," Red Wolf said. "I put it back around her neck, and it activated again when I rubbed it. I still have blood on my hands. It's not about how much you need to sacrifice." He picked up another stone, looked at it, then tossed it into the creek unceremoniously. "I believe Talin's blood only worked at all because she's a Weaver. But the magic in this land is dying. Her magic isn't strong enough."

"Then where do you propose we find a Weaver who's stronger than her? You two could well be the last Weavers left in Kies Tor, and we don't have..." Golmin's voice trailed off. His eyes widened as realisation hit.

"We need the blood of a Hellhound," Red Wolf said, looking down at his hands. "My blood."

"The only way we're getting any of your blood is with a potent enough poison, and those are heavily regulated," Golmin said. "There's not a healer in the Highlands who can sell it to us. Most don't even *have* such poisons in stock."

"Torslek," Red Wolf said quietly. "There must be a supply of torslek at Castle Blackrun."

"The last time you were poisoned with torslek, you almost died," Golmin said.

"I know. I wasn't asking."

He turned away from the creek and strode back to camp, Golmin trailing behind, struggling to keep pace with him.

"She'd never let you do this on her account, you know it," the captain said. "You don't even know if your blood will *work*. This is only a theory—"

"Then I trust you won't let her know about it if it does work." Red Wolf made a sharp turn for the command tent. "Listen to me. It makes sense as a medical device, as a backup in case a Hellhound's powers fail. Given their rapid healing, they'll never activate the necklace unintentionally."

"You..." Golmin hissed through his teeth. "I'm riding with you to Castle Blackrun."

"I won't stop you," Red Wolf said. He ducked into the tent, hoping against the odds that Hurst was still debriefing Aelia.

The Drakel was nowhere to be found, but Hurst was still there, and Red Wolf decided someone else could let Aelia know where he intended to take Talin.

"Captain," he said. "How soon can we expect to reach Castle Blackrun?"

Hurst was still bent over his map and looked up abruptly. "Come again?"

"We need to get Queen Talin to Castle Blackrun," Red Wolf said. "Urgently. I..."

"I know," Hurst said. "But we'll never make it in time, you must understand. Even if we were to start packing this instant, it would take us near a week to reach the castle. I'm sorry."

"I don't intend to ride with the column," Red Wolf said.

Hurst sighed but gave a nod all the same. "I understand." He took a piece of parchment and dipped a pen into his inkwell, beginning to scribble out a note. "This is for the guards. Give it to them, they will let you through—"

"I need access to the torslek stash at Castle Blackrun," Red Wolf said.

Hurst paused with his pen hovering above the page. "The torslek stash...very well. I trust you, sir, but would appreciate it if I was told why." He continued scribbling.

"It may save her life," Red Wolf said. "She has a necklace, a gift from me. I believe it has magic that can only be activated with my blood."

"Ah. Of course," Hurst said. "Take care, Red Wolf. My men will begin the journey back tomorrow and meet you in a week." He sealed the message with wax and pressed his signature into it. Red Wolf took it with a nod of thanks and stashed it under his tunic.

"Rufus, saddle the horses, if you'll be so kind," he said. "Prepare a horse for Ashera and Ettrias too, should they want to come. Arkiel will ride with one of them."

Golmin nodded and muttered a quick 'aye' before disappearing from the tent. Red Wolf turned to follow.

"I don't often say this, sir, but...good luck," Hurst said.

Red Wolf dipped his head. "See you in a week."

He returned to Talin's tent to let Ettrias and Ashera know what was happening. Aelia had joined them outside by now, and she was busy explaining what Hurst had planned for Icari and Marcus. Red Wolf heard something about being granted accommodation at the castle if they chose to ride back that way with the column and something about compensation for what they'd suffered in the arena.

"I'm taking Talin to Castle Blackrun," he told them. "I would ask if you wished to ride with us, but I cannot afford to waste any time, and the three of you would not be able to keep up. Icari, Marcus, if you wish to join us at the castle, I shall see you there. If not, it was good to meet you both." He didn't mention what he intended to do; he doubted that they would understand.

"Likewise," Marcus said, shaking his hand. Icari did the same, and he left them to talk to Ashera and Ettrias inside the tent.

"Has anything happened?" he asked once he was inside.

"Not much," Ashera said. "Whatever magic that necklace has, it's...keeping her alive. For now."

"The necklace is activated with blood," Red Wolf said. "I'm taking her to Castle Blackrun. They have a stash of torslek there that will prevent me from healing so I can use my blood to activate it fully."

"Correct me if I'm wrong, but didn't you almost die the last time you were poisoned with torslek?" Ashera asked. "I might have been twelve years old, but I seem to recall that incident *perfectly* well."

"You can either ride with the column and meet us there in a week, or you can ride with Golmin and I," Red Wolf continued. "We'll only slow when the horses are tired. If you cannot keep up, you're better off staying here and riding with Hurst."

Ettrias scoffed. "Not a chance. We're riding with you. Someone needs to make sure you don't die after voluntarily poisoning yourself."

"I'm coming too!" Arkiel jumped to his feet. "If you're going to save Mother, I want to come."

"Rufus already has the horses saddled." Red Wolf approached Talin's bed and let out a long breath.

"We'll meet at the edge of camp, then," Ashera said. The three of them slipped out of the tent and left him alone with Talin.

"If this doesn't work, I promise I'll find some other way to save you. Whatever it takes." Red Wolf brushed a few loose strands of hair from her face and scooped her up into his arms, grabbing her belongings on his way out. Golmin was waiting at the edge of camp with the others, as they'd agreed, and he slung Talin over the back of his horse, climbing into the saddle behind her.

"We do not stop unless the horses cannot continue," he said. "It's the only way we'll make it in time."

Golmin nodded. "I saddled Talin's horse, too. If yours gets too exhausted, it will be able to bear some of the weight."

The six of them set off at a gallop, Ettrias bringing up the rear with their spare horse. Red Wolf pulled ahead almost immediately and led the way a good few feet ahead of the rest of the group, though he occasionally slowed a little to let the horses breathe and give the others a chance to catch up.

He didn't stop until the horses refused to go further, exactly as promised, and the others kept pace with him without protest. They rode through the night, through searing midday sun, past villages where normally they might stop to rest. He had initially thought that Arkiel would not be able to deal with the exhaustion and hunger, but the boy never complained, eating what little he allowed them to eat when they had the rare break. Talin never woke nor stirred. The wolf necklace she wore continued to give off a faint, ruby glow around the eyes.

I'm losing track of time. How many days has it been?

"This'll be our fourth night," Golmin told him when he asked. "We should be at the castle by morning. How is she doing?"

"Worsening. The necklace won't keep her alive much longer if I don't feed it my blood," Red Wolf said. He rubbed his horse's neck as it lapped up water greedily from the creek where they'd stopped.

"You're better off going alone, then," Golmin said. "We're only slowing you down."

"We came all this way," Red Wolf said. "I'll swap out the horse, get on Talin's. Arkiel, you ride with Ashera to lighten the load on Ettrias' horse. We're so close..."

"Very well, let's continue, then."

"If you need to leave us behind, just go, we'll meet you at the castle," Ashera said. They mounted their horses again, who were understandably reluctant to be put to work again so soon, and left the creek behind. Red Wolf put a hand against Talin's cheek and found her skin unusually cold.

She's running out of time.

"I'm riding ahead," he told them, fighting down a surge of panic. "We will meet at the castle."

"I can keep up; I'll come," Golmin said. "To make sure you're alright after the torslek."

Red Wolf didn't have the energy to argue and spurred his horse on. Golmin, surprisingly, did keep pace with him. They'd been riding for days now, having made a week's journey in half the time without stopping. The horses were exhausted. He was exhausted.

The sun had long since set by the time he emerged from the forest with Golmin, and the two of them glimpsed the castle silhouetted against the waning moon. Red Wolf dug his heels into his horse. Sensing the urgency, the creature galloped on with renewed energy, taking them closer and closer to the front gates.

He heard a shout as he drew closer; the guardsmen must have seen him approach. Golmin still kept pace. Red Wolf touched Talin's cheek again and found she was growing colder. Slipping away. He pulled his horse to a halt in front of the gates and dismounted, pushing Hurst's letter into one of the guardsmen's hands.

"From Captain Hurst," he said. "Get a healer, find a barrel of torslek. GO NOW!"

The guardsmen blinked at him for a moment, but then the one with the letter sprinted off through a side door to relay his request, reading Hurst's message on the way inside. Red Wolf scooped Talin off his horse and set her down gently just in front of the castle gate.

"Hold on. Talin, please, just..." He tried to calm his breathing. "Just hold on. I can't lose you now."

Golmin jumped down from his horse and crouched beside him. "Is she still...?"

"Barely."

The main gate creaked open, revealing a man in healer's robes and two guards carrying a small barrel between them. The healer hurried over to Talin to check her breathing and bandages.

"That's the torslek?" Red Wolf demanded.

"Aye," one of the guards said. They set the barrel down and opened the lid, and Red Wolf drew his dagger, plunging it into the liquid inside. He withdrew it again and slashed the blade across his palm without much thought, cutting his hand almost to the bone, and wrapped his injured hand around Talin's necklace.

"Talin, please." He let go with a gasp of pain.

The jewelled eyes brightened, two burning, ruby lights shining in the dark. Talin stirred a little. Her eyelids fluttered but didn't open.

"I don't know what you just did, but she's breathing normally now," the healer said, looking up at the former bodyguard in astonishment.

"Get her...inside." Red Wolf sank to his knees heavily. Blood dripped from his injured hand and soaked into the ground. In hindsight, he thought, he probably shouldn't have cut his palm, and certainly not so deep. But he supposed it didn't matter as long as it saved her.

"You're alright?" Golmin asked, crouching before him as the guardsmen moved Talin inside.

"Fine. Just...tired." Red Wolf looked at his bleeding hand. "Stings. Heh. Don't think I'll ever get used to losing my healing like this."

"Here, put pressure on it, you idiot." Golmin pulled a wad of bandages from a pouch and pressed them into Red Wolf's hand. The former bodyguard hissed at the contact but took over from Golmin anyway.

"It's really not that bad..." he said.

"Come on." Golmin pulled him to his feet. "Let's get you inside."

XXXIX

The last week or so felt like a fever dream.

Talin remembered being taken to the arena, fighting, sparing Marcus. Then the plan to rebel against the masters and confronting Hargrave in the lower levels. After that, she remembered nothing.

But the fact that she'd woken up in the dead of night with a dying fire in the fireplace to her left and the subsequent realisation that she was in a large, feather bed... It made everything else seem like something out of a fairy tale. How could she have gone from fighting in the arena and sleeping in the shared fighters' quarters to...wherever this was? She looked down at the necklace she wore and found that it was covered in blood. The wolf eyes gave off a bright, ruby glow in the dimly lit room.

Have I dreamed the last few days? Why is this glowing now?

Talin tried to sit up and immediately regretted it as a sharp pain lanced through her gut. Memories came flooding back. Hargrave's knife, a familiar voice shouting for a healer.

How long has it been since?

She realised that laying in bed wasn't likely going to give her any answers. Carefully, so as not to cause herself any more pain, she pulled herself to her feet, using the bed and nightstand as a support. This place felt oddly familiar. She stumbled to the door and exited into the hallway beyond. Here, she recognised the carpeted floor, basking in a soft glow from the torches set into the walls. This was the upper level of Castle Blackrun.

Clutching her gut and gritting her teeth against the pain, Talin headed downstairs to see if anyone was awake. She saw light streaming from under the doors to the second-floor lounge and approached. The door was just slightly ajar, allowing her to hear perfectly what was going on inside.

"How is she doing?" came her brother's voice.

"Still unconscious, but Master Elwyn says her condition has been improving over the past few hours. She's been given one of the guest bedchambers in the upper level." Golmin's voice. "By the gods, Red Wolf, will you stop pacing? She'll be fine."

What...?

Some part of her subconscious told her that this should not be news to her, for she remembered Icari mentioning that her sponsor had met him. But her head spun with the revelation all the same. She wasn't entirely sure she believed what she'd just heard.

Talin strained her ears, listening for a third presence in the room, but Golmin and Ettrias had both fallen silent again, and nobody bothered picking up the conversation. A chair creaked somewhere from within.

"How are you holding up?" Golmin finally said.

"I could sleep for a year." Ettrias huffed a half-laugh. "Gods, I don't think I've been this tired since the war."

"Get some sleep, then."

"Only if you do as well."

"*Tch*. Stubborn," Golmin said. "You know someone needs to make sure this idiot over there doesn't suffer any side effects from—"

A sharp stab of pain lanced through Talin's gut, forcing her to bend almost double. She instinctively stretched out a hand to steady herself and accidentally pushed open the door instead. The entire room fell silent. She saw her brother leaning against the wall next to one of the side exits, Ashera lounging on a sofa with her feet up, and Golmin sitting at the long table half-asleep. Her eyes swept across the room again, drifting over the candles that barely illuminated the back of the lounge, and froze.

There, at the far end of the table where the candlelight didn't quite reach, was Red Wolf.

He looked the same as he had when he left Belanore all those years ago, only more tired and weary. His hair was tousled, and he bore a fresh cut on his cheek where he'd no doubt cut himself shaving, though it took several seconds for Talin to process why that was unusual. He straightened and stepped into the light properly when she took a step forward.

This couldn't be real. She must be dreaming somehow. Talin took another step towards him. Red Wolf's gaze softened.

That was his voice in the arena. He was there.

Talin felt tears springing to her eyes as she closed the distance between them and reached up to touch his face.

"Please don't cry," Red Wolf said, so softly that she barely heard him.

Talin wrapped her arms around him and wept silently into his tunic.

"The world hasn't been kind to you, has it?" he whispered, pulling her into an embrace. "I'm sorry. I'm sorry. I'm sorry."

She wasn't sure what he was apologising for, but she didn't have the energy to ask or tell him he needn't apologise to her at all. Right now, wrapped up in his arms, she wanted to remain like this forever.

Another stab of pain through her gut brought her back to reality—namely, that her wounds were pressed up against Red Wolf's body and that she was soaking through his tunic with her crying. She separated herself carefully but couldn't hide her grimace.

"Ah—apologies, I thought the necklace would have healed you completely by now." Red Wolf reached out to steady her with both hands and guided her to the sofa, where Ashera happily moved so she could sit.

"Where's Arkiel?" she asked. "How are you *here*? How am *I* here? What...happened?"

"Arkiel is sleeping upstairs. He's been given sleeping quarters next to yours." Red Wolf drew up a chair and sat on it backwards, resting his arms against the backrest. "As for the rest, it's...a long story."

Talin listened as he explained how he came to Belanore, how he followed her trail but elected to remain behind and cause a diversion in Dennik—confirming her suspicions that he had been there that night. He recounted what had transpired in the village near Varen, his attempt to pick up her trail again, and how he ended up scouring the Highlands for some sign that she was alive. Golmin took over from there, explaining their attempts to track her down after she'd been taken by the thugs, all the way to Red Wolf's plan to use torslek on himself to activate her necklace.

"You..." Talin hissed through her teeth. "Are you alright?"

"I feel fine." Red Wolf looked at his bandaged hand briefly. "It seems that I don't suffer the physical effects of the venom at all—it's only enough to neutralise my healing."

Talin had a few choice words about how utterly *reckless* it was to even *consider* using torslek, but she knew there was no point in lecturing him on recklessness when they both knew she would have done the same.

"Your injuries were quite extensive," Red Wolf said. "I...suspect that's part of the reason you haven't healed yet. Either that or the necklace has less of an effect on non-Hellhounds."

"Why..." Talin hesitated there, trying to think of the right words. "Why do all of this for me? You suspected the letter and the papers might have been forged, yet you came anyway. You followed a breadcrumb trail for *weeks* and spent over a month trying to track me down, and then you willingly poisoned yourself with torslek to save me. Why?"

"I figured you needed me."

Talin had no suitable response to that.

"Get some sleep." Red Wolf stood. "If you haven't healed yet, you need rest." He offered a hand to Talin, and she allowed herself to be helped from the sofa.

She realised her mistake too late as agonising pain shot through her midsection, sending the world spinning around her. She staggered into Red Wolf with a groan.

"Take it easy." He steadied her again. "Are you able to walk back upstairs?"

"I..." Talin clenched her jaw. She knew when to admit that she'd pushed herself past her limits. "I don't think so. You'll...have to carry m e."

Red Wolf scooped her up without any difficulty and made for the hallway.

"I don't suppose I could trouble one of you to wake Master Elwyn and ask him to brew something to alleviate pain," he said, pausing at the door.

"I'm on it." Ashera jumped to her feet and dashed off through a side door. Ettrias tugged Golmin to his feet.

"We should sleep," he said. "Wake us if you need anything."

Talin allowed herself to be carried all the way back to the upper levels, where Red Wolf settled her back in bed and drew up a chair to sit.

"So..." he began, but quickly fell silent again and dropped his gaze.

"You don't owe me an explanation, or an apology, or anything," Talin said. "I should... I mean, I could have..." She trailed off there and realised their dilemma. What were they supposed to say to each other now, after so long apart?

They were interrupted, thankfully, by a knock on the door. Red Wolf went to answer it and let in a short, bearded man with healer's robes and a balding head. He set a lamp down by the nightstand. Talin didn't miss the way Red Wolf squinted and turned away from the light source.

"It's good to see you awake, Your Majesty. I am Master Elwyn. How do you feel?" the healer asked.

"Awful," Talin confessed. "I feel like my torso's on fire."

"Your wounds were quite severe when you arrived at the castle," Master Elwyn said. He pulled a small vial from one of his pockets and uncorked it. "This is a common pain relief I already brewed. It should help you sleep tonight."

"Thank you." Talin took the potion and drank. Elwyn checked her bandages and picked up his lamp, reminding them to wake him if anything else needed his attention.

"I'll...let you sleep." Red Wolf stood as well once the door had clicked shut. "My chambers are just around the corner if..."

"Wait," Talin said.

Red Wolf paused.

"I...don't want to be a bother, you can say no, it's just..." Talin chewed on her lip. "Stay? Please?"

Red Wolf let out a long breath. "I...can't. I'm sorry. I've barely had any sleep these past few days. It's... Even for a Hellhound, it takes a toll."

"Of course. Apologies, I shouldn't have brought it up—" Talin began.

"No. Don't apologise. I understand. I'm sorry I can't keep you company." Red Wolf took her hand and kissed her knuckles. "We'll catch up in the morning."

"Thank you," Talin said when he reached the door. "For finding me."

She didn't sleep well that night. Though the potion did help relieve the pain in her gut a little, it wasn't enough, and Talin only managed to fall asleep after laying in bed for nearly an hour trying to make herself more comfortable. When she did sleep, her dreams were filled with memories of the arena, of the war she had endured and won. She remembered travelling west with Red Wolf, glimpsing the war-torn ghost towns for the first time. How naïve she had been then, thinking that was as bad as the war would get. Nothing could have prepared her for setting her eyes on the barren north when they crossed the White River for the first time.

Talin jolted awake again with a start and a yelp, heart pounding, the image of Edd's fearful face still seared into the back of her mind. She sat up gingerly and rubbed her eyes.

These nightmares are getting worse.

She dragged herself out of bed after some contemplation and made her way down the hall, turning the corner to Red Wolf's chambers.

I shouldn't bother him, he's probably exhausted...

She paused at the door without knocking. It was unfair for her to call on him again so soon, especially not when he had told her already that he was tired. She ought to go back to bed and at least try to sleep.

The door opened a crack before she could turn and leave. Red Wolf poked his head out and saw her.

"Heard your footsteps," he said.

"I'm sorry, I shouldn't have bothered you, I..." Talin looked away. "...couldn't sleep."

Red Wolf opened the door wider and stepped aside to let her in, and she saw then that he was dressed in nothing but a pair of loose-fitting trousers.

"Oh, gods, I didn't mean to wake you—" she began.

"It's fine," Red Wolf said. Talin stepped into his chambers hesitantly. "You need company. Sleep here tonight if you need."

"Are you...sure?"

"I wouldn't be offering if I wasn't."

She allowed him to steer her to the bed, where he allowed her to settle down before climbing in on the other side. When she reached over to put an arm around him, he took her hand in both of his and kissed her knuckles again. A simple gesture, but Talin understood it all the same. She withdrew her hand.

"Sleep," Red Wolf said. "You're safe now."

And for the first time in weeks, Talin knew it was true.

T hey had their breakfast the next morning in the private dining
hall at Castle Blackrun. Lady Katherine Blackrun, they had all
been told, was on a hunting trip in the mountains, but she had left
instructions that Talin and her companions were to be treated with the
appropriate hospitality and respect should they ever seek refuge at the
castle. She found herself now sipping coffee at Blackrun's dining table
with a plate of eggs and bacon. Arkiel sat beside her with a glass of juice
and a similarly loaded plate.

"Doesn't seem like Blackrun to go on a hunting trip out of the blue,
especially when the north has been dealing with a mass kidnapping and
illegal fighting arenas," Red Wolf said.

"I agree, this is highly unusual behaviour for her," Golmin said.
"She wouldn't abandon the Highlands to go on some hunting trip, not
now."

"I'm more interested in the instructions she left." Talin put a hand on her chin. "From what I know, the entire kingdom thinks I'm *dead*. But she left instructions to shelter us if I ever turned up here—Master Elwyn said she referred to me specifically by name. She suspected all along that I'm still alive. I'm not sure what that means for her relationship with Aldrus."

"Either way, she's not expected to return until tomorrow, and I hear the tavern in town is famous for their ale," Ettrias said. "What say we head down there tonight for a few rounds?"

"You take issue with drinking at the castle?" Red Wolf asked.

"No. Just thought we could do with a livelier atmosphere." Ettrias shrugged.

"People here will recognise me, and I don't want to draw attention to all of you, too," Talin said. "The four of you can go. I'll keep Arkiel company." She rubbed the boy's shoulder.

"Come on, it'll be fine," Ettrias said. "Master Elwyn has cleared you to walk around, hasn't he? Being recognised by people shouldn't stop you from going wherever you please."

"Personally, I think it'll be nice to unwind," Golmin said.

"You can say no," Ettrias added. "If you want to rest, you should."

Talin glanced between her companions. They all certainly deserved a break after the last few weeks, and a few rounds of drinks in the lively atmosphere of a commoners' tavern seemed like the perfect opportunity.

"Arkiel will be safe here," Red Wolf said.

Talin smiled. "If you all insist. I suppose it can't hurt."

"Mother, I'm full..." Arkiel pushed his plate away and stood. Talin piled his leftover bacon onto her plate. "Can I go explore the castle?"

"Alright, make sure you don't pile so much food on your plate next time," she said.

"Red Wolf! Come explore the castle with me, please?" Arkiel asked, tugging on the former bodyguard's sleeve.

"Ah..." Red Wolf looked at the boy, then at Talin, who simply shrugged. "...lead the way, then." He tipped back the last of his drink and stood. The two of them quickly disappeared through the dining hall doors.

"They get along well," Talin mused. She was oddly glad of it and wasn't sure why.

"Arkiel looks up to him," Ettrias said. "I think all those stories we told might have had something to do with it."

She found the two of them again some time after breakfast, sparring in the main courtyard with wooden training swords and padded armour. The boy was huffing and clearly out of breath as he pressed the attack.

"That's it, good form," Red Wolf said, parrying another strike. "Watch your feet."

Talin took a seat on one of the nearby benches to watch.

Arkiel swung again, but she could tell he was growing fatigued; he overbalanced when Red Wolf met his blade with another parry and landed on his buttocks with a yelp.

"Ow...even training with Master Brakis wasn't that difficult," he grumbled as he got back to his feet.

Red Wolf huffed a laugh. "I was trained by Brakis, too. He takes training very seriously. But he is a good teacher."

"Let's go again!" Arkiel said, raising his weapon again.

"I think you need a break," Red Wolf said, still smiling. "You'll wear yourself out if you keep training without any rest."

"But I'm not...that tired," Arkiel huffed.

"Get some water, Arkiel," Red Wolf said. "We can continue once you've caught your breath."

Arkiel reluctantly put his sword down to take a drink from his water canteen. Red Wolf glanced over at Talin and approached.

"How are you feeling?" he asked.

"Much better than I was. Whatever magic that necklace has, it's speeding up my healing. I, uh..." Talin suddenly looked away, feeling her face burn. "Thank you for the company last night."

"About that." Red Wolf rubbed the back of his head. "I...know...it's been a long time. I know you're married to Aldrus, and I know Arkiel is your son. Which is why I need to know where we stand. Who are we to each other now?"

Talin winced. She had expected such a question from him and had been wondering the same herself. But how could she even begin to formulate an answer?

"I don't know," she admitted. "But I'd like to find out, too."

"I thought as much." Red Wolf sat down heavily beside her. "I guess we'll have to find out together."

"Red Wolf, I—" Talin hissed through her teeth. She hadn't imagined that finding the right words would become so difficult after so long. "Please don't think my feelings toward you have changed. They haven't. Or, at least, I...don't think they have. I just don't know if...we can simply pick up where we left off."

"I know." Red Wolf offered her a strained smile. "It's not easy."

"Arkiel likes you, though," Talin said, nodding towards the boy, who had started talking to one of the other soldiers training in the courtyard. "He normally hates swordplay."

"You've been telling him too many stories about me."

"Is that a bad thing?"

Red Wolf huffed a laugh. "As long as you don't stroke my ego *too* much."

Talin couldn't help but laugh as well.

That evening, once she had left Arkiel in the care of Master Elwyn, she made her way down to the castle's front gates to meet with Red Wolf and the others. They had agreed to go into town on foot; five people riding out from Castle Blackrun on horseback would draw far too much attention even if Talin was not recognised.

"I think I see people staring," Ettrias muttered as they made their way through the streets. "So much for keeping a low profile."

Red Wolf shrugged. "Let them stare. We're here under Blackrun's protection. People will have to answer to her if they try to start trouble."

"Still, I'd prefer not to be recognised at all..." Talin said. She stopped in front of the tavern. It was an unassuming building on the main road, with a wooden sign hanging overhead and a smaller promotional sign propped against the wall. Judging from the noise level, there were plenty of patrons inside already.

"I'll buy the first round." Red Wolf pushed open the doors. "I still owe you a drink, after all."

They seated themselves at a table near the front of the tavern, where it was less likely to get too rowdy, and Red Wolf flagged down a passing barmaid. The girl seemed to freeze up momentarily when she noticed Talin, but she thankfully chose not to comment and took note of their orders instead.

"Appreciate the discretion," Red Wolf said when she returned with their drinks.

The girl's eyes widened again. "Your Majesty? So you really are..."

"It's alright. I'm just here as a patron at the tavern tonight," Talin said.

"I understand. Um, would you mind if I informed the rest of the staff?" the girl asked. "We might be able to help you...keep a low profile. If that's what you wished."

"That would be good. Thank you," Talin said.

The girl hurried off again. Golmin took a sip of his ale and raised his eyebrows.

"Not bad," he said.

"So, I know we caught up a little at breakfast, but I have more questions than answers," Ashera said to Red Wolf. "You said you went north after your exile. Did you find anything?"

"Not much. I found people from a tiny village past the border who had heard of Velnora, but since Velnora is still within Kies Tor's borders, I couldn't visit," Red Wolf said. "It was the same story everywhere I visited. People had heard of the place, maybe even knew people from there. But nobody knew *enough*. I don't know who I was, who my blood relatives were...*nothing*." His hands clenched into fists, and he let out a frustrated hiss before relaxing them again.

"I did some research into Velnora, too," Talin said. "I never rode that far north during the war, but...I might have...*something*. I don't know if it'll be useful."

Red Wolf's gaze snapped up to her. "Let...let's hear it, then."

"I told you that I remembered Velnora as the first village to fall to Hellhounds," Talin said. "That much is true, but it...doesn't necessarily line up with your age. I found a report dated a year *before* you would have been taken. Lord Edric Blackrun wrote to my grandfather that...they have heard reports of an invading army of demons ravaging the far northern stretches of the Highlands. He went on to report that they lost all contact with the watchtower at the mountain pass over a month ago."

"The Hellhounds came through the pass..." Red Wolf's voice trailed off.

"The watchtower was at Velnora," Talin said. "It was a strategic position managed solely by House Blackrun as part of their representative duties."

"But they lost all contact, which means there were no survivors." Red Wolf frowned.

"Yes. But this is still huge, Red Wolf. If Lord Edric knew about Velnora, then Lady Blackrun would know something, too," Talin said. "She took over as House Head after Lord Edric's death—she would have gone over all of the old records of her house. She might have the answers you've been looking for."

She caught the barest flicker of hope flash across Red Wolf's eyes as he contemplated her words.

"Maybe," he said softly.

The conversation shifted there, and Ettrias recounted to Red Wolf some of their stories from the war. Talin and Ashera pitched in to add or correct some of the details. Golmin flagged down the barmaid from before and ordered everyone a second round of ale, this time with food to share.

"You should have seen the state of Vill's Crossing," Ettrias was saying. "When we arrived, it was carnage. Rubble everywhere, corpses strewn all over the place. You could barely move a foot in any direction without stepping on bodies or body parts."

Talin saw a brief flash of that scene in the back of her mind—it had been burned deep into her memory the instant she had seen the extent of the initial battle fought there. The Hellhounds had retreated past the southern side of the Crossing by then, but even so, the damage they had left in their wake was immeasurable. She distinctly remembered throwing up her stomach contents into a nearby bush on multiple occasions.

A loud *crash* from somewhere in the tavern sent her to her feet immediately, reaching towards her belt before remembering that she had come unarmed. There was a momentary lull in the chatter around them before the conversations resumed. Talin remained where she was, scanning the room, feeling her blood pounding in her ears.

"Talin. It was just a dropped plate. It's alright."

There was a hand on her arm, firm but gentle. She turned her head to see Ettrias with his hand on her wrist. Ashera and Golmin were both staring. Red Wolf's brow was furrowed, and she could see the concern in his features, despite his attempts to hide it.

"I'm...going to get some fresh air." She picked up her drink with a trembling hand and downed the last of it.

"I'll escort you—" Red Wolf began, rising to his feet. Talin quickly waved him back down.

"That won't be necessary," she said, perhaps a little too hastily, and excused herself from the table.

She felt as if her head had been stuffed with cotton as she made her way out of the tavern and into a side alley, breathing hard. Blood pounded in her ears so loudly that it drowned out everything else. She couldn't *think*. So many were dead at the Crossing, and it was her fault, *her fault*, because if she had gotten there sooner, had accounted for the floods delaying them by so many days instead of waiting like a fool—

My fault that there were so many casualties in the war. I was never fast enough. I should have stayed on the front instead of coming home. I should have donemoretriedharderbeenstrongerledmypeople—

Ettrias was the one to find her eventually, huddled in the alley with her knees drawn up to her chest, crying and shaking and gasping for air. He said nothing, simply knelt before her and pulled her into an embrace. Talin let herself be wrapped up completely in his arms, feeling his chest rise and fall, trying to match her own frantic breaths to his much calmer ones. The two of them remained like that until she had settled enough to talk to him.

"I'm sorry, coming out here was a bad idea," he said.

"It's not your fault," Talin said. She drew in a few shaky breaths. "I..."

"You don't have to explain yourself." Ettrias stood and tugged her to her feet gently. "Red Wolf was worried about you. I figured you didn't want him to see you like this, but..."

"He wouldn't...understand."

Ettrias sighed. "Let's go back to Castle Blackrun. I'll tell the others we're leaving early. They can catch up over more drinks in the meantime."

Talin nodded, and her brother ducked back into the tavern briefly while she waited outside. The two of them made their way back to the castle together.

"You'll be alright tonight?" Ettrias asked once they reached the stairs leading to the upper levels.

"It'll be a while before I feel better, but yes," Talin said. "Thank you."

"Don't mention it. I'm your brother," Ettrias said. "My chambers are right here if you need me. Don't worry about waking me in the middle of the night; I won't be *too* upset."

"Alright. Goodnight, Ettrias."

"Likewise."

She made her way back to her chambers alone. There was a rational part of her mind that knew that Red Wolf would understand what had happened in the tavern, for she was certain she had seen him react the same way to something once before. But another part of her mind insisted that she could not show any weakness in front of him—she had to prove that she was capable of dealing with things on her own. Perhaps, once all this was over, she would explain everything, including her nightmares and memories of the war.

For now, though, she would bear them alone.

XXXVI

Red Wolf could hear the whispers before he even made it half a foot into the front courtyard and caught the concerned looks from some of Lady Blackrun's advisors. He kept quiet and stayed out of their way, finding a shady spot beneath one of the plum trees to observe from afar.

Lady Katherine Blackrun had returned, it seemed, with some kind of news.

"What's the commotion?" Talin asked, appearing beside him.

"Blackrun's home. I don't think she was on a hunting trip," Red Wolf said. It was true; the escort that accompanied her looked ill-equipped for a hunt, and the fact that they had nothing to show for the trip was far too suspicious. He watched as the Head of House Blackrun dismounted to talk to her advisors, a serious expression on her face. She glanced around at one point and noticed him and Talin standing in the shade of the courtyard trees, and he thought he glimpsed a hint of confusion cut through her features, but it was gone so quickly that he decided he must have imagined it. She beckoned to her council and breezed past the two of them without sparing them another glance.

"Something's wrong," Talin said. "Not even a greeting for us…"

"Blackrun never struck me as the type to keep secrets," Red Wolf said.

He had met Lady Blackrun a handful of times in the past, back when Lord Edric was still alive and Arnas was king. They never formally interacted; he had always been there as the king's shadow, and she had always been obligated to show her face as Lord Edric's wife. He didn't remember much of her appearance, but she looked older than he remembered—her dark hair had a streak or two of grey, and there were visible lines on her forehead. His eyes followed her as she disappeared through the front doors of the castle.

"I thought you were friends," he said.

Talin sighed. "It's been a while. A lot of things have happened. But the fact that she left orders to shelter us in the castle during her absence says a lot."

"Let's hope her hospitality remains generous now that she's home," Red Wolf muttered.

The two of them headed back inside to escape the summer heat. Blackrun herself had already disappeared to gods-know-where, but Red Wolf caught Master Elwyn hurrying down a hallway and vanishing as well before he could greet the man.

That's odd. Her advisors seem a little on edge.

A handmaid hurried over to them as he was pondering the situation, bowing to him and Talin and wringing her hands nervously. Red Wolf guessed that she was new.

"Your Majesty? Um, pardon the intrusion. Lady Blackrun requests an audience with you this afternoon," the girl said.

Talin smiled, but there was a glint in her eye that indicated to Red Wolf that she knew more than she was letting on. "We'd best change into court attire, then. Thank you."

The girl bowed again and hurried off.

"I know that look. What's the deal?" Red Wolf asked once she was gone.

"Blackrun's summoning us to discuss the current situation, but there's something more. Something related to her trip," Talin said. She laughed at his expression. "You pick up a few things when you spend your days dealing with politics and brushing shoulders with the nobility."

"You've learned a lot these past fifteen years, I see."

"It hasn't always been..." Talin's voice trailed off there as if she wasn't sure how to end the sentence, and she offered him a somewhat forced smile. "We should go make ourselves presentable for court. I'll see you in the afternoon."

"Wait," Red Wolf said. She stopped two steps from him and spun back around. "Are you alright? After last night, I mean."

"Fine. I'm fine," Talin said. "It was nothing."

"Talin—" Red Wolf began, but she had already vanished down the hall. He let her go.

Later that afternoon, bathed and dressed in a set of borrowed silks slightly too small for him, he met with Talin again outside the doors to the main hall and waited to be ushered in. She had been given an ice-blue dress with semi-transparent sleeves, and through the fabric, he glimpsed the curved line of bite marks on her left shoulder. He felt a brief twinge of guilt.

"I can't say I haven't missed the political intrigue, at least a little," he said. "You look wonderful."

"Ah..." Talin's cheeks coloured slightly. "Thank you."

"Don't suppose you have any idea what Blackrun wants an audience for," Red Wolf said.

"I might have a theory or two," Talin said.

"Hmm. Enlighten me."

"I've long suspected that Katherine wants me to...how shall we put it...cede full control of the north to her, recognising the Highlands as an independent nation. The current political instability gives her the perfect excuse. She probably wants to strike some kind of deal."

"You sound surprisingly calm for someone who thinks they're about to be asked to give away half of the kingdom," Red Wolf said.

"We're friends." Talin shrugged. "I might be able to talk her out of it."

The doors swung open almost as soon as she finished speaking, and they were escorted in by a herald who rattled off Talin's extensive list of titles effortlessly. Red Wolf only recognised the first few; she'd clearly picked up most of them during the war.

"Queen Talin. It's been quite a while."

Blackrun certainly looked more elegant than she had this morning, dressed now in a silver gown with gold highlights. Her hair had been done up in a braided bun, and she had seated herself on the throne at the end of the hall. Blackrun banners hung from the roof of the main hall, depicting the golden wolf of her house.

"My lady, thank you for your generous hospitality thus far," Talin said. "My companions and I owe you our gratitude."

"Spare me the formalities," Blackrun said. "There are matters we must discuss." She glanced at Red Wolf. "And you...the disgraced lord commander with golden eyes. I don't recall inviting you to this audience. Or do I need to remind you that you're not attending this meeting as an extension of the Crown?"

She has a point. It hadn't occurred to Red Wolf until now that he was a third party to all of this.

"If my presence offends you, my lady, I'll excuse myself," he said. Beside him, Talin visibly bristled.

"That won't be necessary," Blackrun said. "I've no doubt your queen will relay everything to you afterwards anyway. We might as well save her the trouble."

"As you wish, my lady," Red Wolf said.

"In any case, I didn't call for an audience to exchange pleasantries," Blackrun continued. "Let me get straight to the point. As you well know, House Blackrun has the power to rally the Highlands. The northern nobles look to me for leadership. I could help you take back the throne by force...but in exchange, you will cede control of the Highlands and recognise, henceforth, that it falls under House Blackrun's independent jurisdiction."

"That's a lot to ask."

"It is my offer."

Talin sighed. "I don't want another *war*, Katherine. We have barely recovered from the last war we fought."

"You might not have a choice. You've been declared dead. Until your boy comes of ruling age, Aldrus is, effectively, king," Blackrun said.

"I'll have to think about it." Talin closed her eyes momentarily. "I need time to catch up on all the news from Belanore. We've been cut off for weeks while on the run. The situation has clearly spiralled while I was away, and it doesn't seem like there's an easy solution to our problems."

"Of course." Blackrun gave a polite smile. "Castle Blackrun will be happy to shelter you regardless of your decision."

"Thank you," Talin said.

"If there's nothing else, I believe our meeting is concluded," Blackrun said. "You can see yourselves out—"

"Wait, my lady, there's something I wanted to ask," Red Wolf said. "It will only take a moment of your time. Please."

Blackrun lifted her eyebrows. "Ask away, then."

"I'm aware that...the watchtower in Velnora was under Blackrun jurisdiction before the village was destroyed," Red Wolf said. "This may be a stretch, but...I wondered if you knew anyone from Velnora."

"An odd question." Blackrun's brow furrowed. He thought he saw confusion flicker across her features when she met his gaze. "I did know...some of the villagers there...but not exceptionally well. Satisfy my curiosity, sir—how do you know of the village, and why do you want to know?"

"I believe Velnora was my home before it was destroyed by the Hellhounds," Red Wolf said. "Or, at least, I have reason to believe I lived there."

There was a beat. Blackrun's expression shifted from serious to shock.

"...Connor?"

My name is Connor Kulos—

My name is Connor Kulos.

My name is—

"Red Wolf," he said almost automatically.

"No, it's...it's you. I'm certain now. I thought I recognised your eyes and that you shared a striking resemblance with your father, but

I couldn't be sure..." Blackrun stood and stepped down from the dais, tears shimmering in her eyes. "Connor, my boy..."

"What...no, *why* do you call me that?" Red Wolf took an instinctive step back when she approached. "That's not..."

My name?

Blackrun lifted a hand to cup his cheek, then dropped it again suddenly. "Of course. You...wouldn't remember me. But surely, your own name...Connor, *please*."

He remembered cold stone floors and locked cages and the scent of medicinal herbs and blood, but beyond that, there was only Red Wolf. Only rage, only pain, and a name to keep himself sane.

My name is Connor Kulos. My name is Connor Kulos. My name is Connor Kulos—

"I..."

Why can't I remember?

"I'm sorry," he said. "I don't remember much of my childhood, if at all. Did you...know...me? Personally?"

"Yes. You could say that." Blackrun let out what could have been a laugh. "Your name...your *real* name...is Connor Kulos Blackrun. My son."

XXXVII

S ilence.

Seconds passed that felt like an eternity. Beside Talin, Red Wolf stilled. She might have mistaken him for a statue were it not for the steady rise and fall of his chest. Nobody spoke, as if the moment was a dream where the illusion of reality might be shattered at the first whisper of a word. Distantly, she recalled that Blackrun had briefly mentioned a lost son once during a conversation long ago, but the topic had quickly shifted, and Talin had never gotten a chance to ask about him again.

It was a shock, certainly, to realise that he had stood by her for so long.

"I thought—" Blackrun began, finally breaking the silence.

"Why was I—" Red Wolf said at the same time. He seemed to suddenly remember how to move, tearing his gaze away and rubbing his head sheepishly. "I... You go."

"This whole time, I thought you were *dead*," Blackrun whispered. Tears fell down her cheeks. "Edric said there were no survivors, that it was a massacre and even the children were not spared..."

"It...it's a long story," Red Wolf said. "I... Gods, this is..." He shook his head. "Why was I in Velnora? I thought...I *remember*...living there. Or I think I do."

Blackrun swallowed. "I think it best if we talked somewhere more private, Connor. You...must have a lot of questions."

Red Wolf's brow furrowed, but he didn't budge, opting instead to look at Talin.

"I'll leave you to it. Come find me after," she said.

"Come with me," he said.

"I..." Talin blinked. She looked between him and Blackrun. "Are you sure?"

Red Wolf gave a tiny nod. Blackrun hesitated, but then she swallowed and exhaled shakily. "If Connor wishes you there, I have no objection."

"Alright." She followed Blackrun from the hall, mind still reeling. Ahead of her, Red Wolf was visibly shaking, though his entire body was tensed, and he barely looked like he was paying attention to where they were going. Talin fell into step beside him and took his hand. He seemed to relax a little at the contact, squeezing back gently.

Blackrun led them upstairs, away from the communal areas of the castle, all the way to the second-floor lounge, where she locked all the doors and immediately crossed to the wine cabinet. Talin sat in an armchair while Red Wolf remained standing, doing his best impression of a statue in the middle of the room.

"Drink?" Blackrun asked.

"Why not," Talin said. Red Wolf gave a barely perceptible nod.

Blackrun poured three cups before seating herself in another armchair opposite them. "Connor...ah, would you prefer 'Red Wolf'?"

Red Wolf hesitated. "I...don't know."

"Connor, then, for now." Blackrun let out a long breath. "You asked why you were in Velnora at all. Lord Edric had wanted to tour the Highlands and took you along with him, and the two of you were scheduled to stay in Velnora for some time before continuing west. But the Hellhounds..." Her bottom lip wobbled. "Lord Edric returned alone and told me what happened."

Then what about his report to my grandfather? Talin thought, but she kept her mouth shut. There was plenty of missing information from the early days of the war, especially given her grandfather's untimely demise a year before she and Ettrias were born.

"Lord Edric...was my father?" Red Wolf asked.

There was a beat. Talin suddenly recalled something about a scandal that surfaced ten years ago, during the war, that she had helped cover up.

Katherine Blackrun hadn't been faithful to Lord Edric during their marriage.

"No," Blackrun said. "Edric was never your father."

Red Wolf looked at his glass and took a sip. "Then who? Someone from the village?"

"Someone from the half-giant clans in the far north," Blackrun said. "Chief Tormod Bjorson of the Kulos Clan."

"Wh...my father's...also still alive?" Red Wolf asked softly. Something in him seemed to break at the realisation, and he swallowed another gulp of wine. "This...whole time...I thought..." He drew in a shaky breath and wiped at his eyes.

"I'm sorry. If I'd known..." Blackrun began. "All those times we'd met, if I'd seen your face..."

"Doesn't matter now," Red Wolf said.

"Connor, there's something else you should know," Blackrun continued after a moment's silence. "House Blackrun has been trying to forge an alliance with the half-giant clans in the Far North since before you were born. That's how I met your father in the first place. But the half-giants are a proud people who have no wish to join Kies Tor or the Highlands. My most recent talks were...unsuccessful, at best. At worst, I've learned that there have been unusual sightings of Hellhounds in the mountains."

"That's what your 'hunting trip' was about," Talin said. She remembered Elder Parya, whom they had met past the eastern border, and the advice she had been issued.

The clans in the Far North...could Parya have been referring to the half-giants?

"I'm guessing you want us to talk to the clans in your stead," Red Wolf said. "You believe I have more of a chance to get through to them than an outsider—but I'm no more half-giant than you. I've never been to the Far North. I know nothing about these clans or how they operate."

"You...are correct, yes." Blackrun swallowed. "But even if you do not wish to negotiate in my stead, you could travel north to meet your people if you so desired." She turned her attention to Talin. "I know you have a lot to consider before you decide on your next course of action. I also value our friendship immensely and would rather we didn't come to blows, so I am making you aware of an alternative path—if you can convince the clans to forge an alliance with us, I will consider the dee d sufficient grounds to lend you the north's support."

Talin thought about it. She knew little of the half-giants, only that there had been clans living in the Highlands before King Braenern's purge. It was unlikely that they would treat her with anything but hostility.

"What do you think?" she asked Red Wolf.

"I..." Red Wolf looked away. "I think the half-giants are likely to be suspicious of you, given what your great-great-grandfather did. That's not...your fault, but..."

"I know, I was thinking the same," Talin said. "But I was asking about *you*. What do you want to do?"

Red Wolf blinked.

"I...think it would be good to visit," he said after a beat. "I'd like to meet my father, at the very least."

"Then we'll head north," Talin said. *And hopefully find out what Elder Parya was talking about.* "The only issue is Arkiel..."

"Your son will be safe here," Blackrun said. "You have my word. Take your companions with you; you'll want an escort. The Far North is an unforgiving place."

Talin's shoulders deflated. "Thank you. I'm sorry to trouble you with looking after him."

"No trouble." Blackrun gave a dismissive wave. "You'd be doing me a favour, talking to the clans in my stead." She looked between Talin and Red Wolf. "I'm aware you are still recovering from the wounds you sustained at the arena. Rest up for now. You can set off once you've healed. My tailor can outfit you and your companions with adequate clothing if you talk to him now. I'd...also like some private words with Connor if that's alright."

Talin gave a nod. "Of course. I'll see you both later."

She found Ettrias and Golmin in the castle library, her brother sitting in the guard captain's lap with a book in hand. Arkiel was sprawled across another couch with his own book. Ashera was nowhere to be seen, but a quick glance between the shelves revealed that she was simply browsing.

"We have another journey ahead of us," Talin said.

"Already? We just got here." Ettrias turned the page when Golmin nudged him. Ashera appeared from between the rows of bookshelves to listen.

"It's important." Talin relayed the situation with Blackrun and the half-giants and the offer she'd made, though she left out the revelation of Red Wolf's identity. That was his news to share—if he chose to do so at all. That done, she approached Arkiel, contemplating how best to break the news to him and hoping to the gods he would understand.

"Arkiel, I have important news to tell you," she said. The boy looked up from his book. "I must leave Castle Blackrun in a few days and ride north to seek out the half-giants. Red Wolf will be coming with me, as will Uncle Ettrias, and Ashera and Captain Golmin. The road is too dangerous for you, so you must remain here where it's safe."

"You're leaving...again?" Arkiel's face fell. "But...but we just got here! And why can't I come? I-I'm old enough now! Where are you going? How long is it going to take? *Why*?"

"We're going into the mountains," Talin said. "The half-giants live up there in seclusion, and Lady Blackrun thinks we will need their help to return to Belanore."

Arkiel's bottom lip wobbled. "But...but...why do I have to stay behind?"

"The mountain paths are far too dangerous, and the conditions are too harsh," Talin said. "I know it's difficult. And I'm so sorry that I have to leave you again." She pulled him into an embrace. "But I promise you. I will return soon. I will always come back to you."

"You...you have to swear it." Arkiel sniffled.

"I swear." Talin kissed the top of his head.

Perhaps it was foolish of her to make such promises so readily, for none of them knew what the mountain roads might hold. But she decided in that moment that she would return to him unharmed, no matter what.

"If it makes Your Highness feel more at ease, I could stay here," Ashera said, coming forwards. She glanced at Talin. "Be good to have someone else here whom the young prince knows."

"Please, Mother?" Arkiel looked to her as well.

Talin considered it. She supposed it couldn't hurt; though Blackrun's bannermen and guards were good, she trusted Ashera more than she trusted any of them. Her being here could also prove to be useful—she'd be able to get the latest news on what was happening in Kies Tor while the rest of them were away and would be able to update them as soon as they returned.

"I don't see any downsides." She shrugged. "Look after him."

"Count on it," Ashera said with a smile.

That night, after Arkiel had been put to bed and the others had already retired to their chambers, she found Red Wolf on the balcony at the end of the hall. He seemed quieter than usual, almost contemplative, with his arms folded on the metal railing in front of him. The sky was almost pitch black in the dim light of the waxing moon. Talin joined him there and leaned against the railing too.

"It's been quite the day for revelations," she said.

"Hmm." Red Wolf didn't turn. Talin wasn't sure he'd even heard her.

"Red Wolf?" Still no response. "...Connor?"

"I hear you."

"What's the matter?"

"I..." Red Wolf's brow creased. "Nothing I would wish to trouble you with. It's unfair for you to bear my burdens too."

Talin cracked a faint smile. "I'm offering to listen. If you wanted to share."

"I know." His frown deepened. "Did you know anything about Katherine—Lady Blackrun—having a lost son?"

"My father knew the Blackruns best. They worked together quite closely when the north was under siege from Hellhounds," Talin said.

"I remember."

"She *did* mention having a son once before, though. We never discussed it. I figured the memories were too painful."

"Katherine's story doesn't add up," Red Wolf said. He straightened with a sigh. "I know she knows my name because I remember it now. But I get the feeling that parts of what she told me don't make sense. She says that Lord Edric toured the outer villages in the Highlands, and our visit in Velnora coincided with the Hellhounds' attack. But the document you spoke of detailed that Lord Edric had lost contact with Velnora, not that the village had been destroyed outright."

"Maybe she's misremembering the details," Talin said.

Red Wolf grunted. "I'd like to believe that. But instinct tells me otherwise."

"Surely she would have no reason to lie to you," Talin said, though she didn't voice her own suspicions.

"I don't know." Red Wolf rubbed his chin. "I thought I'd get all my answers when I learned where I came from. Instead, I find myself with more questions."

"Our route passes through Velnora," Talin said.

"Hmm. Katherine was insistent on a different route. One that avoids Velnora entirely," Red Wolf said. "I thought she simply didn't wish for any unpleasant memories to resurface for me, but now that I think about it, I wonder if she may have had ulterior motives."

"What do *you* want to do?"

"I'd...like to see the village. Maybe I will find my answers there."

"Then we'll take the road through Velnora," Talin said.

"There was one more thing," Red Wolf said. "I am Katherine's only child, and being of ruling age, I could technically be instated as House Head. She wishes to legitimise my claim."

Talin felt a weight drop into her gut. She knew what he meant—a legitimate claim to the Blackrun name meant staying in the Highlands instead of returning to Belanore with her.

"I understand," she said after a pause. "As long as you're happy with—"

"Nothing's been decided yet. I told her I'd think about it," Red Wolf said. "But enough of my problems. How are you faring? The necklace still works?"

"Ah...about that." Talin pulled it from under her nightgown and showed him. One of the jewelled eyes had cracked down the middle, and the glow had faded, so she'd scrubbed it clean again and continued wearing it as a keepsake.

"Hmm. I suppose it was a one-time enchantment, then," Red Wolf said.

"It did its job. I'll be able to travel in a few days."

"Have you decided what you'll do about Katherine's offer?"

"I see no other options," Talin said. "Either I try to take back my throne alone or give away over half the kingdom. Given the half-giants'...complicated history...with the Torrian Crown, I'm not hopeful that an alliance is something they'd even consider—especially if it ultimately benefits me."

"I...may have a solution for you," Red Wolf said. "Though it could very well complicate the situation further instead."

"Well, it can't be much worse than my options right now. Let's hear it."

"I agree to Katherine's wishes to legitimise my claim."

"I fail to see how that helps..." Talin caught on. "Are you propos—" She looked away, face burning.

"Only if you wish it, and not now," Red Wolf said. "I... Like I said, it could complicate things further. Your marriage to Aldrus still stands. I'm still an exiled criminal in Kies Tor." He drew in a deep breath. "I'll not speak of it again if it makes you uncomfortable. But given your current predicament, I thought I'd at least offer you some more options."

"No, you're right, it would solve my problems," Talin said. "You as Head of House Blackrun, marrying into the royal family..." Her face still burned. She smiled awkwardly. "But even *if* you weren't exiled, people will never accept you as king. Regardless of how I see you, you'll always be an outsider to them."

"I know." Red Wolf stared at the railing. "Forgive me. Perhaps I spoke too hastily."

"No, no, it's not that I don't want to marry you, I...guess I'm not opposed to the idea. I haven't exactly thought about it before now." Talin frowned. "I just...don't want you returning to Belanore and being told you don't belong."

"That is my burden to bear." Red Wolf cupped her face in his hands. "My choice to make. Let the masses talk and scream all they want. It doesn't *matter*."

"My people—"

"Forget about what your people want. Allow yourself to be selfish for one moment. What do *you* want?"

The simplicity of the question hit her with the force of a charging bull.

What do I want?

"I...don't know," Talin said. "I want to agree to this. I do. But I need to think about it. I cannot allow myself to be selfish when the entire kingdom is at stake."

"I understand." Red Wolf let go of her. "I know that whatever choice you make will be the right one. Get some rest—we'll talk more in the morning."

"Wait," Talin said as he turned to leave. "If I could make a selfish request tonight..."

"Anything."

"I'd...like to spend the night in your chambers again. If you felt so inclined to share. It's just...last time, your presence helped me sleep."

"Of course," Red Wolf said. "My chambers are yours if you need company."

Perhaps it was foolish to get close to him again now, as it had been foolish fifteen years ago. But right now, in this brief moment of vulnerability, she decided that she would be selfish once again.

Talin slid her hand into his silently, and together, they looked up at the ocean of stars speckled across the night sky.

XXXVIII

They set off for the Far North with their packs stuffed to the brim with cold-weather gear. Blackrun had warned them that the weather in the mountains was unpredictable; the northern summer was deceptive and didn't match the climate up there in the slightest. Red Wolf had been skeptical at first, but seeing the snow-capped mountain peaks in the distance, he'd figured it was safest to exercise caution either way. From what he knew of the Hellhounds' homeland, the land remained frozen almost year-round, only thawing for a few precious weeks during the hottest days of summer. He'd be lying if he said he wasn't looking forward to the cold chill—the winters he'd passed in the Draconian lands had been some of the most comfortable months he'd ever felt.

Tonight, they were camped in the open tundra near the border, less than a day's ride from Velnora. The waning moon bore down on them, reminding him constantly of his powers and curse. He'd shifted in the forest last night without incident, but the memory of what happened in that village near Varen had him on edge for all of yesterday and today despite the knowledge that they were far from any civilisation.

"I'm starting to miss the castle already," Ettrias muttered as he built the campfire. Talin lit it with a spark of lightning.

"You have to admit, travelling like this isn't all bad," she said. "It's hard to find a view like this back at Castle Blackrun or Belanore."

Red Wolf glanced up at the stars, stretching on for what seemed like forever before disappearing behind the silhouetted mountain range. He supposed she had a point.

"You mentioned you never rode this far north," he said.

"No. Ettrias never did, either," Talin said. "We had to push the Hellhounds out of Illyris twice before we could rebuild the bridge at Wycrest, but after we chased them out of this region for the third time, we received confirmed reports that they'd retreated past the border. I'm still not sure why."

"That's unusual," Red Wolf said. "Kehlvor isn't the kind of person to retreat unless he had no choice."

"Maybe he felt that the campaign was lost already," Talin said.

"Maybe."

He suspected there was more to it, but it had been over five years since a Hellhound had set foot in Kies Tor. There was no point in dwelling on these things.

"Alright, enough stories, I want supper." Ettrias pulled their food from their ration pack and divvied it up. "Dig in."

Red Wolf didn't miss the way Talin's shoulders seemed to relax as she accepted her portion of the food.

"You know, thinking back," she said as they ate, "I do remember some kind of scandal that surfaced years ago regarding Katherine. We were in the middle of the war, so we hushed it up to focus on taking back Castle Blackrun...or maybe it was Illyris, but that's irrelevant."

"I don't suppose it had anything to do with her affair," Red Wolf said.

"It might have, but I don't remember the details. You know I'm terrible with court gossip," Talin said. "Not that I paid much attention to it either way. I had my hands full with the war."

"No, you're right; it was about her affair." Her brother swallowed a bite of dried meat. "Why else do you think she was so open about telling you that Lord Edric wasn't your father? Her advisors found out. *Lord Edric* found out."

What...?

"She told me Lord Edric never knew about it," Red Wolf said softly.

"Well, that doesn't add up," Ettrias said.

"Clearly."

"She must have a reason for lying to you." Talin frowned. "If I had to lie to Arkiel...well, it would be a desperate situation, for one."

"I don't think this is the same thing," Red Wolf said coolly.

"I know. You're right. I'm speaking hypothetically, of course. Maybe to protect you? Stop you from going down some endless spiral to look for answers?"

"Protect me from what? The truth?" Red Wolf snapped. "I've spent my life not knowing who I am. I have a *right* to know."

"From what I know of Lord Edric, he wasn't exactly...kind, for lack of a better word," Golmin said. "If he really did find out about Blackrun's affair back then, I doubt he would have let it slide."

"*Tch.*" Red Wolf crossed his arms. "Whatever the case, I deserve the truth."

"We'll know more when we get to Velnora tomorrow," Golmin said. "The town may have been destroyed, but there's bound to be some clues left in the rubble about what really happened there."

They spent the rest of the evening catching each other up on everything; Red Wolf spoke of his travels in the Draconian lands while Talin and the others shared stories of their adventures over the years, and it was well past dark by the time they decided to turn in. The waning moon stared back at them unblinkingly as Ettrias moved to his spot for the first shift. Red Wolf lay down on his bedroll and tried to sleep.

Screams and blood, drowned by the wind.

He linked his hands behind his head and stared up at the sky. Up above, the moon's magic washed over him in waves, mixing with the magic he felt from the earth beneath. He lifted a hand and let golden energy dance across it momentarily. He'd always found it ironic that he should command protection magic when he had his healing powers, though he couldn't deny that it *was* useful for protecting the people around him. Perhaps he was always destined to be a bodyguard.

"Can't sleep?"

Red Wolf turned his head to see Ettrias throw another log onto the fire. "You going to ask me to cover your shift?"

"I was *going* to suggest you get some rest," the younger man said. "But if you're offering…"

"*Tch*. Not a chance."

"Worth a try."

A flash of movement caught Red Wolf's attention. He sat up to see Talin tossing and turning in her sleep, evidently trapped in some nightmare or another.

"Let her sleep," Ettrias said when he rose to wake her. "She might settle. She gets little enough sleep as it is."

Red Wolf hesitated but sat back down anyway. True to Ettrias' prediction, Talin seemed to calm after a minute, slipping back into a more peaceful slumber.

"We all…" the prince began, as if sensing Red Wolf's unspoken question. "We all gave pieces of ourselves to the war effort. Talin…gave up more than most."

Red Wolf dropped his gaze. "I should have been there."

"You did what was necessary. No point in dwelling on it," Ettrias said. "And I know you think you could have helped if you'd been around, but…I doubt there was anything you could have done to ease the burden of the war. The Hellhounds fought back *hard* after their defeat at Belanore, and she suffered the consequences along with everyone else. That's not something you could have prevented. If it's any consolation, though, we tried to look after her in your absence. We all did."

They lapsed into silence. The fire crackled and burned on, making the occasional *pop*.

"She needed you the most. *Needs* you the most," Ettrias finally said. "I don't think she even realises it."

Red Wolf didn't respond. Nearby, Talin started tossing and turning again, this time muttering under her breath. He exchanged a brief look with Ettrias before standing and crouching beside her.

"Talin," he said softly, giving her shoulder a gentle shake. "Wake up. It's alright."

Her dagger cleared its sheath almost too fast for him to catch. He dodged aside just in time to avoid the blade. She swung at him blindly again, and this time, he caught her wrist, controlling the weapon until she stopped struggling against him. He loosened his grip but didn't release her until her eyes fully focused, and he saw the recognition behind them.

"I..." she began, lowering the weapon. "Gods, I'm sorry, I thought..."

"I know," Red Wolf said. "It's alright."

"I...am going for a walk." Talin snatched up her cloak and weapons belt and strode off before Red Wolf could think to respond.

"Talin!" Ettrias jumped to his feet. "*Kust*, she does this all the time."

"I'm on it." Red Wolf grabbed his own weapons belt and took off after her.

In the near-darkness, her scent didn't lead far, cresting a small slope before slanting down to a small creek on the other side of the hill. It was there that he found her, huddled on a boulder with her knees drawn up to her chest, curled almost into a ball. She looked up at the sound of his footsteps on gravel.

"I spent...five *years*...on the front," she said as he approached. "And that was just the first campaign. I was going to stay in Belanore until the south was reclaimed. It took me two years to realise that forgetting about you was hopeless, and the Hellhounds weren't giving up their hold on the south, so I rode west. We pushed them out of the Western Forts, then Vill's Crossing, and then I oversaw the reconstruction of the Wycrest bridge while we protected the workers from Hellhounds on the other side of the White River. In the end, the war was just a distraction from you."

Red Wolf scrambled onto the boulder and sat beside her. She didn't make any objection.

"There was no victory parade when we finally returned home," she continued. "No celebration of all we'd accomplished. Why should there be? They still had Illyris and the rest of the north. We couldn't advance any further—Kadis was returning home for his coronation, and our troops were exhausted." She huffed a bitter laugh. "No. I came home from the war, and the first thing my council told me was that I needed to find a suitor."

Her voice shook. Red Wolf took her hand in both of his, running his fingers over her knuckles, then her palm, and finally lacing their fingers together. She seemed to relax at the contact, stretching one leg out and staring at the water below them for a little while before continuing.

"It wasn't long before the public started talking about it, too. I knew I had to find...*somebody*...if I wanted to keep the people's support. It was good timing that King Darien sought me out for an alliance. I didn't know what else I was supposed to do—even if you *weren't* exiled, they would never have accepted us being together." Talin let out another half-laugh. "Aldrus and I came to an agreement that our marriage was to remain a purely political matter. We married out of duty, not love, and it was out of duty again that Arkiel was born." She closed her eyes. "You're allowed to judge and tell me how wrong I was to choose duty over love. I wonder every day whether I should have chosen differently. He's my son, and I love him more than anything, but there's a part of me that wishes—"

"I set you on this path," Red Wolf said, even though a part of his very soul cracked at her words. "I'd be a hypocrite to judge."

"Kadis returned after Arkiel was born," Talin said. "We received a bird a month later with news that Vill's Crossing had been lost again to Hellhounds. So, I rode out for the front for the second time. It was another three years before we finally drove them out of Kies Tor for good." She shook her head. "It didn't feel much like a victory. I was just...tired."

"I'm sorry."

"No. I'm sorry you have to see me like this. I really was too soft for war." Talin wiped her eyes with a sleeve. "I wasn't strong enough to stomach the things I saw. I wasn't strong enough to help everyone. I t ried...*so hard*..." Her voice cracked. "But you've seen the state of the north. No matter what I do, people still *suffer*."

More tears slid down her cheeks and splashed onto the boulder they sat upon. She didn't lift a hand to wipe them away this time.

"Your suffering is not a sign of weakness," Red Wolf said softly. He let go of her hand to cup her face, wiping away her tears with his thumbs. "It's a sign that you've been strong, that you've kept up that strength for too long—and that it's taken a toll on who you are."

Talin visibly deflated at his words, melting into his touch and wrapping her arms around him. He returned the embrace, pulling her close, rubbing her back gently while she cried silently into his shoulder.

"I missed you," she finally said, voice wavering. "I never...stopped...missing you."

He wasn't sure why his heart ached at such a confession when part of him had selfishly hoped that she would remember him. He felt as if he had glimpsed into her very soul as she laid it bare, and his heart broke again at what he saw.

"I'm sorry." It was all he could say. He wasn't even sure what he was apologising for.

Talin pulled away to look at him. "Don't. Please. It wasn't your fault."

He knew that. Of course he did.

Why do I still feel guilty?

"Let's get back to camp," he said after a moment's silence. "Your brother was worried about you."

Talin sighed and rested her forehead against his shoulder. "I don't want to leave just yet."

Red Wolf wrapped his arms around her again, listening to the steady beat of her heart and her still-shaky breaths. He supposed Ettrias would understand if they took their time returning.

"Take as long as you need, then." He kissed the top of her head. "I'm not going anywhere."

XXXIX

The road was still unfamiliar to him. Red Wolf wasn't sure how to feel about that.

Part of him had prepared for this possibility and had understood that simply visiting the places in his past might not bring back his memories. The other part felt an inexplicable frustration at the fact that he couldn't remember.

Why do I feel this way now? It never bothered me before.

"...Red Wolf?"

My name is—

He blinked. Talin had appeared beside him with a concerned look in her eyes, suggesting that perhaps he hadn't been as good at hiding his emotions as he thought.

"Did you remember something?" she asked.

"No." Red Wolf didn't meet her gaze. "I don't know if that's a good thing or not."

"Don't blame yourself for not being able to remember," Talin said.

"I know. I...need a distraction, if you'll be so kind," Red Wolf said.

"Hmm. You mentioned that you spent some of your exile with Kadis," Talin said.

"I did." Red Wolf let out a short exhale. "After the war, he invited me to join him on a tour of the empire. I'd always wanted to see more of the Draconian lands, so naturally, I couldn't refuse."

"Sounds like you received quite the welcome treatment," Talin said.

"The Drakels...gave me somewhere to stay," Red Wolf answered carefully. "But it wasn't home."

Talin dropped her gaze. "Of course. I'm sorry."

"I don't blame you for what you did, Talin," Red Wolf said. "You should stop blaming yourself."

The two of them lapsed into silence. Red Wolf tried to keep his mind off Velnora, his missing memories, and Blackrun's version of events, but it was impossible. The thoughts looped around in his head on repeat, driving him mad.

What happened there? Why can't I remember?

"You might want to take a look at this!" Golmin called from the front. Red Wolf glanced up at him and found that he had stopped on top of a small hill overlooking the area below. He quickly dismounted and led his horse up on foot, stopping beside Ettrias. Talin was right behind him.

The village, if it could even still be called such, had been completely levelled. From a distance, he could see the blackened remains of some of the houses, crumbled away after so many years, but other than that, it was as if Velnora had never existed at all. Something tugged at the back of his memories, locked away, still out of reach as always. Phantom screams echoed across the cold tundra.

"There's nothing *left*," Talin whispered, and something in him shattered at those words.

"We should keep moving." He let out a shaky breath. "Coming here was a bad idea."

"The mountain pass is on the other side of this village," Talin said softly. "There'll be nowhere to stop until we make it through the pass and into the alps. It's not a journey we can begin tonight."

Red Wolf swallowed. "Right. Of course." He tore his gaze away from the village. "I'll...fetch some firewood for us..."

"Rufus and I can gather firewood," Ettrias said, looping an arm around Golmin's shoulders. "Here's as good a place as any to set up camp."

"Aye, you ought to at least take a look," the guard captain said. "Go on. We can set up camp in the meantime."

"I..." Red Wolf glanced towards the ruins again, then looked at Talin. She sidled up to him and took his hand.

"I'll be right here," she said.

The two of them made their way down the hill together and into the remains of Velnora, treading carefully to avoid disturbing the bones of the dead. Up close, Red Wolf could see some decomposed corpses or whatever was left of them. Most had clearly been eaten by animals or Hellhounds. He approached the village well and ran a hand along the brickwork. More phantom screams echoed through the streets.

"Do you...recognise anything?" Talin asked.

"No." Red Wolf crouched in front of a blackened pile of rubble and brushed aside the overgrown grass. A small stuffed bear became visible underneath. He picked it up silently. "...maybe?"

Talin looked at the bear. "Yours?"

"No. Another boy's," Red Wolf said. He ran his free hand through his hair. "I don't remember his name. It... I couldn't pronounce it. This was...an orphanage?" He put the bear back down.

"An orphanage?" Talin's brow creased.

"I know, it makes no sense," Red Wolf said. "I couldn't even tell you how I know. There's only...fragments."

Talin went back to the main street while he puzzled over the rubble and its surrounds. There were several skeletons lying around here, mostly reclaimed by nature. He was sure some of the bones belonged to children but couldn't confirm how he knew without examination. Perhaps they'd been his friends, and he had seen them killed before his very eyes. It made some amount of sense, certainly, in a village this small.

He hated not being able to remember who they were.

"Red Wolf..." Talin called.

"Still here."

"Katherine told you that you'd gone with Lord Edric on a tour of the Highlands, didn't she?"

"She did."

"I don't see a single weapon, shield, or Blackrun banner here. Lord Edric must have had an escort if he brought you along."

"Then...I was never here...?"

He could smell smoke and iron. The air felt heavy, hard to breathe in. Red Wolf stumbled back to the main street, mind reeling, trying to make sense of the fragments of memory.

"How old are you, boy?"

"He's six! Sirs, please—"

"Red Wolf?" Talin's voice. He turned, and the memory fragment vanished again, leaving only them.

"They...asked us how old we were," he said. "I *was* here. There was a woman. Not Katherine. She lied about my age."

"You're remembering more?" Talin asked.

"I don't...know."

Red Wolf crouched down in front of the skeleton that Talin had been examining and gingerly pulled back the overgrown grass to find its skull missing, severed from the body along with a few vertebrae. Panic seized his chest for some reason he couldn't comprehend. He fell back with a gasp, struggling to breathe.

She's dead. She's dead. She's dead.

He saw the woman fall, clear as day, severed head rolling away in the other direction. The man rushed to her, cursing the attackers, tearing himself free as they tried to grab him. Their leader scoffed and decapitated him as well in a single sword stroke.

No!

I'm going to die here.

The air was thick with smoke. He couldn't draw in a full breath without choking. Red Wolf looked up at the leader of the group and recognised him now as General Kehlvor.

"You're quite tall for a pup of your age," the general said. "Are you really six?"

Some remnant of logic cut through his haze of fear and prompted him to nod.

"What's your name, boy?" Kehlvor asked.

My name is Connor Kulos.

"...got you..."

Some part of his subconscious understood that all of this was ancient history, that nothing he did or said would change what happened. The other part was still trapped with Kehlvor in the past—watching the world end around him.

"...deep breaths, Red Wolf..."

"Connor," he said.

"Sounds Highlander. Could be a half-giant name, though," Kehlvor said. "You're not from one of the clans, are you?"

"I'm...from here..." Red Wolf said. "I was born here."

"Sir? What should we do with him?"

Kehlvor looked him up and down and turned away. "Put him with the others. If he's from the clans, he's been abandoned here."

"...my voice. Focus...my voice. I've got you."

Slowly, painfully so, the voice cut through the fragments, rooting him back in the present. His eyes focused now on Talin, not the woman's corpse. She had cupped his face in both hands and blocked his view of the surrounds so he could only see her. Her face was creased with worry.

"Connor? Red Wolf?" she said softly.

"I..." He drew in a few shaky breaths, squeezing his eyes shut and opening them again. "I hear you. I'm alright."

"Red Wolf," Talin said. She didn't let go of him. He realised that he was still trembling.

"I know what happened here." His shoulders sank. "I remember...enough to know."

His face must have betrayed his emotions in that moment because Talin pulled him into an embrace, hugging his head, fingers stroking his hair gently.

"I'm sorry," she whispered. "I'm so sorry."

Red Wolf rested his forehead against her shoulder for a while, listening to her heartbeat, reminding himself of her presence. She made no move to separate herself.

"There was an orphanage here. It was run by a couple, a young woman and her husband," he finally said, pulling away to look at her again. "I lived there with a handful of other children. Kehlvor was looking for children under the age of six for his alchemists and killing the rest, so the woman lied and told him I was a year younger than I actually was. That's why you and I both thought the year of Lord Edric's report didn't line up." His voice cracked there.

"Then...you're not Katherine's...?" Talin began.

"No, Katherine knew my birthday," Red Wolf said. "Kehlvor wondered if I was half-giant, too, so her affair with Chief Bjorson also makes sense. But there was never any 'tour' of the Highlands. I've lived in Velnora for as long as I can remember."

Talin said nothing.

"There's...only one conclusion...I can draw from all of this," Red Wolf continued. "The real reason that Katherine lied to me...is because I was abandoned here as an infant."

R ed Wolf had barely said a word since they set out for the mountain pass.

He'd been quieter than usual at supper last night, then at breakfast in
the morning, and Talin had figured back then that he just needed some
time to process everything they'd learned at Velnora. But it was now
almost sundown, the two of them were combing through the sparse
mountainside alone for what firewood they could gather, and Red Wolf
still hadn't said a word. She was beginning to worry.

"Are you alright?" she finally asked, breaking the awkward silence
between them. "I know what we found at Velnora was—"

"I'm fine," Red Wolf snapped, then groaned and closed his eyes
momentarily. "I'm sorry. It's... I appreciate the concern, but I'll be fine.
Let's just gather the rest of this firewood and head back to camp."

Talin could tell that he didn't want to get into it, so she dropped the matter for now. He would share his concerns with her, perhaps, once he had made sense of everything in his own head first.

"Did Katherine tell you much about the half-giants?" she asked instead.

"Only what she knows," Red Wolf said as he bent down to pick up a thick branch. "Which isn't much, admittedly. The clans are secretive by nature and aren't the most welcoming. She warned me that we might have to insist a few times before they'll grant us an audience. The Kulos clan, where Chief Bjors— where my father is from, is situated closest to the mountain pass. Their settlements are only accessible in the warmer months when the snowstorms aren't as bad, and we have a few precious weeks of decent weather to get through the pass. Hopefully, anyway. Temperatures are dropping—I can sense it."

"That's it? I imagined that Katherine would know more, given her attempts to form an alliance with them and her affair with Chief Bjorson," Talin said. She scooped up her bundle of firewood and led the way back towards their camp, Red Wolf close behind.

"I guess she's never stayed long enough to fully understand their way of life," he muttered. "Or she doesn't care enough to find out more." There was a hint of bitterness in his voice. He was evidently still upset about Blackrun's deception.

"Whatever the case, we'll know more once we get there," Talin said.

A snowflake landed on the back of her hand and melted. She stopped in her tracks and stared at the spot where it had landed.

"Something wrong?" Red Wolf asked.

"I just..." Talin blinked. "I saw a snowflake. I swear it."

More snow began to fall before her eyes as she stood there. Red Wolf cursed.

"We need to get back to camp. Now. Give me your firewood, and hang on to my elbow."

Talin did as she was bid, and the two of them made their way through the trees towards their campsite. The snowfall quickly worsened into a storm, then a heavy blizzard, covering the ground in a gradually thickening blanket of white. Talin was forced to accept Red Wolf's cloak as an extra layer of warmth against the elements.

"When...Katherine...warned us about the sudden...weather changes..." she began, teeth chattering, "I didn't think it would be...this bad..."

"You alright?" Red Wolf asked.

"I'll live."

The two of them returned to the camp to find Golmin and Ettrias busy packing up their tents and strapping their gear back onto the saddles. Red Wolf quickly grabbed a length of rope to bind their bundle of firewood together and hefted it onto the back of his own horse.

"What are you two doing?" Talin demanded, having to shout to make herself heard over the howling winds.

"We need to get out of this blizzard," Golmin said. "Find some form of shelter. We'll all freeze to death in the open!"

"There's nothing around us!" Talin yelled. "We're surrounded by forest and open tundra! Lady Blackrun even warned us there won't be much shelter from the elements in the mountain pass!"

"We have to find *something*." Red Wolf swung himself onto his horse and led the way at a slow trot. Talin had to squint to see through the biting snow; it stung her face and eyes and blinded them to anything further than a few feet away.

"I thought Blackrun said the weather would be calm enough to travel in the summer!" Ettrias called.

"Well, she's not exactly a prophet, is she?" Red Wolf growled.

The four of them stumbled through the blizzard and quickly fading daylight for over an hour without any landmarks or shelter in sight, to the point that Talin was half-convinced they were travelling in circles. But she also trusted Red Wolf's instincts and Golmin's navigation skills, and if the two of them were unable to find their way to shelter, she knew they were truly trapped in the open.

We're going to freeze to death at this rate, she thought.

Talin glanced at Red Wolf. He looked to be entirely unbothered by the conditions, but from the way he kept looking back at the rest of them, it was clear that he was worried about how long they would last.

"Talin!" he yelled back. "How are you holding up?"

"Don't worry about me," she said. "We just have to..."

Gods, she could barely feel her own fingers. Maybe they would just have to take their chances and try to light a bonfire somehow. Red Wolf sniffed the air and immediately banked right, moving directly against the blizzard. She heard Golmin curse as he forced his own horse to obey.

"Are you mad?" the guard captain snapped. "We cannot head out of the forest! The blizzard will be worse in the open—we'll only freeze faster!"

"I caught a scent!" Red Wolf said. "Wood-smoke and hay. The strong wind is blowing it down to us. There's a settlement this way!"

"Gods, I hope you're right about this." Golmin didn't look happy, but he didn't make any further argument.

"I have an idea." Ettrias pulled some herbs from their ration pack and stuffed them into his tinderbox, drilling a small hole into the side with his dagger. "Think you can light this?"

"Not sure how it'll help, but..." Talin reached over and prodded the dry material with a spark of lightning. Ettrias quickly snapped the tinderbox shut. A thick, red smoke began to waft from it, followed soon by a red glow.

"Trick I learned from Corvan!" Ettrias told her. "He told me some types of herbs have properties that make them burn and smoke in different colours. Ooh, hot!" He almost dropped the box. Red Wolf took it from him and held it up high without hesitation.

"Isn't that going to burn—" Talin began.

"I'll heal."

It wasn't long before they heard distant shouting in what sounded like an odd combination of Old Torrian and the modern Torrian they all spoke. Talin could barely understand what the shouting was but knew enough of both languages that she could respond.

"We're downwind!" she shouted, battling the blizzard and hoping she could be heard. Red Wolf quickly caught on and fumbled for something in his pockets—a wooden whistle. He blew into it repeatedly, still holding the hot tinderbox aloft, slowing his horse to a walk to make it easier for him to spot. The outline of a massive rider and horse loomed into view a minute later, followed by two more.

"Not a lot of elves go past the border," said the first rider in his odd mix of Old and modern Torrian. He wore a hood, and a thick mask covered his mouth and nose, muffling his voice. His companions were similarly outfitted. "Certainly not a lot with good survival instincts. This way."

They were led through the blizzard for what felt like forever before a tall structure became visible, a sturdy watchtower with a massive lantern at the top to light the way for anyone moving through the storm. The riders led them through a set of thick double doors and into the stables. There, the riders finally removed their hoods and masks, allowing Talin to get a good look at their faces. The first rider was a big man even taller than Red Wolf, with dark brown hair tied into a bun but shaved down the sides and back and a magnificent, braided beard. His companions both sported shoulder-length black hair and similar long beards. They all towered over her and her companions.

"This way." The first rider moved off without bothering to look over his shoulder. "My people will take care of your horses. You need warm food and drink."

"Thank you for finding us," Talin said as they walked. "We weren't expecting conditions to get so bad so quickly."

"It happens more often than you think," the rider said. "That's why this watchtower is here—to ensure that we can spot any lost travellers in the area. Your little trick with the tinderbox may have saved all of you. This blizzard is one of the worst kinds we get up here. Visibility so bad you can barely see a thing in front of your own face, temperatures cold enough to freeze water in minutes..."

He pushed open the doors to a lounge area with a fireplace and quickly prepared some warm drinks for the four of them. Talin accepted hers gratefully and drank. It was a delicious blend of hot cocoa and spices.

"Sip it slowly," the rider said, stopping Ettrias from taking another large gulp. "You've been in the cold too long. We need to thaw you out slowly." He looked Red Wolf up and down. "Though you seem unbothered by the temperatures. You don't look like a Hellhound, though—are you from the homeland?"

"No. It's complicated." Red Wolf averted his eyes.

"Now, tell me," the rider said, pulling up a chair. "What are four elves doing in the mountain pass in the middle of a blizzard?"

"Lady Blackrun sent us," Talin explained. "We're on our way to the Kulos clan to discuss the possibility of an alliance."

The rider huffed. "You've found us. Well, some of us, at least. This is one of the clan's watchtowers." He took a swig of his own drink. "Katherine Blackrun wastes her time. I've told her many times of our reasons for refusing. I have to wonder if she truly makes these trips to negotiate an alliance or if..."

"Please," Talin said. "It's important. If you could point us in the direction of your village, we'll be out of here as soon as our task is fulfilled."

"You're going nowhere in this blizzard," the half-giant said. "Once it clears, perhaps—but only because there will be no way off the mountain until some of the snow melts. You passed through a narrow chasm today, yes? It will be completely blocked off. You can shelter at the village for now, but you'll not receive an audience with the chief."

"Is there really no way we can talk to your chief?" Talin asked. "We came all the way here..."

"Let this be a lesson and a message for Katherine Blackrun, then." The half-giant scoffed. "We have no interest in an alliance with a kingdom who began the Inquisition. Kies Tor nearly wiped out all magic in the known world by instilling the fear of magic into the hearts of not just its own people but every other nation on this side of the eastern range."

"Can't you at least hear us out?" Red Wolf asked as the half-giant stood. "What does your chief say about all of this?"

The half-giant let out a long breath and pinched the bridge of his nose. "Choose your next words carefully. You are here under the Kulos clan's generous hospitality. We reserve every right to send you back into the blizzard."

"If you won't negotiate with Blackrun or any of her allies, what about one of your own?" Red Wolf asked.

"You are not one of us."

Red Wolf seemed to hesitate. The half-giant made for the door.

"Just...give him a chance," Talin said.

"My name is Connor Blackrun," Red Wolf said after another pause. "Katherine Blackrun is my mother, and I'm aware that she had an affair with Chief Tormod Bjorson for some time. I'm told he's my father." He paused again and swallowed. "I know the half-giants have good reason to be cautious of Torrians after what King Braenern did. But I'd like a chance to speak with your clan chief in the morning, if possible."

There was a beat, and for a moment, Talin thought the half-giant would ignore his request, but then he crossed the room again and set his mug down.

"You're looking at him," he said. "Chief Tormod Kulos Bjorson. I believe we have some catching up to do."

For the second time since their reunion at Castle Blackrun, Red Wolf looked like he was at a loss for words.

"I...you seem shocked," Chief Bjorson said. "I understand if you have questions for me. I'll answer what I can—though I'll admit, I have plenty of questions of my own."

Red Wolf worked his jaw. His gaze flickered ever so briefly towards Talin.

"I have plenty of questions. For...another time, perhaps," he said. "What do you want to know?"

"Of course. I... Well, what happened to you?" Bjorson asked. "Katherine told me you were dead. We thought...Kehlvor and the Hell-hounds..."

Red Wolf let out a long breath. "It's a long story. You'll want to sit."

Bjorson sat himself down in one of the armchairs, and Red Wolf recounted everything from the beginning—how he'd been in Velnora when the Hellhounds attacked, the experiments they ran, how he came to be in Belanore and the life he'd built for himself there. Talin saw Ettrias and Golmin's expressions slowly shift from curiosity to shock—evidently, he hadn't told either of them about what they uncovered in Velnora. Bjorson was silent for a long while after he finished.

"You've...been through a lot," the half-giant finally said. "I'm sorry."

"Don't be. You thought I was dead. *Katherine* thought I was dead until recently." Red Wolf sighed. "What's done is done. I came to learn who I am. My companions are here as a favour to Katherine."

"Hmm." Bjorson looked at Talin, then at Ettrias and Golmin. "You're all friends of Connor. I suppose I'll have to hear you out if he vouches for you. Kat wouldn't have sent you all up here in her stead if she didn't think you could make a good case."

"I trust them with my life," Red Wolf said. "We came here because Katherine thought you might be able to help us."

Talin let out a long breath. Now was as good a time as any to announce who she was.

"I understand that the half-giants have had a...strained relationship with Kies Tor for centuries, especially House Zylvaris. I... My name is Talin Zylvaris, rightful ruler of Kies Tor. I've come as a favour to Katherine, yes, but I have my own reasons. Your alliance with House Blackrun and the Highlands can help me in taking back my kingdom."

Bjorson grunted. "You are bold to have sought us out. I've no doubt some of the other chiefs would have attacked as soon as they learned of your identity."

"But not you," Talin said.

"I...I am far more lenient to Kat than I should be, perhaps," Bjorson said with a sigh. "Our relationship still stands through the years, by some miracle, and I know if she trusts you to negotiate on her behalf, she must hold you in high regard indeed. Besides, it is by Connor's protection that you remain. Speak your piece."

"I know that the half-giants have every reason to resent me and all of Kies Tor for what my ancestors did," Talin said. "But if you agree to Katherine's alliance and help me take back my rightful place as queen, the Crown would owe you a great debt. You could ask *anything* of us within reason, and Kies Tor will do its utmost to provide."

"Answer me this, Queen Talin of Kies Tor," Bjorson said. "What do you understand of the Inquisition?"

"I..." Talin faltered there. "Not much, I'll admit. I've seen our records of what happened back then, but they only tell my ancestors' side of the story."

"And this is the problem that you and Kat both share." Bjorson flashed her a knowing smile. "You believe you could grant us anything we desire, yet you understand *nothing* of the half-giants. You're no different from Kat. She, too, believed that she had the power to...aid us somehow just because your people call her a 'lady' and treat her with reverence. But the simple truth is this: we do not need your kingdom's favour."

"Then teach me," Talin said. "You're right—I don't understand anything of your people. Many of our records of magic were erased during the Inquisition. But I'd like to learn."

The others all stared at her. She could tell what they were all thinking. *We might not have the time to stay up here.*

But Bjorson had mentioned that they were trapped on this side of the mountain pass, and if they were going to be village guests for the foreseeable future, she could certainly think of worse ways to pass the time than learning from the half-giants.

"What do you know of the White Raven?" Bjorson asked.

"I know it symbolises death in the mountains," Talin said. "I also know it's the royal crest of Kies Tor and the emblem of House Zylvaris, and there's some kind of prophecy surrounding it. I don't know what it all means."

Bjorson heaved a sigh. "Very well. Allow me to propose a deal. I will allow you to learn from my people until the snows melt in the canyon and allow you passage back home. If the elders or myself deem you worthy to drink from the Pool of Prophecy by then, you will learn the truth of the Inquisition, and the Kulos clan will join with Kies Tor in allegiance—if you still wish it by then."

"The Pool of Prophecy?" Talin asked.

"Yes. The source of the white raven prophecy. The place where you will find your answers."

"Alright. I accept."

Her companions exchanged looks. She could tell they were wondering what in the seven hells she had gotten them into now.

"We shall set off when the blizzard dies down in the morning, then," Bjorson said. "For now, you're free to use the lounge. I assume you brought rations with you, but if you require food, you can help yourselves to the cellar. There's firewood in the corner and more in the stables if you run out. Latrines are downstairs." He stood and disappeared through the doors.

"By the gods, Talin, what have you agreed to?" Ettrias groaned.

"We're going to be stuck up here for the time being anyway." Talin shrugged. "Might as well familiarise ourselves with the local culture.

Besides, this is the perfect chance for Red Wolf to learn about his people."

"I—" Red Wolf's ears turned a deep shade of scarlet. "I appreciate it."

The blizzard had settled by dawn, exactly as Bjorson had said, though the freezing temperatures remained. They set off for the Kulos clan village wrapped up in thick layers of fur coats and borrowed masks for their mouths and noses. Bjorson explained that their snot and any moisture on their lips would freeze instantly otherwise.

"How do you deal with the weather up here?" Talin asked as they made their way into the village, past rows of simple huts lined up on either side of the dusty road. "Searing summer heat one minute, freezing blizzard the next...gods, I thought the storms in the south were bad."

"My people have adapted to the mountains," Bjorson said. "Surviving here is second nature to us. Our houses are built with a layer of furs in the walls and ceilings to act as insulation against the elements. We do our farming in the summer months and only grow crops that can survive the harsh climates here."

He showed them to an empty hut close to the village hall, a simple little structure with a small open section serving as the living quarters and a kitchen attached to it, as well as two little bedrooms and a latrine at the end of a short hallway—wildly different from the segregated outhouses Talin might have expected from a similar hut in Kies Tor. No doubt the winter months made it far too cold to exit the building for such an excursion. A fireplace was set into the far wall of the lounge to heat the entire hut.

"I'll leave you to settle in," Bjorson said. "But don't dawdle. I'd like the four of you to join today's hunting party in half an hour. Think of it as your...first lesson on half-giant culture."

The door shut behind him, and Ettrias wasted no time claiming one of the bedrooms for himself and Golmin. Red Wolf didn't move from the doorway.

"Come on," Talin said softly. "We're going to be here for a while yet. You'll have plenty of time to get acquainted with the place."

"I just..." Red Wolf frowned. "Never mind." He adjusted the bag strap on his shoulder and made his way further into the hut. "You ought to claim the bed. I'll take the sofa."

Talin smiled. She'd anticipated that he would be like this. "We could share."

Red Wolf blinked at her. He slowly turned scarlet.

"If...you have no objections..." He cleared his throat. "Alright." He disappeared into the second bedroom while Talin laughed.

It must be a lot to take in, she thought. All of this was certainly difficult to process even for her—all records of the Far North and the Inquisition had mentioned the eventual extinction of giants. Yet their descendants had evidently lived on through it all, hidden from her great-great-grandfather's tyranny.

I should have checked the records more thoroughly. Asked Katherine about what she knew. This kind of history should never have been lost.

They joined the hunters gathering at the edge of the village as agreed half an hour later. The leader of their party, a burly man with a shaved head and full beard by the name of Thorik, explained their intended path through the mountains as he briefed the group. He also handed each of them a spear.

"These smaller weapons are designed for our children, to teach them how to hunt in the mountains," he explained. "They should be the right size for all of you. But we prefer to use bows at range—far more accurate and allows for a second chance if you miss."

"Suits me," Talin said.

"I'm not going to enjoy this, am I?" Ettrias grumbled.

"Look on the bright side." Golmin clapped him on the shoulder with a grin. "There *are* four of us, so if you miss, we can provide a back-up shot and let you take the credit."

Red Wolf snickered. Talin laughed at her brother's incredulous expression.

They moved through the mountainside at a gruelling pace; with the half-giants' height and long strides, they were able to cross the rocky terrain with ease, leaving Talin and her companions to struggle, gasping for air, behind them. Even Red Wolf, who usually never looked out of breath during heavy physical exertion, seemed to be having trouble keeping up.

"Not easy, is it?" Thorik said as he helped them up a ledge far too tall for any elf to clamber onto. He already had three dead rabbits strapped to his bandolier.

"I guess...Kies Tor just...doesn't have this kind of terrain," Talin huffed. "Do you usually lead a hunting party this big?"

"Not normally, no," Thorik said. "We're preparing for a feast tomorrow. You're not the only guests we get up here."

Talin was curious about these other 'guests', but she decided it was best not to pry. Thorik hauled an out-of-breath and sweating Ettrias onto the ledge and continued on his way.

She supposed, looking on the bright side of this exhausting excursion, the half-giants' preference for bows when hunting meant that she was right in her element. She provided a back-up shot for the hunters when they missed, and the unusually agile elk in the mountains made for a good challenge.

"You hunt frequently back home?" Thorik asked as they began the trek back, prizes hauled over their shoulders. Red Wolf happily took the heavier loads and looked almost comical with an elk slung over each shoulder, almost obscuring his face.

"Sometimes. Mostly I just enjoy archery," Talin said.

"I can tell. Your shots are impressive. Clean."

"I'm humbled by the praise."

They had their supper in the village hall that evening, seated at the head table alongside Chief Bjorson. Most of the villagers, like the half-giants in the hunting party, stood at least half a foot taller than even Red Wolf, who seemed oddly relieved that he no longer had to duck his head to go through doorways. Outside, strong winds howled through the streets, but the inside of the hall was blissfully warm. Bjorson explained that they were seated with him tonight as a way to welcome them into the village for the first time.

"This food is delicious," Ettrias said between mouthfuls of roast meat. "Is this some of our hunting haul?"

"Some of it, yes," Bjorson said. "The rest is being prepared for our feast tomorrow."

After supper, the tables in the hall were immediately pushed aside, leaving only the massive fire pit blazing in the centre of the room, providing them with warmth. The villagers gathered around it. Bjorson invited Talin and the others to join them, explaining that this was another tradition—a regular evening gathering where any willing performer was invited to share a song or story.

"Long ago, your ancestors, too, passed down their histories through story and song," the chief said. "No doubt traces of the tradition live on through your bards and storytellers."

"A written system was developed for Torrian even before Braenern's time, and most of our histories are recorded on paper," Talin said. "What you speak of, it's...a lost tradition in Kies Tor now."

"Indeed. It's a shame."

Red Wolf watched the next performer get to his feet with his brow creased. He said nothing.

"I remember when you would sing at the royal guards' talent shows," Golmin said with a grin, nudging him in the ribs.

Talin's jaw fell open. "You can *sing*, and you never told me?"

"It's just a hobby. I'm hardly as good as a bard."

"But he is very good," Golmin whispered.

"Can...anyone join this?" Red Wolf asked, nodding at the gathered villagers.

"Of course. So long as you have a story to tell." Bjorson shrugged.

"Going to perform for us?" Talin lifted an eyebrow.

"You'll see."

The evening continued in a similar fashion, with villagers getting up one by one to perform. Some sang a lively tune that had everyone on their feet and dancing; others sang epic ballads or heartfelt melodies. The rest told stories—some real, some fiction—and wove such incredible tales out of even the most mundane things that Talin felt her full attention drawn to these storytellers.

Another villager finished her song to a round of cheering and applause—and Red Wolf, to Talin's surprise, was the next to stand.

"I have a song," he said. "I wrote it on the road many years ago, not knowing whether I'd ever be able to perform it for the person I wanted. But we're both here tonight, and I'd like to sing it now."

Talin's breath hitched. Red Wolf glanced at her, then opened his mouth, and his deep, melancholic tune would engrave itself into her memory forever. He spoke of Kies Tor, of the Draconian lands, of losing all the people he'd ever loved and leaving the only home he'd ever known. He spoke of her, too, and laid his heart bare before all of them—admitting, perhaps for the first time, that he regretted leaving her behind. In that same moment, she understood why he felt so guilty and why he'd apologised when she saw him again for the first time. He blamed himself for the events that led to their parting fifteen years ago, just as she blamed herself for refusing to intervene.

I'm sorry I left you, his song seemed to say.

I'm sorry I let you leave, she thought.

There was a moment of dead silence when he finished. Red Wolf met her gaze and held it. He looked almost on the verge of tears, and Talin had to fight to keep her own emotions in check.

"Do you want to..." Talin began once he sat, and the next performer took the stage.

"Later." Red Wolf drew in a sharp breath and swallowed. He did, however, reach out and take her hand. Talin bumped shoulders with him lightly and squeezed back.

Slowly, as the night dragged on, the number of villagers at the fire began to dwindle. Bjorson bid them farewell not too long after and told them the hall was open for a while longer, but they were not obligated to stay for any length of time—not all of the villagers joined their communal evenings, and it was common for people to retire to their own homes once it got late. Ettrias and Golmin decided to return to the hut at that, along with Red Wolf, and Talin stayed to listen to one more song before also retiring.

Back in the hut, she found Red Wolf in the bedroom, oiling his blade in the dark. Moonlight glinted off the Draconian steel, a sliver of blue against the patterned metal.

"Red Wolf," she said softly. He paused with his cloth halfway down the length of the weapon.

"I suppose we should talk."

"Please."

Red Wolf wiped his blade down and sheathed it. Talin sat on the edge of the bed beside him.

"We, uh..." He cleared his throat. "I don't know where to start. I'm sorry."

"Tell me about the song, then," Talin said. "You said you wrote it on the road."

"I did." Red Wolf frowned. "Truth be told, I'd originally written it for myself. I was on the road near the western border of Kies Tor and didn't think we'd ever reunite. I wrote the song in a pathetic attempt to move on." He huffed a bitter laugh. "It's funny, really. I spent the better part of fifteen years trying to find out where I came from and who I used to be, but I wasn't nearly as upset about my lack of progress as I was about never seeing you again. I spent fifteen years wondering what I could have done differently."

"That makes two of us, then," Talin admitted. "I wondered, too. What would have happened if you'd let me frame Ettrias again? What if I'd pardoned you instead of allowing your sentencing to go ahead?"

"I suppose we'll never know," Red Wolf said. His frown deepened. "We've been dodging our true feelings for too long. I think it's fair to say we were both afraid that things had changed. But I know how I feel about you, and you know how you feel about me. Have things really changed?"

Talin winced. "I don't know. But you're right. No more secrets."

She cupped his face in her hands and pressed their lips together. Red Wolf hesitated for a fraction of a second, but then he wrapped an arm around her waist and kissed her back hard. She responded by sliding her arms around his neck and pulling him closer.

"Fifteen years ago, I told you that I was yours if you would have me," he whispered when they broke apart. "That has not changed. I have always been yours. I want this, I want *us*, I want what we had back then."

Talin pressed her forehead against his. "Then we'll let the people talk. Let them curse your name and mine. It doesn't *matter*. I am not losing you again."

There was a commotion in the village the next morning.

Talin dragged herself out of bed with a groan and went out to the living quarters, peering through the window to see what was going on. Most of the village, it appeared, was already up; she could see people moving about in the street. There was, however, a gathered welcoming procession along the main road. And making their way up to the village hall in marching columns...

Red Wolf is not going to like this.

"What's with the gods-awful racket?" Ettrias grumbled, appearing next to her and rubbing his eyes.

"See for yourself." She stepped aside to let him pass.

"Oh. *Touvir*. That's not good."

Golmin was next to join them, frowning at the new village guests, followed by Red Wolf himself. He saw the three of them gathered at the window and hummed.

"Quite early for the whole village to be awake, surely," he said. "What's the occasion?"

Talin nodded towards the main road. Red Wolf's gaze drifted over the welcoming procession to the marching column. He froze.

"Hellhounds," Ettrias said.

"These aren't just..." Red Wolf worked his jaw. "I know these Hellhounds. This is General Kehlvor's pack."

"Kehlvor's...?"

Red Wolf was out of the door by the time Talin had processed what he'd said.

"Red Wolf, wait— oh, for the love of the gods."

She threw on a coat and ran after him as he crossed the short distance to the village hall, where Bjorson was already conversing with Kehlvor himself and another Hellhound that Talin had never met before. They looked over at Red Wolf's approach, and Kehlvor stared for a few moments before coughing.

"Perhaps it's best if we continue this discussion another time," the man said, grabbing his companion and quickly excusing themselves. Talin could almost feel Red Wolf's smouldering glare as they made their way into the village hall.

"What in the seven hells is this about?" he demanded. "*Why* are they here?"

"These are our village guests," Bjorson said. "The blizzard you faced had been moving south for some time—it's rendered the entire mountainside almost completely impassable. They were trapped in the area and requested some place to shelter until the snows melt and allow them to move on."

"I don't understand," he growled. "You'd allow Kehlvor and his entire pack into the village after the atrocities they committed in Kies Tor? They don't *deserve* that kindness."

"It is a good thing, then, that this is not your decision to make," Bjorson said icily. "We can speak of this matter in the evening. For now, I expect you to exercise some restraint. They *are* village guests, as are your friends."

Red Wolf's jaw tightened, but he didn't argue. Bjorson turned away and made his way into the hall after Kehlvor.

"What's the occasion?" Talin asked, jogging up. "Why's Bjorson playing host to a pack of Hellhounds?"

"I have no idea." Red Wolf let out a long breath. "But I think it best if we steered clear of them for now. I'm...going to do some training." He stormed off without another word.

Talin cursed under her breath and went back to the hut for her own weapons, figuring that it was probably best to keep an eye on Red Wolf today. She caught up to him on his way to the training grounds on the outskirts of the village.

"I know you're only here to make sure I don't cause any trouble with the Hellhounds today," he muttered. "I'll be fine."

"And can you really promise there won't be trouble?" Talin lifted a brow.

Red Wolf sighed. "You have a point."

They spent most of the morning sparring with the village warriors and shooting targets from horseback. Talin found herself hopelessly outmatched against her opponents; most of the half-giants stood well over seven feet tall and were much stronger than her besides. Red Wolf, on the other hand, seemed quite happy about finally being able to spar someone taller than him, even though it became quickly apparent that none of his usual tactics had any effect.

"You look like you're enjoying yourself," Talin said when he stepped out of the duelling ring, out of breath for once.

"What can I say? It's an experience, fighting someone my own size." Red Wolf grinned. He looked at the shield he'd been holding and ran a hand over the carved wood. "These shields are impressive, too. The craftsmanship is exquisite. If only we had tools capable of engraving metal with the same level of detail and intricacy."

Talin smiled. She had missed Red Wolf's enthusiasm whenever he discussed weaponry; it seemed like he'd already put the morning's incident behind him.

"You'd fit in well here," she said. "You're shorter than the other half-giants, but you'd be welcomed here if you wanted to stay." Her smile faded a little.

Is it selfish to want him to return to Belanore with me?

It was an irrational thought; she knew him well enough to know that he wouldn't leave her again, especially after their conversation last night. Yet some small part of her worried all the same.

"Maybe." Red Wolf's brow creased. "Chief Bjorson seems fine with what I am, but seeing him so friendly with Kehlvor, I don't know if..."

He trailed off. Talin followed his gaze across the duelling ring and found that half a dozen Hellhounds had joined the warriors there. One of the youths stepped into the ring with a half-giant dressed in nothing but a pair of boots and trousers, while the half-giant warrior had ditched his training spear for a metal one.

"You said you recognised the Hellhounds in Kehlvor's pack," Talin said, watching as the two warriors began their duel. "Do you know some of them?"

"I wouldn't go that far," Red Wolf said. "I'm...acquainted with them at best. Didn't exactly have many choices for a sparring partner during my time with them."

They lapsed into silence. In the ring, the half-giant warrior eventually yielded to his opponent's lightning-fast strikes, clutching his arm. Talin winced; she'd sparred with Red Wolf enough times to know that he'd be sporting a nasty bruise there the next day.

"Who's next, then?" the Hellhound asked. His gaze landed on her. "I didn't realise we had *royalty* visiting the village. Care for a round?"

Red Wolf pulled his tunic over his head with a scowl and unsheathed his sword. "Perhaps someone more evenly matched for your speed, *pup*."

"A brother? Well met. Which pack do you hail from?" the Hellhound asked.

I'm not your brother. First to land a fatal strike?"

"Of course."

The two of them collided in a deafening ring of steel, sharp blades biting against each other. Red Wolf quickly freed his weapon and swung again, but the Hellhound brought his own blade back around in a lightning-fast parry. He went low with a feint. Red Wolf met it with a deft counter that slashed his opponent's neck wide open.

"Again," he said. "That was over too fast."

They came at each other again, the Hellhound playing more defensively this time. Talin caught a feint that Red Wolf liked to use that his opponent barely parried. The Hellhound tried to answer with a high riposte. Red Wolf knocked it aside without skipping a beat and drove his blade into the man's chest.

"Damn it, again," he growled. "Don't go easy on me, pup."

They continued for another three rounds, each equally short as the last. It became quickly apparent to Talin that the Hellhound was far outmatched against her ex-bodyguard; Red Wolf moved with a deadly speed and brutality that made her realise he'd been holding back against her all along.

"That's enough," he finally said, freeing his bloodied blade from his opponent's torso yet again. The Hellhound gasped as the wound closed. "We're done here." He turned away and made his way back to Talin with his lips pressed into a hard line.

"Thought you'd be happier about winning," she said.

"I don't…" Red Wolf sheathed his sword. "Too crowded here. Come with me."

He struggled into his tunic as he moved off, and Talin quickly snatched up her bow and arrows before falling into step beside him. He led her all the way out of the village and up a steep hiking trail still half-covered by snow, long legs putting him well ahead of her, forcing her almost to a jog to keep up. The trail led them up to the top of a rocky outcrop overlooking the village, where he finally stopped and gestured for her to sit.

"Something's been bothering you since the Hellhounds arrived this morning," Talin said. "And it's not that you're upset about them being here."

"I know." Red Wolf sighed. "I thought…I was done with that part of my life. That once I left Kies Tor, I could somehow…leave that part of my past behind. But it was just a stupid fantasy." He fell silent for a moment as if trying to work out what to say. "When I saw that

Hellhound fight, I wanted to prove to myself that I wasn't like them because the way they fight is the way I was taught to fight. He was still a youngster, still a pup, but he bested a half-giant twice his height due to his speed. I thought...if I could *lose* to him...I'd finally be able to tell myself that I wasn't as fast as them. I wasn't as strong. I wasn't *one of them*."

"You're not," Talin said. "You won because you were the better fighter, not because you have their powers."

"So was that half-giant warrior." Red Wolf clenched his fists. "I won because I was able to match his speed. His strength."

"Your powers don't define who you are."

Red Wolf turned his attention to the village below. "I know that. But it doesn't change anything."

"Why are you so afraid of being like them?"

"Because I— They're—"

Talin took his hand in both of hers and brushed her fingers over his knuckles. "I've suspected for a long time that Kies Tor wasn't randomly targeted. You'll remember that General Virion made a deal with the Hellhounds fifteen years ago because they supposedly told him the 'truth'. I visited him in jail a few times to ask what they told him to make him turn on us. He spoke in riddles, but from what I've been able to gather, it had something to do with Braenern's quest to purge magic. The Hellhounds and the half-giants call it the Inquisition."

"I don't understand," Red Wolf said.

"I don't know how to explain it exactly," Talin admitted. "But I have a hunch that I can't shake...and I've spent years researching and wondering whether the Torrian Crown was responsible."

"What? How could you be responsible for what Kehlvor did?" Red Wolf asked.

"I'm not saying Kehlvor is blameless, and his actions certainly don't merit defending," Talin said. "But something doesn't add up. Why attack and push south towards Belanore so relentlessly after securing Vill's Crossing? Why did he retreat without explanation at the end of the war?"

Red Wolf's brow creased, and she could see him turning it over in his head, trying to come up with an explanation.

"Fine," he finally said. "Let's say your theory is right. How are we to prove it?"

"Kehlvor's staying at the village for the foreseeable future." Talin shrugged. "Nothing's stopping us from simply...asking."

Red Wolf visibly bristled at the suggestion, but he made no objection. "Be my guest, then. Just don't expect him to tell you anything useful."

"There's...one other thing," Talin said. "I think...it might be worth it if you hear him out too."

"I don't want anything to do with him," Red Wolf snapped, climbing to his feet. "If you want your answers from him, I will not stop you. But I want no part in it." He stalked off.

You're letting your anger cloud your judgement, Red Wolf, Talin thought, but she let him go anyway. She couldn't blame him for his unwillingness to speak with Kehlvor; knowing what she did about his past, even a part of her was reluctant to interact with the pack leader. But she had spent years with the unshakeable feeling that there was more to the Hellhounds' motives than simple conquest, and here was the perfect opportunity to ask the man who'd started the war.

Kehlvor, as it turned out, was surprisingly difficult to track down; she made two laps of the village but hadn't caught even a glimpse of him among the groups of Hellhounds gathered outside. Red Wolf found her in the middle of the main street on her third lap and urged her to give up her search. She relented after he reminded her of her real objective here and mentioned that Ettrias and Golmin had been dragged into helping teach a weapons class for the half-giant children.

"Besides, he'll be at the feast tonight, along with the rest of the pack. You won't miss him then," Red Wolf said.

"I wonder if he's avoiding me on purpose," Talin muttered.

"Wouldn't put it past him."

True to his prediction, with the pack joining them all for supper, the village hall was packed that evening. Talin counted at least half a dozen Hellhound chefs helping with the food. They were seated with the rest of the villagers now, after the welcoming supper last night, and Red Wolf had waited until the supper line was almost empty to avoid queuing with the Hellhounds.

"They clearly have some sort of arrangement with the Kulos clan," she said, nodding at the line when he took his spot opposite her. "This isn't the first time they've been here."

"It doesn't make any sense," Ettrias said. "The Hellhounds live in the furthest reaches of the Far North. What business do Kehlvor and his entire pack have to be travelling so close to the border? Surely they're not...planning another attack..." He frowned at his soup.

"No, I doubt Kehlvor has plans for invasion," Talin said. "They didn't come equipped for battle. It's exactly like Bjorson said—the blizzard just happened to trap them in the area."

"Whatever Kehlvor's up to here, it's nothing good," Red Wolf muttered.

"Kehlvor is standing right behind you, pup."

Red Wolf shot to his feet and spun. Talin jumped up at the same time.

"Red Wolf!" she exclaimed. He froze with a fistful of the pack leader's tunic in his hand.

"My queen wishes to speak to you," he said. "Count yourself lucky." He released Kehlvor roughly.

"I'd heard you were looking for me," the Hellhound said, sliding into an empty spot opposite Talin. Red Wolf scowled and moved to sit on Golmin's other side.

"Let us do away with the formalities," Talin said. "I know you've no remorse for all you did in Kies Tor, and I won't apologise for all I've had to do to your people in defense of my home. I only wanted to ask you *why*."

"Why? Revenge. Justice. To purge the greater evil." Kehlvor shrugged. "Pick one."

"That doesn't tell me anything," Talin said.

"You asked, and I answered."

Talin fell silent for a moment, thinking of another angle. Kehlvor seemed under the impression that she knew more than she did or was unwilling to share the real reason he'd attacked. She needed him to tell the full truth.

"Fifteen years ago, you made a deal with my general," she said. "Do you remember him?"

"Virion? Yes," Kehlvor said. "Deluded. Narcissistic. Naive."

"He said you'd told him about some kind of 'truth' that made him realise he was on the wrong side," Talin said. "What 'truth' could have driven a member of my own Royal Council to turn on Kies Tor?"

"You really don't know?" Kehlvor scoffed. "Perhaps you're just as naive as him."

"Maybe. But humour me."

Kehlvor let out a long breath. "I instructed Virion not to breathe the truth to a single soul because that knowledge is *dangerous*. What do you know of the White Raven?"

There it is again. What does it mean?

"Only that it's the symbol of death, it seems strangely ominous, and I've been hearing the phrase with alarming frequency as of late."

"The White Raven is the symbol of death, it's true. But that's not all. It is the very instrument with which the God of Death enacts his judgement upon the world," Kehlvor said. "The royal crest of your very kingdom is an omen of death."

"But that's what I don't understand," Talin said. "House Zylvaris' crest has always been a white raven, and no dreadful calamity of death has ever befallen Kies Tor. Why is it relevant now all of a sudden?"

"No calamity? What about the millions of innocents killed in King Braenern's name?"

"The...Inquisition...? What does that have to do with you?"

Kehlvor stood. "I owe you no answers. It's better for everyone if you give up your pursuit of the truth. You might actually do some good and save some people that way."

"You invade my home and slaughter my people, and you commit countless atrocities to the innocent civilians caught up in the war," Talin said, rising with him. "I think we all deserve some answers."

"Your people were weak. So are you, for you to have come to me begging for answers to questions you don't even want to ask," Kehlvor hissed. "But it is neither my right nor my wish to tell you the truth. My only hope is that Chief Bjorson also sees enough sense not to tell you." He turned away. "It was good to see you, Red Wolf. Brother."

Talin barely had enough time to register her ex-bodyguard lunging out of his seat before he tackled Kehlvor to the ground.

"Gods damn it." Golmin climbed to his feet as two more Hellhounds rushed to defend their leader. He nailed a punch at the first, but the man quickly recovered and retaliated by shoving him aside. Talin pinched the bridge of her nose.

This is going to be a long night.

"You think you can best me, pup?" Kehlvor huffed a laugh and kicked Red Wolf off him. He slipped behind the ex-bodyguard and threw him to the ground. "You have always been one of us. Your family abandoned you. It was my pack that gave you a new family. A new purpose. Yet you squandered it all."

More people were joining the fight now; Talin saw Ettrias wrestle a half-giant twice his height while Golmin fought off another Hellhound. They were both putting up a good fight despite their opponents' superior size and strength; Golmin threw his opponent down as she watched and went to tackle yet another Hellhound. Some of the half-giants had rushed to break up the fight, but it was no use—the confusion meant that they were inevitably dragged into the conflict as well. Talin dodged a flying plate and watched, almost transfixed, as the scene before her unfolded into pure chaos.

Red Wolf tripped Kehlvor and sent him crashing into a bench. The wood shattered under the strain. He jumped onto the man's back without hesitation and drove a downward elbow into the back of his head, and Talin heard a sharp *crack* from her seat several metres away.

"I am not your brother!" Another elbow. Another crack. Kehlvor threw him off, but he tackled the pack leader again, this time pinning him to the ground and throwing a punch at his face.

"You are not my family! You will never! Be! My! Family!" He accentuated each word with another punch.

"Red Wolf, *stop*," Talin said, starting forwards. He either didn't hear her or didn't care.

"You stole me from the only home I knew," Red Wolf growled, throwing yet another punch. Kehlvor lifted his arms to shield his face, to no avail. "You slaughtered everyone I knew. Everyone I loved." Another punch. "You turned me into a gods damned *experiment* for your gods. Forsaken. Alchemists." A punch for each word. "And you think to tell me that we're *family*?" Another punch. "*Sayu kust shivis.*" Another punch. "You're pathetic. *Sayu kust shivis.*" Another punch.

"Connor!"

Red Wolf drove one more punch into Kehlvor's face and looked up. Dead silence fell across the hall as Chief Bjorson strode forward.

We've really done it now, Talin thought.

"All of you, with me," Tormod said, pointing at her and her companions. "*Now.*"

T he five of them stood in dead silence in Bjorson's living quarters.

Ettrias and Golmin both looked a little worse for wear, with their hair tousled and knuckles bruised, but Red Wolf supposed it was a good thing that neither of them were seriously injured.

Talin, meanwhile, stood with her mouth set into a hard line and her shoulders tensed. He wasn't sure he'd ever seen her truly *furious* about anything before.

Red Wolf looked down at himself. He looked like he'd just come crawling from a battlefield.

He was still out of breath from the fight, but he knew his face and tunic were splattered with blood. His hands were covered in it, too; he was pretty sure he'd split his own knuckles multiple times during his assault. Kehlvor's face had fared even worse—the man had healed, certainly, but it had been little more than a bloodied ruin in the few seconds after Red Wolf had stopped.

That abiyo *deserved it.*

"I thought I was clear," Bjorson said. "You were to exercise restraint."

"And I thought you understood when I told you about what he'd done," Red Wolf said quietly. His hands shook at his sides. He tried unsuccessfully to steady them by clenching them into fists.

"I knew what Kehlvor has done long before you told me—not all the details, mind you, but enough," Bjorson said. "And he has faced his punishment."

"He hasn't faced *enough*," Red Wolf hissed.

"Kehlvor's pack is exiled from the homeland by decree of their elders," Tormod continued, ignoring him. "Forever. They will never be allowed within any other pack's territory, and they cannot seek shelter from any of their kin. The half-giants' settlements are the *only* places in the Far North where they are allowed any form of shelter. They cannot cross the eastern range, nor west into the Draconian lands, nor south into Kies Tor because your people will see it as an invasion."

"They don't *deserve* your hospitality."

"It is not for you to decide what they deserve," Bjorson said. "They have been punished fairly according to their elders. They will continue to be punished for the rest of their lives. It is not my right, nor yours, to punish them further." He looked at Talin and the others. "As for the rest of you—"

"I take full responsibility," Talin said. "These three fall under my leadership. I should have kept them from causing such a disruption."

"It was my fault." Red Wolf stepped in front of her neatly. "I started the fight. If you're looking for someone to blame, blame me."

Bjorson pinched the bridge of his nose and heaved a sigh. "I have no wish to point fingers. What's done is done. Kehlvor's actions in Kies Tor, abhorrent as they may have been, were not without motive. And as usual, the Kulos clan finds itself at the heart of it all." He looked at Talin again. "Remain with us, and I promise you will have your answers."

"I understand," Talin said.

Red Wolf scowled but made no comment.

"If there's nothing else, you should get yourselves cleaned up." Bjorson turned away, a clear sign of dismissal. Ettrias and Golmin both slunk off. Red Wolf remained behind, and, noticing that he didn't budge, Talin turned back around.

"I have questions," he said.

Bjorson gestured tiredly to the armchair. Red Wolf remained standing.

"What's your deal with Kehlvor?" the ex-bodyguard asked.

"I have no specific deal with Kehlvor," Bjorson said. "We half-giants have shared the Far North with Hellhounds for millennia. Out here, in the mountains, we must work together to survive."

"Why shelter them?"

"As I've told you, the blizzards have trapped them here. They cannot make their way to any other settlement until—"

Red Wolf's jaw tightened. "The Hellhounds can brave the frozen wastes north of the mountain range. You're telling me they can't handle a gods-forsaken blizzard?"

"You are letting your hatred for them cloud your judgement, Connor. Some of them might survive. Not all of them will. You'd doom half the pack because of your past grievances with one man."

"Kehlvor's alchemists are just as guilty for attempting those experiments. His warriors are just as guilty for carrying out his orders without objection or thought. They razed entire *communities* to the ground, and you would *defend him*?"

"Red Wolf, let this go," Talin said gently. "I understand where Chief Bjorson is coming from. If you won't trust his word, trust mine."

"You—" Red Wolf hissed through his teeth.

"I know you've suffered because of him," Bjorson continued. "And I am sorry that I will not do more. But you must put aside your hatred. You told me that you came here seeking answers about your identity, and until you can accept your past for what it was, you will never know who you truly are."

Red Wolf closed his eyes momentarily. "Fine, we'll speak of this another time. For now, do you know anything about Velnora?"

"Velnora..." Bjorson frowned. "You've been there already?"

Red Wolf gave a nod.

"Then you'll know what happened. How you ended up there."

"I know I was abandoned."

Bjorson ran a hand over his beard. "Katherine hasn't been...honest...to either of us, Connor. If you blame me for what happened there, I can understand, but—"

"What do you know?" Red Wolf demanded.

"I know that Kat came to me one day with the news that she was with child and that she believed the child was mine," Bjorson said. "I asked her what she wished to do. She told me that she would not be able to hide you from Lord Edric, and so she would try to pass you off as his, but she would find a way to bring you back to the Kulos clan, to your people, when you were older. I do not know what happened next. But she came to me years later telling me that you were lost to the Hellhounds. I barely understood half of what she said, but from what I could surmise, she'd...left you...in Velnora."

"*Why?*"

"That, I do not know."

Red Wolf raked a hand through his hair. "It seems that I'll need to have another conversation with her, then. Thank you for providing what answers you could."

He stepped out of the hut without another word. Behind him, he heard Talin mutter an apology for the village hall fight before jogging to catch up.

"I don't understand," he growled. "You would take my father's side in all this? I thought—" He cut himself off. "I know you have an explanation, at least in your eyes. For both our sakes, I will hear it."

"Bjorson is right. I will not change my mind about that," Talin said. "Kehlvor and his people have already been exiled from their home. To deny them shelter is to punish them further. You, of all people, should be able to understand that—imagine if Kadis had denied you his hospitality in the Draconian lands." She drew in a deep breath. "That said, you should have been allowed to voice your thoughts during whatever trial they stood back home. We all should have been allowed to have a say."

Red Wolf stopped in the middle of the street, brow creased as he processed her words. There was some semblance of logic in them, twisted as it might be; from a purely objective, outside perspective, it stood to reason that Kehlvor's pack had received their punishment for going against the elders' jurisdiction and endangering not only his pack but dozens of other packs in the homeland. But none of them knew the true extent of all the atrocities they'd committed.

"I..." He worked his jaw. "I don't...agree...with the elders' decision, but I recognise that I was never given a chance to attend Kehlvor's trial and that the half-giants cannot be ordered to deny him shelter." He kept moving. "That does not mean I agree with you, either."

Talin sighed. "Are you alright, at least?"

Red Wolf looked down at his hands, then back up at her. "I...need to clean myself up."

Back at the hut, he allowed her to draw up a small bucket of water for him and grab a clean rag. He didn't object when she set about wiping the blood from his knuckles. Red Wolf took the rag from her after a few minutes and finished cleaning himself.

"You're allowed to be angry," Talin said.

Red Wolf didn't look at her. "I— I think I just want to sleep." He set the rag down and made his way into the bedroom, stripping his tunic as he did so. He eventually fell into an uneasy slumber.

The next morning brought another round of snow, rendering the training grounds inaccessible and cancelling whatever outdoor plans Chief Bjorson had for the four of them. Instead, they were taken to a large hut on the other side of the village, decorated with patterned, coloured fabrics. Red Wolf saw a handful of half-giant children gathered on the floor when Bjorson pushed open the door and indicated for them to wait outside. He returned a moment later.

"Good news," he said. "Elder Onja and Elder Lotvik are willing to let you join their class. Have fun. I shall take the four of you out to learn scavenging tomorrow."

Red Wolf pushed open the door hesitantly and led the way inside.

The hut opened up into a large, open section, with several fabric looms pushed up against the walls and the children he'd noticed earlier seated in a semi-circle on the floor. Each of them held a small piece of colourful, patterned fabric, not unlike the decorations he'd seen outside. Facing them was an elderly couple that reminded him, painfully clearly, of the couple who ran the orphanage at Velnora.

Gods, I never even learned their names.

"Ah, you must be the guests that Chief Bjorson was talking about," the woman said. "Welcome. I am Elder Onja, and this is my husband, Lotvik. As you can see, this is normally a class for children, but given your...unique situation...Tormod has asked if we would be willing to take you on as students for the day. Please, take a seat."

"We're thankful for the opportunity," Talin said. "What...exactly...are we learning?"

"Why, fabric weaving, of course."

What have we gotten ourselves into? Red Wolf thought.

Elder Lotvik handed each of them a bundle of loose thread and explained the basics to catch them up to the children's progress, and the four of them quickly moved to the looms to work. Red Wolf got the hang of it easily enough; the finesse required wasn't too different from that of needlework, which he was required to know to repair his own uniforms in the Royal Guard. He glanced at Golmin at one point and discovered the guard captain was also happily making progress.

It was a little amusing to see Talin and Ettrias struggle, though.

"How are you already so far ahead...?" the former grumbled. She was certainly putting in a solid effort, but the fine thread was proving difficult for her to manipulate.

"Here. Just focus on the next step." Red Wolf took the loose thread from her hands and passed it across the taut threads on the loom, pausing after each weave so she could see how it all fit together. Talin reached for it again after a few moments, and he handed the thread back so she could continue with the project herself.

"Thanks. I guess I just don't have the patience for this sort of thing."

"You know, it's odd," Red Wolf said, turning back to his own project. "I... Well, we've only been here a few days, but I almost feel like I'm...well, at home here."

Talin smiled. "It makes sense. These are your people. This is what you have been missing all these years. You could belong here, if you wished it." Her smile faded a little. "They'd welcome you. I'm sure of it."

Red Wolf's brow creased. It was true; the half-giants paid no heed to his height or golden eyes, or even his Hellhound abilities. They simply accepted him as he was—one of them.

He turned his attention to the half-giant children, who had also moved to the looms to continue their individual projects. Was this what his childhood could have been like if Katherine Blackrun had sent him up here to be with his people? Or would he have grown up as a child of House Blackrun, dressed in silks and privately tutored in mathematics and literature and all the knowledge he would require to take over one day as House Head?

Whatever the case, he envied the lives of the children here. They would grow up learning the ways of their people, and they would go on to pass that knowledge down to their children and grandchildren, unlike him. The knew their culture and heritage, unlike him. They knew who they were...unlike him. He envied them, not because he wanted what they had, but because he knew he could never have it.

The half-giants would accept him for what he was. But he was still just a monster.

"Red Wolf?" Talin's voice. He blinked and looked at her. "Something on your mind?"

"Just thinking. About whether I do belong here."

Gods, he wanted to believe he could.

T he half-giants kept them busy over the next few weeks.

Some mornings, they rose at dawn to join the hunting party or foraging teams, enduring long treks across the mountainside to haul back the evening's food. The rest of their time was spent in the village, either sitting in on lessons or helping with chores like food preparation or shovelling snow from the streets. It was gruelling work, and certainly a far cry from the comfortable life she was used to back in Belanore, but Talin found the whole ordeal oddly freeing. It wasn't a life she would choose, given the choice, but she could see why these people chose to live the way they do up here in the mountains.

Red Wolf, too, genuinely seemed happier than she had ever seen him; he talked and joked with the villagers and went out of his way to entertain the children. One of the warriors had taught him how they carved the beautiful, intricate patterns into their spears and shields, and he had spent the rest of the day perfecting his latest project—a wooden shield with a gorgeous rendition of House Blackrun's wolf crest carved into its surface. Even the presence of Kehlvor's pack seemed to bother him less.

But perhaps she should have known that she was never destined for the calm and quiet of this life.

They were summoned, early one morning, to Chief Bjorson's hut with no explanation, interrupting Ettrias' planned sleep-in and forcing Talin to quickly down her coffee and grab a roll of milk bread to eat as they walked. Red Wolf was quiet for the short trek across the village.

"This better be important..." Ettrias yawned. "I was looking forward to not having to wake up...so early..."

Talin had her suspicions about the reason for such an urgent summons. If she was right, then it was likely time to start packing their bags.

"Queen Talin. Connor." Bjorson dipped his head when they entered and gestured for them to sit. Red Wolf took one of the sofa spots next to Talin while Ettrias sat in an armchair. Golmin remained standing.

"Has the snow melted?" Talin asked. "Is that why you've called us here?"

"No," Bjorson said. "I received a letter this morning from Castle Blackrun."

Damn it. That's worse.

"From Katherine?" Talin asked.

"Yes. I haven't opened it. You should read it yourselves." Bjorson produced the parchment and handed it over. Talin broke open the wax.

Talin,

The situation in Kies Tor has changed drastically. At the

time of writing this, Lord Elyr Varkis has just arrived at Castle Blackrun with some two thousand bannermen, including all of the reserve units he had supplied to the Royal Army. With him is Lord Cassius Highett of your Royal Council. They've come to pledge their allegiance to the Highlands and to the rightful Queen of Kies Tor—refusing to recognise Aldrus as king regent. You must understand the gravity of such a decision. I write to you to bid your immediate return to Castle Blackrun, that we might discuss what should come next.

Your friend,
Katherine Blackrun

"Oh, gods," Talin said. She closed her eyes momentarily. "This is bad."

Lord Varkis' decision to turn his back on Aldrus was an incredibly bold move, one that was almost certain to cause offense; pledging his allegiance to her and Blackrun was tantamount to declaring an ultimatum—the proverbial final straw, as it were, demanding for her to be reinstated as the Head of State. House Varkis was ready to declare civil war alongside Blackrun.

"*Kust,*" Ettrias hissed. "How did things even get to this point? When we left, the situation was mostly stable…"

"We need to return." Talin jumped to her feet and began to pace. "This whole situation is a black powder bomb with the fuse already lit—it could explode at any moment." She turned to Chief Bjorson. "I know the canyon is blocked because of the snow, but is there any other way down the mountain? Or a way to move the snow, perhaps?"

Bjorson cleared his throat. He looked guilty all of a sudden. "The canyon...is at a lower altitude to the village and watchtower where we found you. If any snow made it down to the canyon, it would have melted before it even hit the ground. You were never trapped here."

"What?" Talin blinked. "But you said..."

"I know. I had intended to reveal the truth at a later date—once you were almost ready for the prophecy," Bjorson confessed. "Your final hurdle was to be a choice to decide whether you were willing to walk away to protect the truth. But this situation sounds urgent."

Talin let out a long breath. "I'm sorry we can't stay for longer. Perhaps, once things are resolved in Kies Tor, I can return and continue learning from your village."

"No," Bjorson said after a moment of silence. "It's become clear to me, over the past week, that you may be the one the prophecy was intended for. Your words just now confirm this in my eyes. You did not agree to my deal seeking the future—you sought knowledge, nothing more. I will take you to the Pool of Prophecy. Nominate a companion to join you, if you wish, then get your travelling cloaks. I will be in the village hall. Those of you who will not be joining us should pack."

"I nominate Red Wolf," Talin said immediately. Her ex-bodyguard coughed.

"Rufus and I will start packing our gear, then," Ettrias said. "Don't take too long out there."

The four of them made their way back to the hut together, where Talin pulled on every layer of warm clothing she owned, and Red Wolf grabbed his cloak. They left Ettrias and Golmin to pack.

Bjorson was in the middle of the hall when they entered, exactly as he said he would be, along with two of his warriors and Elder Onja, the fabric-weaving teacher. The woman gestured for Talin to step forward.

"Come, come, your hair must be braided," Onja said. "Not by me, mind you. Connor Kulos."

Red Wolf blinked.

"Me? What am I to do?" he asked.

"You will do the braids. I will teach you."

Red Wolf opened his mouth and closed it again. "I..." His gaze flickered towards Talin briefly. "Why me?"

"It is customary among our people for couples to braid each other's hair," Onja said, as if it were common knowledge, turning Red Wolf's ears a deep shade of scarlet.

"Don't overthink it," Talin said with a smile. "I trust you."

Red Wolf swallowed, but he moved behind her anyway, allowing Elder Onja to show him what to do. Talin kept still and let him work. Slowly, at the elder's instruction, he put her hair into what she could only assume was a complicated array of locks and braids. She was always impressed by how fast a learner he was; Onja had fallen quiet after only a few minutes and only chimed in occasionally to give him new instructions or correct a mistake.

"I could get used to this, you styling my hair," she teased. "Almost makes me wish I had you instead of my handmaids in the morning."

"Well, if you...wished it...I could...make a habit of—" Red Wolf spluttered.

Talin laughed. "I'm joking. Unless you want to."

Red Wolf grumbled something about her hair being too long for him to want to make a habit of braiding it.

"Why do you keep your hair so short, anyway?" Talin asked.

He paused. "Hellhounds like to wear their hair longer. Kehlvor rarely let me cut mine."

"I'm sorry."

"Don't be."

It took several more minutes of patience, but Red Wolf eventually finished his work, stepping back to admire her. Talin turned to face him and smiled again.

"You're beautiful," he said softly, and she had to duck to hide her blush.

Bjorson led the way out of the village and turned north, sticking to what looked like a well-trodden path in the mountains. One of his warriors accompanied him at the front, followed by the elder. Red Wolf dropped back to walk with Talin while the other warrior brought up their rear.

Deeper into the mountain, they saw what Bjorson had meant about the blizzards blocking off access through the Far North; an avalanche had collapsed a rope bridge along their route, forcing them off the path to take an alternative route around. Talin had no doubt she would be lost without the clan chief's guidance.

"Hellhounds are built to cross frozen tundra and packed snow," the half-giant said as they trudged downhill. "They will not be able to navigate their way through these mountains without a guide, Connor. I hope you can understand."

"I'm trying to." Red Wolf said nothing more.

It took them several hours and another two detours before the path finally seemed to straighten out a little, giving Talin some respite from the steep slopes and dizzying cliffs. It was an entirely different experience from navigating the tropics, she reflected; though she didn't have to contend with the humidity, she still found herself completely out of breath. By now, Red Wolf had overtaken her and would glance back every now and then to make sure she hadn't fallen behind.

"I could carry you if you wished," he said with a grin.

Talin groaned. "Spare my dignity, Red Wolf. I'll be fine. You're welcome to fix my hair if it's out of place, though."

Red Wolf coughed and looked away. "Your hair looks good."

"You're not just saying that because you did it, are you?" Talin grinned at him.

"It... You..." Red Wolf cleared his throat. "I mean what I said."

Talin decided to give him a break from her teasing for once.

"There was something I wanted to talk about," he suddenly said, slowing to match her pace again.

Talin wasn't sure she was going to like this. Red Wolf rubbed the back of his head, then raked a hand through his hair and sighed. He took her hand.

"If...I was to remain here...with my father and the rest of the Kulos clan," he began. "Would you object?"

"I—" Talin hesitated. "I...would rather that you did not. But I would never object if that was your wish. You should do what you believe is best for *yourself*. Not me."

"Do you think I should stay?"

"How am I supposed to answer that?"

"Honestly," Red Wolf said.

Talin drew in a deep breath. "Then, objectively, I would say that you could belong here. The half-giants accept you as one of their own. I cannot say the same of Kies Tor." She saw something subtle flicker across Red Wolf's face. "But I think you already have your answer."

"We're here!" Bjorson called from the front.

Red Wolf seemed deep in thought as the two of them made their way up to the clan chief.

The Pool of Prophecy became visible as soon as she crested the hill, a glittering blue lake surrounded by greenery and mountain flowers despite the thick snow blanketing the mountainside. The water itself looked almost like it glowed in the sunlight. As she drew nearer, she felt a familiar tingling in her fingertips—that of wild magic gathering around her, begging to be unleashed.

This place was overcharged with magic like she had never felt before.

Talin stole a glance at Red Wolf and knew he felt it too. His eyes seemed to take on a faint, golden glow as he walked, and he kept wringing his hands together uncharacteristically.

"I've never felt magic this powerful," he breathed.

"Places such as this used to be far more common throughout the world," Bjorson said, leading them to the shore. "That all changed when King Braenern outlawed magic in Kies Tor and began the Inquisition. He caused a ripple effect, not just in your lands but *everywhere*. The Fae were the first to follow in his footsteps. Then the Drakels. By the time they realised the consequences, it was too late. And it all began here."

"What do you mean?" Talin asked.

"A thousand years ago, Braenern came to us, to my ancestors," Bjorson said. "He had heard tell of the great magic our sages offered—the gift of prophecy. He wished to know his future."

Elder Onja produced a bowl and crouched, scooping up some of the lake water. It looked strangely ordinary for something that came from a body of water so richly blue. She set it down before her and muttered some kind of prayer in Old Torrian.

"What happened next?" Talin asked.

"My ancestors knew their duty, for a white raven only graces these lands once every millennium," Tormod said. "Braenern was brought here just as you have been brought here. He drank from the Pool of Prophecy, and he was shown all that would come to pass." He took the bowl from Onja and held it out to her. "Before you drink, heed my warning. You will see things—abstract concepts from which you must interpret your version of the truth. But you must *never* assume that the prophecy shows your personal future."

"I assume there's a reason for such a warning." Talin accepted the bowl hesitantly.

"The prophecy is bigger than you and I," Bjorson explained. "To assume that your personal future is shown within it is to start down a dangerous path. Do not make the same mistake as your ancestor."

So, the Inquisition was a direct result of the prophetic visions that Braenern experienced, Talin thought. *That's not exactly reassuring.*

"What kind of...visions...are we talking about?" she asked.

Bjorson shrugged. "I've no clue. You'll only know once you drink."

Red Wolf's nostrils flared, but he didn't object when she lifted the bowl to her lips.

This is it, then.

She tipped the bowl back and drank.

T alin was flying.

She wasn't sure what she had expected to see or what she had expected the prophecy to look like, but she was a raven with snowy-white feathers gliding through the air. Her wings cut through the air like razor blades, and she briefly wondered if she'd always known how to fly, but then she felt herself moving of her own accord. A man in ragged black robes loomed into view. He stretched out a bony hand, and she landed on his forearm, finally catching a glimpse of his face.

I am Lord Caarin, God of Death. And you, little raven, shall be my instrument.

Talin opened her mouth to ask why, why *her*, what did he mean? The only sound that tore from her throat was a raven caw.

The man—the god?—sent her into the air again, and she felt wind brush against her feathers again as she continued her flight. It wasn't long before the landscape changed around her, and she found herself dodging branches and broken trees as she zipped through a dead forest, taken by drought. The ground below her had dried and cracked, and no sign of life could be seen for miles and miles on end. Here, in this forest, magic itself felt dead, empty, forgotten by the world.

What happened here? What could have caused this? Talin wanted to ask.

She approached a clearing bordered by more dead trees. Here, she found herself slowing, landing atop a dying beast covered in blood.

A Hellhound.

It was still breathing, but its breaths were laboured, and she knew immediately that it wasn't long for this world. Blood pooled underneath it, soaking into the cracked earth.

Where are your brethren? Talin thought.

I have no brethren. They're long gone, the Hellhound replied in her mind.

Let me help, she said.

You caused this. I do not need your help.

I don't understand—

But she found herself flying again, leaving the dying Hellhound behind. She zipped past more trees, dodging branches, until she found herself flying across open skies once more, leaving the dead world behind.

A ruined city soon loomed before her, crumbling walls revealing the decaying state of the buildings within. She flew over the wall, down a street, through the city square, circling around what used to be a castle or palace—

It took her a moment to recognise the city layout and buildings.

This was Belanore. She was circling the royal palace.

No, this can't be right. I don't understand!

Talin wanted to yell, to scream, but again, the only sound that came out of her was a raven's caw.

She knew from her childhood stories that prophecies were often a warning. Perhaps that was all this was, despite how much it hurt to see her home in such a state. Just a warning so that she might prevent whatever catastrophe that would befall Belanore.

It was a relief, eventually, for her to leave the ruins behind, returning once more to the open skies. Her head spun with all the information and images she'd been shown. What did it all mean? Who was the true 'White Raven' of the prophecy? Was it her? Bjorson seemed to think that the prophecy was intended for her, but if that were true, how was she supposed to prevent it?

She soared down towards a well in the middle of nowhere, and this time Death greeted her again. He invited her to land on his shoulder, and she had no choice but to obey. Yet even from her perch, she could feel the tingle of magic coming from the well—suppressed and unable to escape.

What is this? she wanted to ask Death.

Death did not respond.

"Wait!"

Talin jolted awake with a gasp and sat up. A bout of dizziness washed over her immediately and almost forced her onto her back again.

She was herself now, no longer a snowy-white raven gliding through the air, and she had been moved to a large bed. Red Wolf sat on a stool beside her while Bjorson stood in the corner of the room.

"What just…" She rubbed her eyes with one hand and looked around. There was nothing particularly eye-catching about the room; it seemed to be the interior of a wooden cabin, with long log beams making up the walls and ceiling supports. The glittering lake was visible through the window, indicating that they hadn't gone far.

"Relax," Bjorson said. "What you just saw was the prophecy. Tell me of the visions."

"I was...I was a bird." Talin's brow creased as she tried to recall everything she'd seen. "There was a man. He said he was the God of Death."

She recounted the visions to the best of her ability, from the dead forest to the ruins of Belanore and the magic well. Red Wolf frowned as she went on.

"Indeed, that matches what others before you have reported," Bjorson said once she had finished. "What do you make of it?"

Talin ran her hands down her face. "I...don't know. It seems like...the White Raven has been marked as an instrument of Death. Wherever it goes, Death will follow. The dead forest, the Hellhound, even Belanore...it all seems to point to some kind of calamity befalling Kies Tor...by the White Raven's hand. By my hand, perhaps."

"And the well? You said you sensed magic within it."

"Magic, yes, but it was sealed away. I don't know what to make of it. I can only wonder...maybe...it symbolises the Inquisition. The destruction and hiding away of magic." Talin let out a long breath. "I knew prophecies tend to be vague, but this is...something else."

"Braenern interpreted the prophecy differently," Bjorson said. "He was warned that he must never interpret the prophecy as his personal future. But he was convinced that magic would be the cause of Kies Tor's destruction...as well as his own death. In carrying out the Inquisition, he became the catalyst for the prophecy."

"Then..." Talin swallowed. "Kehlvor was right. House Zylvaris is the White Raven. The royal family of Kies Tor was responsible for driving half-giants and Hellhounds into the Far North—that's why he blames us. He wanted revenge."

"Perhaps. Perhaps not." Bjorson shrugged. "Kehlvor was never meant to know the prophecy. He came across a series of long-forgotten texts about the prophecy that Braenern had written during his stay here. He believed that Kies Tor was responsible for the destruction of all magic in the known world and that...the White Raven would be responsible for the extinction of Hellhounds. He sought to prevent that from happening."

"That doesn't make any sense," Red Wolf said. "How could he possibly know that—"

"Kehlvor was wrong," Bjorson said. "He went against the Hellhound elders and marched on Kies Tor. By the time he realised his mistake, the Hellhounds knew it was too late—they all feared retaliation from the Torrian Crown. We believed that the world would see another Inquisition, one to wipe out all magic for good. That you did not retaliate is a blessing for us all and a sign of hope that the prophecy might yet be prevented."

Talin's head spun. This was too much for her to take in; she had only endured the trek here to seek aid in taking back her throne from Aldrus. She hadn't come here for retaliation, or a prophecy, or some other world-changing quest. She just wanted to go home.

"I didn't...come here to stop a prophecy," she said. "I don't even know *how* to stop this prophecy."

"I know." Bjorson sighed. "But your arrival here was no coincidence. When you first arrived here, you said you needed allies, that you came on Katherine's behalf to convince us to ally with her in return for her help. If I agree to this alliance, *if* I grant House Blackrun the power to call upon the Kulos clan for military aid, what would she do with that power?"

"She would..." Things suddenly clicked into place.

Blackrun would march on the south and retake Belanore by force. With the half-giants' numbers, as well as the northern banners, it would be *easy*. And Talin would have no say in whom she should call upon for help, for Blackrun's armies were not hers to build, and Katherine Blackrun herself has already set her eyes on war.

And how many will die? How many warriors will the Kulos clan lose before it's all over?

"She would order you to march south to Belanore," Talin said. "Your people would be disposable to her, same as all of her troops. And I would be indirectly responsible."

"Yes," Bjorson said. "We understand each other, then."

Talin looked at Red Wolf. He seemed to be deep in thought and barely noticed when she got to her feet.

"Thank you for your hospitality," she said. "We'll be out of here as soon as we retrieve our belongings."

Red Wolf finally looked up. "That...that's it, then? How do you plan to take back your throne without Katherine's support?"

"I'll think of something. There have to be other nobles willing to take my side in all this, to act as witnesses and vouch for my innocence," Talin said. "I won't drag the kingdom into another war, and I won't drag your people into it." She stopped at the cabin door. "Can we talk?"

Red Wolf's brow creased, but he gave a nod. Bjorson looked between the two of them, then excused himself, a faint smile tugging at the corner of his mouth.

"We're leaving today. Once we return, Golmin and Ettrias will have the bags packed, and we'll be setting off immediately," Talin said. "Which is why I need you to decide this now. Will you be staying?"

It was a question she dreaded asking, despite how irrational she knew her fears were. But she needed to know his decision.

"No," Red Wolf said, and some small part of her seemed to relax at the word. "If you asked me when we first arrived, perhaps I would have said yes. Part of me wants to stay. That same part of me knows that I would be welcomed with open arms and that I could make a life for myself here. But this isn't where I belong. This isn't home." He stepped towards her and cupped her face in his hands. Her breath hitched. "Home is with the people you love, and I love you, Talin." He pressed his forehead against hers. "You don't have to say it back. But I cannot go another fifteen years without telling you."

There was a beat. Talin grabbed the front of his coat and pulled him down for a deep kiss.

"I love you," she said when they broke apart. "I always have. I'm sorry I didn't say it fifteen years ago."

"If you had, I don't think I could have left."

Talin managed a laugh at that, leaning in to peck him on the lips again. "That might have been a good thing."

Back at the village, they gave Ettrias and Golmin the quick version of events, and Chief Bjorson poked his head into their hut briefly to call Red Wolf away for something. Talin wasn't entirely sure what the clan chief wanted to discuss, but when her ex-bodyguard returned, he had met her gaze and quickly looked away with a cough. She could only assume that the conversation had something to do with her.

"Something the matter?" she asked as he hoisted his pack over one shoulder.

"Nothing...particularly catastrophic."

"But you're not going to tell me?"

He only responded with a shrug.

C assius almost wished that Corvan and the others were here for him to gloat.

The first thing he had learned upon arriving at Castle Blackrun was that Queen Talin was indeed alive and well, and that the crown prince was also perfectly safe within the castle walls. The second thing he had learned was that the queen had rejected Blackrun's plans to march south with an army—at least for now—and rode north instead to seek out a clan of half-giants. She had taken her brother and captain, and of course, the former lord commander, leaving behind Prince Arkiel and Ashera.

The latter had insisted on attending the meeting they now held, citing the fact that the queen would want to hear a direct report from her about the details. Blackrun had sided with her and called her advisors in so they might discuss their next steps. Among them was a Drakel who had introduced herself as Aelia Cato.

"...doesn't have the numbers to face us in open battle," Lord Varkis was saying. "By instructing the entirety of the Highlands to pull their reserve banners from the Royal Army, you can deprive the south of almost all of its cavalry. Aldrus cannot advance north without risking significant casualties. This is the perfect opportunity to strike. "House Varkis holds a huge section of the Western Forts. If we can cross the White River at the western border..."

Blackrun sighed. "I will admit, I have been toying with the idea of open war for quite some time. But I value my friendship with the queen, and she still wishes to settle things without bloodshed."

"Think about it, my lady," Lord Varkis said. "Any hope of diplomacy between the north and south has broken down completely. Aldrus will not yield to your demands. You refuse to accept him as king regent. Civil war is the only option left."

"We have just finished fighting a different war," Cassius said coolly. "You cannot honestly tell me that dragging the nation into *another* war is the most sensible outcome."

Blackrun was silent. Cassius could tell she was considering her options, trying to find the best possible solution to this whole mess. But then he recognised the steely glint in her eyes, and his heart sank.

"I will send out word to the rest of the Highlander nobility," she said. "We will gather our banners. If Queen Talin wishes to march south with an army, we will be ready, and if not...well, we will still be ready in case of retaliation from Aldrus."

"My lady, this is not a course of action I would recommend," Aelia said. "There must be an alternative. Rallying the Highlands is sure to be seen as another act of provocation—Lord Varkis marching his banners north was bad enough. This could drive Aldrus to do something radical, especially with what we know of Darien's involvement."

"I agree," Ashera said. "I don't know much about the situation, I'll admit, and politics certainly isn't something I'm familiar with. But only a fool would assume that Aldrus wouldn't take offence to something like this."

Thank you, some semblance of reason in this meeting hall, Cassius thought. Gods, if only they'd waited until the queen returned from her trip into the mountains, she would have given Varkis and Blackrun a talking down about how *eager* they were to shed blood.

But the queen wasn't here, and they needed to make a decision—before Aldrus made the first move.

"There...may be a third option," Aelia said carefully. All eyes turned on her. "If Aldrus can't make any progress with swaying the north to his side, Darien is sure to march his own armies into Kies Tor to pacify us by force. That's tantamount to a full-scale *invasion* if my lady hasn't yet declared independence."

Cassius could sense where this was going.

"Emperor Kadis isn't likely to take kindly to an unauthorised Fae presence in Kies Tor," Aelia continued. "He'd be obligated to send his own troops into the kingdom, as per the treaty."

"That's true," Blackrun allowed. "But according to Aldrus, he will have allowed Darien's presence as king regent."

"We have no official treaty with Astaria," Cassius said. "Aelia's idea could work. Our alliance with the Fae was built on a political marriage—that was all. Without a treaty, Torrian law *and* Draconian law both forbid a regent from approving a foreign military presence within the kingdom, and the Torrian-Drakel treaty reflects that. Only the royal family has that kind of power—even if the monarch is under investigation. Not even the High Court can overrule it."

It was the one power Talin deliberately withheld from the High Court, and it was part of the reason she had agreed to marry Aldrus. Ostensibly, their alliance with the Fae was no different from their alliance with the Drakels. But she had told him that she'd done all of this as a fail-safe, preventing what she had termed a 'pacifist invasion' in case of a situation exactly like the one they were facing now.

The Drakels, she trusted—Kadis' interests and views aligned with her own. The Fae had been a different matter. She had been cautious, and rightly so, it seemed.

"Alright," Blackrun finally said. "Aelia, you will ride for the Draconian capital immediately to explain the situation in Kies Tor and implore Emperor Kadis to rally the legions. Lord Varkis, if you truly wish to fight for the Highlands and for Queen Talin, I must ask you to march your banners back home and allow the Drakels free passage through the Western Forts."

Cassius closed his eyes momentarily. *This is it, then. War seems inevitable now.*

"Consider it done." Varkis dipped his head. "I'd best prepare."

He disappeared through a side door, along with Aelia, leaving Cassius with Blackrun, Ashera, and the rest of her advisors. The spymaster let out a long breath.

"Speaking on behalf of the Torrian Royal Council, my lady," he said, "I hope you know what you're doing."

"I hope so too," Blackrun said. "If you're wrong about this, the Torrian and Astarian royal armies will rip the north to shreds."

XLVII

Their return to Castle Blackrun was met with quite the commotion, to say the least. Talin wasn't sure what she had expected.

For one, the surrounding town was far busier than usual, with dozens of soldiers passing by them as they led their horses through the streets. Talin could see mostly Blackrun bannermen, but the distinct pale green of House Highett caught her attention—as far as she knew, Lord Lorvan Highett had no reason to station his troops at Castle Blackrun. She saw the deep purple banners of House Whitehall, too, and wondered for a moment whether she was seeing things. Red Wolf's tensed shoulders and tight lips had suggested otherwise.

"Looks like Katherine rallied the Highlands already," he said. "This isn't good."

Talin's brow creased as they made their way through the courtyard. She could see other Highlander bannermen, too, and counted at least half a dozen different noble houses before her gaze landed on a dark-skinned woman and a black-haired man with grey eyes and long stubble on his chin. The two of them stood together to the side, keeping out of the way of the bustling traffic.

"Icari?" she said. "And Marcus?"

The two of them broke into a grin when they saw her, and Icari rushed forward to pull her into an embrace but quickly separated herself awkwardly.

"Sorry. I imagine it's not proper to hug royalty like that..." She cleared her throat. "Gods, it's so good to see you, though. Red Wolf told us he was going to try and bring you here to save your life, but we had no idea if he was successful. You look...great."

Talin smiled. "I owe him a lot. What brings you two here?"

"We *were* on our way home," Marcus said. "We'd made it halfway to Fallbjorn, where we were going to go our separate ways, but we heard rumours of civil war and wanted to pledge our support to the one who freed us from the arena. So we turned around."

"I..." Talin wasn't sure how to respond. "I'm grateful for the support, but I'm...hoping...that we might *avoid* a scenario where the entire kingdom ends up at each other's throats."

The front doors flew open at that moment, and Arkiel practically threw himself down the steps, barrelling into her with a hug. She laughed as she picked him up and spun him around before setting him down again.

"I missed you!" the boy said. "You were all gone for *so long*. Ashera was worried that something might have happened, but Lady Blackrun said she thought you'd be fine. What did you do in the mountains? Where did you go? Was it interesting?"

"We met the half-giants," Talin told him. "Red Wolf found out where he came from, and we all got to experience what life is like up in the mountains."

Arkiel's eyes went wide. "That sounds *amazing*. You have to tell me all about it! Please?"

Talin laughed again. "Of course. We'll..."

She trailed off. The front doors had opened again, this time revealing Blackrun, Ashera, and one Lord Cassius Highett. Her smile faded a little.

"How about this, Ark? You make sure you get your daily weapons practice with Captain Golmin," Talin said, "and we'll spend the whole evening telling you all about the half-giants and our journey north."

"This way, Your Highness." Golmin stretched out a hand, inviting Arkiel to take it. "I'll teach you some tricks that even Red Wolf doesn't know about."

"No way! Really?" Arkiel skipped off with him eagerly. Talin sighed internally and made a mental note to thank Golmin later. She bid Icari and Marcus farewell, too, promising that she would find the time to catch up once she was free, and made her way up the steps to Blackrun.

"Now, then, what's the occasion?" she asked.

"Your Majesty. It is *very* good to see you," Cassius said. "Most of the kingdom believes you to be dead. I was glad to learn that my doubts were proven correct."

"You'll have to catch me up on what's been happening in Belanore," Talin said. She stripped off her cloak as she led the way inside. A servant at the door took it away. "And, of course, what all of this...activity...is about. I saw your uncle's banners outside, along with banners from half the Highlands."

"I can explain," Blackrun said.

"I certainly hope so."

Blackrun gave her the quick version of events, from Lord Varkis' appearance and Cassius fleeing Belanore to gathering her banners, sending Aelia west, and everything the spymaster had learned back in the capital. Talin looked to Cassius and Ashera to confirm. Their grim expressions told her everything she needed to know.

"*Orrlát*," she muttered. "Katherine, I told you I don't want another war. We have barely recovered from the Hellhound invasion. A war could tear this kingdom apart!"

"I understand your reservations," Blackrun said. "But at this stage, we have no choice. You know of Darien's involvement in this—it's a clear violation of any alliance we might have held with the Fae. Why do you still insist on resolving things peacefully?"

"Listen to me." Talin pinched the bridge of her nose. "Darien's involvement is exactly what we need to prove my innocence and allow the court to reinstate me. It's not worth...going to war...when all we need is the evidence. Cassius can easily come forward as a witness, and if you and the rest of the Highlander nobility can vouch for my innocence..." She sighed. "Perhaps it's best if we talk in private, Katherine. You too, Red Wolf—this is relevant to you."

"Wh—hey, as one of your advisors," Ettrias began, "I really think I should—"

"Please trust me," Talin said.

Ettrias crossed his arms but didn't argue. "Fine. Come on, Ashera, I guess we're not welcome."

"What about your negotiations with Chief Tormod? Were you successful?" Blackrun asked once he'd disappeared down the hallway with Ashera in tow.

"No," she said. "I will not enlist their help. They showed me some things and taught me much more about their way of life than any Torrian texts have ever documented. Out of respect for them, I cannot let them join an alliance with the Highlands or the south."

"I see." Blackrun sighed. "Allow me to remind you, then, of my previous offer. The support of the northern bannermen in exchange for the Highlands."

"I think you'll want to hear what I have to say first."

They reached the small hall, and Blackrun pushed open the double doors, gesturing for them to enter first. Red Wolf locked the doors again behind him. Talin pulled up a seat at the table and indicated for her companions to sit, but Red Wolf remained standing, lips pressed into a thin line.

"I...have a confession to make," she said.

"You forged the documents," Red Wolf said.

Talin was stunned into silence.

How could you possibly have known about that?

She had spent countless hours on those documents, had made certain the court's stamp was replicated perfectly and all the signatures matched their owners exactly.

"If you're wondering how I knew," Red Wolf continued after a beat, "I've had my suspicions for a while. Katherine's right. It shouldn't be difficult to ask me to come forwards and explain how the documents were forged. But you can't do that because you don't want to ask me to lie to the High Court again."

Blackrun rubbed her eyes. "Am I to understand that we are in this mess because you really *did* send forged documents to bring Connor back into Kies Tor?"

"It's complicated," Talin said. "I take responsibility for the documents' existence. But I never sent them."

"I don't follow."

"You are aware that the Fae were well-versed in illusory magic before the Inquisition, yes?"

"I am," Blackrun said.

"Some of their craft has survived through the years. I enlisted Aldrus' help to craft the fake documents for Red Wolf's return...as a backup plan, many years ago, in case things spiralled out of control and I found myself in desperate need of allies," Talin explained. "We had to do it in secret. The court would never have agreed to such a contingency. I hid the papers afterwards and never told him where, but he was the only person until now who knew about them. He must have told his brother about them and then been instructed to find and send them as a way to frame me."

"Then your goal isn't really to prove your innocence directly," Red Wolf said. "If you can prove that Aldrus acted with outside influence, reason dictates that you should be innocent, at least in the eyes of the High Court. You don't want to drag the kingdom into a war because you know this was...essentially...your fault."

Talin winced. "Yes. I should never have made those documents. It was stupid, impulsive, far too reckless. I was...never mind." There was no sense in justifying herself. She had been drunk, about to march north for her second campaign against the Hellhounds, and she had missed him.

"The point is, I have to fix things without bloodshed," she continued. "If war breaks out in Kies Tor, then all the lives lost, all the blood spilled...will be on my hands."

And the White Raven will become the agent of Death, just as the prophecy warned.

"Why tell me now?" Blackrun asked. "If you're after my help in rallying nobles to your side, even as witnesses, you know I cannot give it for free."

"Because you deserve the truth. Both of you."

"I don't know about this, Talin," Red Wolf said. "Do you have any idea how much damage this would do to your plans if one of us were to leak the information?"

"I'm...counting on my personal relationship with both of you to ensure it doesn't leak."

"Why keep it from Ettrias?"

"Ettrias...is terrible at keeping secrets," Talin said. "He would want to tell Golmin and Ashera, and someone would inevitably overhear."

Red Wolf raked a hand through his hair. "I have a few...choice words...about how utterly *reckless* and *naive* you were to make those documents," he growled. "But without them, I wouldn't be here. So I suppose I cannot complain too much."

"I will gather the northern lords and convince them to vouch for your innocence in court, then," Blackrun said. "In the meantime, Castle Blackrun is always open to you and your companions." She gestured around her. "The same goes for you, Connor. Have you thought about my offer?"

"I'm...still undecided." Red Wolf cast a brief sideways glance at Talin. "But there was something else I wanted to discuss."

Blackrun blinked, evidently caught off-guard. "Of course. Anything."

"We passed through Velnora on our way to the half-giants' village," Red Wolf said. "What really happened there?"

Blackrun was silent. Talin felt a growing sense of dread settle in the pit of her stomach.

"I'm not sure I understand," Blackrun finally said.

"Don't lie to me." Red Wolf scowled. "We were there. We found no evidence of Blackrun bannermen *anywhere* in the village. There was nothing to suggest that Lord Edric ever visited!"

"I... That's not...possible," Blackrun said.

"Katherine."

Blackrun gave a defeated wave of her hand, gesturing for Red Wolf to sit. "I... Lord Edric never visited the village on a tour. It's true. But...before I explain...you must know the full story."

Red Wolf crossed his arms. "I'm listening."

"As you might know, Lord Edric was not a kind man," Blackrun said. "He was well-known for losing his temper over even the most...trivial...of matters. I knew that...if he were to ever find out you were an illegitimate child...he would not have taken the news well. I knew I couldn't hide your parentage forever, so I made arrangements for you to head north to the Kulos clan if Lord Edric found out the truth. I'd hoped to keep the secret for many years, but..."

Red Wolf glared.

"He found out sooner than you expected," Talin said softly.

"Yes." Blackrun looked at Red Wolf, then dropped her gaze. "Connor, you were barely a month old. I don't know how Edric found out or who told him, but he was...*furious*. I was given an ultimatum: either I send you far, far away from Castle Blackrun, or he would kill you." Tears shimmered in her eyes. "Please understand. I had no choice."

Talin saw the exact moment Red Wolf's steely composure cracked and splintered. His glare melted away in an instant, replaced only by betrayal.

"You...*abandoned me*...in Velnora...instead of taking me *home*. To my *people*." His voice shook.

"It was the dead of winter," Blackrun whispered. "You wouldn't have survived the trip even if I could cross the mountain pass into the village. Connor, please understand...those people I left you with, I trusted them with my life. I would have arranged for someone to take you to the village when you were old enough. I was going to. But a month before I was due to set off...we received a report detailing what we now know to be the first Hellhound attack on Kies Tor."

"Then *why* would you *lie* to me?" Red Wolf hissed. "Why go to such lengths to hide the truth?"

"Because I failed you. And I was too ashamed to admit it." Blackrun looked away. "I'm sorry, Connor. I'm so sorry."

Red Wolf shoved his chair back and strode from the room. The door slammed behind him with a loud *thunk*.

"Red Wolf— and he's gone." Talin sighed. "I'll find him."

"You must think I'm such a terrible mother." Katherine huffed a bitter laugh. "You'd be right." She turned away to wipe her eyes.

"What's done is done. And from what I hear, you tried to keep him safe," Talin said, pausing at the door. "Don't worry, I'll talk some sense into him."

It took her half a lap of the entire castle before she bumped into a servant who told her that Red Wolf had left the castle, headed north through the forest on a stroll. She passed Marcus sparring with Icari on her way out and had to quickly excuse herself by explaining that she had a personal matter to attend to.

Red Wolf was still on the castle grounds when she eventually found him, only a few minutes walk from the front gates, sat on a small hill overlooking a forested valley below, knees drawn up to his chest. He looked up when she approached but then buried his head in his hands again.

"She just...left me there." His voice cracked. "As if my childhood didn't even *matter*."

"I don't think it was like that." Talin took a seat on the grass beside him. "Maybe, looking back on it, there were other options she could have taken. But I know Katherine. I know that if she left you in Velnora, in the care of that couple, it was because she felt like she had no choice."

"She could have...kept me safe! Gods, in all that time, she never even *visited*, and I'm supposed to believe that...she would have simply showed up one day to take me home?" Red Wolf snapped. He jumped to his feet and ran his hands through his hair. "No. She should have...she should've..."

Talin watched him pace back and forth silently, breathing hard.

Think! He's surely not angry at Katherine alone.

"You told me once that to protect the things we love, we must be prepared to let them go," she said gently. "Katherine Blackrun didn't reject you as her son. She loved you. She still does."

"You..." Red Wolf stopped and glared at her but quickly faltered. "How could you possibly know that?"

"Because if that's what it came down to, I would do the same for Arkiel."

Red Wolf sank to his knees on the grass with a yell that seemed to echo through the entire forest.

"I'm not...angry...because she left me there," he said, voice barely audible despite her proximity. "I'm angry because it's not *fair*." He bowed his head, and Talin saw his chest heave as he sobbed quietly before her. "It's not fair. Why did Lord Edric have to find out? Why did I have to be born in the middle of winter? Why Velnora?"

Talin knelt beside him and pulled him into an embrace. He buried his face in her shoulder.

"I don't know what I expected," he continued. "That I was born into a happy, normal family who loved me? That I somehow simply...didn't have a life before the Hellhounds? Gods, I was naive. I was always an outsider, even to my own family. To think I could be anything else..."

"That's not true." Talin pulled back to look him in the eye. "Forget about your past for a second. Forget about who you were and whoever you think you are. Who do you *want* to be?"

"I..." Red Wolf's brow creased. "I don't know. I just..." He let out a shaky breath. "I just want to be...myself. Connor Blackrun was the scared little boy taken by Hellhounds. Red Wolf was their failed experiment. I can't deny myself any part of that."

"You have your answer, then," Talin said.

"I suppose I do," Red Wolf said softly. "But it doesn't make it any easier to accept." There was a pause. "Thank you, though—for being here."

Talin straightened and kissed the top of his head, and he rose too, only to take a knee before her.

"Once upon a time, I was the Crown's shadow. I was its shield from foes who would seek to destroy it," he said. "And I would take up that mantle again, if not in title, then in duty and in service once more to the Queen of Kies Tor."

Talin understood.

"Then I accept," she said. "From here on until—"

Footsteps sounded behind her. Talin turned to see Golmin hurrying up the hill towards them.

"I hate to interrupt whatever private moment between you two, but this is urgent," he said. "We..." He looked between Red Wolf, still on one knee, and Talin standing in front of him. "Oh, gods, this is a really bad time, isn't it?"

"What?" Talin glanced back as Red Wolf got to his feet. Her eyes widened. "No, it's not like that! We were...talking..." She winced. There was no way to explain the conversation they'd just had. "Never mind. What's the news?"

"Blackrun just received a bird from Vill's Crossing," Golmin said. "Aldrus has marched the Royal Army north and issued an ultimatum—they were only intercepted by Lord Varkis' troops marching south through the Crossing. He's listed two options: either Blackrun accepts him as king regent and bends the knee, or he marches into the Highlands to pacify her by force." He heaved a deep sigh. "Your Majesty, he knows Blackrun isn't going to yield. This is a declaration of war."

XLVIII

T alin wasn't sure she'd ever seen Blackrun this upset.

She and Red Wolf had barely made it two steps into the castle before Blackrun had stormed past, announced that she was marching her banners to Vill's Crossing, and gave them half an hour to pack—or be left behind. Talin had tried to talk some sense into her to no avail.

From what she could gather as they had moved out, Lord Varkis' troops had put up resistance, but the Royal Army managed to push them back in the end, occupying Vill and the southern tower of Vill's Crossing. Varkis' banners, as well as Lord Dragonfall's men, had been forced to retreat to the much smaller northern tower. The two groups now stood in a stalemate over the northern bridge, neither side able to advance without the defenders shooting down at them from their respective towers.

It only takes one wrong step for the situation to collapse completely, Talin thought as she was shown into the war room in the northern tower. With so little time to prepare, she had been forced to leave Arkiel once again, in the care of Castle Blackrun's servants and staff. There was no way she could risk bringing her own child to what she was sure would soon become an active warzone. She hoped he'd be able to forgive her.

"Not to say I don't appreciate the reinforcements, but even with all of the Highlander banners in the kingdom, we won't storm the northern tower without siege weapons," Lord Dragonfall was saying. "Begging your pardon, my lady, but I should know—it was my men that held Vill's Crossing against the Hellhounds for so long."

Blackrun paced back and forth at the head of the meeting table and didn't respond.

"I don't want this to devolve into an all-out conflict," Talin said. "Regardless of who holds which tower, if we fight, attempting to breach either fortification will result in massive casualties. You say that Aldrus himself led these soldiers?"

"Please don't tell me you still want to *talk* your way out of this." Blackrun stopped to glare. "This is no ultimatum. This is *war*. Aldrus has marched into the north with an army and wishes to pacify us by force. The time for negotiation has long passed."

Talin crossed her arms. "I don't want to talk. I want to surrender myself."

"Here we go." Red Wolf groaned and rubbed his eyes with one hand while the rest of the room erupted.

"You *cannot be serious—*"

"We are only here because of you—"

"That's enough," her bodyguard snapped. "I assume you would prefer a solution that doesn't involve your *actual* surrender?"

"I'll do what's necessary," Talin said. "But if you have an alternative, I'd be happy to hear it."

"If you're adamant about walking out across what's essentially a shooting range for the Royal Army archers, I know better than to stop you," Red Wolf said. "But we may be able to negotiate a...better outcome."

"I'm listening."

"Am I correct in assuming that your plan hinges on the Drakels being allowed through the Western Forts without bloodshed?" Red Wolf asked, looking at Cassius.

"That's correct," the spymaster said.

"I propose we give up the northern tower. Aldrus obviously wants the Crossing to prevent Highlander forces from pushing into the south," Red Wolf explained. "In exchange, they allow Lord Varkis and his bannermen to return home—under...'house arrest' at the Western Forts, shall we say."

"That...could actually work." Ettrias frowned. "Once the Drakels make their way through the Forts, we can hold them there as reinforcements. Darien wouldn't dare march into the kingdom with the might of an entire legion at our disposal. And if, gods willing, Talin's trial goes well, we won't need to fight at all."

Talin considered it for a moment. It was a solid enough strategy; Aldrus' occupation of Vill's Crossing would prevent Blackrun from marching her armies into the south from this direction, and the Royal Army garrisons situated in the southeast would be able to meet them if they tried to cross at Wycrest. Meanwhile, the Drakels at the Western Forts would serve as a deterrent for Darien in case he attempted to march into Kies Tor, forcing everyone into another stalemate. It would buy her the time she needed to expose Darien's involvement and Aldrus' motives in investigating her.

"Correct me if I'm wrong, but doesn't this strategy technically still involve your surrender?" Blackrun asked.

"Well...yes and no," Talin said. "I'll need to return to Belanore eventually to face the High Court and present my evidence. But this way, we'll have time to make a case. Can we get word out to the southern tower?"

"It shouldn't be difficult," Lord Dragonfall said.

"Good. Then I suppose I'd best prepare," Talin said.

"Talin," Blackrun called when she reached the door. "You must understand that if *anything* does not go according to plan down there, I will order my banners to attack. I cannot risk losing the Crossing with nothing to show for it."

"I understand," Talin said.

"I'll come with you," Red Wolf said. "If something does go wrong, you'll want my protection magic."

"I...don't know if you should be showing your face..." Talin began. A pointed look from him silenced her. "Stubborn."

"Reckless."

The two of them made their way down to the armoury first, where they donned some light armour before heading out onto the bridge. At the top of the southern tower, Talin could see dozens of archers, completely filling the wall—ready to shoot down at any who dared to try and take the fort. But they stayed their hand as she came to a stop in the middle of the bridge.

So far, so good.

A minute passed, and then the gates before her swung open, revealing Aldrus flanked by two Royal Army officers. He, too, had donned some armour; one of his officers carried his helm for him as they approached.

"By the gods..." he said, approaching her slowly. "Lord Dragonfall's message did not deceive us, then. You're alive—back from the dead."

"Oh, please, we both know I was never dead," Talin said. "I came to negotiate. The last thing I want right now is to start a civil war. I'm sure you feel the same way."

"It's a bold move, you know, coming here with Red Wolf," Aldrus said. "If nothing else, it's proof that he has returned to Kies Tor against his exile."

"I'm here under Katherine Blackrun's protection," Red Wolf said. "You would be wise not to test us. We are here for diplomacy, but Lady Blackrun does not answer to my queen. Do not provoke her into attacking."

The corner of Aldrus' mouth twitched. "You're exactly as Talin described you. Blunt with your words, perhaps, but direct. What are your terms?"

"Lady Blackrun orders all of her banners to retreat, including Lord Dragonfall and his men," Talin said. "Royal Army soldiers will be allowed to occupy the northern tower and control the entire Crossing. In exchange, you allow Lord Varkis and his three thousand troops to return home. Place them under supervision at the Western Forts, if you wish, but let them go—Blackrun has no wish to provoke the south further by turning House Varkis against the Royal Army."

"That cannot be all," Aldrus said. "You'd give up the Crossing *and* three thousand men for...what purpose, exactly? Placing Lord Varkis' troops behind enemy lines?"

"Perhaps. But they won't be of much help to us there." Talin shrugged. "Besides, I'm the real bargaining chip. You'll have the Crossing, and you'll have Varkis' banners under surveillance, but you won't have me. You will agree not to advance further north than Vill's Crossing, nor will you attempt to cross the bridge at Wycrest, and you will give up your attempts to bring me into custody. I plan to face the court's judgement eventually—but until then, you will allow me safe refuge in the Highlands."

Aldrus sighed. "You cannot avoid the court forever, Talin. What you did..."

"I don't plan to avoid it forever. But I will face the judges on my own terms, not yours."

"I don't know about this."

"Aldrus, please," Talin said. "I know you don't want to fight. Let's resolve this peacefully."

Her husband looked between her and Red Wolf, then looked up at the northern tower.

"Fine," he said, turning his attention to her again. "I accept your terms. Prepare your men to move out and send Lord Varkis through."

They quickly agreed on how exactly they should handle the exchange—Talin and Red Wolf would relay the news to Blackrun first, ensuring that she was on the same page. Then, as a precaution, they would remain in the northern tower with a handful of northern bannermen, waiting until Lord Varkis had made it safely through the Crossing and Blackrun's people cleared out of the tower completely. If Aldrus failed to honour the deal in any way, the northerners would be able to keep the northern gates to the tower open and allow Blackrun to re-occupy the defensive fort. If Blackrun failed to honour the deal, Talin and her meagre team had no way of locking down the northern tower fast enough to prevent Aldrus from gaining access. It was, in many ways, a perfect plan. One that should have gone off without a hit ch.

"I can't believe we're giving up the north's most valuable defensive position," Red Wolf muttered as they made their way from the northern tower, flanked by Blackrun bannermen. Behind them, Talin could hear thundering footsteps as Aldrus marched the Royal Army into position. Archers and crossbowmen immediately took up position at the top of the tower.

"Lord Varkis' troops have made it through the Crossing," she said. "Our deal is done. Aldrus wouldn't dare march further north—Illyris is open farmland and tundra. Blackrun's cavalry will trample them to bits if he even tries. We must now honour our word."

"Something's off about this situation." Red Wolf's brow creased. "I don't know how to explain it. It just feels too...easy."

Talin understood what he meant. From what Cassius had told them, Darien liked to meddle in foreign politics as a way to destabilise prospective kingdoms for conquest, only marching his armies in if absolutely necessary. Resorting to brute force felt entirely out of character for him.

Could Aldrus be working separately for some reason?

"Talin..." Red Wolf said. He was looking up at the top of the tower. "Get down!"

Talin barely had time to process his words before a flicker of golden energy exploded in front of her eyes.

What in the seven hells...?

Red Wolf didn't hesitate. He spun, nocked an arrow, and sent it up at the archers on the wall. One of them toppled from the tower...and dropped an empty crossbow as he fell. Talin suddenly understood the situation.

They shot at us! Why?

But it was too late to be pondering; she could already hear Blackrun yelling orders at the other end of the field, organising her men, readying a cavalry charge.

"*Orrlát*! Red Wolf—" Talin began.

"We'll deal with Blackrun later! MOVE!" Red Wolf grabbed her by the hand and took off at a sprint. The tower gates creaked open behind them as Aldrus sent out his pikemen to meet Blackrun's attack. Talin quickly realised they were trapped.

The problem was, she thought, they couldn't fall back—meeting Blackrun's cavalry charge put them at risk of being trampled, at best, and put them in what would no doubt become a death zone filled with arrow-fire from the tower. Nor was staying put an option, for they would inevitably be caught in the middle of what was about to become a bloodbath between the charging cavalry and defending pike formation.

"The river!" she exclaimed. Passing directly by the tower and making for the riverbank was the only option that gave them enough time to avoid the cavalry. She took a sharp turn without hesitation, pulling away from Red Wolf, and saw one man from her escort also move. Hoofbeats clicked on the paved road as Blackrun's men drew closer.

Gods, I hope Red Wolf is behind me. Talin skirted around the row of pikemen and threw herself aside moments before the two groups clashed together in a grating screech of metal and death.

The first thing she smelled was blood.

Talin remembered the scent of blood well. It was always the first thing that overpowered the senses when they fought the Hellhounds because the wolves always knew exactly where to strike and how to go for a fatal blow. They always tried to draw first blood, thinking they had the advantage...until they realised that the Royal Army's weapons had been dipped in torslek.

But it wasn't always enough. It wasn't enough *now*. Sometimes, the Hellhounds' ferociousness won out despite everything they threw at the enemy, and sometimes, the mistakes were on Talin's head. She was responsible for these lives lost—if not to Hellhounds, then her own naivety and foolishness. Some small part of her registered that more units were joining the fray and sent to die on Blackrun's orders, their fates sealed by her hand. They were in a death zone. A shooting range. The soldiers before her were nothing but *target practice* for the archers above.

Someone came swinging at her with an axe. Talin barely registered that she was moving to dodge, then counter, then step around the body and move on.

Focus! There has to b—

She couldn't breathe. Couldn't *think*. Arrows rained down on them, and she was caught in the middle of it all, unable to do *anything*. Their troops would all die here, and she would be helpless to stop it. Blood pounded in her ears, burning hot, drumming a deafening beat.

Where's—

"Talin! Breathe. We need you." Ettrias' voice. "Talk some sense into Blackrun, *please*."

Talin found herself staring into her brother's eyes through a narrow slit in his helm. He was splattered with blood.

"Blackrun," she repeated as her mind caught up to their current predicament.

She's upset about losing the Crossing. She's upset that they shot at us.

Talin understood why the Highlander woman wanted to continue the advance so badly. But in her haste to march for Vill's Crossing in the first place, they had come unprepared, with no siege weapons to show for it.

And if the Crossing almost held *Hellhounds* without siege weapons indefinitely, a few thousand Highlander soldiers had no chance of taking it back from Aldrus' men.

"She's at the back of the formation!" Ettrias yelled. "I don't care how you persuade her; just call off the attack!"

Talin grabbed a nearby riderless warhorse and made for the back of their ranks at a gallop.

Gods, I hope there's still time to save some of these men.

As it turned out, Blackrun wasn't difficult to spot among the rows of Highlander infantry held in reserve, her silver and gold colours standing out in a sea of deep purple. It was no surprise that she kept Lord Whitehall's banners back; his infantry were some of the best they had in the north. Talin pulled her horse up before the older woman as she paced her own steed back and forth, shouting orders, reorganising her troops.

"This is madness," the queen snapped. "Katherine! You know as well as I do that attacking the Crossing won't even make a *dent* in their defensive efforts, especially without siege weapons."

"Aldrus marches on the Highlands with an army and then fails to honour our deal, and you would let it slide?" Blackrun demanded. "He has no *right* to—"

"It doesn't matter." Talin glared. "As your friend, I understand your frustrations. But as a *leader* working alongside you...I cannot condone this course of action. Our duty is to our people."

Blackrun hissed through her teeth, and for a moment, Talin wondered if she hadn't gotten through, but then the Highlander woman cursed and wheeled her horse around.

"Fall back!" she yelled. "Back to the rendezvous!"

"Thank you," Talin said and rode off to relay the order to anyone who might listen. She didn't see Red Wolf in the chaos that followed.

Where is he?

Come to think of it, she hadn't seen him since Blackrun sent out that first cavalry charge...

Talin fought back a wave of bubbling panic as she scanned the ranks of gathering troops at their rendezvous, a stretch of farmland on the far side of a hill that overlooked the Crossing. Colourful northern banners stretched across the land as far as the eye could see, but there was no sign of a half-giant with golden eyes among the officers rounding them up.

Oh, gods.

"Have you seen Red Wolf?" she asked Ettrias when he passed her.

"No," he said, then paused and doubled back. "That's odd. I don't think I saw him with you when I found you in the middle of the battlefield, either. There's no way he would have left you on your own like that..."

Talin drew in a shaky breath. "We must have gotten separated somehow. I don't know. Maybe he's just organising t—"

"Have either of you seen Connor?" Blackrun asked, appearing in front of them. Talin felt her blood turn to ice.

"Something must have happened to him," she said quietly. "I don't...we were separated during the charge...he wasn't there when I turned around and..."

By the gods, she was such a useless fool. If only she'd paid more attention to her own surroundings instead of getting distracted by ghosts, she might have seen something or been able to help him somehow.

If Aldrus makes it back to Belanore with Red Wolf as evidence, the court will never believe my innocence. We'll both be found guilty.

"Finish the headcounts and round everyone up," Blackrun was saying to one of her advisors. "We need to retake the Crossing at any cost—if Aldrus thinks he can get away with taking my own *son* from me, he will pay for his mistake with his *life*."

"No," Talin said.

"I beg your pardon?" Blackrun fixed her with a hard glare.

"You won't retake the Crossing; it's too strong a fortification," Talin said, forcing herself to focus. "And I know I won't change your mind about this—you think you've failed him again. Which is why I'm sorry for what I'm about to say, but we have to do it my way."

Blackrun opened her mouth to respond.

"I accept your offer. You will give me full command of your banners and the allegiance of the Highlands in exchange for half a kingdom," Talin continued. "You rallied the north to show your support for me. Now, I ask for your trust."

Blackrun hissed through her teeth. "Sometimes, I forget who I'm friends with. Well-played." She sighed. "My banners are yours to command. But how do you plan to march south without retaking the Crossing?"

"I already thought of that," Talin said. "The Royal Army is lacking manpower since the Highlands deserted. I'm willing to bet that Aldrus had to pull resources from all the garrisons to even have a *chance* of marching on Vill's Crossing. That means the other watchtowers in Kies Tor are significantly weakened."

"And this helps us because...?"

"We're not going to take Vill's Crossing. We're going to cross the bridge at Wycrest."

XLIX

T alin didn't like how quiet the area was as she halted her banners at the edge of Wycrest, facing the bridge and the Glass Forest beyond. In the dry season heat, the river before her had lost its usual foaming rapids, reduced to a slow trickle below the riverbank. She supposed it was a good thing in these circumstances; anyone who fell in wouldn't be swept away immediately to their watery demise.

"This bridge is a terrible place to fight," Ettrias muttered. "Too narrow for us to make good use of a cavalry charge. It's a bottleneck, and an exceedingly *long* bottleneck at that. If we're attacked before we can get across..."

"Better to fight here than forcing our way through two fortified towers and a fortified, gated city." Talin scanned the glass trees in the distance. "It doesn't make sense, though. I would have thought that we'd run across *some* resistance. Aldrus isn't a fool—he must have anticipated that we'd try to circle around near the western border or take the Wycrest bridge."

"If you're worried about an ambush, you could always send a few scouts ahead," Ettrias said. "I'm sure Rufus would be more than happy to help."

Talin glanced at the gathered bannermen behind them. She didn't want to risk giving away their presence if the Royal Army wasn't yet aware of their plans, but if they were ambushed on the bridge, there would be no way to save all of their siege weapons. She hadn't spent precious time rerouting to Castle Blackrun for their trebuchets only to lose them to a stupid mistake.

"Find Golmin and have him round up a team, then," she said. "They're to search the Glass Forest for any attackers or enemy forces camped in the area. We'll cross the bridge once we can determine it's safe."

Ettrias nodded and moved off, and she saw a small team begin their trek across the bridge a few minutes later. Among their number were Icari and Marcus.

"You could have sent me with them," Ashera said, riding up beside her. "I hate waiting around."

"Golmin chose the team, not me," Talin said. "Besides, I need you here. As 'acting lord commander', if you will."

Ashera snorted. "It's fine. You're allowed to say I'm a substitute for Red Wolf."

"You're not," Talin said. If—once—they rescued Red Wolf and dealt with matters once and for all, she would have to ask him to take up the mantle of House Head. He would become *Lord Blackrun*—making him lord commander at that stage would be an insult and demotion.

She needed a new royal bodyguard, and truthfully, there was only ever one other person she could have considered.

The minutes ticked by. Talin found herself watching the tree line intently, waiting, hoping to see *some* kind of movement, good or bad.

"I can tell you're worried about him," Ashera said. "You're worried about this war. You don't know if you're doing the right thing, and you're worried you chose wrong because you followed your heart instead of thinking it through."

"And you're not worried?" Talin asked.

"Of course I'm worried." Ashera turned her attention to the forest. "But I trust you. Come on, I spent three years squiring for you, and a year of that was on the front. You make mistakes sometimes, but you fix them. Trust yourself more."

A war-horn rang out across the river. Talin recognised it immediately as the Royal Army's.

"Cavalry!" she yelled. "Into position! On my order!"

There was a mad scramble of hoof-beats and shouting as the officers organised their men.

"You should probably get ready, too," Talin said to Ashera.

"I'm ready whenever you need me."

Half a dozen soldiers in northern colours came sprinting out of the forest ahead—Golmin, followed by Marcus and Icari, and the three Whitehall infantrymen who had gone with them to scout ahead. One of the infantrymen was limping and quickly falling behind as they reached the bridge.

Oh, gods, there really was an ambush.

Talin hesitated—perhaps foolishly so. The limping soldier stumbled as she looked on and fell to one knee. One of the Royal Army crossbowmen broke free of the tree line and shot him in the back without hesitation.

"Archers, loose!" Talin commanded. "Cavalry, hold!"

"I can lead a smaller squad ahead to help the scouts," Ettrias said. His gaze was fixed on the other end of the bridge. "Talin. Please."

He just wants to help Golmin. A small squad won't do much except give the archers more targets to shoot at.

"Go," Talin said. "Bring Ashera with you."

Ettrias spurred his horse on. Ashera followed hot on his tail. Arrows sailed down over the bridge as her archers loosed shot after shot at the attackers, providing Golmin and the others the precious time they needed to get behind Ettrias' charging squad.

"Cavalry!" Talin yelled. "On my mark! Infantry, move with them! Forward!"

Her cavalry surged across the bridge, dodging around Golmin and Ettrias' teams and colliding with the advancing Royal Army soldiers at breakneck speed. Talin winced. She was reminded, once again, of charging Hellhounds during the war, of the sheer brutality of those battles and all the lives lost. It always looked different from a distance. Part of her always longed to charge down there and help somehow.

But she knew her place was here, overseeing the battle instead of fighting in its midst. She had learned, early on in the war, that people would throw aside all caution and self-preservation to protect her, risking everything to keep her safe even if she didn't need their protection. Her presence on the battlefield served as a distraction more than anything else.

Her cavalry split and circled back for a second charge, slamming into the enemy lines again and forcing them back ever so slightly. Her infantry was there to fill the space left behind when the riders broke off again this time.

It was a quick and brutal battle. Without the element of surprise, their northern banners far outnumbered the Royal Army soldiers stationed in the Glass Forest just south of the bridge. Talin had ordered a shield wall to form at the front of the infantry lines, and with them pushing forward slowly, it was inevitable that her forces would advance past the bridge into open ground before the tree line—not much ground, but enough for their infamous cavalry to effectively charge. Talin crossed the bridge as the battle was nearing its end, finishing off any wounded soldiers along the way so they wouldn't have to suffer. She saw Ettrias with Ashera just ahead and rode up.

"What's the situation?" she asked.

"We have them on the run," Ettrias said. "I think a few scouts have already run ahead—warning Fort Clements and Fort Voraine of our imminent arrival, no doubt."

"And they'll send word ahead to Belanore," Talin muttered. "Damn it."

"I could round up teams to pursue," Ettrias said. "Not sure how much use they'll be, but anything's worth a try if you want to maintain the element of surprise."

"No, that won't be necessary," Talin said. She glanced back at their siege weapons. "They'll be expecting us to take the roads. It's the only way to get our trebuchets to Belanore without literally cutting a new path through the wilderness."

"You...have an alternative?" Ashera asked.

Talin put a hand on her chin. "We'll send our siege weapons along the road as normal, along with their crews and enough infantry and archers to protect them. The cavalry and leftover troops will come with us. We'll cut through the Glass Forest and Stormwood—and march in a straight line directly to Belanore."

"That...might actually work." Ettrias blinked. "Ah—*before* you go off to celebrate and make preparations, dear sister, I have to point out that you need to send most of your army with these siege weapons along the road. Our goal is to make it to Belanore as fast as possible, as discreetly as possible. Only our cavalry will be able to keep up."

"I'd send a few cavalry divisions with the main army, too," Ashera added. "Remember—the northerners are *known* for their cavalry units. It'd be far too suspicious if your army marched past Fort Voraine without a horse in sight."

Talin let out a long breath. "You're both right. But that would deprive us of numbers and manpower. We need both if we're to stand any chance of forcing the city into lockdown and beginning the siege."

"It's a risk. We can go organise the troops on your command, but you have to decide." Ettrias shrugged.

Talin cursed. Logic and reason dictated that she should keep marching south as planned and arrive at Belanore with her entire army. But Red Wolf might not have that kind of time. At best, the trial would go ahead, and the High Court would find him guilty of conspiracy, treason, breach of his exile, and a dozen other crimes for which he was innocent. At worst, Aldrus might consider him a prisoner of war and do something radical.

I lost him fifteen years ago. I won't let that happen again.

"Split up the men and relay my orders to Blackrun," Talin said. "We ride for Belanore at dawn."

D own in the dungeons beneath the royal palace, the conditions were surprisingly decent. It was a far cry from what he had anticipated; Red Wolf would go so far as to say he was impressed. Evidently, in the fifteen years since his departure, Talin had dedicated no small effort to making improvements and renovations to these cells. Instead of the narrow, wooden bench that used to serve as a bed, there was now a proper cot, complete with a simple straw mattress. Where he once might have expected a constant cold draft from the cell window, he found now that there was glass to block the elements and steel bars when he opened the window to look beyond. He had no doubt that these renovations had cost a fortune.

It's impressive, though.

Red Wolf had to admit he was a little proud.

His meals still consisted of the usual prison slop—leftover stew of some kind with tasteless stale bread. Given the circumstances, he supposed it was better than whatever disgusting sludge they used to serve to the prisoners, but he still found himself craving proper food. He remembered being locked in the lower levels, in solitary confinement, back when Wormwood had them arrested on their return to Belanore. This was barely an improvement.

He had lost track of the days he'd been here by the time he received a visitor—and judging by the footsteps, there was the usual large detail of extra security. The door swung open not long after to reveal a dozen royal guards armed with crossbows, who quickly surrounded him and forced him to his knees, shackling his wrists behind him and chaining him to the floor. Behind them came the king regent himself.

"Evening," Aldrus said. "I hope you've not been too uncomfortable."

"Save your formalities. What are you doing here?" Red Wolf asked.

Aldrus shrugged. "I wanted to formally meet you. Talin always spoke exceedingly highly of you—it's a shame that our first proper conversation has to take place like this, but from the reports I've read, I'm sure you can understand if I take certain...precautions. Despite what Talin might say."

"I served the Crown since her father's time. I know my reputation. I know it was all earned—and deserved."

"Most nowadays would call you a disgrace."

"Earned and deserved, as I said." Red Wolf shrugged. "Or did Talin never fill you in on the specifics of my trial?"

"You misunderstand our relationship," Aldrus said. "I only know what she deems important for me to know. Nothing more. Whatever assumptions you might have, I can tell you now they're not true."

"*Tch.* Enlighten me, then," Red Wolf said.

"It was, at its core, a strictly professional one," Aldrus said. "She was under pressure to find a suitor; my brother wanted to get rid of me. Our paths happened to cross at the right time."

Red Wolf glanced at the crossbowmen. "Bold words for someone trying their best to hold onto the people's support."

"It's the truth. It's no secret." Aldrus stepped into the cell. "But I didn't come all the way down here to indulge in small talk." He waved the soldiers out. Red Wolf watched them leave.

"What do you really want?"

"Answer me honestly. You were in a romantic relationship with her fifteen years ago, were you not?"

Red Wolf scowled. "Why do you care?"

"Because someone spread rumours about the two of you all across Kies Tor. As far as the High Court is concerned, that's sufficient motive for Talin to have forged the papers for your return," Aldrus said.

"Motive, certainly," Red Wolf said. "But you were going to tell them that regardless."

"I only want to tell them the truth," Aldrus said. "And I would hope that someone of your reputation knows better than to lie to the court again."

Red Wolf closed his eyes momentarily. It seemed, then, that the consequences of their decision had finally caught up to them.

"Talin seemed to think you were the one who spread those rumours," he said. "You're telling me she never told you the truth?"

"Not directly, no," Aldrus said. "I had my suspicions, but I certainly didn't know the details that these rumours go into. Now, for the sake of your trial, I'd like to hear it from you."

"I don't have to tell you anything," Red Wolf said.

Aldrus huffed a laugh. "Do I detect a hint of jealousy, Lord Commander? Perhaps over the fact that I got to her before you did?"

Red Wolf growled.

"Relax. My only interest in your queen is to bring her to trial and prove her innocence or guilt." Aldrus crouched before him. "So I ask again. Were you in a romantic relationship with her fifteen years ago?"

Red Wolf headbutted the man in the face and heard a satisfying *crack* as his nose broke. He stumbled back immediately with a scream. The half dozen royal guards he'd sent away thundered into the cell a moment later.

"Your Majesty, are you alright?" one of the guards asked.

"Fine. I'll be fine." Aldrus straightened with a groan, holding his nose. Blood dripped from it onto his hand, then onto the floor. "I would have expected more civilised behaviour from you, Lord Commander."

"Perhaps you should think twice about demanding an answer from me about such private matters," Red Wolf said. "My queen's personal life is none of your business if your relationship with her is exactly as you say."

"No matter. I have my answer." Aldrus turned away. "I'll see you again soon, when it's time for your trial—"

A single horn blast echoed through the city, audible all the way down in the dungeons. Red Wolf smiled.

"One blast," Aldrus said. "That's an invading force."

"Sounds like it came from the northern gate, Your Majesty," one of the crossbowmen said.

"The northern alliance." Aldrus' lips pressed into a hard line. "Get him up. It seems like we'll need to have a chat with my wife."

The guards unlocked Red Wolf's shackles and bound his wrists again behind his back, and he was marched from the cells without another word. At the northern wall, he was forced onto his knees once more, where his escort was doubled, and he could see exactly what it was that had sent all of Belanore scrambling into a panic.

To the naked eye, there was no opposing army outside the gates. But his enhanced eyesight could pick out the soldiers hiding in the forest on either side of the main road, waiting silently. They had no doubt made themselves visible, only for a moment, as a way to panic the City Watch guardsmen. From the wall, there was no way to see their numbers. No way to know exactly what the city was up against.

Well played, Talin. Red Wolf smiled.

Aldrus joined them a few minutes later, clad in plate and mail, his nose now fixed with strips of thick cloth tape to hold the bone in position. He approached the edge of the wall immediately to look at the road and forest beyond.

"They're in the trees," Red Wolf said. "Maybe thousands. There's no way of knowing."

"Hmm." Aldrus turned away from the wall to look at him. "The reports from Fort Clements and Fort Voraine mentioned that Talin was marching south with siege weapons, and there is no way she could have hidden them all in the trees. I can only assume she split her army and cut through the wilderness. I suspect she only brought a small number of soldiers with her, but the city has no defenses prepared, and the rest of her army will arrive soon. I cannot hold Belanore for long." He leaned forwards. "That's where you'll come in."

"What, you're going to use me as a bargaining chip?" Red Wolf laughed. "Do you honestly believe that Talin would choose *me* over her people? She chose to sacrifice me fifteen years ago to do the right thing.

She is responsible for defeating the Hellhounds because she cares about her people more than her own *life*. She recognises the Crown's need to put duty first, above all else, above even her own wishes." He gazed into Aldrus' eyes. "You and I both know she would sacrifice me again if that's what it came down to."

"And you would let her?" Aldrus asked.

"I would. In a heartbeat," Red Wolf said.

"I suppose we'll see." Aldrus turned back to face the forest. One of his crossbowmen shoved Red Wolf forward until he was visible to whoever was watching from below.

This is it, then.

"I know you're there, Talin," Aldrus called. He drew his sword and rested the blade against Red Wolf's neck. "I took the liberty of lacing this blade with torslek. Show yourself, or he dies."

"What do you want?" Talin asked.

"Just to talk. Perhaps we can come to an arrangement," Aldrus said.

"Short of handing back my crown and my lands, you have nothing I want."

"I'll kill him."

"Red Wolf dies, and my banners attack," Talin said. "The city will not last long against a siege. You have no defenses prepared, no provisions, and no numbers. I know most of the Royal Army is still garrisoned at Vill's Crossing—you only brought a small company back to Belanore with you."

Red Wolf focused on her voice and quickly pinpointed her location in the trees. He glanced in her direction.

"It's alright, Talin," he told her. "Do what you have to."

"Well, then, if you've made up your mind..." Aldrus' sword dug further into his neck, drawing blood. Red Wolf closed his eyes and resigned himself to whatever came next.

"Wait!"

His eyes flashed open again.

Talin had left the cover of the trees and sprinted into the open, dropping her weapons belt and bow on the grass as she did so. She held her hands up in surrender.

"Put the sword down. We'll talk."

What?

"They want you out in the open!" Red Wolf hissed. "Are you out of your mind? Don't take another step towards those gates, Talin. I swear to the gods—"

The bite of steel disappeared from his neck as Aldrus lowered his blade.

"It seems that you were wrong, royal bodyguard."

Below them, the gates swung open, allowing half a dozen crossbow-men to spill out, directing their weapons at Talin. Aldrus turned away from the wall.

"Come, now," he said. "I'm sure she's anxious to see you."

Red Wolf followed him down from the wall and through the open gates, stopping just behind the crossbowmen. Seeing him approach, Talin started forwards but quickly stopped when the soldiers tensed.

"Are you alright?" she asked.

"I'm fine," Red Wolf said. "You shouldn't have done that."

"As if I would have done anything else."

Red Wolf had no suitable response to that. He knew, deep down, that she was right; there was never any question about whether or not she would risk everything to save him.

"You wanted to talk," Talin continued, looking at Aldrus.

"I'd like to propose a trade," the Fae said. "I will return your former lord commander to your ranks unharmed. In return, Katherine Blackrun will march her banners back into the Highlands and remain there. She and the nobility who support her will await trial for treason and conspiracy. You will submit yourself into the Crown's custody to await trial for the same. Arkiel will be returned home to the royal palace, where he will continue his tutoring and be crowned king once he reaches ruling age."

"Not exactly a fair deal," Talin said.

"No. But Red Wolf faces execution as a prisoner of war otherwise," Aldrus said.

Talin's jaw tightened. "You can't execute a prisoner."

"Yes, yes, it's bad form, I know how to wage war." Aldrus scoffed. "But there is nothing stopping me. And I know you can't take that risk, no matter what the price."

Talin looked at Red Wolf, then at Aldrus. She said nothing.

"Don't," Red Wolf said. "I'm not worth all of that."

"I know." Talin closed her eyes momentarily. "I cannot guarantee Blackrun's cooperation in this deal, even if I command her to turn her banners around. The rest, I can agree to—on one condition. Red Wolf is to be released immediately."

"Done." Aldrus stood aside, and the crossbowmen parted for Talin.

"Relay my order to stand down," she said, pausing as she passed Red Wolf. "Tell Blackrun we've come to an agreement."

"Talin."

"That's an order, Lord Commander."

Red Wolf bowed his head. "As my queen commands."

"Trust me." Talin took his hand briefly, and then she stepped past the crossbowmen to stand before Aldrus.

I always have, Red Wolf thought.

At the edge of the trees, he stopped, turning back to watch as Talin and her escort disappeared through the gates. Ettrias and Golmin were at his side a moment later.

"Evening," the prince said cheerfully. Red Wolf responded with a growl.

"I cannot believe you let her make that deal, *gods*, you're both—" he began.

"Relax," Ettrias said. "Come with us. Everything is going to plan."

They led him deeper into the forest, to a map roughly drawn in the dirt, where Blackrun and her generals were gathered, along with Ashera, Icari, and Marcus. Red Wolf immediately recognised the map—it was an approximation of the layout of Belanore, not perfect, but close enough. The Stormwood tunnel entrance at the northern wall had been circled.

"What's this, then?" he asked.

"Talin went into this with a plan," Ettrias said. "She knew Aldrus would use you as a bargaining chip. We needed a way into the city, so we came up with something. Talin would agree to whatever deal that Aldrus came up with and seek an audience with him, keeping him occupied while the rest of us get into the city through the Stormwood tunnel."

"The tunnel you circled is blocked," Red Wolf said.

"At the fork to the palace, yes," Ettrias said. "The path to the exit near the city square is still open. We can get in, open the gate for the rest of our forces, and take over before Aldrus can mobilise his men." He nodded at Icari and Marcus. "We have a team. All we need is someone to lead it."

Red Wolf considered it. There was a good chance that the plan would work; not many patrols would be wandering through the city tonight with everyone at the wall. Assuming Talin could keep Aldrus occupied, this could very well be their easiest way into the city.

She really came here with a backup plan for everything, he thought. She had asked him to put his trust in her, and now, it seemed, he needed to honour that trust.

It was time to retake control of Belanore in her name.

They made their way through the streets and back to the palace, Talin escorted at arrow-point by the half-dozen crossbowmen from earlier. Aldrus led the way in silence. Even in the evening quiet, she could hear whispers from the crowd still out and about at this hour—it wasn't the first time, after all, that she'd returned home with an escort pointing weapons at her back. Some of the city folk had even left their homes to see the commotion.

"Aldrus, there are things we need to discuss," she said.

"Indeed there are." Aldrus glanced over his shoulder at her without stopping. "But not here. I'm sure you'd rather some privacy."

Talin said nothing and tested her chains instead. They'd taken the precaution of binding her hands, probably in an attempt to stop her from using her lightning, but her fingers still had enough wiggle room to grab or touch whatever she could reach. Her bindings were entirely useless. But she supposed she could go along with it for now if it put Aldrus and the crossbowmen more at ease.

In the palace, she was marched directly into Aldrus' office instead of a tower or the dungeons, exactly as she'd predicted. She now had to keep Aldrus occupied while Ettrias and Red Wolf snuck into the city. In theory, it was simple enough, but in practice...

Ettrias knows what he's doing, and they'll be moving under cover of darkness. They'll be fine.

Still, she had to admit to herself that the plan was far riskier than she would have liked. Under normal circumstances, she wouldn't have agreed to it at all.

I was a fool for rushing here. All to stop Red Wolf facing trial.

She didn't regret her decision—not when it came to saving him. But she did regret how easily she'd thrown all caution aside for his sake.

I cannot afford to be selfish at a time like this, she told herself. Blackrun's banners waited outside the city gates for the signal to attack. If a bloodbath happened in the streets of Belanore because the plan failed, she would be responsible for it all.

"Sit," Aldrus said, indicating the chair opposite. Her escort left him with the key for her chains. He freed her hands once the guards had left, and she sat down hesitantly.

"There is something you must know," he said carefully after a moment's silence. "I...have known, for quite some time, that...the assassins you faced were sent by my brother."

"Yes, I already know," Talin said.

Aldrus opened and closed his mouth. A moment of silence passed between them.

"How long have you known?"

"Ettrias told me when he returned from his trip to Astaria. He'd uncovered some kind of royal conspiracy in the south but left before they could target him."

Aldrus sighed. "Of course. But you must understand, I had nothing to do with those assassins. Darien wanted to provoke you into sending those papers. I...when I found out he was the one who tried to kill Arkiel, I no longer wanted a part in his plans. But things were already in motion. People were saying you were dead, the reports from the search parties said the same, and as far as I knew, Arkiel was missing. I had to continue playing my part as king regent."

"Trying to garner sympathy for the mess you've caused?" Talin lifted a brow. "I might have been on the run, but I still know how to play politics back home. Lord Cassius updated me on everything he learned before you ordered his arrest."

"You know everything, then," Aldrus said.

"Enough to know your part in Darien's plans of conquest," Talin said. "Your goal all along was to undermine my rule."

Aldrus let out a half-chuckle and sipped his drink. "I...will admit, I was working with him for a time. But I saw that Kies Tor was, perhaps, better off with you in charge—until you sent those papers to Red Wolf. As I said, I resented my brother for sending those assassins. You might have been the one who brought your bodyguard back, but Darien was the one who made you desperate enough to do it. And with you on the run, or dead, or whatever the rumours and search parties were saying...someone had to take over."

"Oh, please. You just wanted to be in charge." Talin scoffed. "You know as well as I do that I didn't send those papers. The timing doesn't line up. More likely, *you* were the one who sent them."

"I don't understand," Aldrus said.

"Aldrus, think about it," Talin said. "Your assumption is that I sent the papers after that second assassination attempt, correct?"

"Yes."

"And three weeks passed between then and my attempted arrest in Belanore. It's at least five weeks to the Draconian capital. How could Red Wolf have received the letter *and* made his way all the way into Belanore in time?"

Aldrus' brow furrowed. "But I didn't send for Red Wolf. And from what you're telling me, it seems like you didn't either."

Talin fell silent, mind racing. If Aldrus was telling the truth, then a third party must have lured Red Wolf home—and in doing so, had wanted to pit Aldrus against her.

"It doesn't make sense," she said. "I'd suspected it couldn't be you, but there's no one else who had motive...oh, gods."

Aldrus' eyes widened, and she knew then that he was thinking the exact same thing. "That first assassin...attacked you in your study, yes?"

Talin nodded. "He was waiting there when I entered and fled before I could call for backup."

"Then he...wasn't an assassin at all. He had another objective. My brother sent those papers, Talin. It's the only thing that makes sense."

Everything slotted into place. "He wanted us to turn on each other. And once Kies Tor had destabilised to the point of civil war, he would swoop in with his own army and take the entire kingdom by force. To the people, he would be *saving* them from us both."

Alarm bells sounded in the city below them, indicating that invaders had broken through the outer wall. She knew immediately that Ettrias' team had been successful. Aldrus jumped to his feet.

"You planned for all of this," he hissed. "Is that the only reason you wished to talk? To distract me?"

"*Wait*," Talin said, rising as well. Aldrus paused with his hand on the doorknob. "Aldrus. If my suspicions are correct, we must negotiate a truce. *Now.*"

"We can negotiate later. It'll be a massacre if we don't tell the troops to stand down." Aldrus threw open the door and took off at a sprint, Talin on his heels.

The two of them made it to the stables in record time, where they quickly saddled two horses and made for the northern gate as fast as their mounts dared to go. It wasn't long before Talin spotted the fighting; Blackrun's bannermen had gained significant ground in the short time since the alarm bells had first sounded. She cursed how effective their plan had been.

"Stand down!" she yelled, forcing her way through the battle. Aldrus split off to give the same order. "Stand down! Blackrun banners, stand down!" She barely heard herself over the clashing of steel.

Where in the seven hells are Red Wolf and Ettrias?

She spotted her lord commander quickly enough, cutting down Royal Army soldiers with an arrow lodged in his shoulder. She clicked at her horse and made a beeline for him, shouting for their banners to stand down at whoever could hear, hoping to the gods that it wasn't too late to stop the bloodbath.

"What's the occas—" Red Wolf began, lifting the visor of his helm as she neared.

"Stand down! Tell everyone to stand down!" Talin snapped. Sensing the urgency, Red Wolf moved off immediately to relay the order, his own voice ringing out over the cacophony.

Slowly, painfully so, the battle died down around them, leaving groups of opposing soldiers facing each other uncertainly, weapons still held between them. The tension in the air was suffocating. Slick blood already painted parts of the dimly lit streets. Talin could see bodies strewn all the way to the northern gate—the invasion force evidently hadn't been as undetected as she'd hoped.

Gods, what have I done?

None of this bloodshed had been necessary. If she hadn't been so hasty to rescue Red Wolf, if she had seen Darien's plans earlier, if she hadn't been a damn fool and fallen for his trap...

Talin covered her mouth with one hand and stifled a rising sob.

Focus! The important thing is we've stopped ripping out each other's throats.

Two horn blasts echoed through the city, this time coming from the southern gate, indicating unannounced friendly forces. Talin felt her blood run cold.

"*Please* tell me that's not your brother's army," she said to Aldrus.

Her husband grabbed the nearest City Watch guard. "Go to the southern gate. Tell them not to let anyone through under *any circumstances.* MOVE!" The guard scrambled off with a nervous "yessir", and Aldrus turned back to Talin.

"He's not going to wait around patiently while we get the city ready for siege," she said.

"I know." Aldrus winced. "Let's get back to the palace. I'll send someone to free Corvan and Lord Wyndove from the dungeons. It's about time we negotiated that truce."

They gathered before dawn in the war room in the dim light of hastily lit candles and oil lamps, Talin at the head of the table with Aldrus to her right. Blackrun soon joined them, too, along with Ettrias and Golmin and a handful of northern nobles. Red Wolf sat in one of the armchairs being tended to by Corvan. He had revealed, on the way back to the palace with the arrow still in his shoulder, that his healing powers weren't working—Aldrus' torslek-dipped blade had scratched his neck at the wall. Talin had sent him to find a healer and snapped at him for being too reckless when he insisted on joining the war meeting instead.

"Thank you for gathering, all of you. We don't have much time to prepare," she said. "I'll get straight to the point. How big of an army do we have?"

"I brought some Royal Army soldiers with me from Vill's Crossing, but the rest are still garrisoned there," Aldrus said. "I can put out word to Fort Saria—they'll be ready to march immediately and should arrive within a few days."

"Not fast enough," Talin muttered. "What of our northern banners?"

"Still en route along the road," Ettrias said.

"The Drakels are on the march by now, too," Blackrun added. "We had a bird from Castle Blackrun yesterday. They should be almost here."

"I remember," Talin said.

"It's all well and good that we have so many reinforcements on the way," Red Wolf muttered, "but you're forgetting one thing. Darien's army is at the gates *now*. None of those armies are of any help to us from half a week away."

"We'll have to hold out until they arrive, then," Talin said. "What about our current numbers?"

Aldrus winced. "It's...hard to say. We suffered significant losses during the skirmish at the northern gates."

"As did my banners," Blackrun said. "Still, we have reinforcements arriving."

Talin closed her eyes momentarily. "How many casualties did we suffer from that fight?" she asked.

The meeting table was silent.

"*How many*," Talin repeated.

"Two hundred and three," Ettrias finally said.

Talin wanted to scream. Once again, it seemed, others had paid for her mistakes. Two hundred and three others, to be precise. Far too many.

"That brings our total to under a thousand," Red Wolf said. "Not exactly promising numbers to hold off a full-scale siege."

"What if we just...wait out Darien's army?" Lord Wyndove asked. "They don't yet know they're unwelcome here. If we can stall until our reinforcements arrive..."

"It's a nice idea, but not one that will work, I'm afraid," Aldrus said. "Darien will assume the city has fallen under northern occupation if we don't let him in soon, and then he will order his banners to attack. We might be able to stall him for an hour or two, but not nearly long enough."

Talin considered their options for a moment. Either they try to stall Darien by waiting, or they begin their siege preparations and prompt the Fae to attack. She wasn't exactly thrilled about either choice.

But there is a third way.

She glanced around the table. Everyone here had gathered for the sake of the city—for *her* sake. She had no right to ask them to fight in her stead. If she was going to go through with this, she had to do things herself.

"Darien doesn't know I've returned with the northern alliance," she said. "Why don't we announce my return by challenging the Astarian Royal Army to a duel?"

The silence that greeted her this time was deafening.

"Hear me out," Talin continued when it became apparent that nobody else was going to speak. "Even if Darien refuses the duel, it buys us time to secure the gates, at the very least. But I'm willing to bet that someone with such an inflated ego isn't going to refuse. We could settle this with minimal bloodshed."

"Who do you plan to send as a champion?" Aldrus asked.

"I'll do it," Red Wolf said. "Let me fight."

"You're injured," Ettrias said. "Send me. I'm one of the best swordsmen in the kingdom. You know I stand the best chance of emerging victorious."

"No." Talin straightened. "I nominate myself."

"Wh— absolutely not," Red Wolf hissed. "We need you. You're our *leader*. We need you alive."

"And who would you ask to risk their life in my stead?" Talin said softly. "Fifteen years ago, you duelled Kehlvor in my stead and almost died for it. Who am I to dictate which man's life is worth so little that I would be willing to throw it away in a duel?"

"We are all here because we...follow...*you*." Red Wolf stood with a grimace, despite Corvan's protests. "Our banners rally to *you*."

"Our banners rally to the Crown," Talin said. "It's not. About. Me. It never was. People rarely ever rally to a single person; they rally to a cause. It was true when I rallied my banners fifteen years ago. The people wanted to see their kingdom reclaimed. It was true when Blackrun rallied her people to march south. They wished to see the Highlands free. It is true now. We all wish to see Belanore safe."

"I cannot let you do this," Red Wolf said. "You speak of challenging Darien to a fight to the death—"

"You won't *let* me? You would issue commands to your queen?" Talin glared. Daring him to object.

"My duty is to protect you," Red Wolf said. "From yourself, if necessary, and it would appear that it *is* necessary right now."

"Enough!" Talin snapped. "You undermine my decisions in front of this entire war council, and you have the gall to presume I need *protection* from such decisions—as if I haven't already weighed the consequences and understand the risks. I will tolerate no more of it. Your duty is to the Crown. Do not forget that."

"The Crown." Red Wolf scoffed. "You wish to speak of *my duty* to the Crown? I have lied for the Crown. Killed for the Crown. I've dedicated my *life* to the Crown. And it was never out of loyalty to your father; it was out of love for you! So please, *forgive me* if I am slightly opposed to an idea that involves your self-sacrifice."

Dead silence fell over them like a blanket. Red Wolf swayed on his feet and sat back down heavily, finally allowing Corvan to finish stitching his shoulder.

"Darien will take the city by force if he has to," Aldrus said carefully. "I'm not sure that even winning this duel will convince him to stop."

"As I said, we only need to buy ourselves some time," Talin explained. "If his banners still attack, we'll be ready."

Red Wolf was silent. Talin couldn't tell if it was because he was upset or because he saw no way to convince her not to risk her life. Maybe both.

"We should fortify the walls, then," Blackrun said. "Organise the guard rotations. Prepare the palace for siege."

"Yes, it's time to get moving." Talin flattened her palms on the table. "Corvan, if I could trouble you to send the challenge to Darien once you're done with Red Wolf..."

For the next half hour, they went through a map of the city and the palace blueprints, identifying possible weak points and deciding on the best way to defend everything. It was eventually decided that Blackrun and a small team would reinforce Hesar's men at the northern wall while Ettrias and Lord Whitehall kept the south wall secured. Golmin would remain in the palace to coordinate the royal guards, and the rest of their troops would be spread out through the city, blockading strategic points along the main roads to slow down the Fae army in case they ever broke through. Lord Wyndove was responsible for evacuating civilians out of the city.

But until Darien graced them with a response to her challenge, Talin had nothing else to do but wait.

She wasn't entirely sure what exactly drove her to visit the royal crypt beneath the palace; it had been a long while since she last paid her respects to the sovereigns of Kies Tor's past. But she was here now, making her way through the wide, open chambers, past her ancestors' tombs. Every ruler who had ever worn the Torrian royal crown was buried here, leaving behind a legacy that stretched back two thousand years. The sculptures of them almost seemed to stare as she walked.

Talin had never liked feeling the weight of that legacy when she visited.

She eventually stopped before her parents' tombs, looking up at their sculptures and failing, as usual, to conjure up memories of her mother's face. Arnas had said to her before that he didn't think the stonemason fully captured Queen Elora's beauty, but Talin was grateful to know her face at all. She took in the woman's elegant features, her slightly pointed ears, her long, braided locks. Talin liked to imagine that her mother's hair was some shade of blonde or light brown and that her eyes were the same shade of blue as Ettrias' eyes.

"I didn't bring anything today, I'm afraid," she told them. "I'm not entirely sure why I'm here. But I guess this might be my last chance to visit."

She trailed her fingers over the engraved stone lids sealing away her parents' coffins., tracing the Old Torrian script along its edges.

"*Nori shivis trev nádáv retour var Kou Yumal, nori shivis siyal nádáv retour var drar,*" she said softly. *May your spirit be returned to the Moon*

Goddess; may your soul be returned to the land. A beautiful line from an age before magic was shunned.

"I don't know what to do," she confessed after a long silence. "I don't know...how else...I can save everyone. Every mistake I make has consequences for the people around me. I'm responsible for the massacre at the northern gate before the siege even began. My mistakes are the reason Kies Tor is once again threatened. I can't keep doing this." She sank to her knees before them. "I needed you both. I needed your counsel, your wisdom, your kindness. I can't do this alone. Please, *tell me*, how do we get through the siege?"

Silence.

Coming here had been a bad idea. She wasn't sure what answers she was looking for, but she knew there were no answers to be found with the dead.

Footsteps rang through the crypt behind her. She stood and turned to see Ettrias approach, torch in one hand and a handful of flowers from the central courtyard in the other. He brushed past her to lay the flowers at their parents' feet, then stepped back to join her.

"I was wondering who brought flowers for Father the last time I was here," Talin said.

"The dead deserve some dignity," Ettrias said. "Even if it's Father."

A moment of silence passed between them. Ettrias set his torch down in an empty bracket and looked up at Elora's face.

"Do you remember what she looked like?" Talin asked.

"No," Ettrias said.

"Me neither."

"I found one of Mother's old violins in the storage rooms," Talin said after a beat. "It's the same one I broke. Father must have replaced the string at some point. I didn't think he was the sentimental type."

Ettrias huffed a half-laugh. "I remember you sneaking off with that thing when the palace staff weren't looking. Father was furious—didn't you almost take your own eye out when the string snapped?"

"Not the brightest idea I've ever had, I'll admit." Talin smiled. "If I survive the duel and we make it through this siege, I think I want to learn how to play it."

"We'll get through this," Ettrias said. "Don't think about 'if'. You're going to win, and we're going to kick Darien all the way back into Astaria."

More footsteps echoed through the crypt, almost too soft even for the echoing walls to amplify. She turned her head as Red Wolf approached.

"It's time," he said. "Your messenger's returned. Darien has agreed to the duel."

T hey made their way to the southern gate on horseback as the first traces of dawn light broke across the horizon, passing only the on-duty soldiers as they rode through the city. Red Wolf tried to lighten the mood with stories of hers and Ettrias' childhood, but Talin only felt growing dread with each step her horse took. She tried unsuccessfully to swallow the lump in her throat.

In theory, this was a good idea. In practice...

Thinking about the duel was only making things worse. She did her best to focus on other matters, like the siege preparations and the warm-up spar with Red Wolf earlier. It was gods damned impossible.

She'd gone with as little armour as she could get away with and settled for an open helm, knowing that the dry season heat would make it impossible to fight for any prolonged period in full plate. It was a risk, wearing so little protection, but she knew she could outlast her opponent if she just kept up the defense.

Darien's champion was already waiting for them when they stepped through the gates and out to the grassy field between the city and the southern forest. He stood at the edge of a makeshift duellists' ring marked with blades stuck point-first into the ground, clad in full plate, holding his helmet under one arm. He was a taller opponent than her, with a youthful face and a tuft of curly hair, and he reminded her, painfully clearly, of young Edd from the arena.

"You don't have to do this," Red Wolf said.

Talin huffed a quiet laugh. "Still trying to change my mind? You know that's a futile effort."

"Worth a try anyway. I'll see you afterwards."

Behind her, the wall had been crammed with on-duty soldiers looking to see the action for themselves. Ettrias had shown himself, too; she saw him watching with the troops on the battlements. Aldrus waited for them in the middle of the ring, ready to signal the start of the duel. Talin could see Darien's banners waiting in the distance, thousands of soldiers poised to attack. The Fae king himself stood next to his champion.

"What are the terms?" he called.

"It's simple enough," Talin said. "If I win, you will turn your armies around and cease to trouble our lands any further. Aldrus will be stripped of all titles he holds in Kies Tor for aiding in conspiracy against the Crown. If I lose, Belanore offers its unconditional surrender."

"Very well. I accept." Darien waved his champion forward. "Aldrus! Little brother. Do not stand with these elves in the coming siege. Join your people."

Talin looked at her husband.

"No," Aldrus said. "You tried to kill my son. *You* are the cause of Kies Tor's political instability these past few months. I will not play your games any longer. I stand with a people who value justice and fairness and a ruler who would rather protect her own than seek out new lands to conquer." He turned to the Fae generals gathered behind Darien. "Lord Bayesh, Lord Auwin, General Gorin. You stand with a tyrant who cares not for his people—only power. Know this before you march into battle alongside him."

He turned on his heel and strode back through the southern gates. Talin stared after him.

Just like that? I didn't think he'd turn his back on Astaria so readily.

Ashera approached and held out her sword and shield, allowing Talin to unsheathe the weapon and fit the shield to her arm. She stepped out to meet her opponent in the middle of the ring.

"Before we begin, I'd like to know my opponent's name," she said.

"Sir Artin of House Willoric, representing King Darien," the champion said. "And yours?"

Ah. So he doesn't know who I am.

"Queen Talin of House Zylvaris. Representing myself."

She saw her opponent's eyes widen for the barest fraction of a second before he composed himself. He lowered his helm and visor.

"It's an honour, then."

"Likewise."

Talin closed the distance with a swing at her opponent's neck.

He met her blade with a deft parry, metal ringing together as their weapons clashed. Roars of approval went up from both sides. Talin quickly changed angles, sidestepping the riposte and going for the back of the champion's leg. He saw the strike and dodged just in time. Talin ducked under his swing and parried the follow-up.

He's good. Probably better than me. I have to end this quickly.

She stepped to the left again, trying to change angles, but he followed her effortlessly, quickly forcing her on the defensive with a lightning-fast jab at her exposed neck. She suddenly felt glad of her earlier spar with Red Wolf—it was the perfect preparation for fighting against a taller opponent like Sir Artin.

Talin feinted right. Her opponent followed but recovered quickly enough to parry her strike from the left. He punished her mistake immediately with another swing and hissed through his teeth when the blade skittered off plate armour mere inches from her throat. She glimpsed Red Wolf letting out a sigh of relief from his spot at the top of the wall. He met her gaze momentarily and gave a nod.

Talin ducked under her opponent's next strike and aimed another low cut at his legs. The tip of her sword made it into an armour gap and drew a grunt of pain from him, but he didn't falter, shoving her back out of range with his free hand so he could recover. She saw his limp despite his best efforts to hide it.

There has to be an opening I can exploit.

But the champion was giving her none of that. His next attack came so fast that she barely had time to parry, knocking the blade away from her neck. It went high and scored a scratch across her cheek. She saw Red Wolf wince out of the corner of her eye and muttered a silent apology for making him worry. Her opponent was on the offensive again almost immediately, the blade glinting in the morning light. She ducked and feinted left again. He followed as she'd expected and recovered again to parry her real attack—much slower this time. She noticed that he wasn't pivoting so much on his wounded leg anymore.

They both knew he wouldn't be able to keep up with her forever.

Talin could see desperation building up in his movement, in the way he grew increasingly aggressive as the minutes dragged on, hoping to end the fight before his leg gave out completely or he collapsed from exhaustion or blood loss. She had the perfect chance to drag things out—to simply defend until he could no longer fight. The cold, rational part of her knew it was the wisest move.

Instead, she distracted him with a jab to the neck and kicked him in the back of the knee.

He let out a grunt and staggered hard but recovered in time to knock aside her next swing. Sweat dripped from his forehead under his helm when he lifted the visor. She knew immediately that he was not accustomed to fighting in such high temperatures. Though Astaria was situated in the same tropical region as southern Kies Tor, its people did not have to spend years contending with Hellhounds. Her young opponent had likely never seen combat in his life and had certainly never tried to fight in full plate in the dry season heat. The armour that was supposed to protect him now only served to hasten his demise.

"You won't last in these conditions," she told him. "You're wearing too much armour. Yield now. I don't want to kill you."

"This is a duel...to the death," Sir Artin said. "I will not disgrace myself by yielding."

He lunged forwards again, aiming for her neck, but the blade glanced off her left pauldron when she sidestepped. Her riposte found an armour gap above his elbow, effectively disarming him. He dropped his weapon with a grimace and immediately tried to reach for it with his other hand. Talin snatched it up before he could. He drew the dagger at his belt and managed to parry one more strike before sinking to one knee.

"Do it, then." He ripped off his helm with one hand and looked up at her. "Just make it quick."

"Keep your life." Talin tossed his sword back. "It's clear enough that I'm the victor. I've seen death, and there's no honour in it."

The champion looked at his weapon, then at her. He didn't move. "Then I thank you for giving me my life."

Talin turned away as Darien rushed up to help Sir Artin to his feet. An outwardly kind gesture, no doubt, to make himself look good.

"Kill her. This is an order from your king."

She stopped in her tracks and turned back. Darien offered her a strained smile and clapped Sir Artin on the shoulder. The knight looked at the dagger in his hand.

"Please don't," she said softly.

A single arrow sailed down from the wall behind her and punched clean through Sir Artin's neck.

Talin spun in an instant, about to order her archers to hold, and saw Red Wolf lowering his bow. He was the only one armed.

Damn it.

She understood immediately; with his enhanced hearing, he must have overheard Darien giving Sir Artin the order to kill. But he would be the only one other than her to have heard it—other than Sir Artin, now dead at her feet. Darien backed away, and she caught the faintest trace of a smile on his lips before he schooled his expression into one of false anger and outrage.

"Liar!" he shouted. "You say you would spare my champion, then go back on your word and execute him after he offered his gratitude?" He turned to his generals and the waiting army. "Belanore does not deserve our honour. We will *attack*."

"You ordered him to kill me while my back was turned—" Talin began. Ashera was at her side a moment later, tugging her back towards the open gates as the Fae soldiers began to chant. She could see teams of archers already lining up their shots at the back of the army, ready to shoot at a moment's notice.

Darien planned for all of this.

She didn't have much time to ponder it; the first wave of arrows sailed overhead, almost blotting out the sun, arcing over their heads. Talin knew from experience that plenty would fall short—and she and Ashera were directly in their path.

Something slammed into her with the force of a charging bull moments before the arrows landed. She saw a flash of golden energy before her eyes.

"Red Wolf...?"

"Go!" He gave her a shove and sent her stumbling forwards, under the gate's archway, where the arrows couldn't reach. She looked around and saw that Ashera had also made it. Red Wolf was a moment behind her, golden energy flickering around him again and failing as he stumbled under the arch.

"You...reckless..." she began. "Your healing—"

"Me?! You two almost died!" Red Wolf growled, yanking his helm off his head. He pinched the bridge of his nose. "Are you both alright, at least?"

"Fine." Talin let out a long breath.

"I'm alright," Ashera said.

Red Wolf sighed. "We need to get back to the palace—"

"Talin!" Aldrus jumped down the steps to the wall three at a time. "Are you alright?"

"I'm fine," Talin said. "I don't understand. Darien ordered Sir Artin to kill me after the duel, and..."

"I did warn you that my brother was willing to do whatever necessary to take the city," Aldrus said.

"Watch your tongue," Red Wolf growled. "My queen won that duel—it's not her fault your brother refused to honour it. Whatever the outcome, we bought enough time to prepare our forces for the siege. The plan *worked*."

Talin could sense some kind of tension between the two of them and decided she didn't have the energy to deal with it. "That's enough, both of you. We can only look forward. Aldrus, you addressed Darien's advisors directly. Why?"

"They're reasonable people, unlike my brother," Aldrus said. "I thought there might be some way to...sway them, convince them to stand with us before the siege began. A childish fantasy, now that I think about it. They face charges of treason if they dare step out of line."

"It's only treason if your actions fail to depose the sovereign," Talin mused. "I'd like to talk to them, if possible."

"Gods, you must be mad." Aldrus let out a deep sigh. "Negotiations might have been possible *before* they started shooting arrows at us, but now?"

"There has to be a way," Talin said. "Would they listen to us if we explained the truth about Red Wolf and Darien's meddling?"

"I...suppose there's a possibility," Aldrus admitted. "I can't believe I'm suggesting this, but I can write a letter to Lord Bayesh—he'll probably be the most receptive out of Darien's remaining generals now that Sir Artin is dead. The only issue is delivering it to him. We can't risk having a messenger pass it on, or it'll likely go through Darien first. I can only think of having one of our people sneak all the way through the camp and delivering it in person."

Talin thought about it. She could sneak into the camp herself and deliver the letter, certainly; as long as she didn't reveal herself, there was no reason for any of the soldiers to suspect that the leader of the opposing army was in disguise in the middle of their camp.

"I know that look," Red Wolf said. "You'll be recognised instantly. We need to send someone more...discreet."

Talin sighed. "Maybe you're right. But who...?"

"It can't be anyone here," Red Wolf said. "There's a chance we'll all be recognised."

"Icari and Marcus." Talin's eyes widened. "They'll be perfect. I think Marcus knows some Faerie, and Icari knows Old Torrian—it'll be enough to get by."

"I'll have someone send for them," Red Wolf said.

"And I suppose I'll get to writing that letter." Aldrus let out a long breath. "I hope this works, Talin."

I hope so, too. Talin didn't voice it out loud. *Anything to prevent this siege.*

She was tired of these games. Tired of this fighting. She had no energy left to organise everything, to lead everyone, to pretend that every inch of her wasn't unravelling like a ball of yarn dropped off a cliffside. She wanted to crawl into bed instead and pretend that the rest of the world didn't exist. But she knew her duty. They were at war, and she could no longer show any weakness, for weakness did not exist in wartime. From now on until the siege saw its end, she was the Queen of Kies Tor, highest authority of this land.

There was no room in her heart for weakness.

R ed Wolf wasn't happy about being forced off-duty, to say the least.

Upon returning to the palace, Talin had forced him to strip his armour immediately, putting him on stand-down orders to prevent him from rushing out into combat until his healing powers returned. He'd protested, but all it did was earn him a pointed look and a lecture about how he needed to be more careful without his powers. He was more likely to ignore a potentially fatal injury, there was a good chance he'd forget his powers were gone, his usual aggressive fighting style wouldn't work...

She did, much as he hated to admit, make some very good points.

He was so absorbed in his thoughts that he barely registered Icari and Marcus running down the hallway in the other direction and managed to dodge aside just in time to avoid a collision. The two of them were still clad in their Fae disguises and looked out of breath.

"What are you two doing here?" Red Wolf asked. "I thought you were supposed to be delivering that letter."

"We did," Marcus gasped. "Couldn't find Lord Bayesh, and we didn't really want to show ourselves, so we left the letter in his tent. But we have a situation."

"Situation?" Red Wolf asked.

"Aye," Marcus said. He paused to catch his breath before continuing. "We passed a battle map on our way out of the tent, thought we'd take a look. It's...from what I understood, Darien's sent out a smaller team to circle around the city and break through the northern gate."

That's not good. Red Wolf cursed. Talin *had* stationed a few guards along the length of the city walls, but not enough, it seemed. Anyone determined enough could easily camouflage their troops and siege weapons in the forest and sneak right past. They hadn't imagined that Darien would go to such lengths.

"Find my queen in the war room upstairs and explain the situation," he said. "I'll handle this in the meantime."

He turned back the way he came and geared up in the armoury, grabbing a war-bow and extra quiver of arrows on the way out. He made for the stables without a second thought. No doubt Talin would give him another lecture later about pushing himself too hard, but for now, they had an attack to fend off.

By the time he arrived, Blackrun was at the top of the battlements at the northern gate already, shouting orders, trying to organise their troops into some semblance of cohesion while Hesar rounded up the infantry at the bottom of the wall. The City Watch Commander saw Red Wolf and waved him over.

"Oh, thank the gods, some backup," the man said. "They didn't bring that many siege weapons, but with our limited numbers, we're overwhelmed here. We need reinforcements!"

"My queen should be aware of the situation by now," Red Wolf said. "Help is coming. What about the civilians?"

A massive stone sailed over their heads and slammed into one of the houses behind them, crushing the roof and top floor. He hoped that nobody had been in the way.

"I've already redirected them towards the palace," Hesar said. "Lord Wyndove is still overseeing the evacuations. I don't suppose we can use those secret tunnels again."

"We'll have to see." Red Wolf doubted they could use the same evacuation plan as they did fifteen years ago, given the Astarian soldiers no doubt watching Stormwood for any sign of movement, but he figured that Talin could come up with something. He left his horse with Hesar at the bottom of the wall and made his way up to Blackrun.

"Katherine, you've got to be mad!" he called. "We have trebuchets flinging stones and archers shooting up at us, and you insist on being at the top of the wall?"

"Someone has to organise the troops up here," Blackrun said. "Besides, I don't see you taking precautions either."

"I have *magic*," Red Wolf said. "You have...this." He gestured to her helmet. Another stone sailed over their heads. "But we can argue about risking our lives another time. What's the situation?"

"See those trebuchets?" Blackrun pointed to where the enemy siege weapons were grouped. "If we had some of the Drakels' explosive arrows or any of their black powder bombs, we could destroy a good number of them. It's the only solution I've come up with so far. We were far too under-prepared for a full-scale attack at this gate."

Red Wolf nodded. "It'll have to work. Let me talk to Hesar—"

An ear-splitting *crack* sounded to their right as one of the stones struck the weak section of wall directly above the gate—dead on. A second follow-up shot from a ballista was all it took for the gates to crumble.

"Ah, *touvir*." Red Wolf drew his sword and took the steps three at a time, making it to the bottom landing as Fae soldiers rushed up the steps to take out their archers. He parried a strike and slit his opponent's neck. Blackrun was at his side a moment later to parry and counter a second soldier.

"I didn't know you had weapons training," he said.

"I taught myself."

The two of them held the steps for as long as they could, but it was no use; with Red Wolf's healing powers not yet returned, he was forced on the defensive and backed up the stairs with Blackrun as the fight dragged on. He barely managed to knock aside a blow that would have gone through his neck and felt it glance off the side of his helmet instead.

An archer fell to his right with his hand halfway to his sword. The Fae soldier who'd dealt the killing blow moved on to challenge Red Wolf. He sidestepped the swing and drove his dagger into the man's throat. Another opponent replaced him immediately and forced him all the way up the steps onto the battlements.

There are too many. Where's Talin?

Two of the advancing soldiers before him fell in quick succession. He caught a glimpse of the blue-and-white arrow fletching sticking out from the first man's neck moments before he tumbled off the wall and out of sight.

"Took you long enough!" the bodyguard shouted.

"You're welcome!" Talin called from the bottom of the wall. Ashera was right behind her, covering her back from any approaching infantry. Red Wolf stabbed another soldier under the armpit and began pushing to the stairs again. Talin picked off unsuspecting enemies with her bow.

"We need to fall back," she said when he finally reached her. "Are you alright?"

"Fine." Red Wolf ducked under an axe swing and took off his opponent's head. "If we fall back, we'll trap your brother and whoever else is at the southern gate. It'll be a massacre."

Talin winced. "I know. I was planning on riding there and getting word out. What in the seven hells are you doing out here? You're supposed to be—"

"On stand-down, yes, save the lecture," Red Wolf said. "I couldn't sit there and do *nothing*."

"Well, since you're here now anyway, I need you and Ashera to head back to the palace and prepare the defenses there," Talin said. "Katherine! Can you and Hesar divert all your troops to the blockades throughout the city? We need to buy as much time as possible for our forces at the southern wall."

"I could—" Red Wolf began.

"Consider it done!" Blackrun called.

"Fine." Red Wolf whistled for his horse. "We'll meet back at the palace, then."

"Be careful," Talin said.

"You too."

At the palace, he and Ashera quickly moved to organise the troops, rounding up anyone in the front courtyard and sending them up to the wall. Red Wolf made it halfway up the stairs after them before Ashera threw out an arm to block his way.

"Sorry," she said. "I have orders from Talin. She was very clear that I wasn't supposed to let you on the wall."

Red Wolf sighed. "Of course. But how exactly does she expect me to help defend the palace if I'm not allowed on the wall?"

"Not a clue." Ashera shrugged. "But I'd rather you didn't get me into trouble, so..."

Seeing no choice, Red Wolf held up his hands in defeat and made his way back down the stairs. He supposed, at the very least, he could help with organising the civilian evacuations...

People were already streaming into the palace; he could see the crowd of civilians cramming themselves through the front gates, through the courtyard, and up the main doors into the palace. Lord Wyndove and Lord Mornus stood on either side of the crowd to direct traffic. It really was a logistical nightmare.

Now I know how Talin felt during the last siege.

There was nothing for it. These people were trapped in Belanore for the foreseeable future. He knew from fifteen years ago that they *could* theoretically fit everyone into the palace, but with so many civilians, it would become a hindrance for their own troops trying to navigate through the hallways. And the worst part, perhaps, was that they couldn't even use the Stormwood tunnel, or Darien's forces would notice the fleeing civilians and start targeting them to further strain the city's resources.

He was, however, in luck. Following the line of people moving into the palace led him to Aldrus, who was directing civilians up a flight of stairs along with a handful of off-duty soldiers. Red Wolf hurried over.

"Royal bodyguard!" Aldrus said. "This is...a lot of civilians to fit into the palace. Should we start turning people away?"

"We did this fifteen years ago. Everyone will fit, but it'll be cramped," he explained. "You've lived in the palace for eight years. I don't suppose you have any ideas."

Aldrus looked up and down the line. "We're assuming the Stormwood tunnel is unusable?"

"For now, yes," Red Wolf said.

"We can try filling the crypt and dungeons," Aldrus said. "It'll be uncomfortable for some of the townsfolk, but there's plenty of empty space there. If these people are here to stay for the time being, we might as well clear the hallways as much as possible."

"Can you start directing people there?"

"I'll handle it, never fear. Let Mornus and Wyndove know the plan, too, if you run into them."

Red Wolf gave a nod and made for the stables, intending to ride out again and try to find Talin on her way back to the palace or at least help Blackrun and Hesar with their defensive efforts in the city north. Talin was sure to lecture him yet again, but he needed to make sure she was alright.

By the time he reached the stables, northern bannermen and Royal Army soldiers were everywhere, and Ettrias was shouting orders in the middle of it all. He was splattered with blood and dust, as were most of the other troops with him. There was no sign of Talin.

"Before you panic, she's fine," the prince said as Red Wolf approached. "Left without a word. If she's not at the armoury, she'll be upstairs somewhere."

There was a hint of...something...in his eyes that gave the bodyguard pause.

"Please talk to her." Ettrias' shoulders slumped. "Or at least find her. I don't think she should be alone right now."

Red Wolf nodded and quickly left the stables again.

A lap of the armoury and then the upstairs hallways yielded no results, but he found her in her chambers eventually, braced over a pail of water on a wooden chair with a bloodied rag in her hand. She was visibly trembling and practically gasping for air.

"Talin," he said.

She looked up sharply and saw him, and he saw a brief flash of panic across her eyes before she tried to compose herself.

"I'm just...cleaning up," she said, but even her voice shook. "I'm fine. You don't..."

"You're not fine." Red Wolf pried the rag from her hand and put it aside, along with the pail of water—

Something in her seemed to simply...snap.

She backed away slowly, still gasping for air, tears beginning to roll down her face as she curled up on the floor at the edge of her bed. Red Wolf knelt before her and tried to lift her chin gently, but she only hugged her knees tighter and muttered something incoherent about everything being her fault. He sat next to her and pulled her towards him, hugging her head against his chest so she could hear his heartbeat.

"Listen," he said. "Focus on my heartbeat. Focus on my voice. I'm real. I'm right here."

It took almost half an hour of quiet talking and stroking her hair before she finally seemed to settle, breaths becoming steady, heartbeat slowing. Red Wolf waited until she was ready to extricate herself before straightening and leaning back against the edge of the bed.

"I'm sorry—"

"Do not apologise. You are not at fault."

Talin wiped at her eyes. "No, I'm sorry you have to see me like this again. You must think I'm ridiculous. Too weak to stomach the realities of war."

"You are not weak." Red Wolf pressed his forehead against hers. "Don't ever think that. I understand what you're going through—believe me, I do."

Talin buried her face in his shoulder and cried silently into the front of his armour.

"I can't do this," she said. "I can't do it. I can't...lead. I hate fighting. I hate killing. I hate...that every mistake I make...has consequences for everyone else. I'm tired of pretending I'm alright."

"I know." He kissed the top of her head. "But you *can* lead your people. They've depended on your leadership for fifteen years, and you never faltered. You're stronger than you realise, Talin."

"I..." Talin pulled away and looked up at him. "How do you...deal with it?"

Red Wolf shrugged.

"One step at a time, I suppose. Throwing yourself into work and battle are *not* coping mechanisms."

Talin managed a laugh at that, a genuine sound that seemed to dissolve the tension between them, at least a little. Red Wolf brushed a few loose strands of hair from her face.

"I didn't want anyone to think that...I wasn't capable," she admitted. "I didn't want to show anything that might be perceived as weakness. So I...kept going. Even when I knew I couldn't."

"It takes a toll," Red Wolf said. "More than you realise."

"I don't have a choice," she said. "My duty—"

"Forget about your duty for one moment." Red Wolf said. "What do you think is best for yourself?"

Talin looked down at her hands. A moment of silence passed between them.

"I'd like to sit here for a while, then," she finally said. Red Wolf allowed her to settle in his lap and wrapped his arms around her.

"Stay as long as you need," he said softly. "I'm not going anywhere."

The first few days passed without incident. With their defenses secured and all the remaining civilians safely housed inside the palace, Red Wolf had forced Talin to rest instead of throwing herself back into work, and the two of them had spent most of the evening yesterday curled up together in her bed. She had taken the time, albeit reluctantly, to explain everything, from the nightmares to the panicked response to clarifying what had happened that night in the tavern outside Castle Blackrun. She had half-expected Red Wolf to dismiss it all, to tell her to get over it, but he only held her tighter and told her that he was here if she ever wanted to talk. She fell asleep eventually, her head on his shoulder, and slept soundly through the night for the first time in a long while.

When she woke, the first rays of dawn light were streaming through her window, and Red Wolf was standing on her balcony in nothing but a pair of loose-fitting trousers. With the rising sun wreathing him in a golden, almost ethereal glow, he looked majestic. Talin wanted nothing more than to capture the moment forever in a painting of some kind.

"Morning," he said, turning his head.

"Mmm." Talin rolled over to look at him properly. "I don't want it to be morning just yet."

"Day's still young," Red Wolf said. "Sleep well?"

"Better than I have in years," Talin said.

Red Wolf turned his attention back to the sunrise with a smile. Talin watched him for a few minutes longer, admiring him, before getting out of bed to join him on the balcony.

"I had to take Katherine's deal," she said. "She was adamant about besieging the Crossing. I didn't want them to put you on trial, so..."

"You did it your way instead," Red Wolf finished. "I understand."

"I know you proposed an...alternative...to giving away half my king-dom," Talin said. "I was wondering if that offer is still on the table."

Red Wolf blinked.

"I...of course," he stammered. "Anything for you."

"Red Wolf." Talin cupped his face in her hands. "I want this to be something *you* want as well. Please don't do this just because it's convenient for me."

"I do want this," he said softly. "There is no one I would rather spend the rest of my life with." He pressed his forehead against hers. "If—*when*—all this is over...I don't want to hide anymore."

"Open the gates!"

Talin sighed and pulled away from Red Wolf to look down at the front gates. Ettrias had just dismounted in the front courtyard, it seemed, rich red cloak flapping behind him. He tucked his helm under one hand as he made his way up the steps, and Talin turned away from the balcony to don her armour and equipment.

"Duty calls, I suppose," she said.

Ettrias had already made it halfway to the war room by the time she stepped out of her chambers, so she fell into step beside him instead and accompanied him into the meeting hall. Red Wolf trailed behind her silently.

"Please tell me you have some good news," Talin said as they walked.

"Our lines are still holding," Ettrias said. "The north side of the city is almost completely blocked off by rubble created by their own trebuchets. There's no way for them to get their siege weapons through, and they haven't made it through the southern gate yet. But I don't know how long that's going to last."

Talin pushed open the doors to the war room to find Aldrus and Blackrun already hunched over the maps, several open letters on the table beside them. They both looked up when she approached.

"Morning," Blackrun said. "I was just about to send someone to wake you. We have news from our reinforcements. They're almost at the gates—another day's march, and they'll be here to bolster our lines. They've linked up with the Drakels coming in from the west."

Talin let out a breath she didn't realise she was holding. "Things are looking good, then. We just need to hold out until tomorrow."

"The Fort Saria garrison should be here later today, too," Aldrus said. "They'll be able to put pressure on the attackers from the south—we won't get them through the enemy lines, but they can force Darien to divide his resources."

Things are going a little too well, Talin thought. She knew from experience not to get her hopes up early.

"With those numbers, we'll easily repel Darien's forces," Red Wolf said.

"There's more." Aldrus tapped another piece of parchment on the table. "Lord Bayesh has graced us with a response. He wishes to meet outside the city walls, under cover of darkness, to discuss things face to face." He huffed a short exhale. "I'd thought you mad for wanting to negotiate in the middle of a siege, Talin, but perhaps I underestimated how much Darien's advisors hated him."

The corner of Talin's mouth twitched. "It seems I'd best go see him, then. He's risking a lot simply by responding. We ought to honour that."

Red Wolf crossed his arms. "This could very well be a trap, you realise."

"I know. But I'd rather we reach a resolution to this conflict before there's another massacre to rival that of the first siege," Talin said.

"Let me come with you, then," Red Wolf said.

"No. You're needed here, coordinating the defensive effort," Talin said. "Same with you, Ettrias. Don't worry yourself—I'll be fine."

"If you require an escort, I'm willing," Blackrun said.

"You're needed at the front. Most of the soldiers holding our defenses in the city are Blackrun bannermen—they respect you the most."

"If it would put your bodyguard at ease, perhaps I could join you," Aldrus said. "Lord Bayesh and I are well-acquainted. You might even have a better chance of swaying him to your side with me present."

Talin looked between him and Red Wolf. The latter scowled but made no objection, and she understood then that the odd tension between the two was *jealousy*.

I have enough to deal with right now.

"I need you focused, Red Wolf," she said. "I'll be safe with Aldrus."

"I understand." Red Wolf dropped his gaze.

"It's settled, then." Talin straightened. "See to your duties."

The siege continued throughout the day with little improvement. The Royal Army reinforcements from Fort Saria arrived as planned just after noon, but even with their numbers diverting Darien's attention, the barrage of attacks on their defensive lines never ceased. Talin remained in the war room for most of the day, keeping the maps updated and watching as their northern lines were pushed further and further back. Part of her longed to ride out to assist.

My presence would be more of a hindrance than help.

She glared at the map pins. Her duties dictated that she lead her people no matter the cost, that she see the bigger picture and make the decisions that could decide the fate of thousands. One lone person couldn't possibly hope to make a difference on the front.

Yet she felt so *helpless* standing safe behind the palace walls.

"Have you even eaten today?"

Talin looked up. Aldrus sighed and stepped through the doorway fully, clutching a wrapped bundle in one hand.

"It's almost time. I brought you some meat pastries." He set the bundle down in front of her.

"I..." Talin rubbed her eyes with one hand. "Thank you."

Aldrus seated himself in one of the meeting table chairs while she ate.

"So," she said between mouthfuls, "you know Lord Bayesh. Any...useful tricks for dealing with him?"

"You could try appealing to his sense of honour," Aldrus said. "He's a good man. If you can convince him of everything that's happened in Kies Tor because of Darien, there's a good chance he'll take your side against my brother."

"You told me that people in Astaria are afraid of speaking against their monarch," Talin said.

"Yes. But this siege has given the Royal Council an opportunity—one in which Darien is captured by enemy forces, and the council has the perfect chance to dispose of him," Aldrus said. "Have you thought about what you're going to say?"

"I have. I'm ready." Talin wiped her hands on the pastry wrapper and reached for her weapons belt. "Let's go."

The meeting spot that Lord Bayesh had picked was a small grove in Stormwood, not far from the western side of the city, almost completely hidden by thick clusters of bushes and foliage. Talin brought her weapons but left her helm and gauntlets; she wanted to show that she had come with the sole purpose of negotiation but left her hands uncovered so she could still use her lightning if the situation called for it. Aldrus accompanied her with a sword hung at his waist.

"Your Majesty." Lord Bayesh dipped his head. "And King Aldrus—an unexpected pleasure."

Talin opted to keep her distance for now and looked the Fae noble up and down. He was a short man with shoulder-length black hair, a small goatee, and steely green eyes that seemed to pierce right through her.

"Sneaking through Stormwood to meet here was risky," Talin said. "I hope you have a reason for picking a location so far from the gates."

"I know you have a tunnel that leads directly into the forest," Lord Bayesh said. "Besides, this was a necessary precaution. I'm sure that, like me, you'd prefer if King Darien didn't find out about this meeting."

Talin stepped closer. "You said you're willing to hear me out."

"I will be direct." Bayesh clasped his hands behind his back. "You may be aware by now that the Astarian Royal Council bears no love for our king. But speaking of such things openly is treason, and we are still loyal to his cause—uniting the western kingdoms under a single ruler. If you wish for the council's help, you must have a good reason prepared."

Talin exchanged a look with Aldrus.

"My husband tells me you're an honourable man," she said. "If you have no wish to serve Darien, help me lift the siege. I can tell you now that this attack was a last resort. His meddling goes far beyond what you can imagine, and I wish to see him brought to justice in the Torrian High Court."

She explained everything that had happened, from the attempt on Arkiel's life to the forged documents and Aldrus' involvement in it all. Bayesh listened to it all in silence with his lips pursed.

"This is...an entirely different account from what we have been led to believe," he said carefully. "Darien told us that Kies Tor was on the brink of collapse because of your actions, that joining with Astaria was the only way to save this kingdom." He let out a long breath. "I must ask for proof."

"The Fae assassin he sent is still in the dungeons beneath the palace," Talin said. "That should be proof enough. Aldrus is also willing to corroborate everything I've said."

"It's true," her husband said. "I acted under Darien's orders for a time because he promised it was for the good of the kingdom. He promised me that I could make things better here by being in charge. But it was all a lie."

Bayesh swallowed. "Turning on our monarch... I mean, it's high treason, no matter how justified. But...if you can *promise* that you can capture him at the end of this siege..."

"I cannot guarantee anything," Talin said. "Help me end the siege. We will have a much better chance of capturing Darien if I have his advisors and generals on my side."

"I can talk to the rest of the council," Bayesh said. His gaze flickered towards Aldrus. "We will be in contact if we decide to work with Kies Tor."

"Thank you." Talin let out a breath she didn't know she was holding. "I hope the rest of the Royal Council are as reasonable as you—"

A deafening *crack* split the air, echoing from the east. Talin whirled around to look in the direction of the city.

"You must return," Bayesh said when she turned back to him. His eyes were wide. "I...had heard that Darien wanted to launch a night-time attack, but I didn't think he would go through with it..."

Talin cursed. "Can you do something about it from your end?"

"I...don't know," Bayesh admitted. "It's too late to call a halt, but I might be able to slow things down."

"Do what you can," Aldrus snapped. "Talin?"

"If they've resumed their attacks, we need to get back *now*." Talin spun on her heel and took off back the way they came, Aldrus right behind her. She knew those sounds couldn't have reached them all the way from the southern gate—at least not so clearly. There was only one explanation.

Darien's siege weapons were targeting the palace itself.

The outer wall of the palace was in complete chaos by the time Talin made her way to the top.

Half a dozen trebuchets lined the square directly in front of the main gate, sending wave after wave of massive stones at the palace. A seemingly endless barrage of arrows sailed at them and forced anyone on top of the wall to take cover. The troops at the top of the wall were doing what they could to slow down the Fae advance, but it barely seemed to have any effect; the assault continued without pause despite their own ballistae taking out some of the trebuchets. Talin could see more stones flying over from behind buildings in the distance. No doubt more trebuchets were placed there, where they couldn't be targeted.

"By the gods, Talin, are you mad?" Red Wolf growled. "It's suicide up here!"

An arrow glanced off his helm almost as soon as he finished speaking and forced him to duck lower to avoid being shot. Talin spotted Ettrias and Golmin further down, huddled together and shouting orders at the archers and crossbowmen on the wall.

"*Kust*—I swear, if I have to drag you off the wall—" Red Wolf began.

"Save the lecture for later. What's the situation?" Talin joined him behind the merlon while Aldrus ducked behind another one. One group of crossbowmen nearby poked their torsos out to shoot down at the attackers before quickly getting back under cover. The last man wasn't fast enough and fell backwards with an arrow through his eye.

"Not sure!" Ettrias called. "I was about ready to turn in for the night when Blackrun returned with what's left of her banners. Said they'd launched a surprise attack in the middle of the night and overwhelmed our lines and that they were clearing the rubble as we spoke. They were on us within minutes."

"They've been planning this." Talin beckoned for Red Wolf's helm, and he passed it over silently. She used the reflective surface to get a better look at the Fae numbers.

"You have a plan?" her bodyguard asked.

"Maybe," Talin said, tossing the helmet back. She wasted no time in making one of her chain arrows. Red Wolf grabbed her arm before she could nock.

"You'll give away your position the moment you send that shot," he said. "The trebuchets will switch their aim to *you*."

Talin hissed through her teeth. "I have to do *something*. Those trebuchets will tear us apart otherwise."

"I know." Red Wolf let go of her arm. "You only have one shot. Make it count."

Talin tried her best to remember the layout of the trebuchets below. She couldn't possibly hit them all with a single shot; her lightning was nowhere near powerful enough, and the weapons were spread too far apart. But perhaps...

She turned her attention to their own lines and quickly spotted a crate of explosive charges—leftover souvenirs, so to speak, from the Drakels' time in Kies Tor.

"Red Wolf, I need you to throw one of those charges on my mark," she said. Her bodyguard reached over and snatched one up without question, narrowly dodging an arrow. She took his helm again and showed him the line of trebuchets in its reflection.

"Aim for the gap between the middle two."

Red Wolf gave a nod, and she pulled back the bowstring, readying her magic at the same time.

"Now!"

The explosive charge sailed past her and arced down towards the line of trebuchets. She could see immediately that it was going to fall short; Red Wolf had a good throwing arm, but the charge wasn't nearly heavy enough. And she had no time to ponder her choices—there was only a tiny window of opportunity for her to duck out of cover and hit her target dead-on.

Talin let her arrow fly.

She couldn't tell whether the shot had struck until a deafening *boom* shook the air and sent her sprawling. Her ears rang painfully with a high-pitched whine. She found herself scrambling to her feet, still half-dazed, and stumbling to the edge of the wall to see what had happened.

Her arrow had struck perfectly if the carnage before her was any indication. Her lightning had supercharged the explosive and increased its lethality tenfold; she could see four trebuchets lying in pieces down below and bodies strewn everywhere around them. The other trebuchets, as predicted, began to swivel, changing their aim to her.

"We need to *go*." Red Wolf grabbed her hand and half-led, half-dragged her back towards the palace as heavy stones began to rain down on the area around them. Each hit seemed to echo like rolling thunder. One struck the wall directly beneath her feet, and she physically felt the ground beneath her begin to crumble. Red Wolf grabbed her and pulled her forward just in time as a chunk of the battlements fell away under her.

"Thanks," she breathed.

Another stone sailed over their heads so low that she was sure she could have jumped up and touched it. Red Wolf scowled and tugged her onwards.

"Ettrias and the others—" she began.

"They'll have to find another way off the wall." Red Wolf didn't slow.

"We need to regroup in the rear courtyard."

"Understood."

The rear courtyard, despite being the furthest point from the outer wall, was the only defensible position in the palace in case of a breach—it was the only courtyard not surrounded by towers and tall palace walls that might collapse on them when enemy siege weapons inevitably weakened the structural integrity of the building. It was also the location of the remaining Stormwood tunnel and their only hope of escape should they find themselves surrounded.

"We'll have to split up," Talin said. "I'll inform Corvan of the situation and have him start making preparations to move the wounded.

The civilians in the palace will have to be moved, too. I think it's time we reconsidered using the tunnel."

"Darien's banners should be completely focused on the palace by now," Red Wolf said. "The tunnel should be safe—or at least as safe as we'll get it. I'll find Ashera and have her round up a team to send ahead, then let Lord Wyndove know about the plan."

"We'll meet again in front of the tapestry," Talin said.

They split up at the next fork, Talin making for the stairs to the second level while Red Wolf moved off towards the northern side of the palace. In the throne room, she quickly located Corvan in the middle of the crowd, applying a tourniquet to a screaming soldier with a missing hand, and fought back a wave of nausea and panic at the sight of blood. She elected to wait until Corvan had finished treating the man before approaching.

"Ah, Your Majesty. You'll have to forgive me for greeting you in...this state." The old healer gestured to his blood-splattered apron. "We've sustained heavy casualties these past few days. What brings you here?"

"The walls aren't going to hold for much longer," Talin said. "We need to start evacuating the wounded. We'll buy you as much time as we can, but you'll need to have everyone in here moved to the rear courtyard by dawn."

"That's...not much time," Corvan said.

"Can you do it?" Talin asked.

"If I had a dozen more pairs of hands..."

"I'll have Blackrun find some people."

She stepped past the rows of wounded soldiers and pushed open the doors to the meeting hall, where Blackrun was pondering over the city maps and palace blueprints. Her brow was furrowed as she stared at the pins at the front gates of the palace.

"During the second Siege of Castle Blackrun, we'd bunkered down with six months' worth of supplies and held the outer wall for half a year," she said. "I believed we could have held it forever if we only had the food to spare. But here...it's been less than a week. I don't know if we can last the night."

"We can. We have to." Talin joined her at the table. "I'm giving the order to fall back to the rear courtyard—we'll barricade the hallways and bottleneck Darien's forces there. Corvan needs a dozen men to help move the wounded."

"Most of my forces are at the northern wall," Blackrun said, pointing to the north side of the palace. "Ettrias has just asked me to divert some men to help defend the eastern side and the main gate. I've had to reorganise all the northern banners. I can spare you half a dozen."

"That'll have to do," Talin said. "Once you're done, get yourself to the courtyard."

"Understood. What about you?" Blackrun asked.

"I need to make sure nobody gets left behind."

"If you see Connor—"

A *boom* shook the very floor beneath them and knocked dust from the ceiling beams above them. Both of them looked up at the same time.

"I'm going to find him now," Talin said, and took off through another side door.

Red Wolf wasn't at the tapestry yet when she skidded to a stop in front of it. She knew she couldn't wait for him for too long, given everything she still had to oversee, but a stubborn part of her insisted that she stay until he showed—just to make sure nothing had happened to him. The building shook every time a direct hit landed against the inner wall.

The minutes ticked by. Talin found herself pacing.

He better not have—

"Talin!"

Her head snapped up. Red Wolf appeared at the far end of the hallway and began to run. She moved forwards to greet him as another *boom* shook the palace.

"Run, damn it!" he snapped.

What?

Talin looked up as a creaking sound came from the ceiling. The section directly above her cracked almost as if on cue, spiderwebbing across the entire width of the hallway.

This isn't good. She took off at a sprint towards him.

Red Wolf stretched out a hand as the ceiling crumbled above them, golden energy flickering briefly in his palm, and she felt his fingertips brush her arm—

But then there was nothing at all.

LXVII

H er head hurt.

Her other senses returned slowly as the floor swam into focus, reminding her, painfully, that she was still alive. Something was putting pressure against her eyebrow and making her head hurt more. She slapped it away without thinking, but it quickly returned, so she tried once more to slap it away. Someone grabbed her wrist.

"Quit it. I'm trying to stop the bleeding."

Talin groaned. The floor was oddly comfortable.

"I know your head hurts. Take it easy." She recognised the voice as Red Wolf's.

"What...happened?" she asked, taking over from him to keep the wad of cloth pressed against her head.

"You hit your head. My magic wasn't fast enough to absorb the impact," Red Wolf said. "The palace is falling apart—after the ceiling came down, we were trapped with no direct path to the rear courtyard. I brought you here to avoid the soldiers."

Talin struggled off the floor with another groan. They were in some kind of storage closet, in semi-darkness; the only light she could see came from the gaps between the door and doorframe. The ceiling was low, and Red Wolf had stayed crouched when she sat up, no doubt to avoid having to hunch in the tiny space.

"We can't stay here," she said. The room seemed to spin.

"You're not going anywhere with that injury, not with Fae soldiers all over the palace by now," Red Wolf said.

"What's your plan, then?" Talin asked. Her bodyguard was silent.

He's right. I'm hardly in any condition to fight.

But staying here certainly wasn't an option; even if they could remain undetected for the entire time, the full moon was tomorrow, and Red Wolf couldn't shift in such a cramped space. They had to regroup with the others in the rear courtyard.

"Maybe you should go without me—" Talin began before her mind caught up with the ridiculousness of her own suggestion. Red Wolf levelled a pointed look at her.

"Alright, maybe not. But our situation isn't going to improve if we stay in a storage closet."

"I..." Red Wolf hissed through his teeth. "Fine. I can...bandage you up as best I can. We'll try to stay out of sight. If it comes to a fight, let me handle it."

"I can work with that." Talin squeezed her eyes shut as a fresh wave of throbbing pain split her skull. Red Wolf bandaged her head with strips of cloth from his tabard before pressing his ear against the door. Talin waited in silence.

"It's clear." He pushed open the door after a minute and led the way down the corridor.

Talin wasn't sure what she had expected, but she certainly hadn't expected so much rubble to be scattered through the palace. Huge chunks of ceiling had collapsed in some places, completely blocking off further access through the corridors, forcing the two of them to detour and take a longer path around. Red Wolf's enhanced senses kept them out of sight of any Fae soldiers that came their way.

"How are you feeling?" he asked when they stopped at a fork.

"I'll be fine. Just keep going," Talin said. "We're almost—"

She was cut off by a child's wailing in the distance.

"Please, we haven't done anything..."

"There are civilians still in the palace?" Talin asked, looking at Red Wolf.

"I...don't—" her bodyguard began. She didn't bother waiting for him to finish. "Oh, why do I bother..."

Talin skidded around the corner to find a family of five cornered by half a dozen Fae soldiers. One of them had forcibly torn the father away from the rest of the family and was busy searching him for weapons.

"You know the way to the rear courtyard?" another soldier demanded.

"N-no! We're civilians; none of us have ever set foot in the palace in our lives—" the man said.

Talin loosed an arrow at the nearest soldier before she could give herself time to think.

Her shot sailed wide unexpectedly, clipping the man's armour instead and clattering harmlessly to the ground, and the soldiers all turned in unison. Red Wolf cursed.

My coordination is off. This damned head injury...

She adjusted her aim to compensate and sent her second arrow into the soldier's eye. Red Wolf charged past her to parry and counter a strike aimed at her head. His opponent fell with a gash in his neck. Her next shot sailed low and bounced off her target's breastplate instead, but he stumbled anyway, giving Red Wolf time to take his head clean off. The remaining three backed up a little, evidently more cautious now, but it was too late; her bodyguard took out the next two with alarming speed and precision and let her put an arrow through the eye-slit of the sergeant's helmet.

"Your Majesty?" the woman gasped. "Oh, gods, thank you—"

"Thank me later," Talin interrupted. "Are there other civilians near-by?"

"I...there must be, yes," the woman said. "We were on our way to the courtyard when part of the ceiling came down, so we were separated. Then the soldiers came through the palace while we were trying to find our way..."

"You'll have to take the long way around now," Talin said. "Go back the way we came, then turn left at the fork and continue. Don't stop until you see a raven statue—no, that might be too damaged. It's the second turn on your left. This side." She pointed at the woman's left hand when it became apparent that these people couldn't tell the difference.

"Talin, we don't have time to be rounding up civilians," Red Wolf said.

"I'm not leaving my people behind."

They encountered more groups of Fae soldiers as they moved through the nearby hallways and rooms, all of them searching for an open path to the rear courtyard. Talin did her best to dispatch them, but being slightly disoriented, Red Wolf ended up being the one to take out most of the soldiers in their path. The corridor eventually ended in a pile of rubble too tall to climb over, so the two of them turned back and headed in a different direction instead. In one of the empty guest bedrooms, they found a boy huddled under the bed, and Talin managed to send him off with instructions on how to get to the rear courtyard. Red Wolf's jaw tightened ever so slightly as he watched the boy's fading form.

"Something on your mind?" Talin asked.

"Nothing important." Red Wolf tore his gaze from the boy and adjusted his weapons belt.

Further down the hallway, they came across another squad of Fae soldiers looting the civilian corpses strewn before them. One glance at their injuries told her that they had been cut down by the same swords these soldiers carried. Talin nocked an arrow.

"Don't." Red Wolf grabbed her arm and pulled her back around the corner before she could loose it.

"What are you doing?" she hissed, yanking herself free. "We can't just—"

"There's nothing you can do for those people. We need to focus on surviving the night." Red Wolf tugged her away from the soldiers. She followed along reluctantly.

No matter what I do, I still can't help everyone. It's not fair.

Deep down, she knew that Red Wolf was right; there was no sense in picking a fight with a team of Fae soldiers who weren't threatening or trying to kill anyone. All she would achieve was vengeance—and there would be time enough for that later. With more and more enemies closing in on the rear courtyard, there was no more time to help the civilians, and escape was now the only option left. Talin decided to turn back for the rear courtyard with a knot in her stomach.

She heard a shout as soon as they skirted around a tall pile of rubble. Red Wolf reacted before she fully registered the situation and recognised the huge group of Fae soldiers standing around just ahead, blocking off their path to the courtyard. She reached for her bow as her bodyguard yanked her back behind the rubble and narrowly dodged a cluster of crossbow bolts.

"They're reloading. Why aren't you shooting?" he hissed.

"In case you hadn't noticed, my aim isn't exactly up to standard tonight," Talin said. "I'd be wasting arrows. You shoot."

Red Wolf took the bow from her hands without question and loosed a handful of shots. She didn't dare peek out to see if they'd struck. A second cluster of bolts zipped past them and thudded into the wall thirty feet behind them. Red Wolf ducked back behind cover just in time with a scowl.

"If I had my healing, this fight would be over by now."

He grabbed another handful of arrows and leaned out to shoot.

"Stand down!"

Talin poked her head out cautiously to find Darien at the far end of the hallway, partially hidden behind a shield wall. Red Wolf loosed a shot at him, and his men quickly moved to block the arrow.

"Don't do this, Talin!" Darien called. "We outnumber you. I'd prefer to keep you alive. This doesn't have to get messy."

Red Wolf growled at him. Talin pulled him back and motioned for him to stand down.

There are far too many of them, she thought. *Red Wolf doesn't even have his healing.*

She checked her remaining arrows. Less than half her quiver remained; she'd broken or blunted far too many arrows on steel plate or the environment when she misjudged her shots. This wasn't a fight she and Red Wolf could confidently win, even if she could hit every target with her remaining shots and Red Wolf could heal through everything. But if Darien truly wanted them alive, he would no doubt try to use them as a bargaining chip or take them back to the Fae lines outside the palace. And with the full moon bearing down on them tomorrow night...

"You can't seriously be thinking of surrender," he hissed.

"I have a plan," Talin said. "Of sorts. Granted, it's not a *good* plan, but it's infinitely better than one or both of us dying here. Trust me."

Red Wolf sighed. "I always have."

"How can you guarantee you won't shoot us as soon as we step out?" Talin called.

"I can't. All you have is my word. But I should think that we both know you're far more valuable to us alive than dead," Darien said.

He's got a point. She and Red Wolf would make for good bargaining chips if nothing else.

"I want your crossbows to drop their weapons," she said. There was a pause, then a clatter, and she looked to Red Wolf for confirmation. He gave a nod.

"Alright. We're stepping out." Talin dropped her weapons and stepped past the pile of rubble with her hands raised. She heard Red Wolf do the same behind her.

"A good choice," Darien said and turned away. "Bind their hands. It's time we paid a visit to your friends."

They were marched through the palace hallways with an escort of half a dozen crossbowmen led by Darien himself. Red Wolf glared at the man's back and growled at anyone who tried to touch him or Talin, so the soldiers quickly gave up and let them walk freely with only their hands bound behind their backs. Talin, meanwhile, was more preoccupied with where they were going; she knew this route led to the rear courtyard and understood that Darien planned to use her to force the others to surrender too.

But with the power of the full moon about to unleash the wolf's rage and ferocity upon the world, she knew that making any kind of deal wasn't an option—at least not with Darien.

"Are you planning on telling me about this plan anytime soon?" Red Wolf muttered as they walked.

Talin shook her head. "Not here."

They were stopped eventually at a corner, just before the hallway straightened out past the courtyard entrance, and Darien signalled for the rest of his men to hold while one of them stuck a white cloth around the corner. There was a beat of silence.

"Approach and speak your piece!" someone yelled in Torrian. "General Ettrias will grant you an audience."

Darien stepped out carefully. Two of the crossbowmen moved to shove Talin and Red Wolf forwards and earned another growl from the latter. He seemed to calm a little when he met her gaze.

A few yards down the hallway stood a solid barricade of rubble, stone, and anything else the soldiers had managed to scrape together from the surrounding area. A few archers and crossbowmen poked their weapons out over the top, ready to shoot if need be, while Ettrias stood in the middle with his head and shoulders just visible. Talin had to give her brother some credit; he'd been incredibly efficient while she and Red Wolf had been trapped running in circles in the ground-floor hallways.

"I was hoping we could have a civilised discussion," Darien said. "Tell your troops to stand down. My two prisoners are both in their line of fire. We wouldn't want any...accidents, would we?"

Ettrias waved for his archers to stand down. "What do you want? A deal? Some kind of trade?"

"Yes," Darien said. "I am willing to return Queen Talin and Red Wolf to your ranks unharmed and allow you to leave the city without further bloodshed. In exchange, you will surrender Belanore to me and hand over Aldrus."

What does he want with Aldrus? Talin thought.

"That's a lot to ask for two prisoners," Ettrias said, stealing a glance in her direction. She gave a subtle shake of her head.

"How long do you imagine you can last in your current position?" Darien asked. "A few days? Less? I have soldiers in Stormwood to round up your fleeing civilians, and your few dozen guards won't be enough to stop them. Think about it. You could save them."

Ettrias looked at Talin again. She flicked her eyes to Red Wolf, and her brother seemed to understand immediately.

"Give me a day to think about it," he said. "Halt your attacks and pull your troops back from the palace interior. Return at dawn tomorrow, and I'll have an answer for you then."

Darien's eyes narrowed, but he turned away with a scoff all the same. "Fine. One day. These two will remain behind our lines until then."

Talin could practically feel Ettrias' gaze burning into the back of her neck as she was escorted away.

Outside the palace, the full extent of the damage to the building became apparent; sections of the outer and inner walls had crumbled completely, and parts of the interior were visible from their position just outside the front gates. The healer's tower had partially collapsed and was completely inaccessible, and two smaller spires branching off the eastern wall had also collapsed. Talin's heart ached at seeing the palace in such a state. It reminded her, clear as day, of the prophecy she had seen.

Is this it? The destruction of Belanore?

She looked out towards the city. Parts of it still smouldered from the siege, smoke rising up into the dawning sky. There was no denying that the sight was near-identical to the ruins in that accursed prophecy.

I don't understand. Did I fail? Has the prophecy come true after all?

It wasn't possible. She'd done what she thought was right by refusing the half-giants' help, and she had interpreted the prophecy as objectively as she could without assuming that any part of it could pertain to her personal future. What did she miss?

No. This wasn't over yet. She would not give up on this city while she still lived.

"Not pretty, is it?" Darien asked. "If your brother will not see reason, perhaps you will. My men will reduce Belanore to dust if they have to. It's up to you to prevent it."

Talin didn't respond. Darien glanced back at her, hummed, and continued walking.

At the Fae encampments facing the palace, the Fae king quickly disappeared in the direction of the command tent, leaving his crossbowmen to escort Talin and Red Wolf all the way to the far end of the camp. She saw Lord Bayesh as they passed the officers' lines and made eye contact with him for the barest fraction of a second before they were marched past another tent and out of sight.

"Don't suppose you convinced him to switch sides," Red Wolf muttered.

"I'm not sure." Talin turned her head to search for the Fae noble, but it was no use; between the various tents between them and the soldiers milling about, it was impossible to see where he was now. She hoped, if he truly was an honourable man, that he would pay them a visit later—to tell her of the other council members' position, if nothing else.

Here's hoping they see reason.

The soldiers led them into an empty tent at the back of camp, where their hands were briefly freed so they could be chained around two of the wooden posts lined along the sides. Their weapons were dumped in a small chest in the corner. That done, their escort left them, leaving two guards just outside the tent flaps to ensure they didn't escape. Talin wriggled her hands to test her new shackles and discovered that they were *heavy*. She sat down with her back against the wooden post. Red Wolf slammed his shackles into the post he'd been chained to in an attempt to break something and free himself.

"Red Wolf," she said. He stopped struggling. "Your powers haven't returned yet. Don't hurt yourself."

He sank down into a sitting position as well. "What's the plan, then?"

"The full moon is tonight. We're in the middle of the enemy encampment," Talin said. "If you shift here, you could cause some serious damage and escape before they even realise what's going on. I plan to use that as leverage."

"Against whom? Darien isn't exactly receptive to anything other than total surrender of the city into his control," Red Wolf said.

"We're not dealing with him. We're dealing with Lord Bayesh," Talin said. "I'm sure he'll visit us later. Until then, I suppose we'll need to find a way to keep ourselves entertained."

Red Wolf grunted. "I'm not exactly thrilled about being chained up."

"I know. I'm sorry." Talin winced. "I'll make it up to you some other way."

"I'll be fine."

"Can I ask you something?" Talin said after a beat.

"Go for it." He didn't quite meet her gaze.

"You know Kier Dekkel, Old Torrian, and a bit of Faerie," Talin said. "How come?"

"I'm not exactly fluent in any of them, but I guess you could say I know them," Red Wolf muttered. "Call it a...job benefit from occasionally listening in on yours and Ettrias' tutoring lessons. Corvan also helped me practice."

"Impressive," Talin said. "I remember it took me years to understand Kier Dekkel."

"It's easier for me—I knew Demonic from the Hellhounds. Both of them have their roots in Draconic. Just as Torrian and Faerie both came from Old High Elvish."

"I...didn't know that."

"Both are lost languages because of the Inquisition," Red Wolf said. "Braenern thought that Elvish, being such an ancient language, was closely tied to magic and witchcraft and tried to destroy all records of its existence. It didn't have a written component, being so old, so it truly is lost. All we know now is that it once existed. I guess Braenern wasn't that successful in wiping it out completely."

"And Draconic?" Talin asked.

"The ancient language of the dragons," Red Wolf explained. "It's said that only dragons are able to communicate in Draconic because it was developed long before any other race walked this earth. It was lost all across the known world when the last dragons flew east five hundred years ago."

The Inquisition was far worse than I'd ever known, Talin thought. No doubt, her great-great-grandfather had gone to lengths to ensure that the full extent of his actions would never be known to the kingdom so as not to tarnish the royal family's name. So much history lost—all because Braenern was too selfish to acknowledge the prophecy and instead sought to prevent a false calamity from befalling himself.

He wasn't even successful.

Talin could have laughed at the irony. In the end, Braenern had died anyway, from a bout of severe and sudden illness that many had attributed to a curse. Perhaps it had been retribution from the gods themselves to punish him for what he did.

"Something on your mind?" Red Wolf asked, snapping her out of her thoughts.

"The prophecy," Talin admitted. "You saw the state of the palace. The state of the city. Part of me can't help but wonder if I failed. I know we still have a fighting chance, and I know I can't give up on my plan just yet, but...what if all that destruction was set in stone?"

Red Wolf's brow creased. "I can't answer that. My father—Chief Bjorson—told me some things. Clan secrets that the White Raven must never know before it's time. His words, not mine."

"It's alright. I don't expect a miracle solution," Talin said. "You don't have to reveal anything solely for your people to know."

"Well, what do you believe?" Red Wolf asked. "Do you believe that there is such a thing as fate? Destiny? Prophecies set in stone?"

"I don't believe anything is set in stone before it happens," Talin said. "We have the power to write our own destinies if we so desire. It's duty that dictates what we do and ties us down."

"Yet you value duty above all else," Red Wolf said.

"I think my duty is more important than anything else. I know you feel the same about yours."

"Then I suppose our duties tie us both to our fates. For better or for worse."

Footsteps drew to a halt outside the tent, followed by quiet voices in Faerie too soft for Talin to pick out. She saw Red Wolf tilt his head a little to listen to the conversation. Lord Bayesh ducked through the flaps a moment later and strode towards them purposefully.

Finally. Just who I've been waiting for.

"Your Majesty," he said. "I'm sorry to see you in such a situation." He frowned at her head injury and the makeshift bandages that Red Wolf had used. "If you need a healer, I could see if any of my army healers are available..."

"Never mind me for now," Talin said. "You've talked to the other lords in Darien's council?"

"I have," Bayesh said. "I'm afraid it's...not the news you might have hoped for. Lord Auwin and General Gorin are...unwilling, shall we say, to go against our king. Without their support, I cannot hope to act on my own. I'm sorry."

Talin sighed. "It's alright. I can't force you to work with me. But I *am* glad to know I have an ally on the opposing side."

"What of your banners?" Red Wolf asked. "I know you're here without Darien's knowledge, else you wouldn't have lied to the guards. Let's say you gathered your courage and deserted. Would your men follow?"

"They'll follow me to the death, sir," Bayesh said. "But just as my men are loyal to me, Lord Auwin and General Gorin's men are both loyal to them. You'd still be facing most of the Astarian Royal Army. And that's assuming Darien *doesn't* notice a quarter of his troops suddenly deserting."

Talin thought about it. Red Wolf's idea, though ridiculous in its current form, did have some basis; turning Darien's *army* against him would be an easy way to end the siege.

"What about Sir Artin?" she asked. "Who do his people follow now?"

"Darien commands them directly, along with the other Royal Army soldiers who don't fall under any of the council's banners," Bayesh explained. "They're sworn to follow him, and I doubt many of them care for the kind of politics we play in the royal courts."

"Is there no way to convince them to follow you?" Talin asked.

"Oh, I'm sure it's possible. But not in the middle of a siege everyone believes they're about to win." Bayesh scoffed. "I truly am sorry, Your Majesty, but you'll not receive any help from the inside. Not like this."

Talin let out a long breath. "You have to do *something*, my lord. Tonight is the full moon, and my lord commander here will transform into a deadly creature capable of massacring half this camp. I don't want more people to die, and I'm sure you feel the same. We have to make some kind of deal before sunset."

"I've heard the stories," Lord Bayesh said. "It all seems a little far-fetched to me. Besides, I'm not exactly authorised to make any deals with you—barring treason, of course, and that's not something I'm risking without more inside support."

Of course. He hasn't seen what Red Wolf is capable of. They've only ever heard stories of the Hellhounds in Astaria.

"Then perhaps the threat of reinforcements will change your mind?" Talin lifted a brow. "We have Drakels on the march. Northern siege weapons and thousands of infantry. You must have seen the southern front by now—Royal Army reinforcements are still trying to push through to the palace. That should be proof enough."

"Your Drakels have to march for weeks through the south to reach you," Bayesh said. "My scouts in Stormwood tell me there are no signs of any reinforcements on the march. I doubt they'll arrive in time." He looked between the two of them and heaved a sigh. "Look, I know that your brother has asked for a day to think on Darien's offer, but given that you're trying to make a deal with me, I can assume that all he's been instructed to do is buy you time. And given that I cannot help in any other way, I feel it is my duty to tell you that Darien is planning to do whatever it takes to win. Once your brother refuses his offer, he will throw everything he has at your little defensive position in the courtyard."

"I know," Talin said. "We'll be prepared."

"I hope so. For your sake." Bayesh turned away. "I'll find a healer to treat your injuries. Your lord commander needs new bandages, too, I should think."

"Thank you."

"Thank me if you win the siege. King Darien will not take kindly to finding out I've helped you in any way."

He left them with that, and Talin heard him pause just outside to talk to the guards again, speaking once again in low voices. She thought she heard the jingle of coin and looked to Red Wolf to confirm. His expression proved unreadable, as usual.

"He bribed the guards, if that's what you're thinking about," her bodyguard muttered. "Something about making sure Darien doesn't know. Couldn't understand the rest."

"I'm getting conflicting motivations from him." Talin stared at the tent flap. "He says he doesn't want to go against Darien, then helps us and goes out of his way to cover the evidence. Whose side is he really on?"

"Either way, I doubt he's going to be of much help like you hoped." Red Wolf scowled. "And if I shift here tonight—" He cut himself off. "I don't want what happened at that village to happen again. It... I... That was the exact situation I'd been trying to avoid for decades. If I turn on you..."

"You won't," Talin said. "You never have."

Red Wolf hissed through his teeth. "Things have changed. You can't *know*—"

"I know *you*. Trust me. Please."

He sighed. "I always have."

The rest of their day passed uneventfully, other than a healer entering before midday to treat Talin's head injury and bandage it properly. The man explained, after some painful probing and examination, that she may have a small fracture in her skull, but there wasn't much to be done other than rest and continued monitoring to ensure her condition didn't worsen. He returned frequently to re-examine her condition and had been kind enough to offer to change Red Wolf's bandages too, but her bodyguard had insisted that it wasn't necessary and told him to save his supplies for the Fae soldiers.

Sun's going down fast.

Talin knew, from the first time he'd been poisoned, that he might shift at any time between dusk and midnight without his powers, and his account of the village massacre had confirmed that the torslek in his system *did* delay his shifting for a few hours.

"Feel anything yet?" she asked. A soldier had come in earlier and lit an oil lamp in the tent to give them some light. As far as she was aware, it was already pitch black outside.

"I feel the call. Not so strong that it drowns out everything else, but getting louder—too quickly for my liking. It's...hard to focus." Red Wolf squeezed his eyes shut momentarily. A low growl escaped his throat, wild and unrestrained. "Inside, it's easier to suppress. Out here...all that separates us is a sheet of canvas." He looked up at the tent c eiling.

"Remember, the plan is to get back to the rear courtyard as quickly as possible. Kill as few soldiers as you can," Talin said.

"You're assuming the wolf can remember anyth— argh!"

He strained against his restraints as the transformation took over, muscles rippling and bones reforming. Talin heard a sharp, metallic *snap* as his shackles gave like cheap wood. The two guards standing outside the tent charged in to see what was going on and reached for their swords when they saw the broken manacles—

Too late.

Talin barely had time to blink. The wolf lunged himself at the closest guard, claws shredding his throat like paper and spraying blood across the tent floor. The second guard didn't even have time to draw his weapon; he was met with the same fate before the first guard had even hit the ground. Talin was entirely unsure she had understood what just happened.

The wolf licked his paws clean before sniffing around the bodies, quickly lifting a set of keys with his teeth. He passed them to Talin with a carefulness that completely contradicted the sheer speed and brutality she had just witnessed.

"See, I knew you liked me." She let out a nervous half-laugh. Truthfully, she hadn't been sure that the wolf remembered her at all, let alone remembered her as an ally. But she'd always had a hunch that he retained some of Red Wolf's memories and wasn't driven purely on instinct.

With her hands freed, she snatched her weapons from the chest in the corner of the tent and strapped Red Wolf's sword to her back by using his belt as a bandolier. The wolf helpfully poked his head out of the tent before looking back at her to signal the all-clear.

They snuck around the edge of camp, dispatching any sentries placed around the perimeter, though Talin had to admit that it was the wolf doing most of the work. He moved with a frightening amount of grace and efficiency for a creature so huge, each kill as brutal as the last yet made with perfect precision.

She had seen Hellhounds during the war. She understood how they moved, their speed and their ferocity, particularly when they were at their strongest, drinking in the power of the full moon. Yet some part of her, perhaps, had never thought that *Red Wolf* could be capable of the same.

This is the part of him that he always tries to deny.

Seeing him now, she understood why; the wolf was a terrifying force to be reckoned with, even when he was prowling silently beside her. Red Wolf, perhaps, knew that better than anyone. She could only imagine how it must feel to know that he wouldn't be in control of his own body when all that pent-up rage and power unleashed itself under the full moon.

Alarms began to sound in the camp as they neared the front, and the outline of the palace became visible under the light of the full moon. A squad rushed forwards to intercept them. One of them landed an arrow in the wolf's side, but that was all; he darted between them and slashed open the archer's throat first—taking out the biggest threat. The next two soldiers both fell in a similar fashion. Talin took out the fourth with an arrow to the eye while the wolf tackled another man and tore out his throat. The final soldier dropped his weapons and fled in the opposite direction.

"So much for escaping undetected," Talin muttered. The wolf huffed through his nostrils and tore out the arrow in his side with his teeth. His ears twitched, and he spun, taking off in the direction of the palace without waiting for her. Talin sighed and jogged to follow.

There were no soldiers in the palace hallways, as Darien had agreed, and navigating the debris-filled hallways was all too easy with the wolf's help. Part of her was oddly glad of his company; he could have easily outpaced her to the courtyard and left her to make her way through the palace alone. But he had stayed, driven, perhaps, by Red Wolf's duty.

"Wait," she said as they neared the rear courtyard. The wolf stopped just before rounding the corner and cocked his head at her. "They might shoot at you reflexively—you *do* look like...well, you know."

If she didn't know better, she might have thought the wolf had just rolled his eyes.

"Stay here for now," she continued. "I'll make sure they're stood down."

She stepped out from around the corner slowly with her hands raised. The sentries at the barricade immediately lowered their weapons when they recognised her.

"Your Majesty!" the sergeant exclaimed. "Gods, we're glad to see you. General Ettrias said to look for your return."

"Red Wolf is with me," she told them. "Don't shoot him, please."

The soldiers looked puzzled—until the wolf padded around the corner, and they all visibly jumped. The youngest of them, a rookie who barely looked like he was old enough to be in the army, reached for his crossbow. The sergeant in charge slapped his hand away.

"The general is in the courtyard, Your Majesty," the sergeant said. "I expect he'll be pleased to see you, too."

They shifted part of the barricade to make it easier for her and the wolf to clamber over, then sealed the gap again behind them. Most of the soldiers jumped out of the way for the wolf when they passed and refused to come near. Some put their hands on their weapons and remained tensed until all they could see was his tail.

"Don't take it personally," Talin said. The wolf looked away.

"Talin!"

She barely had time to turn in the direction of the voice before Ettrias barrelled into her with a hug.

"I knew you'd make it out somehow," he said with a grin when they separated. "I suppose we have Red Wolf to thank, though."

"I'd love to regale you with the story, but there's not much time," Talin said. She looked past him to see Golmin and Ashera gathered around the palace maps on the stone courtyard table, along with Blackrun, Aldrus, and a handful of northern nobles.

"I take it that means your talk with Lord Bayesh was unsuccessful," her husband said.

"Mostly. He let me know that Darien is planning to send everything he has at us if we refuse his deal—and now that they no longer have Red Wolf and I as a bargaining chip, I'm willing to bet that's exactly what's going to happen," Talin explained. "We need to make sure we're ready. The remaining civilians are all evacuated by now?"

"A few stragglers left in the crypt, but otherwise, we're clear," Aldrus said. "We'll still need to defend the tunnel from this end until everyone is safe. Shall I find Corvan to look over your injury?"

"I'll be fine." Talin waved him off. "You know Darien best. What's he likely to hit us with?"

"Could be anything." Aldrus shrugged. "They won't have black powder weapons—weapons trade is highly restricted between the Drakels and Fae. I guess Emperor Kadis doesn't trust my brother to put them to good use. Other than that, I expect they'll try to use fire to burn whatever barricades we have set up. Maybe a few smaller battering rams designed for breaking down locked doors, but I've never seen them used on fortified structures."

"We can work with it." Talin turned her attention to the maps. "From what I understand, there's only one way into the courtyard, correct?"

"Aye, everywhere else is blocked by rubble," Golmin said. "I led a team out to search the perimeter, just in case the Fae might have found a secondary entrance. We're completely sealed off except for that hallway." He nodded towards the existing barricade, barely visible through one of the shattered courtyard windows in the corner.

"Good. That gives them fewer entry points, and we'll have less work. If we can salvage some more material from the nearby rubble, I think we could build a second barricade..."

It took most of the night to complete her project, but they managed to construct another barricade in the end, this one directly in front of the courtyard entrance and a little sturdier than the first. The wolf spent his time dragging heavy stones and digging. Golmin and Blackrun took it upon themselves to board up every accessible window in the courtyard, making sure that the only way in for Darien's forces was through the bottleneck they'd set up. Talin eventually relented and allowed Corvan to re-examine her head injury, though he came to the same conclusion as Bayesh's healer, giving her a potion for the headache and recommending as much rest as possible before the battle.

At the break of dawn, right on cue, they heard the marching footsteps. Talin stood and made her way past the snoozing wolf to the outer barricade.

I suppose this is it, then.

Ettrias quickly joined her, followed by Blackrun, then a clothed and armoured Red Wolf a few minutes later. He grumbled about still being disoriented and mentioned that his jaw hurt from dragging around so much heavy material.

"I don't suppose Darien is planning on playing nice," he said.

"The defenses are ready." Talin checked her weapons. "Whether we succeed now will depend on ourselves."

A white flag appeared around the corner.

"Approach, then," she called. "Though you should know I'm not exactly in the mood to negotiate."

A shield wall moved out across the hallway, followed by Darien, safely protected behind them.

"It doesn't have to come to this, Talin," he said. "Lay down your arms now. We can negotiate surrender and the proper treatment of your people."

"No," Talin simply said. She glanced over her shoulder at the gathered troops. "I liberated Kies Tor from the threat of a similar tyrant years ago—General Kehlvor of the Hellhounds. He sought to destroy us just as you do now. He failed, not because he was weak, but because my people were willing to die for their queen." A collective roar of affirmation rose up behind her, and she inclined her head towards them. "What say you all? Will you stand with me?"

There was a beat of silence.

"To the death!" Red Wolf yelled, lifting his sword straight into the air. The soldiers behind them responded with another collective roar, quickly escalating into a chant that clearly unsettled the shield bearers in front of Darien.

"DEATH! DEATH! DEATH! DEATH!"

"Well, then, Your Majesty," Talin said, nocking her first arrow. "My people have given their answer."

L I X

The first attack hit them with the force of a charging bull.

Darien had immediately sent out his shield-bearers, exactly like Talin had predicted, countering the archers and crossbowmen they'd posted at the front of the formation. She aimed for the gaps between their shields while Ettrias shouted for their explosive charges. A team of specialists was given the responsibility of priming and throwing them.

And they had been effective at first. With the Fae soldiers entirely unprepared for such weaponry, it had been easy to take out the shield wall and make short work of the infantry hiding behind them, but Darien quickly countered with archers of his own, forcing Talin to duck low to avoid being shot. Red Wolf tossed their remaining explosives down the hallway and took out a handful of crossbowmen. He was forced to duck moments later when a bolt clipped his helm.

"Worth a try," he said.

Talin peeked through a small hole in the barricade and saw that the archers were now fitting fire arrows to their bows—no doubt ready to burn through their cover. She decided she might as well let them try. It was hardly going to do any damage; Blackrun had insisted on having a team make several round trips to fetch water from the kitchens and douse both barricades with it, and for good reason, too. Her simple trick had completely nullified the fire from the Fae arrows, rendering them effectively fire-proof. Talin saw a lick of flame flicker ever so briefly at the top of the barricade before dying out.

So far, so good.

But she knew better than to get her hopes up. They had barely half the number of Darien's troops, and this wasn't some fortified castle where they could bunker down—this was a shoddy, improvised, last-ditch defense while Lord Wyndove and Lord Mornus finished seeing to the evacuations.

And a last-ditch attempt to stop Darien from taking the city, I suppose.

She had to admit that her expectations weren't high.

"More shields!" Ettrias shouted. Talin risked peeking over the top of the wall and saw another shield wall advancing, this time locked in a tighter formation. She reached for her second quiver. During the battle preparations, she'd taken the liberty of fitting as many chain arrows as she possibly could, figuring that she could use her lightning to take advantage of the Fae soldiers' metal armour and the cramped space in the hallway.

All she needed to do was land a solid hit through the wooden shield wall.

Her first chain clipped the edge of a shield and set the wood alight in an instant, forcing the soldier to drop it with a yelp. She sent a follow-up that landed square in the gap between his breastplate and pauldron.

Lightning lashed out across the corridor faster than anyone could react, jumping between the soldiers' armour, sending lethal jolts of energy through their bodies. The archers at the front of the formation turned away to shield their eyes. The scent of burning flesh filled the air. Talin's fingertips tingled a little at the fading contact.

I'm sorry, she thought with a wince and forced herself to move on. For now, their most effective defense against the advancing troops was her lightning.

"One might argue your lightning is a little *too* effective," Blackrun muttered.

Talin checked her arrows and guessed she could take out another four groups with good aiming, but she wasn't entirely sure her coordination had returned to normal quite yet. If she missed her first shot again like last time…

Whatever the case, more soldiers were coming. She nocked another chain arrow and sent it past the shield wall this time—dropping the entire formation in the blink of an eye. One of the crossbowmen providing ranged support was unlucky enough to poke his head out when she nocked her next arrow. Talin sent it into his eye without hesitation and heard the crackling and screaming as anyone unfortunate enough to be next to him was also hit with her lightning.

Two more arrows left.

Another shield formation came out to meet them, this one accompanied by a hail of arrows and crossbow bolts. Red Wolf yanked Talin down behind the barricade as she was aiming her chain, and it thudded harmlessly into the wall instead of past the shields as she'd hoped.

"You could have used your protection magic..." she grumbled.

"Just trying to keep you alive," Red Wolf said.

Talin nocked her final chain and poked her head out again for just long enough to send it through the shield wall. The soldiers went down instantly.

"You'd think Darien would learn after the first few times," her bodyguard said, looking over the barricade again. Another bolt clipped his helm. Talin pulled him back down.

"Please don't get shot again."

"I'll make an effort." Red Wolf turned his attention to the rest of the waiting northerners. "Shields and infantry to the front! Move!"

They scrambled into position immediately, forcing Talin and the other archers back as they formed their own shield wall over the top of the barricade. A row of spears poked their weapons through the gaps to stab at anyone who tried to get near. Red Wolf drew his sword but remained at her side.

"Once they break through here, you need to retreat past the second barricade," he said. "I know better than to convince you to leave through the tunnel, but—"

"I know. Stop worrying yourself."

Talin picked off whoever she could trust herself to hit without accidentally hitting any of her allies, but her ammunition was running low; they only had what supplies they'd brought with them during the retreat, and she had elected to prioritise arming the other archers. In her current state, she was sure her aim would be far worse than the Royal Army marksmen in their ranks.

Bodies were beginning to pile up on their side now. Each time there was a break in the shield formation, another shield-bearer or spear would move to replace the fallen soldier, but it was a losing battle.

More and more Fae infantry were crowding the hallway, some of them slashing at the shield wall, others hacking away at the barricade with axes or maces. It was only a matter of time.

She saw the exact moment their formation scattered, both all at once and in slow motion. One of the Fae soldiers grabbed a shield and pulled it down to stab the man in the neck. He leapt over the barricade without pausing, dodging a spear thrust, and took out a second shield-bearer before anyone could fill the gap. Talin's arrow took him out too late.

Two more swordsmen had jumped the barricade by the time she realised she was out of arrows. Red Wolf cut down another charging soldier who made a beeline directly for her.

"Go!" her bodyguard snapped. An axe buried itself in his neck. He tore it free and stabbed his opponent under the armpit.

No. I can't leave everyone to fend for themselves.

Talin drew her sword, snatched up a shield from a fallen soldier, and slammed it into the nearest Fae swordsman's face. She followed through with a slash that opened his throat from ear to ear.

"Really!" Red Wolf growled. He parried an incoming strike with his sword and dagger. "And you tell *me* off for not following orders..."

"The difference between you and me is that you can't tell me what to do," Talin said.

Red Wolf grumbled something that sounded like, "Stop talking and fight." Ettrias glanced over his shoulder, saw them, and began backing towards them to cover Talin's left. The three of them stood together with what remained of their front line as they were pushed further and further down the hallway.

Another axe-wielding soldier swung at her. Ettrias knocked the strike aside and crippled the man with a slash to the hamstring. One of their spears finished him off. A shield-bearer fell just ahead of her, and two more Fae soldiers filled the space to continue the advance. Red Wolf cut one down, but the other landed a solid stab to his neck, cutting off his air supply. Talin cut down the Fae while he ripped the dagger free with a cough.

We're losing ground too quickly.

"Back!" she yelled. "Fall back to the courtyard!"

The northerners behind her began to move, making space for their retreat. Red Wolf remained ahead of her to stop anyone from getting too close, swinging what would normally be a heavy, two-handed longsword in one hand like it weighed nothing. The Fae soldiers were understandably cautious as they approached him.

Slowly, with the hallway clearing up, they managed to reach the second barricade, still fending off advancing swordsmen and spears. Here, they were reinforced by more archers, giving Talin some breathing space and allowing her and Ettrias to scramble over the barricade while Red Wolf kept the attackers from advancing further. He joined them moments later with a final jab at the nearest soldier.

"Morning," Ashera said cheerfully as they allowed fresh teams of shield-bearers to the front. "Been having fun without us?"

Talin wiped her sword on a sleeve. "I'm not sure I'd consider any of this 'fun'."

"Just trying to stay positive." Ashera drew her sword. Golmin joined them a moment later with his own blade at the ready.

"I thought you were at the other end of the tunnel," Ettrias said.

"I was. We were pushed back," Golmin said. "Soldiers all over Stormwood. We got the civilians out just in time before they swarmed us, but..." *There's no way out now.* Talin didn't need him to finish the sentence.

"We're trapped in the courtyard, then," she said.

"Well, this day just keeps getting better." Ettrias scowled.

Red Wolf lowered his visor. "Let's make it count."

Once again, Talin saw their formation collapse; a single instant of inattention had been enough to allow one soldier through their lines. It was understandable. Everyone remaining in the courtyard was exhausted, from the hasty preparations last night to the non-stop fighting. She glanced back at Blackrun and Aldrus and saw that they had both drawn blades, too.

To the death. She lowered the visor of her own helm.

The first Fae soldier to rush at them received a longsword to the neck as Red Wolf cut him down without missing a beat. He turned his blade on another opponent and left Golmin to cover his back. Talin remained with Ettrias to provide him with some shield cover; he held a sword in one hand and dagger in the other and was entirely exposed to any stray arrows. Ashera picked up a second sword as she watched, using it to brutal efficiency, dancing through opponents effortlessly.

A Fae soldier swung a mace at her. Talin ducked and slashed his leg with a low cut. Red Wolf finished the man off with a thrust that pierced his abdomen. On her left, she saw Ettrias parry and counter another strike, taking off his opponent's head with the force of his swing. He moved on without hesitating and forced Talin to move with him to cover his back. Out of the corner of her eye, she could see attackers slowly circling, pushing past the edge of their formation, trying to surround them. Red Wolf had evidently seen it, too, because he also moved, dropping one soldier with a kick to the stomach and stabbing him in the neck with his dagger.

But it wasn't enough—three more slipped past him and tightened the circle in the time it took him to dispatch his next opponent. A particularly hard mace swing sent him staggering back. Talin heard metal crunch and saw him rip off his helm. He wiped blood from his nose. Fae spearmen began to push forward, tightening the circle further and forcing them to group together.

Think! a voice in her head scolded her. *The Hellhounds used this exact trick, circling us, surrounding us. You had a solution for it.*

"Spears to the front!" she yelled. "Form a circle!"

Their remaining spears scrambled into action—just in time.

"Spears, hold!" came a command.

The opposing Fae spearmen halted, unable to advance further without risking retaliation. They stood there uncertainly instead, trapped in a stalemate in the middle of the courtyard against what remained of her own soldiers.

"It seems we're at an impasse," Darien called. Talin saw the rows of infantry part ways for him. He was flanked by Lord Auwin and General Gorin, though there was no sign of Lord Bayesh. It was odd, to say the least.

"It would seem so." Talin kept her weapon raised.

"My offer still stands," Darien said. "Surrender now. Give up the city and keep your lives. There's no way out."

"My answer is still no," Talin said. "I hope the seven hells take you."

Darien scoffed. "Don't be stubborn. You'd be dying for *nothing*."

"Better dying here than being executed."

"Where's Lord Bayesh?" Red Wolf asked. "I see the rest of your advisors, but he seems to be missing."

Darien smiled wryly. "Lord Bayesh was kind enough to warn me about what you so conveniently told him—that there are reinforcements marching on the northern gate as we speak. I've stationed him there, along with all of his men, to prevent them from reaching you."

That doesn't make sense. Bayesh didn't believe that our reinforcements would arrive on time.

Talin exchanged a look with Red Wolf. If Lord Bayesh really *had* believed her back at the Fae camp, then he must have also believed that Red Wolf would transform last night under the full moon. And yet he hadn't warned Darien about the latter...

Come to think of it, none of the sentries we ran into last night wore House Bayesh colours.

Her head spun. From what she could tell, Bayesh was the only one of Darien's generals who had been stationed at the gate instead of participating in the final attack—perhaps at his own insistence. Could it have been a subtle way to avoid participating in the battle to come? What was his angle?

Bayesh has scouts in Stormwood—he probably knows about the Drakels' proximity to the city better than we do.

Red Wolf tilted his head ever so slightly. She saw his ears shift as he tuned out of their conversation and honed in on whatever hidden sound he could pick up in the distance.

Perhaps what we truly need to do is buy time. Trust in Bayesh.

Talin lowered her sword. "Tell your men to stand down. Let's discuss the terms of your surrender."

Darien let out a chuckle. "I think you misunderstand the situation, Your Majesty. You have no reinforcements coming. We outnumber you three to one. It is your surrender that we should be discussing, not mine."

"I don't think so. I trust the people closest to me. Can you say the same about yours?" Talin asked. She could hear fighting now, quickly getting closer. All heads turned in the direction of the courtyard entrance—

Just in time to see a sand-coloured Drakel charge into the Fae lines with a roar.

More Drakels swarmed into the courtyard like a flood, accompanied by elves in northern colours, outnumbering the Fae infantry. Behind them came the familiar teal of House Bayesh—exactly as Talin had hoped.

"What is this...this...treachery?" Darien demanded.

"This isn't treason. This is a takeover." Lord Bayesh stepped forward to face the Fae king. "King Darien of House Dalkarth, House Bayesh no longer recognises your authority in Astaria."

Darien opened and closed his mouth several times, looking almost like a dying fish on land.

"So," Talin said with an easy smile, "shall we negotiate your surrender?"

T alin found herself, after countless months, seated on the throne
again.

With the arrival of the Drakels and their northern reinforcements,
Darien had no choice but to surrender; his armies were no match for the
full might of the Draconian Legions. Heading the bulk of the force was
Bo'Kata, one of Kadis' most trusted generals and an old friend. Talin
was glad to see her again; it had been years since they fought together
in the war. They'd quickly agreed to negotiate the terms of Darien's
surrender in a more formal setting, and by some miracle, most of the
throne room had survived the siege.

"...should take him back to Astaria for execution," Lord Bayesh was
saying. "Kies Tor has no death penalty and—"

"No," Talin said. "The Torrian Crown exercises its right to justice—as the ones wronged, we will deal with Darien in our own court.

He will be offered a fair trial and sentenced to life behind bars. If the Astarian Crown wishes for him to be returned home, it will have to wait until after the sentence has been carried out."

It was a risky move, seeing as she didn't have any legal power and technically nobody held the Astarian Crown at present, but she refused to let Darien return home for trial. The courts there could just as easily favour him and let him go without punishment, undoing Lord Bayesh's attempt at a takeover and condemning the man to death for treason.

"You have no authority to make such a claim," Darien hissed.

"And you have no authority to refute it." Talin shrugged. "Your Royal Council must represent the Astarian Crown—and Aldrus, technically, represents Kies Tor." She looked at her husband.

"I concur with Talin," Aldrus said. "As King Regent of Kies Tor, it is my wish that my brother be tried here. What say his council?"

"Aye," Lord Bayesh said.

"What do you plan to do with us?" Lord Auwin asked.

"That depends." Talin looked between him and General Gorin. "I know neither of you wished to serve Darien. But your refusal to aid Kies Tor cannot be forgotten."

"Then I say try him here," Lord Auwin said. "Let him be found guilty of his crimes and left to rot away in prison forever."

"I don't care what happens to him," General Gorin said. "But Astaria needs a new ruler. Someone capable, who can lead the people, instead of throwing aside all responsibility in pursuit of conquest."

Talin glanced at Bayesh. She knew he must have gone into this with an agenda in mind and understood that he must already have an idea of who to crown as the new ruler of Astaria. But that was a discussion she preferred to have with him in private, without the other lords listening in or trying to influence their decision.

"It's decided, then," she said. "Darien will be taken to the dungeons to await trial. My lords, we'll also have to house you in the dungeons for the time being—at least until the palace towers are repaired. You'll be provided with decent accommodations, as will all of the captured Astarian soldiers. The court will decide your punishments, or they might let you go." She nodded towards the doors. Red Wolf, Golmin, and Ashera grabbed a man each and escorted them from the throne r oom.

"I suppose that leaves me," Bayesh said. "Given that you didn't have me dragged off, can I assume that I'll be allowed to leave freely?"

"Your aid this morning was commendable, but I haven't decided yet." Talin frowned at him. "I would hear Bo'Kata's thoughts about you first."

"I say you can trust him." Bo'Kata stepped forward. "He was nothing but helpful when we arrived at the gates. We almost mistook his men for an enemy blockade, but he explained the situation and just...let us through. He was even kind enough to update us on the numbers we were expected to face."

"So...all of that talk about not wanting to make a move, telling us you couldn't do more..." Talin said. "That was all a farce?"

Lord Bayesh swallowed. "I will admit, I had...hoped...that the other lords were more receptive to my proposal. Without them, it was risky for me—getting caught was a real possibility. I pretended my hands were tied in the hope that you would not treat me with hostility but also wouldn't...reveal something by accident if Darien ever came to interrogate you."

"If I may," Aldrus said. "It was my idea to put you in contact with Lord Bayesh in the first place. I can vouch for him."

Talin exchanged a look with Ettrias.

"You worked to betray your king, yet Aldrus seems to trust you," her brother said. "What are you not telling us?"

Talin held up a hand before either of them could reply. She knew where this was going and had suspected since Aldrus offered to write a letter personally to Bayesh, but she'd had no way of confirming until now.

"I'd like to propose a deal," she said, getting to her feet and making her way down from the dais. Bayesh swallowed again, but Aldrus made no move, lips pressing into a hard line.

"What happens in Astaria now is no longer your business," her husband said carefully. "Who we decide to put in charge of the kingdom is an internal affair. Let us handle it."

Talin let out a humourless laugh. "Let's not forget that you worked *with* Darien to undermine my rule for *years* before having a change of heart. I will not forget that. With all the evidence we have, it wouldn't be terribly difficult for the court to sentence you both behind bars. My council remains loyal to *me*. They would represent the Crown in my stead." She stopped directly in front of Aldrus. "If you want your brother's throne, I'd advise you to think this through."

Aldrus seemed to shrink a little. "Fine. Speak your piece."

"You are, under Torrian law, married to the Head of State," Talin said. "My first condition is that we end our marriage and negotiate a proper treaty of alliance between Astaria and Kies Tor. For all intents and purposes, this kingdom cannot allow the Head of State of another nation to have any kind of administrative power here."

"Sounds reasonable," Aldrus said.

"My second condition is that you appoint an entirely new Royal Council," Talin continued. "I leave it up to you to decide who to choose. But Lord Bayesh, Lord Auwin, and General Gorin must be removed from office, regardless of what the Torrian High Court decides of their fate."

"*What?* I helped you—" Bayesh began.

"You're disloyal, gullible, and quick to jump behind whichever side suits your interests," Talin said without looking at him. "Your fellow council members are both cowards, too afraid to challenge the Crown's authority. None of you are fit to serve as the Crown's advisors."

"No." Aldrus drew himself back up to full height. "Auwin and Gorin, I will remove from office. But what you say of Lord Bayesh isn't true. He stays."

Ah, so he can *stand up for himself.* Talin smiled. "Perhaps. Perhaps not. Either way, it's clear to me now that you trust each other. I leave the choice to you. Lord Bayesh, you're free to go, as are your men. I'll send my husband to you soon."

"Then I thank you for your generosity," Bayesh said with a deep bow. "I hope the next time we meet, it will be under better circumstances."

"If there's nothing else for me, I should also go round up my men," Bo'Kata said. She broke into a grin. "It was good to see you again. We'll have to catch up sometime."

"Pass my regards to Kadis, too!" Talin called after her. Ettrias followed her from the throne room as well, muttering something about keeping some semblance of organisation with so many factions in the city, leaving her alone with Aldrus. Her husband went to the window with a sigh.

"There's more to this deal that you haven't said, isn't there?"

"About the papers, yes. And Red Wolf."

Aldrus hummed. "I'd be dropping the investigation against you either way—that should be enough to clear your name. No one will ever have cause to think that Darien *didn't* forge them."

"Red Wolf is still exiled according to the High Court. Once you're gone, no one in the kingdom will have the power to undo that sentence," Talin said. She joined him at the window. "But we're still married until everything is finalised. You're still the king regent until you and the court officially clear my name." A faint smile tugged at the corners of her lips. "And given that *you* were technically responsible for this whole ordeal in the first place...I feel like you owe me a favour, no?"

Aldrus, to his credit, let out a chuckle. "You're making a habit out of finding these loopholes. Ever considered making it a career?"

"What, an entire profession dedicated to finding legal loopholes?" Talin asked. "Who would possibly have the patience to comb through so many official documents and codices?"

"Anyone, if you pay them well enough."

Talin snorted. The two of them turned their attention back to the window and the ruined central courtyard below. There was a beat of silence.

"I have a confession to make," Aldrus finally said. "I told your lord commander that I never had any interest in you beyond our professional relationship. I may have...said that...just to stay on his good side." He let out a long breath. "I think, in truth, over time...I really did start to develop feelings for you." Talin opened her mouth to respond, but he quickly interjected, holding up a hand to stop her. "I know what you're going to say. And I don't expect you to return those feelings. I guess I'm telling you this now because I want to make it clear that I never intended to make your life so difficult. For most of these past few months, I was convinced that you wouldn't have run if you truly were innocent."

"Well, maybe I *did* overreact a little." Talin winced. "I never should have asked you for help to forge those documents."

"Who else knows the truth about them?"

"People I trust. Katherine Blackrun and Red Wolf."

Though I probably should get around to telling Ettrias the truth now that the situation has been resolved. Talin made a mental note to apologise for keeping such an important secret.

"You're not worried about Darien revealing the truth at trial?" Aldrus asked.

"He won't be believed."

"And...Arkiel? I...know my duty is in Astaria now, but I wouldn't want to neglect my duty to him..."

Talin thought about the stories that the others had told him on the road, about the way he'd dragged Red Wolf off to play on their first morning at Castle Blackrun, and about the few weeks that Ashera had spent as his bodyguard before any of them had understood the full extent of this entire conspiracy.

"He's stronger than you think. He'll be fine," she said. "But you're always welcome here if you'd like to visit."

"Likewise. Once things settle down in the south, you're free to visit whenever you wish," Aldrus said. "Though I think we both have long rebuilding efforts ahead of us."

Perhaps. Talin's gaze swept across the ruined courtyard. In the days that followed the First Siege of Belanore, she'd barely slept, between the nightmares of the battle and endless stacks of rebuilding permits to approve and two court cases to prepare. This time, oddly enough, something felt different. She wasn't sure if it was the reassurance that she'd already done all of this before or the knowledge that, for once, she could be a little selfish without consequence. They'd saved the city and prevented the prophecy. It was cause enough for celebration.

This time, whatever happened next, she felt ready to face it.

T he first thing Red Wolf felt when he set foot in the front courtyard was the full force of an eight-year-old child tackling him in
the legs.

He managed to extract himself with some difficulty, though it
turned out there was no need; Arkiel quickly moved on to trap Talin's
legs in a similar hug when she appeared through the doors behind him.
Accompanying the boy was Lord Cassius and half a dozen Blackrun
guards.

"Mother! Red Wolf! I missed you both so much!" he exclaimed.
"You *have* to tell me all about the battle, please? It must have been *epic*.
All I know is that you managed to convince one of Uncle Darien's advisors to switch sides, and that already sounds amazing! What happened
to your eye? Did someone hit you there?"

Talin laughed and kissed the top of his head, hugging him tight. "I missed you too, Ark. I'm glad you made it back here safe. And no, I got hit by some falling debris, not someone's weapon." She released him again. "You'll have plenty of stories to listen to—*after* you go and bathe properly! You've been on the road for weeks. Get yourself cleaned up."

"Wait," Arkiel said when Cassius began leading him into the palace. "What about Father? The letter you sent said he had to go home to Astaria to be the king there. Are we ever going to see him again? I didn't get to say goodbye…"

"Of course we'll see him again." Talin smiled. "We'll both be quite busy these next few months, but once things are settled down again, you can visit as often as you like. He'll try to visit us here in Belanore, too. Now, go! Princes need to have some respect for their own hygiene, Arkiel."

"I have to admit, I've missed him." Red Wolf grinned as the young prince was finally tugged into the palace. He saw Talin's hand briefly touch the half-healed cut above her eye.

"It's good to have him home," she said. "Though he's certainly enthusiastic with the questions." Her gaze swept across the courtyard. "You have a moment?"

"For now, certainly," Red Wolf said. "But I suspect I'll need rescuing from Arkiel once he's cleaned up. Something tells me he's not going to be satisfied until I've given him *all* the details of the siege."

Talin let out a chuckle. "Walk with me, then. There's a lot we haven't had the chance to discuss yet."

Red Wolf fell into step beside her as they made their way through the courtyard. With so much of the city in ruins and so much to do in the wake of the siege, they rarely got to see each other on a good day; he distinctly remembered their last conversation had been the briefest exchange of pleasantries as she'd brushed past him in the hallway with armfuls of documents. That had been last *week*.

"Regarding your...proposal, shall we say," she said as they walked. "I...was wondering if it still stands. Given all that's happened since our last conversation about it..."

"Of course," Red Wolf said. "If it's something you still wish. I suppose we'll have to start making wedding arrangements."

"Not...quite yet." Talin's cheeks turned pink. "The rebuilding efforts have to remain my priority, as ever. But we *will* need to announce our engagement at some point—and I imagine you still need to talk to Katherine about legitimising your claim to the Blackrun name."

"Hmm." Red Wolf put a hand on his chin. "An official announcement...I guess it's unavoidable. I assume you're planning on using the upcoming tourney to distribute such earth-shattering news?"

"Naturally. Unless you have a better idea?" Talin asked.

"I know you and Ettrias have always had a penchant for mischief," Red Wolf said with a grin. He dug into his pocket and produced a silver-banded ring inlaid with tiny gems. "And I just so happen to have a ring I procured from my father—a parting gift when we left the clan's settlements. He told me it was a priceless family relic and to only give it away to someone who will understand the value of such an item. I'd like to make a formal proposal at the tourney. Assuming I win."

Talin lifted a brow. "You understand this could cause a city-wide scandal that will take anywhere from a few months to several *years* to die down?"

"I figure there's going to be a scandal either way. Why not have some fun with it?" Red Wolf shrugged.

"Oh, you know me too well." Talin laughed. "Alright. If anything, it'll be nice not taking all of the unwanted attention for once. But

I'd best talk to Lord Wyndove all the same. Hopefully, we can keep the...unruliness in the crowd to a minimum on the day."

"Have you thought about who you'll appoint as lord commander once we're married?" Red Wolf asked.

"Not yet. But I have a candidate in mind."

Ashera, then. He knew that neither of them needed to say it. The girl was the only one who could possibly succeed him, and there was no one else he quite trusted to do his job.

They caught each other up on a few of the things they'd gotten up to in the past week before parting ways; Red Wolf needed to find Blackrun before she returned north, and Talin had a delivery of new carpet to sign off on. He made his way to the freshly reconstructed half of the palace, passing construction teams along the way in search of the Highlander woman.

He found her eventually in the guest bedchambers where she'd been staying these past few weeks, half-folded clothes strewn across the bed with a travelling pack almost filled. The door was open, but he knocked anyway, and she looked up sharply before waving him in.

"Leaving already?" he asked. "I thought you'd be staying for the tourney."

"My work is done here," Blackrun said. "The north has officially been recognised as an independent state. I'll be crowned Queen Katherine once I return home. From there, it'll be a matter of reorganising our administration. You could join me, you know. Take the crown as King Connor."

"I already have plans," Red Wolf said. "But it seems I was right to seek you out today, or I might have missed you. There were a few things I wanted to discuss. Well, two things, to be precise."

"Of course." Blackrun continued folding clothes.

"First, I wanted to take you up on your offer," Red Wolf said. "I'd like to officially be recognised as Head of House Blackrun—on the condition that I keep my clan name as well."

Blackrun looked up again, eyes widening. "Truly? You'll be returning north with me, then?"

"That's...the other thing." Red Wolf took a deep breath. There was no going back from this now. "I'd like your blessing."

"Blessing...?"

"For my marriage to Queen Talin."

Blackrun stared at him. Red Wolf braced himself for her to rescind her offer once more and refuse to recognise him as a member of House Blackrun, but she did none of that. Instead, a small chuckle escaped her throat, quickly turning into a laugh.

"So, she outplayed me after all," she mused. "Rather, you both did."

"I'm doing this because I want to," Red Wolf said. "The political convenience is secondary, and the political *repercussions* might well end up outweighing any benefits my queen would gain."

Blackrun only smiled. "I know. Of course you'll have my blessing."

"I... Thank you." Red Wolf was taken aback. "Just like that?"

"Connor. You're my son." Blackrun cupped his face in her hands. "Only a fool would deny their child happiness. I only have one request—see for yourself our rebuilding efforts without the support of the Torrian Crown. Understand *why* we wished to do things on our own. If, after that, you still trust Talin to fix things in the north, I won't get in your way."

"Very well," he said. "It's only fair."

"I wish you luck, then," Blackrun said, releasing him. "I'll miss you. Come visit if you have the time, won't you?"

Red Wolf came forwards on impulse and pulled her into embrace. "Count on it."

The next few weeks were equally busy; Red Wolf found himself running errands for Talin almost every day or otherwise helping the palace builders with heavy loads. They were barely given a few minutes of free time to talk on a good day, preoccupied as they were with their respective duties. He was almost worried that Talin would push herself to the point of exhaustion, but she seemed entirely in her element, despite rushing back and forth all over town to take care of business. He had never seen her so focused.

Maybe that's a good thing, he thought. *We could all use a distraction from the siege. Talin more than most.*

There was no need to speak of it between the two of them; he knew that she was still haunted by the war, just as he was still haunted by his past. But she genuinely seemed more like her old self when she busied herself in her work, so he left her to her devices, opting instead to help lighten her workload.

Besides, the tourney should provide them with plenty of time to unwind—at least before they officially announced their engagement to the world. Red Wolf wondered how the people would react.

With outrage, most likely.

But he found that he didn't care. He and Talin deserved some happiness after all they'd been through, especially her, and he had no reason to care for the opinions of some sheep who would never understand the sacrifices she'd made for them. Whatever happened next, they could weather it together.

And what about Bjorson's warning? Talin thinks it's all over.

Red Wolf pushed the thoughts from his mind. It *was* over, as far as he was concerned; Darien failed to destroy the city, Talin prevented the prophecy from coming true, and they would have their happy ending now.

And yet—

No. It's over. There's no need to worry about warnings or prophecies anymore.

He pulled the ring from his pocket, transferred it to a pouch on his weapons belt, and elected to forget all about whatever irrational fears he might have about this whole situation.

Tomorrow, he had a tournament to win.

Epilogue

"**H**onestly, it baffles me why you'd sign up for the open melee," Ettrias said with a grin. "Wouldn't it be, I don't know, unfair for everyone else?"

Red Wolf strapped his armour on in silence. Nearby, Ashera and Golmin both busied themselves with getting ready. They'd agreed to gear up together before the start of the open melee, allowing the four of them a chance to talk and catch up, given the past few weeks of chaos. What he hadn't expected was so much teasing from the others.

"I think it's perfectly fair," Ashera said. "Red Wolf is such a big target, I'd say it's more unfair for *him* to take part than anything else. Just think—everyone gets a chance to hit you without having to crowd around." She laughed.

"If I knew the three of you were going to be like this, I would have geared up alone," Red Wolf grumbled. "All jokes aside, I *do* have a lot hinging on actually *winning* the open melee, so if you could all go easy…"

"In your dreams." Ettrias scoffed. "I, for one, have a reputation to maintain as the most feared swordsman in the kingdom."

"Nobody thinks that," Golmin said immediately. Ashera nodded in agreement.

"Wh—" Ettrias spluttered. "You…are all the worst. I will have you know I'm one of the *few* people who can defeat Red Wolf in honourable combat."

"If he's holding back, maybe." Ashera snickered.

"Why do you care so much about winning this thing, anyway?" Golmin asked, looking at the bodyguard. "I know it's been decades since we were in a tourney together, but you've never cared much about winning before now…"

Red Wolf sighed. "If you must know…" He dug into his belt pouch and pulled out the ring. Ettrias squawked indignantly and grabbed his hand as if the item might be some illusion he could get to the bottom of. Golmin and Ashera both fell deathly silent.

"No. You're… That's a joke. You're jesting. Aren't you…?" the prince squinted at the ring in his palm. "Do you *realise* how much of a scandal you'll cause—"

"We're both aware," Red Wolf said.

"B-both!" Ettrias turned away to inhale deeply before beginning to pace. "What kind of a sister is she? *Gods,* I'm going to kill her for not telling me. And to think she had the audacity to apologise about the papers…"

"To be fair, we've all been busy." Red Wolf pocketed the ring again. He gave them the quick version of events.

"I mean, it makes *sense*, it all just seems...sudden," Golmin said once he was done. "And I'm not exactly expecting it'll be well-received by the crowd, either." He let out a long breath. "If you want help making it to the final round..."

"Oh, no. I'm winning this tourney. And for keeping...*this*—" Ettrias gestured to Red Wolf's belt pouch— "a secret, I'm half-tempted to knock you out *first* just to see how you'll announce your engagement then."

"Talin has plans on announcing it herself anyway," Red Wolf said. "I figured that formally proposing would place more of the attention on me so she doesn't take all the heat. Besides, we all know you couldn't keep a secret if your life depended on it."

"*Orrlát*, I hate it when you have a point," Ettrias grumbled. "But I'm still not teaming up with you."

"Well, my solemn duty as your friend and partner dictates that I give my help willingly and of my own volition." Golmin thumped Red Wolf on the back with a grin. "Sorry, Ettrias."

"Wh—this is betrayal!" Ettrias put a hand to his heart in mock offence. "Rufus!"

Ashera laughed. "It's alright. I'll team up with you."

"Thank you, *someone* who knows how to use common sense. Rufus, I'm breaking up with you and courting Ashera from now on."

Golmin snorted. "I'll make it up to you later."

"Alright, time's up! Enough chatter, time to fight! Get out there!" Brakis shooed them from the combatants' tent. Red Wolf pulled his helm on and lowered the visor.

"Good luck," he said. "May all of you walk away with minimal bruises and no life-threatening injuries."

"Likewise," Golmin said.

"Personally, I hope you have to get carried out of the arena unconscious, Red Wolf," Ettrias muttered.

"You can dream."

The open melee was exactly as the name suggested—a massive free-for-all fought in an equally massive arena for the entertainment of the masses. Anyone able to hold a weapon could take part, though blunted blades were the only weapons allowed in the arena to prevent serious injury. The goal was simple—hit your fellow opponents until they yielded.

Red Wolf kept out of the way for most of the first round as he always did, preferring to let the rest of the combatants take each other out before swooping in, though he was forced to beat one man over the head repeatedly until he begged him to stop. With how easy it was for most of the combatants to sustain injuries, King Arnas had been the first to introduce timed 'rounds' into the rules, forcing all fighting to cease every three minutes so the healers could tend to any injured combatants. Unconscious combatants were also dragged off during these intervals so they wouldn't be trampled. Red Wolf honestly wasn't sure it made *that* much of a difference to the frequency of the injuries sustained, but he supposed at least they were getting prompt medical treatment.

Ettrias *was* right in a way, he mused as he forced another opponent to yield under his brutal strikes. His healing powers meant that even the heaviest of blows were unlikely to be anything more than a mild inconvenience, and his high pain tolerance made it easy for him to endure whatever beating he took. Really, the only way to beat him in the open melee was to knock him out instantly—a feat that was far easier on paper than in practice. It was the main reason he avoided participating in tourneys before his exile and only ever went easy on his opponents when he did sign up.

It was almost too easy for him to win otherwise.

It took only four rounds for he and Golmin to be the only ones left standing; Ettrias had gotten himself beaten early on, and Ashera was only able to last for so long in a one-on-two against them.

"Just don't hit me too hard," the guard captain said as they circled each other.

"That depends on how good your acting is."

Their blades met with a ring of steel. Red Wolf went on the offensive immediately, driving Golmin towards the edge of the arena, landing two solid hits before his friend slipped under a swing and smacked him in the back of the head. He turned with a third strike that sent the man staggering.

They treated it like a slightly more violent sparring session, with Golmin landing most of the heavy hits and Red Wolf trying to regulate his enhanced strength. It was hard work to keep himself in check; Golmin kept landing the most infuriating hits and forced him to spend all his concentration on keeping the wolf tamed.

Light hits, light hits, light hits—

He parried a low cut and followed through with a riposte that sent his opponent to the ground instantly, coughing. Red Wolf hesitated but lifted his sword to swing again anyway.

"Stop, I yield!" Golmin held up a hand. Red Wolf lowered his blade. "Sorry."

"I'll be sore tomorrow. But you're forgiven." Golmin picked himself back up gingerly with a groan. "Have fun with your proposal. I'll be...over there. Regretting picking a fight with you."

He limped off, and Red Wolf turned to face the spectators' stands, raising his sword in a salute. Talin stepped forwards to address him, with Arkiel a few steps behind.

"Remove your helm, sir," she said. "I would see the face of our champion."

Red Wolf eased his helm off his head and let it fall. "Connor Kulos Blackrun, my queen. Representing House Blackrun and the Highlands." He took a knee.

"Lord Commander," Talin said. "You know the rules of victory. Ask any one favour of me, and I will do my utmost to fulfil it."

"My request is simple." Red Wolf lifted his head. "I'll not bore the crowd with flowery prose and overwrought speeches today. My queen, we have stood together through countless hardships. We rode west to seek help from the Drakels and overthrew a tyrannical insurgency who cared only for power. We saved Belanore twice—first from bloodthirsty Hellhounds, then from the threat of invasion to the south. We travelled north for knowledge and learned that magic has survived against all odds up in the mountains. What I'm about to ask is well within your rights to refuse if you so wish. But if you do find it in you to accept..." He produced the ring. A few gasps went up among the spectators. Whispers began in the stands. "I would ask for your hand in marriage."

All chatter in the crowd ceased in an instant. In the long beat of silence that followed, Red Wolf had the time to think things through and realised, for the first time, that he had always hated the city gossip. Then he wondered if perhaps he should have thought about something more useful, like how best to pacify an angry mob or the fastest route back to the palace—

But that was the last moment of quiet introspection afforded to him before the crowd erupted.

Acknowledgements

Wow, okay, book two. Where to begin? I think, first of all, I have to thank my fellow writers in the original Cabin in the Woods Discord server (you know who you are) for planting the sequel plot bunnies in my head and basically spawning this entire book. Yes, as depressing as it was, book one was supposed to be a standalone and Red Wolf and Talin were simply never going to see each other again. We might not be in touch as often anymore, but you guys were the writing group that really set my mind on eventually publishing my books, and none of this would have been possible without you.

To my other Discord servers, thank you for the community and support throughout. Indie publishing is tough, but you've all been amazing, and thank you in particular to the Melbourne writers' group for putting up with my antics and writing woes. I really don't have the words to describe how much I appreciate you guys, from the online and in-person events to all the memes, jokes, and everything in between. So—thank you. To Scribs, Chaos, Fires, Meg, and Kate: moderating the server with you is a blast, and I truly do love our little corner of the internet. Here's to more server shenanigans in the future. To Scribs in particular: thank you for beta reading, and I'm not sorry for all the trauma I put your favourite characters through in this book.

I'd also like to thank my editor, Charlie, for going through this entire 140,000-word manuscript and doing line edits. Even just going over the edits is a slog—I have the utmost respect for you and all the other editors in this industry for having the patience to improve our manuscripts and polish them up as much as possible. Thank you also for helping me finally understand how commas work and for explaining the difference between 'toward' and 'towards' (honestly, why can't English spelling and grammar be simple?). This book probably wouldn't look nearly as good without your help.

To the Knox Writers group: you guys are awesome, so thank you for the support and brainstorming help despite also being professional distractions. Hanging out at the library is always a blast, and the Knox Library staff are always super chill and supportive, too (thank you, library staff!). Working on this series wouldn't be nearly as fun without your help.

Finally, I'd like to thank *you*, the reader, for picking up this book and giving it a read. If you've been following this series, I hope the sequel satisfied you, and if you're new here, I hope you enjoyed this book! Your support and reviews are what make it possible to continue doing what I love and write more books—we wouldn't be here without you.

About the Author

T.C. Smith (he/she/they) is a criminology undergraduate trying to make a career out of creative writing instead of the degree they graduated with. *Stories of the Ancient Lands* is their debut fantasy series, which pays tribute to the sci-fi and fantasy stories they read and watched as a child. Their hobbies include writing, digital art, and gaming, but their favourite activity is procrastinating both of the former two by spending several hours playing *Baldur's Gate 3* instead. They're inspired by pop culture and any form of media they can get their hands on, and remains a stalwart fan of *Star Wars: The Clone Wars* even though the entire series makes them cry.

Liked this book? Leave a review!

Books in this series:
Song of the Wolf
Scars of the Raven
Souls of the Dragons